Saint Ben

The
Saints'
and
Angels'
Song

"Absolutely loved *Saint Ben* . . . was moved to tears several times. Your characters are beautifully constructed, the anecdotes real, and the honoring of each person's soul-search-for-integrity brilliant . . . comparable in impact but more emotionally powerful than John Irving's *A Prayer for Owen Meany* . . . a well-paced, continually engaging, and captivating piece of business."

Noel Paul Stookey

"John Fischer has created a cast of lovable characters, a plot that twists and turns, and poignant commentary on legalistic Christianity in his first novel, *Saint Ben*."

Moody Monthly

"Combines a realistic setting, little-boy delight, humor, and the gift of surprise."

Terry Whalin, *Bookstore Journal*

"I just finished recording *Saint Ben* for release on our twenty-station network. As I recorded the last episode, I struggled. I would read for a few minutes . . . stop and cry . . . turn on the recorder . . . read for a few minutes more. I had to stop several times . . . [John] is a great storyteller."

Wayne Pederson,
Executive Director
Skylight Satellite Network

"*Saint Ben* will leave you laughing, choking back tears, and best of all, thirsting for the real faith of a nine-year-old. Fischer's style, wit, and wisdom are a welcome addition to Christian fiction."

Phil Callaway, *Servant* magazine,
Prairie Bible Institute

SAINT BEN

The SAINTS' AND ANGELS' SONG

JOHN FISCHER

BETHANYHOUSE
MINNEAPOLIS, MINNESOTA

Saint Ben
Copyright © 1993, 1994
John Fischer

Previously published in two separate volumes: *Saint Ben* © 1993, and *The Saints'
and Angels' Song* © 1994.

Cover illustration and design by Bill Chairavalle

Pascal quotation in Author's Note from Blaise Pascal, *Pensées*, trans.
A. J. Krailsheimer (London: Penguin Books, 1966).

Published by Bethany House Publishers
A Ministry of Bethany Fellowship International
11400 Hampshire Avenue South
Bloomington, Minnesota 55438
www.bethanyhouse.com

Printed in the United States of America by
Bethany Press International, Bloomington, Minnesota 55438

Library of Congress Cataloging-in-Publication Data

CIP data applied for

ISBN 0-7642-2522-7

JOHN FISCHER, pioneering musician, songwriter, and popular speaker, is also the award-winning author of many books. For years his insightful columns have been a favorite monthly feature in *Contemporary Christian Music Magazine*. A graduate of Wheaton College, John and his family live in California. For more information about John, visit his Web site at *www.fischtank.com*.

Books by John Fischer

FROM BETHANY HOUSE PUBLISHERS

Ashes on the Wind

On a Hill Too Far Away

Saint Ben

The Saints' and Angels' Song

True Believers ~~Don't~~ Ask Why

12 Steps for the Recovering Pharisee (like me)

SAINT BEN

MAN . . . IS A THINKING REED.

—Blaise Pascal

Author's Note

Although the quotation that forms the basis for this book, "There is a God-shaped vacuum in every human heart," has been attributed to Blaise Pascal, hours of research, even consultations with experts on Pascal, have failed to turn up the original source. The following words from Pascal's *Pensées* come as close as anything I have found thus far.

> *What else does this craving, and this helplessness, proclaim but that there was once in man a true happiness, of which all that now remains is the empty print and trace? This he tries in vain to fill with everything around him, seeking in things that are not there the help he cannot find in those that are, though none can help, since this infinite abyss can be filled only with an infinite and immutable object—in other words, by God himself.*

Perhaps this "God-shaped vacuum" we are so familiar with is nothing more than a modern summary—an evangelistic caricature, if you will—of what was obviously a far more complete and eloquent statement.

Contents

1

First Sunday

At first glance he looked like a normal boy dressed up against his will for church—hair slicked down, ears squeaky-clean, and a body forced to wear a suit that had worked its way down through two older brothers and was now being pressed too soon into service on his thin, wiry shoulders. But something about Ben made him stick out in the middle of this family and this church like the cowlick on his nine-year-old head.

They made an almost perfect picture, all five of them standing there on the platform in much the same pose as the one in the picture tucked into the bulletin that Sunday morning. The proud father and two of his three sons each wore a small red rosebud, while the mother had been decorated with an orchid corsage on this their first Sunday as the new first family of the Colorado Avenue Standard Christian Church.

The *almost* of the *almost perfect picture* was Ben. He wore no rosebud, and I imagine, now that I think about it, that he had probably removed it the first chance he got and impaled it to the bottom of the pew with the long pearl-headed pin that had briefly held it fast to his pale-blue seersucker coat. It wasn't only his bare lapel that signaled something different about Ben; it was his angular stance, his eyes all twisted up in a squint, and his head cocked to one side as if listening for another voice with ears too large for a face that would never catch up to them. Very little about Ben matched the perfect picture that his family—indeed that the whole church—was trying to fit into that morning. Ben was what was wrong with the picture. He was the only one in the whole church who was not smiling. He wasn't smiling in the picture inside the bulletin either, the one that introduced his family to the church and his father as the new pastor.

It was the picture in the bulletin that we saw before we saw the real Ben, and seeing the real Ben made you understand about the picture—that it hadn't been a mistake and that this was probably the best picture anyone could get of Ben Beamering through the eye of a camera—or any other eye, for that matter.

I had been up there on that same platform myself, and I had smiled just the way Ben's older brothers were smiling. That I-want-to-be-just-like-my-father look. Joshua and Peter Beamering possessed the fewest of their father's physical features, and yet they longed the most to be like him. You could tell that morning how proud they were to be there, just as you could tell how desperately Ben wanted to be somewhere else—anywhere but on that platform, looking out at all those smiling people. Ben's brothers were clearly in their element that Sunday morning in March of 1958. Ben, however, with every strand of his hair held against its will by wave set, obviously had other thoughts.

The sermon that morning was long and full of all the things that would make a Standard Christian congregation proud and certain they had made the right choice in their new pastor.

Ben's father, Jeffery T. Beamering, Jr., had some very large shoes to fill. In just twelve short years, the pastor before him, T. J. Barham, had brought this small struggling church to life, winning a respectable amount of people back into the traditional white clapboard building that had suffered, before he came, from a painful church split. Jeffery T. Beamering, Jr. was inheriting a pulpit that epitomized all that made these faithful churchgoers proud to be Standard Christians and certain that they were smack-dab in the center of the perfect will of God.

Jeffery T. Beamering, Jr. was young, in his mid-thirties, and he had the same fervor that Pastor Barham had possessed when he first came—at least that's what I heard. Many of the older members hated to see their beloved pastor go, but if the bounce in Jeffery Beamering's step and the fire in his voice were any indication—well, they were in for even greater things than they had basked in for twelve years under T. J. Barham.

So on this splendid Sunday morning in March, with the bright sun bouncing off freshly painted white colonial columns, and the choir sitting tall in its loft and the people sitting tall in their pews, everyone was smiling. Everyone, that is, except Ben Beamering.

The new pastor delivered well that morning. Some said it was the best sermon they had ever heard from that pulpit. It was definitely Jeffery T. Beamering's best and his favorite—a sermon that would become the most reliable in his repertoire. It was based on a famous statement by the seventeenth-century mathematician and scientist turned religious philosopher, Blaise Pascal, in which he likened man's spiritual condition to a God-shaped vacuum in the human heart—an empty longing that only God can fill. It was also a sermon of great portent for Jeffery T. Beamering and his family.

Though I would hear that sermon later in many variations, I only heard about it that first Sunday, because, as usual, I didn't stay for the sermon. I was in children's church watching Leonora Kingsley get her first taste of what it was going to be like having Ben Beamering in her class.

The first thing we all noticed was that Ben didn't do any of the hand motions to the Sunday school songs. In fact, he didn't sing any of the songs. He just sat in the front row with his arms folded.

Now, we had our share of malcontents, like Bobby Brown, who was always drawing attention to himself. His favorite trick was to reverse the hand motions (motion wide when we sang "deep" and deep when we sang "wide") and to sing loudly on those notes where we were supposed to only motion and not sing. Then everyone would turn around and point and laugh, which was exactly what Bobby wanted.

Bobby and his little band of eight-year-old deviants always sat in the back row. If they could have invented a row farther back, they would have sat there. That's what made Ben's behavior seem so strange. Though he had the outward demeanor of a deviant, he sat right down in the front row, alone, directly in front of Miss Kingsley.

No one ever sat in the front row.

Because I was sitting directly behind him in the second row, I couldn't help but notice that his ears looked even bigger from the back than they did from the front. From the back, it was easy to see that the problem with Ben's ears was not just their size; it was also their shape. They were cupped like radar screens facing forward, as if designed that way by God for better reception.

We were all thinking it, but it took someone like Bobby Brown to say it.

"Hey, Dumbo!" he yelled from the back of the room, and we all froze.

Ben didn't flinch. Miss Kingsley glared at Bobby and began playing the piano vigorously, directing our singing, as she always did, with her head and torso while her hands were busy up and down the piano keys. She seemed more nervous and intent than usual. Probably because the new pastor's son had positioned himself right in front of her.

> Deep and wide, deep and wide,
> There's a fountain flowing deep and wide.
> Deep and wide, deep and wide,
> There's a fountain flowing deep and wide.

Miss Kingsley's head went deep and wide, and we all motioned appropriately with our hands. Bobby sang where he wasn't supposed to, and Ben didn't sing at all.

"Hey, what's with Dumbo?" hollered one of Bobby's henchmen from the back row, gaining courage from his leader's earlier success with the comparison. Miss Kingsley ignored the disruption and plowed ahead into the next song.

> We are climbing Jacob's ladder,
> We are climbing Jacob's ladder,
> We are climbing Jacob's ladder,
> Soldiers of the cross.

Ben continued to sit there stoically, arms folded.

Leonora Kingsley, growing increasingly nervous over his nonparticipation, stopped the song abruptly and tried the direct approach.

"Class, most of you probably know we have a new child with us today. He's our new pastor's son, Ben Beamering. Ben, welcome to children's church."

No one moved or made a sound except for a few snickers from the back row.

"Ben, are these songs new to you?" asked Miss Kingsley,

knowing they couldn't have been foreign to the son of a Standard Christian minister, but trying her best to deal with the awkward silence.

"No, ma'am."

"Is there some reason why you can't sing with us, then?"

"Yes, ma'am. I don't like these songs."

"Is there a song you'd like to sing?"

"No, not really."

"Would you care to tell us why you don't like these songs?"

I figured Leonora was taking a big chance with this question—and I hadn't even heard the answer yet.

"They're not true," said Ben, "and they don't make any sense. Have you ever been on Jacob's ladder? Do you know anyone who has? I bet no one here has ever even seen Jacob's ladder. It's just a dream some guy had in the Bible. If we are never going to see it or be on it, then why are we singing about climbing it?"

Everyone sat there stunned for the longest time. Even the back row was quiet, including Bobby Brown. We'd never heard anyone our age speak to an adult in such a straightforward manner.

"Well, how about 'Jesus Loves Me'?" Miss Kingsley said, faltering. "Surely there's nothing wrong with that song—" and she started right into the introduction to move us through the bottleneck.

This time, as we all started to sing, Ben began to sing too. In fact, Ben sang out so clearly that I had to stop singing. I'm not sure why, except that suddenly I was aware that my own voice was grating against something much more beautiful—unlike anything I had ever heard before.

I wasn't the only one with this reaction. One by one, everyone else dropped out, and you could tell, right before they stopped, that they heard it too. As if suddenly they were elbowed by perfection—interrupted by beauty—caught unawares by the voice of an angel. They each stopped suddenly, in the middle of a vowel, and looked around the room to find the source of that mysterious, rounded, bell-like, haunting sound.

Even Miss Kingsley stopped, which was most obvious because her loud, warbling vibrato always dominated our singing sessions. She was the last to drop out, and for a moment her

throaty voice was clashing with that pure tone coming from the
boy with the big ears in front of me. Clashing, but not over-
powering. Right up against the tone, in and around the tone, but
never touching it.

By the time we got to the chorus, Ben was singing all by
himself:

> Yes, Jesus loves me.
> Yes, Jesus loves me.
> Yes, Jesus loves me.
> The Bible tells me so.

Somehow, Miss Kingsley managed to keep playing the piano
through all of this, and when she finally stopped, everything was
quiet. Nobody moved. We all just stared silently at Ben, at the
back of his head, at his radar screens turned inward. Ben, however, seemed unaware that everyone had stopped singing. As if
his voice had carried him off somewhere so far away that even
though his body was still there on the first row, his spirit hadn't
quite made it back yet.

"That was very nice, Ben," Leonora Kingsley finally said, and
we all slowly came to and returned to the rest of the program as
if nothing had happened.

It wasn't something you could comment on anyway. Wherever Ben's voice had taken us, it was not a place we could remain
in very long, nor a place we could talk about once we returned.
In fact, no one ever said anything about what happened that
morning in children's church. Except that from then on, whenever anyone who wasn't there that day suggested we sing "Jesus
Loves Me," there was a loud chorus of disapproval. There would
be no singing of "Jesus Loves Me" unless Ben Beamering was
not around. We all made sure of that.

2

Iced Tea

In the car on the way home from church, my mother let us know that the Beamerings were coming over for dinner. It didn't seem right, she said, that the pastor's family didn't have a dinner invitation on their first official Sunday. Besides, they had just moved in over the weekend, and she had a hunch Mrs. Beamering hadn't been able to prepare anything.

"We always have more than enough roast, and Mrs. Beamering's going to bring a salad," Mother said. "We'll just make do."

My heart sank when I heard this. I didn't like it when we had guests over on Sundays. That was our time together as a family. Sundays had a routine that was close to a ritual for me. It was the best meal we had all week. Mother would start early in the morning by browning the meat and cutting the vegetables while my sister, Becky, and I set the table. The roast was put in the oven before we left for church so that right about the time the pastor stepped into the pulpit to preach, the oven clicked on and started cooking the meat. By the altar call, juices were bubbling in the bottom of the pan and the wonderful smell would be permeating the house. The first whiff of that aroma as I walked in the door after church was a major part of Sunday. It signaled home and comfortable clothes and reading the funnies and fine china and lace tablecloths and iced tea with sugar piled up in the bottom of the glass and long iced-tea spoons clanking around in the granular swirl. I wanted all this for myself. I didn't want to have to share it with anyone. And I didn't want to have to perform for anyone.

That's the other thing I didn't like about having guests on Sunday. When we had guests, we sat differently and talked differently. I had to keep my tie on until dinner was over, and no one ever talked to me, and I had to be careful not to eat too much. "Family Hold Back" (FHB) was the motto when we had guests for Sunday dinner, and I resented that. I liked being full and eating one more piece of meat just because it was there and it tasted so good. I liked not having to hold back and still having some left over. FHB applied to more than just food. We held back ourselves. We held back what we really wanted to say. We held back any right to deserving this time for ourselves. My parents' time was in great demand at the church during the rest of the week, so it was only natural that we would want them all to ourselves on Sunday.

My father was the Minister of Music for the Colorado Avenue Standard Christian Church in Pasadena, California. Before I was born, he had been a high school music teacher and band leader. Stories that sometimes surfaced made me wish I had been around then, because that man sounded like a lot more fun than the version I grew up with. Apparently my father had once been quite a hit with the students and even earned the nickname "Lips Liebermann" for the trumpet solos he used to play in the student dance band he had formed and conducted.

Something must have gotten lost when "Lips" traded in his horn for the ministry, because the man I knew always seemed preoccupied with worry, which I could never figure out, since he was in essence such a kind and good man.

The only time my father ever showed any real emotion was when he was directing the choir. He would step up to the little podium in the choir loft and infuse every eye with a charged wave of anticipation, and by the time his hands went up and came down for the first note of the organ introduction, he had sprung out of his small world of worry and become larger than life.

"We'll need to put a leaf in the table," said my father as we waited at the signal light on Huntington Drive.

"We'll need to put all three leaves in," added my mother. "There are five of them, you know."

"Is Ben coming?" I asked.

"Of course. Why wouldn't he?"

"I don't know," I said. "He's kind of strange."

"In what way, dear?" asked my mother.

"I don't know. He's just not like the rest of the kids. He doesn't smile a lot."

"It's always hard to move to a new home. You don't know because you've never had to, but Ben is in a totally strange place without any friends. He's probably just shy."

Then my sister spoke up. "He's not shy."

"Oh? Why do you say that?" asked my mother.

"Didn't you see him on the platform this morning?" Becky said, sliding up on the edge of the backseat and resting her arms on the dip in the middle of the front seat of our '57 Ford. "He looked like he was way too big for his britches, that's what I think."

"Now, Rebekah," said my mother, "don't go jumping to conclusions. You haven't even met the boy."

I knew what it was like up on that platform. Every time they introduced new members to the congregation, all the families of the church staff had to go up there and greet them. I always hated having to do that.

"Remember to smile, Jonathan," my mother would say, "and keep your hands at your side. Don't fidget." And then she'd fidget with my collar and my tie and my hair, and she'd lick her thumb and wipe off the sugar that was still on my face from the donuts they served every Sunday in the fellowship hall. My favorites were the big soft glazed kind that collapsed into my face when I took the first bite.

I always smiled on the platform, but it was only because my mother wanted me to. It was a silly smile, though. A fake one. When I look back at my childhood pictures, at least the posed ones, and compare them to Ben's pictures . . . well, there's no comparison. In my pictures I'm smiling all right, but I'm not really looking at anyone or anything. It's not me. It's just a look that doesn't seem to be connected to me in any way. In fact, if you thumb through the book of family photos that our church began publishing that year, you can find that look everywhere. It was the expected Christian look. Christianity at the Colorado Avenue Standard Christian Church was full of expected looks.

Ben's look was something else entirely.

In the backseat of the car, I pulled the bulletin out of my Bible and stared at the photo of the new first family. Ben was staring right into the camera, but his eyes were focused some-where just behind the lens, as if he were questioning the photo-grapher's right to be taking this picture.

"Look, Mom," I said, handing the picture to her, "look at his face."

Becky, still leaning over the front seat back, stared for a mo-ment at the picture my mother was holding, just as my father turned the car into our driveway. "I've seen that look before," she said. "You know when we have missionaries come on Sun-day nights and show us all those boring slides from the mission field? Doesn't he look just like one of those natives who don't want to have their picture taken? They think the camera will take away their spirit or something."

She was right. Ben had that same look. Like he was refusing to give anything of himself away.

We were certainly giving a large part of our Sunday away to the Beamerings, and I regretted it; but like most of my real feel-ings, I kept that inside, at least as much as a nine-year-old could. I walked into the house and smelled the Sunday roast and got put to work immediately without even getting to loosen my tie.

"Okay now, if everyone pitches in, we can get this done," said my mother.

Becky and I had to undo the table, put the leaves in, and reset it for nine. My father cut up the roast as he usually did, and my mother got going on the vegetables and the iced tea. There was a whole lot of clanging and banging going on in the kitchen as seldom-used pans and serving dishes were dragged from their hiding places and put into service. I could tell I was not the only one who resented this intrusion on our normal Sunday ritual. Some bangs from the kitchen were louder than they needed to be.

"Where are we going to heat up the water for the iced tea?" said my father in his high-pitched anxious voice. "There are no more burners on the stove!"

My father's books were always balanced, his car and his yard were always cared for, and his serving nature was an example to all, but his real feelings often banged around inside him and never came out.

"It's okay, dear, we'll just set the beans aside for now and put them back on right before we're ready. See if you can find another teapot. I think there's one above the refrigerator way in the back."

"I'll have to get a chair," I heard him say. "It's too far back."

"They're here!" shouted my sister from the living room.

"That's all right," Mother said calmly. "We'll just make two batches. Let it go."

"They're here!" Becky repeated, running to the door, and she and I were the first to get there. There was a clog of Beamerings in the front hallway as they all seemed to come through the door at the same time.

"Hi, Walter . . . Ann," said Pastor Beamering over the tops of our heads as he saw my mother and father coming behind us from the kitchen. "And this must be . . . Jonathan, right?" I nodded and smiled and shook his hand. It was a big, warm hand, and up close his smile seemed to cover my whole body with a kind of syrupy glow. "And this of course is Becky." He patted my sister on the head. "Now let me introduce my children." He patted their shoulders as he introduced them, like descending a scale on a xylophone. "This is Joshua, Peter, and . . . and . . ." His hand went for the final note, but there was nothing there. "Honey, where's Ben?"

Mrs. Beamering didn't answer because she had passed everyone at the door and made her way to the kitchen with a heavy salad bowl in her hand.

As for Ben, he had slipped through the traffic jam in the front hall and headed straight for the chocolate kisses on the coffee table in the living room. Three foil wrappers already lay there next to the candy dish.

"Ben, get over here. I want you to meet these people. And no more candy before dinner." Ben shuffled back to the front hall, and his father took hold of both his shoulders and planted him directly in front of us. "Ben, this is Mr. Liebermann, and this is Jonathan and Becky," he said, turning Ben's whole body slightly to face each person as if he were positioning a camera on a tripod.

"Hi," Ben said in a remote way along with something like a half wave, his head cocked to the side.

"Well, come in and sit down," said my father.

"Walter, that choir was wun-der-ful this morning," said Pastor Beamering as we all took seats stiffly. He talked just like he did in the pulpit, as if a large number of people were listening to him and taking notes. It made you want to look around the room to make sure a crowd hadn't gotten into the house somehow without being detected. "Took me right to the gates of heaven. We should have just sent everybody home after the anthem."

Not a bad idea, I thought. I looked at Ben, and something told me he was thinking the same thing.

"So, how is the moving going?" asked my father.

"As well as can be expected. If it wasn't for your kind invitation, we'd be eating beans and Spam off cardboard boxes right now."

"We wouldn't think of having you go without a dinner invitation on your first Sunday," said my father, borrowing my mother's words and sentiment. "Speaking of 'first Sunday,' that was quite a sermon you gave this morning. Had me on the edge of my seat. That's the first time I ever heard about . . . what's his name? . . . Pas—"

"Pascal," said Ben before his father could get the words out of his mouth. "Blaise Pascal. He was a seventeenth-century French physicist."

Becky and I looked at each other in amazement. I couldn't even say "physicist" without getting all tied up in the "s" sounds.

Pastor Beamering continued the conversation as if interruptions of this kind were a common occurrence. "Yep. Mr. Pascal was quite a guy. For all his scientific experiments, his concept of the God-shaped vacuum in every human heart is what made him famous. A perfect picture of the condition of man, wouldn't you say, Walter?"

"Oh yes, I think it captures it perfectly."

They went on to discuss their excitement over the Brooklyn Dodgers moving to Los Angeles while we all got more and more fidgety.

"Johnny," my father finally said, "why don't you show the boys your room and the backyard. There's probably a few minutes yet before dinner. And Becky, I'm sure Mother could use some help in the kitchen." Becky, very much aware of the older Beamering boys, reluctantly veered off to the kitchen with a red face as we all filed through the dining room.

Our house was small, with only two bedrooms, but my dad had turned the back screened-in porch into a bedroom for me. The walls were all windows, the dining room opened into it with double French doors, and it was also the main thoroughfare from the front of the house to the back, but it was still my room. I could close the doors and pull the curtains for privacy if I wanted it. But not today. With three leaves in, the dining room table butted into my room, putting my father's chair right in the center of it.

I led the three Beamering boys by the table with its nine iced tea coasters waiting for the arrival of their dripping wet glasses, and I started to feel a little better about having guests. Seeing the table all ready and hearing noisy conversations going on in the house suddenly made everything take on a holiday spirit.

Joshua and Peter immediately found my football and left for the backyard. Ben just stood there and inspected my room. The bunk bed against the wall, the built-in bookcase that contained more toys than books, and the desk on the other side of the room, presently cut off by the table.

"That's my bed up there," I said, too shy to be anything other than obvious. "Do you collect baseball cards?" I asked, fishing my pile of cards from a drawer under the bottom bunk.

"No, I don't care for sports very much. I like to read. Do you have any books?"

"I have some Hardy Boys."

"Yeah. I read all those when I was seven. I like Sherlock Holmes now."

"Who's he?"

"You never heard of Sherlock Holmes?"

"No," I said.

"He's a detective, like the Hardy Boys, only better. You can borrow my books if you like. What's that?" he asked, pointing at the bookshelf, and I started taking down the dusty model airplane. "No, not the plane, the car. I've never seen one like that. Is it a model? Did you put it together?"

"No," I said, proudly pulling down my favorite toy, a 1957 blue and white Ford Fairlane just like our own family car. "You buy them like this. They're better than models. You could never play with it if it was a model. They break too easily. Here."

Ben handled the car as if it were a museum piece, turning it over carefully. He examined it from every angle, peered in at the interior and rolled the wheels. It was the first time I saw his face brighten. "Wow, it's even got a dashboard and a steering wheel— and an instrument panel!" Then he set it down on the floor and rolled it back and forth. He laid his face against the floor and brought the car right up to his eyes until it bumped into his nose. "I like it from the front most of all. A chrome grille and clear plastic headlights! Where did you get it?"

"At the dime store across the street from my school. I stop by almost every afternoon to see if they have anything new. There's a '58 Edsel there right now."

"An Edsel? Really?"

"Yeah. It's been there for a while. No one seems to want to buy it. They're having trouble selling the real ones, too."

"I'd drive a real Edsel right now if I could. The Edsel is Ford's greatest idea."

Somehow it seemed right that Ben Beamering's favorite car would be an Edsel. I thought they were pretty ugly. Different, but ugly.

"It even has suspension," Ben observed as he rolled the Fairlane back and forth across the rag rug in my room and watched the wheels follow the bumps up and down. I couldn't believe that he noticed the suspension right away.

"I know. Doesn't it act just like a real car? You want to try it outside? I have roads and everything."

"Roads? Really? Sure, let's go!"

From that moment on, my whole view of Ben changed.

Ben was the first person to share my love of playing with cars. My other friends had graduated to making models to look at. But these detailed reproductions were much sturdier than any models; they were made for the road, and there were still plenty of miles left on my imagination. An inexhaustible wealth of adventure, from making roads and going on long trips, to engineering gas pumps and car washes. From the beginning, I could tell that Ben had the imagination to find all this in a car and more.

Actually, I didn't have many friends. Eric Johnson lived right behind us and we played together sometimes, but Eric was Catholic and went to a parochial school, and my parents tried to discourage me from spending much time with him. I grew up believing there was something wrong with Catholics, though no one ever explained what it was. I just had this general feeling that I might catch something bad if I hung around them too long. The same went for my friends at school, actually. None of those friendships went beyond the boundaries of the schoolyard, which was only a block from my house.

My parents were careful to make sure that any opportunity I had for a close relationship was at church, and since church was fifteen minutes and two school districts away, this presented some difficulty. Perhaps that was why I had learned to entertain myself and play for hours in a world of my own making.

When I discovered that Ben's imagination ran on the same wavelength as mine, it was like opening the door to a world that had only existed in my mind. I took him outside and showed him the roads I had drawn on the concrete with chalk and he could see all the things I saw. He noticed the no-passing lines around the curves, the left-turn lanes, and the STOP printed at the intersections. I had a whole system of roads that followed the walkways around the back of our house, down the driveway, and even along the curb out front. That was my favorite part. I imagined it a daring mountain road that dropped off into a rushing river below, which was actually runoff from the sprinklers of other houses up the street.

Ben loved it all, especially the curbside mountain highway. At dinner, he made a big deal about my roads and my Ford Fairlane and about the fact that there was an Edsel currently unaccounted for at the dime store, which initiated a discussion among the adults as to the fate of the unusual car.

"I don't think it has a chance," said Ben's father, making loud clanking sounds with his iced-tea spoon. "It's too far of a departure. It's a wonder it got off the drawing board."

"I don't mind the back," said my father. "It's the grille I can't stand. It's awful. It looks like a barracuda with its mouth open."

"Or an Oldsmobile sucking a lemon," laughed Pastor Beamering.

"I *like* the grille," Ben interjected between the tinkling

sounds of silverware and the stirring of tea. Ben's father was still working on his, and the way he was beating his glass, I thought for sure he was going to break through the bottom any minute. "It's my favorite part of the car."

"What do you suppose got into them to design such a thing?" said his father, and before anyone else could even give it a try, he answered his own question. I soon learned that this was a recurring aspect of any attempted dialogue with our new pastor. "I think they got carried away. Look at how the designs have been going. Bigger fins, more and more chrome—each new design becoming more outrageous. It was only a matter of time until someone reached a point of no return. Enter the Edsel. Or maybe I should say, exit the Edsel. Ha! How about that? Could be prophetic. Exit the Edsel. Kind of has a ring to it, don't you think?"

"Unless it's a false prophecy."

"Ben!" said his mother, and I tipped my tea glass slightly, catching it but sloshing some of its contents on the table. I was just settling it down when I caught a slight twinkle in Mrs. Beamering's eye as she reprimanded Ben. I dared not even steal a look at Ben's father, though I know exactly what look he had on his face because I saw it so many times afterward; it's printed on my memory. It was the look he always got when Ben crossed him in some way—a look made up of equal parts of anger, exasperation, embarrassment, and impatience, but with a dash of admiration.

"Ben," Pastor Beamering said in a very controlled voice, "maybe you would like to instruct us all about false prophecy since you know so much about it."

It got very quiet at the table. The pastor stopped stirring his tea, but Peter and Joshua took to stirring theirs, as if to pick up where their father left off. I couldn't take my eyes off Ben. I wondered what the critic of Sunday school songs was going to come up with now.

"Actually, Dad, it was a marketing problem. There was an article in the *Saturday Evening Post* last week that said the problem with the Edsel wasn't looks, but the fact that they created it on the results of a detailed study but didn't actually get the car out until five years later. By the time the car arrived, the market had completely changed."

Silence settled over the table like the undissolvable sugar floating to the bottom of Pastor Beamering's glass. Ben's brothers absorbed themselves in their food. My sister, as usual, was somewhere else with her thoughts and relatively disinterested. The two mothers exchanged glances. My father stared into his iced tea glass, trying to avoid the uncomfortable moment. Mr. Beamering raised his eyebrows, cleared his throat, and stared at his son with the look. And Ben was cutting a fresh piece of roast.

My mother finally broke the silence. "It sounds as if we have a future businessman on our hands here."

Or president of the Ford Motor Company, which was what I was thinking right then.

3

The Perfect Gift

"Mom," I said on the following Friday, "can Ben sleep over tonight?"

Becky and I were eating our Cheerios in the breakfast nook while my mother ironed in the kitchen. My father was rarely around for breakfast during the week. He always had early meetings at the church. T. J. Barham had started that tradition, and it looked as if Jeffery T. was going to continue it. Most Standard Christian pastors were highly driven and demanded the same from their staff as they did from themselves. Today we'd probably call these guys workaholics, but in 1958, in the Standard Christian Church, they were merely "dedicated to the Lord." Though I never heard her speak about it when I was a child, I know my mother wondered a lot about a dedication to the Lord that kept a man away from his family seventy to eighty hours a week.

"I think it would be fine to have Ben sleep over," she said, "but not tonight."

"Why not tonight?" I was anxious to play cars with Ben. Since the Beamerings lived in the next school district, we couldn't see each other at school, and we certainly couldn't play at church.

"Because your father is going to be home at a decent hour tonight, and I'm planning a nice dinner and a family evening at home for a change. Saturday is the church picnic, and you know what Sundays are like. Tonight is our only chance for some family time together this weekend. Maybe Ben can come over next Friday."

"What about me?" said Becky. "Can I have someone over?"

"I knew you were going to ask that," I said.

"You both know you can't have sleep-overs at the same time. Our house just isn't big enough for that. You may have a friend over another time, Becky."

"You know, Mom, I've been thinking about that Edsel car that's at the dime store. The one I told you about."

"Yes," she said, holding up a shirt and then smoothing out its sleeve on the ironing board. "After last Sunday, that car is pretty famous."

The steam from the iron was making small beads of perspiration form on her forehead, which she wiped off with the sleeve of her blouse. My mother was the most beautiful woman I had ever seen. She had clear, translucent skin and long, shiny brown hair that she usually folded back into a twist. Soft tendrils would break loose and fall over the smooth white temple of her face— a clean midwestern face, acquainted with hard work but soft in its appearance. She had grown up on a farm in Minnesota and met my father when he was in college there.

"I've been thinking how great it would be for Ben to have that Edsel," I said. "Then we could play cars together."

"Well, I'm sure he'd really like that."

"I was thinking maybe someone could get it for him. You know, maybe you could talk to Mrs. Beamering or something. It's only five dollars."

"No," my mother said as she set down the iron. "I'm not doing anything of the kind. If the car is that important to you, then you'll have to figure something out. You've got some money saved up from your allowance, haven't you?"

"Yeah, but only two dollars and fifty cents, and I was saving it for the Chevy that's coming in week after next. Abe says he thinks it will be a red '58 and that's the car I've been waiting for for months, Mom."

I stared at her hopefully but there was no sign of sympathy. "Sounds like you have a decision to make."

"But even if I did get him the Edsel, I couldn't get it by next weekend. I'd have to wait at least two more weeks."

"Aren't you getting a little ahead of yourself? We don't even know yet if Ben can come over next week. And if he can, you've got a week to earn some extra money. Maybe you should talk to your father about doing some work around the house."

"Okay, Mom," and I kissed her and she hugged me and Becky, and we went off to school like we always did—with the faint scent of her perfume clinging to where we last brushed against the side of her face.

School was only a block away from our house. On days when I was home sick, I could hear the recess bell and the voices in the playground. We were that close. I had a favorite rock I would kick to school and back, always leaving it in the same place so I could find it again. The trick was to get it back and forth with as few kicks as possible and without losing it in the bushes or the street. This particular rock had lasted since the end of Christmas vacation. A record. Becky thought it was silly, but I didn't care.

"So, are you going to get Ben the Edsel?" she asked. "That Chevy sounds like a beauty. Just think, it could be there right now all red and gleaming and—"

"Aw, cut it out!"

"Don't be so nasty," she said and kicked my rock clear out into the street. Then she laughed and ran off to her classroom. Sometimes I hated having a big sister.

All day long I thought about the Edsel. All day long I thought about the red '58 Chevy with the shiny grille, the rounded fins, and the six pointed taillights. After school I went directly to the dime store.

"Hey, Johnny. You'll be lookin' at the Edsel, eh?" Abe Dewendorfer greeted me.

Abe talked funny. He prided himself in thinking he was the only "down-easter" in California. Abe had come out from Maine to be near his daughter after his wife died, and ended up staying and managing this store.

The dime store on the corner was a small neighborhood variety store that thrived on its close proximity to the grammar school across the street. The well-stocked candy rack next to the counter made it a popular after-school hangout. But the first place I looked whenever I walked in was the shelf behind the counter where Abe kept the model cars. As far as I knew, these cars were something Abe concocted out of thin air. I never found them in any other store, anywhere. Lately, there had only been one car there, and that afternoon Abe had the Edsel out and waiting.

The cars came in boxes with cellophane windows, and each time I would ask if I could take the Edsel out so I could look at it up close. The flap on the end of the box was barely hanging on after all the opening and closing, but Abe always let me look.

The Edsel was all white with a long gold scoop down the side of each back fender. The interior was gold too and, unlike any of the models I had seen up to that time, it had two-toned upholstery—red and white. The real surprise, however, was when I discovered that the top came off with a snap. Just that fast, it became a convertible.

"When did you say you might have a '58 Chevy in?"

"Oh, hard to say. Probably a week or two. I'm gettin' half a dozen in with this order, but you can't always tell what they'll be. I just take what they send me. Like I said, I think at least one of them will be a Chevy. Most of them will be '58 Fords. Fancy that Chevy, eh?"

"Yeah." I certainly didn't like the '58 Ford—1957 was the last good year for the Ford. I'd take even the Edsel over the '58 Ford. As I stood there rolling it back and forth across the counter, I knew I had to have this car for Ben.

"I'll be back next week, Abe."

"Suit yourself. I'm sure it will still be here. I'm having about as much luck selling this car as they are at the Edsel lot down on auto row."

That afternoon I got the rock home in three kicks. The only

way I could do that was to have the last kick skip across the street, jump up over the curb, and scoot perfectly under the bush on the other side of the sidewalk where I always left it. I'd only done it once before.

"Hi, Mom."

"Hi, Jonathan! Come give me a kiss. How was school?"

"It was okay."

"Just okay?"

"Yeah . . . Mom? I want to get the car for Ben."

"That's nice, Jonathan. Especially when you hear what I have to tell you. Here, help me with this basket. I'm going to bring the laundry in."

The screen door slammed behind us as I followed her out to the clothesline. Our backyard was small but private, surrounded on all three sides by brick walls green with ivy. We had a covered patio, a large sycamore perfect for climbing, and two smaller fruit trees at the rear of the yard. Behind the garage was a permanent clothesline, and my father had rigged up a way to string three more lines between the fruit trees and the garage for days when my mother did sheets and bedspreads. Clothes dryers were just gaining popularity then, but my mother preferred the fresh smell that a day in the sun imparted to the laundry, especially the sheets and towels. This was a sheet day. They waved in the breeze like the tail of a giant kite trying to get up off the ground.

"I talked to Mrs. Beamering today," she said as I helped her fold the sweet-smelling, billowing white cloth.

"Can Ben come over?"

"Yes, and not only that, it's his birthday next Saturday," she said. "They aren't going to celebrate it until Saturday night, so she said it would be all right for him to sleep over on Friday, as long as he's home by noon."

A corner slipped out of my hand and the sheet settled on top of my face. I heard the screen door slam.

"She was actually very grateful because Ben doesn't know enough people yet to have a big birthday party. Coming over here will be something special, kind of like a party. I thought I'd bake a cake for him. What kind do you think he'd like?"

"Chocolate. With white frosting and coconut," I said, over-joyed.

"I thought you'd say that."

"What's this about a party?" Becky said, coming up behind us.

"Hi, honey. Give me a kiss. Why don't you get the other basket out of the garage and come help us."

"We were talking about next weekend," my mother continued as Becky fell in line with another empty laundry basket. "Ben's sleeping over, and it's his birthday on Saturday."

"What about me?" said Becky.

"You just had Julie over. It's Jonathan's turn."

I stuck my nose in the air, and she wrinkled hers at me. Becky was two-and-a-half years older and never let me forget it. She was much taller than me, though I was close to being stronger. I always assumed the mental domination my sister held over me was just one of those things you accept about having an older sister.

"What if I got invited somewhere? Julie was talking about maybe asking me over. She has to check with her mom."

"It's all right with me. Have Mrs. Flory call me."

"Now, that's what I call a good trade," I added, thinking that Ben and I could have the run of the house without my big sister around. "Gee, Mom, that car is really important now."

"Yes, it would be the perfect gift. Talk to your father tonight about earning that extra money. There. You two take the baskets inside while I take down these lines."

"Did you get your little rock home okay today?" my sister teased as we struggled with the screen door and the baskets.

"Yes," I answered, proudly. "Only three kicks."

My father was late coming home that night. By the time we sat down for our "family evening," it was almost eight o'clock. The chicken, which was going to be barbecued by my father outside on the grill, had been prepared by my mother in the kitchen.

"Jonathan, didn't you have something you wanted to ask your father?" my mother said as I cleared away the plates and she and Becky got the dessert.

"Oh, yeah. Dad, I was wondering if maybe there was something I could do around the house. What I mean is—I need to make two dollars so I can get a car for Ben for his birthday."

"It's Ben's birthday?"

"Yes, dear," my mother said. "We talked about that a few minutes ago. Ben's coming over next Friday night and Jonathan has the perfect gift in mind."

"Oh? What's that?"

"It's a '58 Edsel model car," I said.

"Oh . . . I see . . . yes, that is the perfect gift, isn't it? Let's see . . . mmmm . . . look at that!" he said, temporarily distracted by the strawberry shortcake Mother and Becky were bringing in from the kitchen.

"What about the windows?" said my mother. "I've been asking you to do them for weeks."

"I don't know if that would be a good idea," my father said.

I said I agreed with him, but he ignored the vote of confidence. "I don't think Jonathan's big enough to reach all the windows."

I agreed with that, too.

"We have a stepladder," my mother said, more and more pleased with this new angle on getting clean windows, after all. "He could get started in the morning while you're doing the yard, and you can check up on how he's doing."

"You know what's going to happen," said my father. He'd been through this many times before. Jobs that we started but he had to finish—or worse, do over. My father was a believer in the axiom that if you want something done right, you'd better do it yourself. My mother, on the other hand, always wanted to give someone else a chance to learn. Becky and I were always getting caught somewhere between these two philosophies.

"Yes, I know exactly what's going to happen," said my mother in a cheery, musical voice. "I'm going to get my windows done!"

"Can Becky help me?" I asked, seeking any backup I could find.

"If you want to pay me," she said, narrowing her eyes.

"Then I wouldn't have enough for the car. I need the whole two dollars."

"Don't forget your allowance," my mother added. "You've got fifty cents coming on Sunday."

"I know. I already figured that in."

"Okay," my father finally said, with little enthusiasm. "The windows for two bucks."

If he'd had a clue about how much this little agreement would end up costing him, I'm sure he would have gladly given me the two dollars right then and there and let it go at that.

As it was, I started out the next morning on the windows in my parents' bedroom. Dad suggested that I vacuum around the windows and sills first to get up all the loose dirt, so I got out the Electrolux and went to work. We only had the morning to accomplish our chores because the church picnic welcoming the Beamering family was at one o'clock. Things went pretty well until I got to a corner above one of the windows that had a nasty spider web in it. I could almost reach it, but the suction of the vacuum wasn't strong enough to make up the distance. I suppose I could have used the stepladder my mother had mentioned, but that didn't seem as much fun as the other idea I had.

I had seen my father do something with the vacuum to reverse the flow and make it blow out. He did this sometimes when he was trying to hurry up the coals in the barbecue. If I could do that, I was sure I could blow that spider web right out of there. I thought I knew how to set this, but unfortunately something went wrong. When I turned the Electrolux back on and pointed it up at the window frame, a black cloud started to form. It took me a few seconds to realize where it was coming from—that I was, in fact, blowing out the contents of the bag.

I dropped the hose and ran out of the room, coughing and wheezing, while whatever was left in the bag continued shooting into the room.

"Mom, I think there's something wrong with the vacuum cleaner."

"Oh? Why?" As soon as she saw me, a look of horror came over her. "What is that all over your face?"

"I don't know, but there's black stuff coming out of the vacuum cleaner."

"Oh no!" she said as she reached the bedroom, yanked the vacuum plug out of the wall, and stared at the mess in a state of shock. "Go get your father!" My mother was much better than my father at handling emergencies, and I could tell she wasn't doing well at all with this one.

"Dad, I think you'd better come inside. There's been an accident."

"An accident? Is anyone hurt?" he asked, dropping his broom and running on ahead of me.

"No, it's your bedroom."

"My bedroom?" he said as he ran down the hall. I stayed back as far as I could in the hallway.

"What on earth? What happened?"

"What did happen?" said my mother, looking for me. I slowly crept up to the door.

"Well, I tried to blow a spider web out of the corner of the window—"

"Blow?" my father yelled. "What do you mean—blow?"

"Well, I couldn't reach it and I thought I could—"

"Why didn't you come get me? We have a stepladder, you know . . . blow?"

"Just let it go, dear. It doesn't matter now," said my mother, a little calmer.

"There's more than just dust here. Why is it all so black?" My father's voice was still at screeching level.

"I vacuumed out the barbecue yesterday," said my mother.

"The barbecue? Why on earth would you vacuum the barbecue?"

"I wanted it nice for the barbecue dinner we were going to have last night, remember?" Now my mother's voice was picking up a little steam.

I slowly started retreating toward my bedroom. My sister was no comfort at all. She thought it was all pretty funny—until she got assigned a portion of the cleanup duty.

"Do you realize what this means?" I could easily hear my father's voice from my bedroom. "This means there is grease mixed in with all this! The carpet is probably ruined. Not to mention the curtains and the walls and the ceiling and the bedspread." At that point they hadn't even noticed yet what happened under the bed where they had storage boxes.

We (mostly *they*) spent the next three hours cleaning the room. The curtains had to come down and be taken to the cleaners, the bedspread had to be washed, the bed had to be taken completely apart—the stuff had even blown up into the box springs—and everything under it had to be gone through and cleaned individually. Some of the boxes had been open. The sheets we had taken off the line the day before had to be washed again. All this had to be accomplished in three hours because "We can't be late for the picnic" (my father said) and "We certainly aren't going to come home to this" (my mother said). In all of the excitement, my window job was totally forgotten by everyone but me.

Of course it wasn't funny then, but by the time Sunday morning rolled around, Pastor Beamering had gotten wind of the story and found a way to work it into the morning service.

"You all will recall my sermon last Sunday on the God-shaped vacuum in every human heart?" he began in the welcoming portion of the service, which he was trying to establish as an informal, lighter moment. "Well, it seems that the Liebermann family has found a new twist on the God-shaped vacuum." I sat in the pew and listened in utter horror. "It seems that Jonathan Liebermann was trying to help his parents do a little spring cleaning yesterday, when he got the hose hooked up to the wrong end of the vacuum and blew the contents of the vacuum bag all over his parents' bedroom."

There were groans and laughs everywhere. All the choir members were bobbing up and down, back and forth, trying to see around the people in front of them so they could find me out in the congregation. The eyes of the whole church were on me. I didn't know whether to laugh or cry.

"Now believe it or not, there's a lesson here for all of us. You folks all know that each and every one of us has a God-shaped vacuum in our heart, but some of us are not bringing God into that vacuum. We've somehow hooked the hose up to the wrong end, and we're blowing Him out of our lives. And if God's not there, I'm afraid the stuff that comes out is going to be pretty ugly, just like Jonathan Liebermann found out."

I'm sure Pastor Beamering could hardly believe his good fortune in having this anecdote dropped in his lap on his second Sunday at Colorado Avenue. He probably even credited God with providing it, but I didn't think God had anything to do with it.

Now Pastor Beamering turned around and talked right to my

dad. "Did you ever get it all cleaned up, Walter?" My father shook his head and kind of chuckled with his upper body—the kind of chuckle you could see from a distance. He must have been in on this. Somehow my father had managed to laugh about what had made him so angry the day before. Not just because he had gotten over it, but because he had given up something of himself for the glory of being used as an example by the pastor, even at his family's expense. Especially at my expense.

Pastor Beamering then turned back around and leaned into the pulpit for what appeared to be his main point. " 'The heart is deceitful and desperately wicked,' says the Bible. So what Jonathan has reminded us all of here is that we must be careful that we have the hoses of our lives hooked on the right way so that we're bringing God in and not blowing Him away. How about it, Jonathan? I know you'll get it hooked up right next time."

I looked up when he said my name, then quickly buried my face in my bulletin, where I was to find my second great shock of the morning.

Colorado Boulevard Standard Christian Church
Pasadena, California
A Standard Christian Church
Raising High the Standard of the Word of God
Pastor: Jeffery T. Beamering, Jr.
Assistant Pastor: Virgil Ivory
Minister of Music: Walter K. Liebermann
Organist: Milton Owlsley

That's the way the bulletins always started out, and I loved to read that header and see my father's name there. It made me proud—except for this morning, that is. My eye followed down the page until I got to "Offertory." Suddenly I remembered that I hadn't tithed in a whole month. I had decided last week, before all this stuff with the Edsel came up, that I would just wait until this week and put in a quarter. That would cover for today and the month I was behind. But if I tithed a quarter today, I wouldn't have enough money left over for Ben's car.

My father paid Becky and me a fifty-cent allowance every Sunday morning before church. He usually gave it to us before we dressed for church, so sometimes I'd forget and leave it on my desk. I was hoping this was one of those mornings, until I remembered that he had given me two shiny quarters in the car on the way to church. I hated the fact that those quarters were in my pocket.

Right up to the moment the offering plate passed under my nose, I wrestled with this. Didn't God know how much I wanted to do this for Ben? Didn't He think this was okay? Wouldn't He maybe see this as a kind of tithe? I had gotten behind before and made it up. Maybe we could make a deal . . . which in the end was what I did. I vowed to give Him my entire allowance the following week, ("more than ten percent, God") and passed the offering plate by as two quarters burned in the pocket of my pants.

And then I wondered, as the plate reached the end of the row, if I had just reversed the vacuum and blown God out of my life.

All the way to children's church, I was hounded by comments. "Way to go, Jonathan!" "Nice job, Johnny." "Hey, Johnny, why don't you come over and vacuum our place sometime. It's already a mess." Much to my surprise, I had become an instant hero with Bobby and the back row. "You'll have to tell us how to do that, Johnny, so we can try it."

Only Ben seemed to understand how I felt. "Well, Jonathan, you just got a little taste of what it's like to be a preacher's kid. He does that kind of thing to us all the time. Sometimes I wonder if I'm living my life or if someone's making it up for me."

The rest of Sunday came and went with no mention of the window job that had started all this vacuum business, and I didn't have the nerve to bring it up to my father. On Monday morning, I finally mentioned the subject to my mother.

"Mom, remember I was going to get paid for doing the windows? What do I do now?"

"You made an agreement with your father. I haven't heard anything that would change it. You'll just have to get busy after school."

"But do I have to do all the windows?"

"That's the way I heard it."

"But, Mom, I don't know if I'll have enough time. And I think Little League practice starts this week."

"You'll just have to get at it this afternoon then. Jobs like this move quickly once you get them down to a system. Just promise me one thing—that you'll use the stepladder this time."

"Promise."

That week a system did develop. Each day after school I would do a few windows, and when my dad came home in the evenings he would check them out to make sure they were done well, without any streaks. What this amounted to was that he did them all over again. He told us he was only polishing a few smudges I'd missed, but we all knew better. My mother didn't care. By the end of the week, she had the cleanest windows in town. And I didn't care either, because by the end of the week I had five dollars in my pocket.

All day Friday I was conscious of those four dollar bills and four quarters in my pockets. At times I was sure one of those quarters, the tithing one, was still burning a hole. Then I would push the guilt aside and finger the four dollar bills, imagining the car and the look on Ben's face when he saw it. My hand hardly ever left my pockets all day except to pull out the dollar bills, unfold them, smooth them out, count them, and then fold them back up and return them to the watch pocket of my jeans. The rest of the time I was rolling the quarters around with my fingers, numbering them over and over, making sure they were all there.

I was sure everyone knew I had five dollars in my pocket and that any moment some bully was going to make me cough up the money, or that somehow it would fall out of my pants or disappear through a hole in my pocket. I think I was afraid God was going to punish me by making something happen to the money. I didn't even play kickball at recess. I just stood around with my hands in my pockets.

At the final bell, which I was sure would never come, I was out of there like a shot. In all my worrying about the money, it had never even occurred to me to worry about whether the Edsel might still be there. As he was wrapping it up for me, Abe said, "It's a good thing you came by today because, believe it or not, someone else is very interested in this car. Somebody your age was just in here looking at it yesterday with his mother."

"What did he look like?"

"Oh, he was about your age, maybe a little smaller than you."

"Did he have big ears?"

"Well, now that you mention it, they were kind of large. At least they stuck out. Why, do you know him?"

"I think so. If it's who I think it is, he's the one I'm buying this for."

"Well, here you are," he said, handing me the Edsel all gift-wrapped and snug and mine in a paper sack. "You're going to make one boy mighty happy."

"I know," I said with a grin. "I can't wait."

Ben was due at our house around five, and I convinced my mother to let me give him the car right away instead of after supper with the birthday cake. "By then it will be too dark to play outside," I said. So as soon as Ben got there, I took him to my room where I had his present waiting for him on the bottom bunk.

"Happy Birthday!" I said.

"For me? How did you know it was my birthday?"

"My mom found out."

Ben tore off the wrapping paper, and when he got his first glimpse through the cellophane window, he froze. He didn't scream, or shout, or tear the box open to get at the car, or run and tell his mother before she left. He didn't do any of the things I had imagined him doing as I had rehearsed this scene over and over throughout the week. Instead, he set the box down reverently in front of him and stared at it for the longest time—with wonder, with eyes turning slightly wet, and with what I can only describe as a certain sense of worship.

"It's a miracle," he said finally. I didn't know how to respond. "When did you get this?"

"This afternoon," I said, puzzled.

"Did my mother know?"

"No," I said. "I've been planning it all week."

"This was the only thing I wanted for my birthday. My father said I couldn't have it. My mother said she called the store and it wasn't there anymore so I should forget about it, and I knew she wasn't just saying that. She wouldn't lie to me about something like this. Even to surprise me. So you know what I did? I prayed. I've never prayed for anything like this before—anything that I thought was impossible. In fact, I never pray very much at all."

Ben slowly removed the worn flap and rolled out the shiny new Edsel as if he were driving it out of its garage for the first time without any miles on it and wanted to remain a few hundred feet away from anything that might potentially mar it. A huge smile finally came over his face; it seemed to raise his ears a few inches.

We played with our cars for hours that night, or so it seemed. We ran errands, made luggage carriers for long trips, got our cars dirty and washed them. We ran out of gas and filled up a hundred times. My father had to come out and practically drag us in for supper. Afterward, we discovered a way to make the headlights shine by inserting small penlight flashlights under the front fenders so the light would come through the clear plastic head lamps. Ben never grew bored or tired of this like Eric Johnson or other kids I'd had over. His imagination and appreciation for the details of play were the same as mine. We were like one person.

Except when it came to coconut frosting. He scraped all of it off his piece of birthday cake.

"You know," he said that night as we were lying in bed with our cars propped up on the bed rails so we could study them in the moonlight, "this has been the best birthday I've ever had."

"Yeah, me too," I said.

"It's not your birthday."

"Well, it's the best one I've been to, then."

When my mother came in to say good-night, she prayed that we would have "sweet dreams" and thanked God for "Jonathan's new friend," and asked Him to "bless Ben's family in their new home." Then she kissed us both. The room was quiet for a while after she left, until Ben spoke up.

"You know the grille on my car? You know what it looks like?" I leaned over the edge of the top bunk and looked down. Ben was lying on his side staring at the front end of his Edsel. "A kiss," he said. "It looks like someone all puckered up for a kiss." I rolled back in my bunk chuckling.

"Do your parents do it?" he said after another long silence.

"Do what?"

"You know. Do your parents have sex?"

"Do yours?" I said, trying to dodge such a direct encounter

with what had been for me, until then, a very indirect subject. I also didn't want to let on that I didn't know something he might know.

"Of course," he said glibly. "Sometimes I can hear them from my room. They make a lot of noise, especially my father."

"How do you mean?" I said, leaning over the edge again and looking down at Ben.

"You mean you don't know?"

And it was from that vantage point that I received my first course in sex education. Not from my father or mother, but from the graphic mind and the dexterous hand gestures of Ben Beamering, viewed from the top bunk of my bedroom in the moonlight.

"Where did you learn all this stuff?" I asked.

"From books," said Ben. "I walked in on my parents once too, and it's just like it is in the books. It's gross."

I rolled over on my back and stared at the ceiling, which was only a few feet from my face, and slowly fell asleep with only one thing on my mind. *They do that?*

4

Magnetic Field

It happened again. It happened too fast for any of us to do anything about it. It wouldn't have happened except that Miss Kingsley, for some reason, abruptly quit teaching children's church. Her temporary replacement was a young college student with an accordion. He led us in a number of songs that morning. In fact, he got us worked up pretty good, especially on a couple of spirituals. We were so used to Miss Kingsley pounding away on the stationary piano that the new teacher's ability to walk around the room while he played kept us spinning in our seats. Once he even let us gather around him and push the buttons on the side of his accordion. For a while, we punched the chords while he improvised melodies on the keyboard. We were all so enthralled that it caught us totally by surprise when he started right into "Jesus loves me, this I know" without any warning.

Once again, Ben's clear angelic voice took over. Once again, Ben had the whole song to himself. As soon as we heard the opening strains of the familiar chorus, we turned to statues in our seats, and the young man with the accordion went on playing a thin, exposed accompaniment to the sensitive boy soprano voice that seemed to come from another world.

Except this time I noticed something different. This time I wasn't so taken aback by the whole experience. This time I realized that Ben had his own version of "Jesus Loves Me." The verse was the same, but when he came to the chorus, he sang:

> Yes, Jesus loves me,
> Yes, Jesus loves me,
> Yes, Jesus loves me,
> But I will tell me so.

It sounded so much like "The Bible tells me so" that it was easy to miss.

I played the words over a number of times in my mind. They didn't make sense. "But I will tell me so." Maybe I wasn't hearing correctly. Maybe Ben's voice had played some kind of trick on me.

Ben's singing had the effect of heightening the spiritual nature of the room much like an electrical storm carried a highly charged magnetic field along with it. This latest foray into the ethereal sent our new accordion-playing teacher off on an impassioned sermon on the love of God, as if he were speaking to an evangelistic crusade of thousands instead of only fifteen squirmy grade-schoolers in the basement of a church. He even gave an invitation and played "Just As I Am" on his accordion. Normally he would never have gotten away with this kind of thing, but Ben's strange magnetic field was still hovering in the room. At least that's the only way I could account for Bobby Brown going forward—and, of course, the whole back row with him. But by the time they were up there and the teacher was asking them why they had come—was it to receive Christ or rededicate their lives?—they weren't sure, except that they did want to push the buttons on his accordion one more time.

Was Ben conscious of the effect his voice had? And had he really sung those strange words? These questions bothered me for the remainder of children's church. They bothered me all the way home and all through Sunday dinner. I determined I would bring up the subject the next time we were alone.

It wasn't until the following Saturday that I finally got my chance.

"Can you believe those guys went forward last Sunday?" I said, thinking Bobby Brown's momentary lapse into conversion might be a handy back door into the subject I was determined to tackle.

"It was probably a temporary loss of memory," he replied.

"Memory of what?"

"Of their calling as bullies."

"What do you suppose would make them lose their memory?" I said, prying at an opening. Ben didn't reply.

We were lying on our backs in my backyard, taking a break from playing with our cars. It was an unusually warm day in May, carrying with it premonitions of summer and long days to play together. Ben and I spent as much time planning as we did actually playing with our cars.

In the dirt that surrounded the bases of the peach and plum trees that sat side by side behind our patio, we were going to build our own suburbia. We each had our own property, mine under the peach tree, Ben's under the plum. Everything would be authentic, down to the smallest detail. We would even use our Tonka toys to dig dirt and haul it away. It was perfect: I had the truck and Ben had the bulldozer. That day we had been working on lines of demarcation for our properties, marking areas with matchstick stakes and string. At the moment, we were discussing the placement and construction of the backyard swimming pools. Ben wanted to use real concrete, but I thought concrete would be too coarse for such a small model pool. We should try something smoother, like plaster of paris. Ben's busy mind was already working on a miniature filtering system.

His lack of response to my last question made me certain that he did not want to discuss what had happened on Sunday, but I wasn't going to let it go that easily.

"Do you think the song had anything to do with it?" I asked after a long pause, taking a big chance.

"What song?"

Staring up through the long fingerlike leaves of the peach tree with its small green balls of fruit, hard and clustered in their early stages, I tried to figure out a subtle approach to the delicate subject. I decided there was no way to be subtle.

" 'Jesus Loves Me,' Ben . . . you know, the song that seems to make everything stop every time you sing it? Why is it that you only sing that one song? And why does your voice have such an effect on everyone?"

There. I had asked just about everything I could think of except for his rewrite of the last line. Since he wasn't answering right away, I decided to finish what I started.

"And why did you change the words to the last line?"

Ben was quiet for a long time. In that silence, still staring up through branches into tiny patches of blue sky, I was wondering if I had said too much.

"I don't believe it," Ben finally spoke.

"Believe what?"

"I don't believe that Jesus loves me. Show me where the Bible says 'Jesus loves you . . . Ben.' I can't find it anywhere. The song should really be 'Jesus loves us.' Now that would make sense. Too many people sing 'Jesus loves me' and they don't really mean it or they don't even know what it means. I'm not going to say anything I don't mean, especially with God standing around listening. That's why I changed the last line. The Bible doesn't tell me 'Jesus loves Ben,' and until I can tell myself that, I'm not going to sing about something that I can't believe is true."

"But didn't He die on the cross because He loves everybody? Isn't that the point—I mean—aren't you and I in there some-place?"

"Yeah, but that's everybody. He died for everybody. But I'm not everybody. I'm Ben Beamering. I get lost being a tiny part of everybody."

Suddenly I thought of Ben's face in the picture of his family and Ben's face in church on the platform that first day, and I understood something new about that strange expression. It was the look of someone lost—lost among people who looked like they were all so happy to belong.

Ben lost me, too, when he talked like this. I was quiet for a while, wondering what made Ben so smart—it would not be the last time I wondered this. He always seemed to be thinking about things that I wouldn't be concerned with for years. The resulting effect was either to make me feel dumb or to make Ben seem like he came from somewhere in outer space. More often than not it was a combination of the two.

To counter my uneasiness, I jumped up and tried to pull a small green peach off the tree. In its premature stage, the stem was so strong that it broke off higher up on the branch, yielding me a handful of leaves and a few clusters of unripe fruit.

"Why do you bother singing it at all, then?" I asked, snapping off the hard, golf-ball-sized peaches and throwing them as far as I could into the neighborhood, "and why only that song?"

"It's the only song I believe in . . . with the change, that is."

"Do you think you'll ever be able to believe Jesus loves you?"

"If I do, you'll be the first to know."

"But I still don't understand why that song has such an effect on people when you sing it," I said.

"I don't understand it either," he said. "I wish I could, because I know it frightens everyone. It scares me too sometimes."

5

The Master Key

Other than playing with our cars and our suburban development, our next favorite thing was the activity Ben and I referred to as "spying." Because our families were always the last to leave the church on Sunday, we usually had forty-five minutes to an hour of prime-time spying after both Sunday morning and Sunday evening services.

For this clandestine endeavor, the entire church was enemy territory, and to be seen by anyone was tantamount to death. Thus, in a desperate attempt to stay alive, no closet, room, hall, or passageway was left unexplored. By the time school was out, we knew every beam of that church intimately. We drew up detailed maps of its inner structure and kept a log of the regular movements of staff members—especially the janitor, Harvey Griswold, or "Grizzly" as we called him because of his reaction upon finding us anywhere he thought we were not supposed to be. (Which soon came to be anywhere at all.) He would growl and hold his arms out in desperation, and when you're hiding in a dark place, whoever discovers you is almost always going to be backlighted, and Mr. Griswold's wiry hair, outstretched arms, and throaty voice yielded an imposing bearlike silhouette. Hence, the nickname.

Though at first we were frightened of him, we soon discovered we had nothing to fear. Harvey Griswold was a deaf-mute and easy to fool. The throaty growl was the only sound he could make. He was also deathly afraid of heights, so we could always lose him by going up. Grizzly was so afraid of heights that he wouldn't even go up into the balcony, a phobia which necessitated having a volunteer to clean that part of the sanctuary and created a bother that many on the board of deacons wanted to solve with a new janitor. But too many church members loved Harvey and knew that if he lost this job, he would not likely find another.

Our church had been built in the early 1920s, and though it had gone through some remodeling and stood on one of the busiest corners in Pasadena, it still had the charm of an old wooden church in the country. Had we been at all familiar with the Northeast, we would have recognized it as a typical New England white clapboard church, quite unusual for southern California. To us, however, it had no architectural identity apart from being a fortress that housed a heavenly host of childhood imaginations.

As summer approached, our system of surveillance became

more and more sophisticated, and soon turned into a major operation.

We found the perfect headquarters in what had once been the bell tower. A number of years earlier, the bells had been replaced by loudspeakers, and there hadn't been any activity in the tower since. About halfway up there was a ledge, a sort of landing, where a vent afforded a clear view outside to the front of the church; opposite that we discovered a tiny four-by-six-inch window where we could look down into the sanctuary from high up the wall behind the balcony. The window must have allowed the bell ringer to see when the benediction was over so he could commence ringing. That was one tradition that still lived on: the ringing of the church bells immediately following the benediction, only now this sound was cued electronically from the organ.

Which left the bell tower to us. Ben even found a secret compartment, the size of a bathroom medicine cabinet, where we hid our maps of the building, our logs of activity, our flashlights, and a private stash of candy and gum. Of course, the location of our headquarters, over two stories up a somewhat rickety, vertical, wooden ladder, was forever safe from Grizzly's scrutiny. I must admit, I had a few queasy moments myself climbing that ladder until I got used to it. We did make sure, however, that we always lost the growling janitor before ever entering the closet that led to the entrance to our headquarters, figuring this would keep him from suspecting that we might be using the tower as a hideout.

Until the day when, after a mad dash to the closet, we found the door locked.

"What are we going to do?" I asked Ben.

"Don't worry, I'll think of something."

"Who do you suppose did this?"

"Probably Grizzly. Maybe he finally figured it out. He's not ever going to go up there himself, but he's probably thinking he can keep us out. But never mind. This has given me an idea. This could turn out even better for us."

Ben was always turning adversity into an opportunity for something better. His mind was always working to rethink apparent setbacks. I never once found Ben stuck without an option.

Our assumption that it was Grizzly who locked the door was confirmed by finding a number of doors locked that day. Apparently Mr. Griswold was coming up with some maneuvers of his own.

"You know," said Ben, "he's probably not as dumb as everybody thinks. He doesn't know where we are, but he's going to limit our hiding places and flush us out. Not bad for old Grizzly."

The following Sunday during the offering, Ben, who had been allowed to sit with me during the first part of church, produced his idea. While we were all reaching into our pockets for money, Ben reached into his pocket, motioned with his eyes for me to look down, and there, partially out of his pocket and shielded by his cupped hands, displayed, for my eyes only, was a brand-new, shiny key.

"To the closet?" I whispered with wide eyes.

"Better than that," said Ben with his mischievous smirk. "It's the master key to the whole church!"

"How did you ever get that?"

"I took it off my father's key chain."

"You can't do that!" I said a little too loudly. The woman in front of us turned around and gave us a nasty look.

"You've got to put it back!" I said more softly but with much more intensity.

"I already did," said Ben with that cocksure look he got when he knew he'd won. "I copied it at the hardware store."

Now we had carte blanche to the whole church. Not only could we enter rooms at will, but we could lock them behind us, a development that proved to be helpful later on when Bobby Brown and his buddies wanted to get into the spy business with us. Ben and I liked keeping our espionage activities to ourselves. With a master key in our possession, we were definitely moving to a new level of investigation. With it, we could keep Grizzly from knowing we were even around.

———————

We were lying under the fruit trees again a few weeks later in early June. The peaches were now halfway between the size of a golf ball and a tennis ball. The plums were just coming out. Our miniature suburbia was developing more rapidly now that school was out. It had been only a week, but already we had graded our driveways, dug around our foundations, and "poured them," which really meant we had laid down the square concrete slabs Ben's father let us have when he remodeled their patio with brick. The slabs turned out to be the perfect size for foundations for our future homes.

"I know what we can use for the driveways," I said as we surveyed the construction site. "Sand. Sand will look just like gravel."

"Perfect," said Ben. "And we have some of that too. I'll bring it tomorrow."

With school out, we played together almost every day. Ben's parents had started letting him ride his bike to my house. The trip from his house to mine was downhill almost the whole way, so it took him only fifteen minutes. Once we tried to ride back to his house together, but that was uphill and it took us almost forty-five minutes. As much as we valued our independence, we didn't want to work that hard, so my mom got into the habit of driving Ben and his bike back home in the late afternoon, and at least once a week Ben would stay over. Mrs. Beamering continually brought up the inequity of this arrangement, but my mother kept insisting that it was no trouble at all since we played so well together. Plus, we kept assuring Ben's mom that we wanted to be near our construction site. So Ben and I spent almost every waking hour, and quite a few sleeping ones, together that summer.

Meanwhile, our little backyard suburbia was taking shape in much the same way it would in the real world. Slowly. After grading the property and laying the foundations for our two-unit housing tract, we began construction. For Ben and I being in the process of making something was more fun than having it completed, so we took our time and spared no detail. Our houses were not just going to look authentic on the outside; they were going to be completely finished on the inside. When you looked through the windows, you would see rooms and doorways and halls and ceilings.

We made the houses entirely of balsa wood and glue, and we

made them "from scratch," as we used to say. We copied the floor plans from award-winning houses we found in my parents' *Better Homes and Gardens* magazines. The floor plans had to be drawn to a scale to match our cars, of course, and we constructed the walls with two-by-four studs and proper bracing for windows and doors. That first summer we never got further than the framing. Having a long-term project like this meant we always had the option of working on the houses—which we did in my garage—or taking them out and putting them on their foundations and then driving our cars up as if we were visiting the construction site, inspecting the progress of the work, and anticipating when we would be able to move in.

Ben continued to cherish his Edsel. When we were going through the magazines looking for floor plans, he would take note of every Edsel ad. One day he found a new one in the current June issue of *Life* and asked if he could clip it out.

"Sure," I said. "You can take all the other ones, too, if you want. I'm sure my parents won't mind."

"I don't need to. I already have those."

"You do? You mean you saved all those other ads?"

"I've saved everything I could find on this car."

"How come?"

"I want to see how it comes out. I want to see how long it lasts. Do you know that they sank 250 million dollars into research and marketing for this car? Ford had been working on developing a new line of cars since 1948. And then, after ten years and all that money, they came out with this. Doesn't that make you wonder?"

No. Because I didn't get it. But I didn't say anything.

He picked up his Edsel and held it right up to my face. "You have to admit it. *This* is an ugly car. Look at it. Can 250 million dollars sell this car to the American people? Either the Edsel is one big mistake, or someone's trying to pull one over on us."

"But . . . I don't understand. I thought you liked this car," I said, trying to hide my hurt over the fact that Ben would treat my hard-earned gift with such contempt, not to mention my shock over this sudden about-face in his affections.

"Oh, I do. I like this car a lot. That's just the problem. I'm trying to figure out why. What made me start liking something so ugly? Look at this," he went on, pointing to the current ad. The photograph was a picture of two Edsels, one of them a convertible, parked near a marina with a few fun-loving affluent people standing around unwilling to leave their cars for their boats. Then he read the caption out loud: " 'In less than one year, Edsel's outstanding design has become as familiar as it is distinctive. In fact, you can recognize the classic Edsel lines much faster, much farther away, than you can any other car in America!' Well of course you can! You can spot that lemon-sucking grille from a mile away! This car is all puckered up and ready to puke! Anyone can see that. It's a wonder that anyone would buy one of these," he said. "Did I ever tell you I went to the showroom last September when they pulled the covers off the cars for the first time?"

"No," I said, still in a mild state of shock.

"I can't remember when I was ever more excited. I was close to the front, and I was up on my father's shoulders when they pulled the cover off the first car. It was the strangest feeling, looking at that ugly grille and those beady headlights. . . . I loved it and hated it all at the same time. I get the same feeling when I look at myself in the mirror."

This would be the first of a number of conversations Ben and I had about the Edsel, none of which I really understood at the time. As much as I loved our models and appreciated certain classic designs, I couldn't fathom his fascination, his growing obsession with the fate of the Edsel—as if it meant something to him personally.

6

Operation Mercy Canary

"I've got an idea," announced Ben, suddenly sitting up. It was a few days after our conversation about the Edsel and we were both stretched out underneath the fruit trees, taking a break from our building.

"What?" I asked, thinking he had some new scheme for our suburban neighborhood.

"I know how we can wake everybody up in church."

"What do you mean?" I said. "I didn't know they were asleep."

"Of course they are. They sit there every Sunday and everything happens just like it says in the bulletin. Mr. Mason is usually asleep before we leave for children's church. I even heard my dad complaining the other day about how everyone was sleeping through his sermons. Well, we'll just have to wake them up, that's all."

"How?"

"How do people wake themselves up in the morning?"

"An alarm clock?"

"Exactly. That's what we'll do. We'll set off an alarm clock."

"In church?" Now I was sitting up as well.

"Yes. In church. Remember when we were spying in the church offices last night?" He didn't wait for my nod. "Well, I saw the bulletin plan for next week on my father's desk and noticed the Scripture reading for Sunday. It's in Ephesians 5 somewhere. I read it last night. Go get your Bible."

Wondering what Ben could possibly be up to now, I ran into the house and came back out with the Bible I had won for Scripture memorization in Sunday school in the first grade. Ben found Ephesians and started fingering through the words.

"Here it is," he said. "Listen to this: 'And have no fellowship with the unfruitful works of darkness, but rather reprove them. For it is a shame even to speak of those things which are done of them in secret. But all things that are reproved are made manifest by the light: for whatsoever doth make manifest is light. Wherefore he saith, Awake thou that sleepest, and arise from the dead, and Christ shall give thee light.'"

Ben looked up at me from the Bible as if I was supposed to get it. I didn't.

"So?" I said.

"'Awake thou that sleepest,'" he quoted. "That's when we'll do it."

"Do what? What are you talking about?"

Ben's face suddenly took on the look of someone who had just tasted a morsel of indescribable goodness—only in Ben's case it was a thought-morsel, an indescribably delicious idea.

"I bet we could make an alarm clock go off in the front of the church right when my dad reads that part. Just imagine: 'Awake thou that sleepest' and suddenly from out of nowhere comes 'Brrrrrrrrrring!' And no one can do anything about it!"

"You're crazy!"

"Listen. We can do this. It'll be a cinch. Remember the scaffolding we found behind the organ pipes so the repair people can work on them? We could set it off from there and they'd never find it until the clock was run down."

I looked at Ben's excited face and thought of all the negatives. "But you'd never be able to hear from back there," I said. "The organ would be too loud. Mr. Owlsley always plays during Scripture reading. How would you know when to set it off?"

"Hmmm," Ben's mind went on undaunted. "Maybe you could signal me somehow."

"How would I do that without someone seeing me?" I was trying to throw up as many barriers as I could think of. "Ben, you have a lot of great ideas. That one you came up with yesterday for the windows on our model houses, that was great, but this time—" I shook my head.

"Wait a minute!" he whispered excitedly. "That's it! You could signal me from the little window in the tower!"

"Oh, great. What am I going to do, wave a white flag?"

"You could flash the flashlight from up there, just like we do when we're playing Morse code when no one's around. All we have to do is find a place behind the organ pipes where I can have a clear view of the window."

"But someone would see that—someone from the choir or someone on the platform. They'd be after us so fast."

"No, they wouldn't. It would catch everyone by surprise. They wouldn't know what to do. They'd spend all their time trying to find the alarm clock; they'd never find us. I could be out of there as soon as I set it off, and you'd be safe in the tower."

"Sure, as long as no one saw a flashlight go off from up there. No, Ben," I said. "This just isn't a good idea . . . and what about children's church? Won't they miss us?"

"I thought about that, but that new teacher they have hates me. She'll be so glad we're out of her hair, she won't say a thing."

Ben let the force of his argument settle in. He had thought of everything.

"Oh, come on, Jonathan. It's just a joke. My dad does the same thing from the pulpit all the time. What about the big deal he made over you and the vacuum cleaner? We're just going to give him a little of his own medicine, that's all. Besides, we're going to help him wake everybody up!"

"But I've never gotten in trouble before, at least not on purpose. I don't think I want to start now."

"Oh, I see. Don't want to mess up your record, huh? What about mine? I'm the preacher's kid, remember? If anyone should be worrying about their record, it should be me. You worry about stuff like that too much. You need to care a lot less about what other people think and a lot more about what you think."

"Well . . . my dad's the choir director. There's not much difference, you know. They're both on the front of the bulletin."

Ben shook his head and laughed at me. "What are you so afraid of? Even if they did catch us, what would they do? What could they do? Kick us out of the church? We'd probably have this big session with my dad, and he would give us some kind of warning, and that would be the end of it."

"They could keep us from playing together." I was trying to think of the worst.

"So? Even if they did, that wouldn't last for very long. Our parents like us being friends too much."

"You're probably right about that," I said, weakening slightly. "Do you really think we could pull it off without getting caught?"

"I'm telling you, we can," he said eagerly. "So you'll do it?"

"No, I didn't say that."

"I have an idea," he said. "Why don't you at least do a trial run with me tomorrow night after prayer meeting. We can see if there's a place behind the pipes where I can see the flashlight, and then I can check from the choir loft and the platform to see if I can even see the flashlight from there. Would that make you feel better?"

"Well, okay, but I'm only agreeing to a tryout."

Later that night I overheard my mother and father talking about Ben and me while they were doing the dishes. My father had commented on how it was often the case in Standard Christian churches that new senior pastors spent the first year watching everyone like a hawk and deciding which of the existing pastoral staff to keep and which to replace.

"You don't think Jeffery is thinking of replacing you, do you?"

"I don't know. He's hard to predict. If we have anything really going for us, it's as much the result of Ben and Jonathan's relationship as it is my job. I assume he likes what I'm doing. He says he does, but I'm never sure if he's just saying that. I do know he likes the fact that Ben has found a friend in Jonathan. Apparently the boy hasn't had too many friends in the past."

"Speaking of Ben and Jonathan, guess what I saw today?" said my mother. "I saw them in the backyard studying the Bible together, of all things. Isn't that wonderful? And on their own initiative, too.

"I like Ben, don't you?" she added.

"Well, he has some strange ideas, but I guess I like him. I like who he's related to more."

"I wish you wouldn't talk like that. It sounds so mercenary." (Except that I didn't know the word *mercenary* when I overheard this. To me it sounded like "mercy canary.")

"I'm sorry, dear, but it is a job, and in my position it's a job that depends solely on the whim of the senior pastor. I hate living like this, but it always feels like I'm one false move away from another church."

"Walter, stop that. You're too good at what you do to talk like this. Besides, Jeffery likes you a lot. I don't think you have anything to worry about."

"You think so?"

"I know so. You know what Martha told me a few days ago? That Jonathan was the best, best friend Ben had ever had."

" 'Best best friend?' Is that what you meant to say?"

"Yes. That's just how she said it: 'best best friend.' "

"Like I said, I think my job owes a lot to those kids."

"Have you ever heard of a mercy canary?" I asked Ben the next night when we got to prayer meeting.

Prayer meeting was something I never did understand. Hardly anybody ever came, except old people. It was almost as if the whole evening was designed with the dim-spirited in mind, to insure that they could indeed be Christians with their lights on low. Even Pastor Beamering was less than enthusiastic on Wednesday nights. I actually think he was waiting for the old guard to die off so he could yank Wednesday nights out of the church calendar, or at least replace this worn-out service with something more appealing. Once in a while a new, excited convert would show up, but they soon caught on to the fact that this was not a place to get too excited about anything more than praying for your dying aunt, your dying spouse, or your dying self. Luckily Ben and I never had to attend prayer meeting, but we would often go to church with our parents and play in the Sunday school rooms or in the basement. More often than not, of course, we were up in the tower, spying on the smattering of white, gray, and balding heads.

"No. I have no idea what a 'mercy canary' is," said Ben as he checked the batteries in our flashlights. "Where did you hear about such a thing?"

"I overheard my parents talking about us last night, and Dad said he liked you because you and I were one of the main reasons why he still had a job here—that your mom and dad liked us being together. And then Mom called him a 'mercy canary' for saying that."

"Well, I don't know what a 'mercy canary' is, but that's exactly what I was talking about yesterday. That's why we don't have anything to worry about. Our parents like us being together."

"But it could work the other way, too," I said. "If anything ever happened between us, my dad could be out of a job."

"Then we'll just have to see to it that we stay best friends," said Ben.

After that, anything that had to do with keeping us together came to be known as a "mercy canary." We decided if we didn't know what it was, we could make up our own definition.

When prayer meeting was over, I watched from the tower as the last of the midweek remnant filed out. Soon I saw Ben's flashlight beam bouncing around behind the organ pipes, gleaming through the vertical tubes of the giant silent xylophone. I turned on my light and waited until I could see his flashlight pointed straight at me, which would be the signal that he had found a spot where my light was clearly visible.

As I pictured Ben back there on the scaffolding, intent on his work, I thought about his alarm clock idea. It seemed like such a preposterous plan, and yet it was so important to him. I was content to keep our imaginary games to ourselves in my backyard, but Ben wanted to carry them out on a grand scale. It was like he wanted to play out something big with his life, and I decided right then and there, up in the tower, that I did too. By the time Ben's flashlight caught my eye and I signaled back with mine, I had decided this wasn't such a bizarre idea after all. He's right—I told myself, thinking about all those gray heads—most of these people could use some waking up.

Satisfied that he had located the exact spot that afforded him a clear view of the window, Ben soon appeared at the front of the church to see if my flashlight could be seen from the platform or the choir loft. He walked around a bit and then returned to the tower.

"Perfect," he announced as he came up the ladder, his voice sounding close and delivered right to my ear by that small space in the tower. "When you hold your light back in from the window frame like you did, I can't see it from anywhere except behind the organ pipes; and even then, there's only one place where I have a clear shot of the window through all the pipes, the way they're stacked." He was out of breath and flushed from running and trying to talk faster than he needed to. "That took a long time to find."

"Yeah," I said, "and while you were up there, I decided that I want to be a part of this. I think we should call it 'Operation Mercy Canary.' "

"Yahoo!" Ben shouted. I tried to quiet him down for fear someone would hear us in the tower, but it was hard to control Ben's glee. When he was really happy, which wasn't often, his smile would grow so big that I was sure his ears would touch at the top of his head.

Sunday morning, however, I woke up with lots of second thoughts—third and fourth thoughts too. The closer I got to the actual moment, the more I realized that our imaginations were about to bump into a lot of people's Sunday morning expectations, and I started to worry about the repercussions.

"Are you feeling okay this morning, Jonathan?" my mother asked in the car on the way to church. "You hardly ate any of your cereal."

"Yeah, I'm fine," I lied. "Just wasn't hungry."

"Probably because he and Ben finished off the last of the Frosted Flakes yesterday," said Becky. "What is that new stuff you got, Mother?"

"Oh, Krumbles? Don't you like it?"

"Yuck."

"I like it," I lied again, only for the sake of disagreeing with my sister. Krumbles was a ribbonlike wheat cereal put out by Kelloggs that enjoyed a short shelf life in the '50s and '60s. I could see why. I was always afraid I was going to get one of the sharp strands stuck in my throat. But it wasn't Krumbles sticking in my throat that Sunday morning in June; it was the knowledge that I was about to signal a rude interruption of the sacred order.

Ben and I had set it up so that we wouldn't even see each other beforehand; we would just take our respective positions and do the deed. So there was no way I could back down now. Even if I didn't do my part, I knew Ben would still do his, and it would be even worse because it wouldn't be timed properly. At least if he did it at the right spot, it would make sense.

Something was still stuck in my throat as I took my place in the tower with my heart pounding and my Bible opened to Ephesians 5. Every few minutes I checked the flashlight to make sure it worked as I followed along with the order of service in the bulletin. Pastor Beamering's voice came through the glass just fine, but the assistant pastor, Mr. Ivory, was a different story. He had such a low, soft voice that I couldn't hear every word. I wished they had thought to make the little window so you could slide it open. I prayed that it would be Ben's father reading the Scripture, because sometimes they traded off. I prayed that God would forgive me for what I was about to do if indeed it was wrong to do it. I noticed my prayer didn't make me feel a whole lot better.

The first hymn was "Crown Him With Many Crowns," and as Milton Owlsley touched his keyboard and filled the pipes full of air, I wondered what it was like for Ben back there right next to them. I imagined him covering his ears.

I was relieved to see Ben's father get up when it came time for the Scripture reading. At least that prayer had been answered. I picked up the Bible and held the flashlight poised just above my shoulder, two feet from the window, aimed at the organ pipes.

" 'And have no fellowship with the unfruitful deeds of darkness,' " he began, and suddenly a wave of guilt swept over me. What if I was about to do an unfruitful deed of darkness? " 'For it is a shame even to speak of those things which are done of them in secret.' " And here I was in a secret place. All at once, all the things I had been taught about respecting God's Word came rushing to my memory, and Pastor Beamering's voice was lost in the fear of that moment, drowned out by the other voices bouncing off the walls of my head. *God's Word is God's Word, don't ever let anyone alter it . . . don't ever put other books on top of the Bible . . . the Bible is holy . . . treat it with fear and respect. . . .*

I would have missed my cue entirely had it not been for Pastor Beamering's own plans that morning. A master at sermon theater, and a bit miffed over his lethargic congregation, as Ben had observed, he had decided to pull out the stops on this one. So when he got to verse 14, Jeffery T. Beamering, Jr. leaned into the microphone and read very softly, " 'Wherefore he saith—' " and then he paused, filled his pipes, and shouted as loud as he could, " 'AWAKE THOU THAT SLEEPEST!' "

His voice broke through the frozen state of my fear, and my hand involuntarily tightened its grip on the flashlight, squeezing the button. In an instant an alarm went off from the organ pipes on the other side of the church. Except it turned out to be more than an alarm.

What Ben hadn't told me was that he had found a public address outlet at the back of the choir loft and had run a cord up from there to a microphone that he held right up to the alarm clock. When it went off, it sounded more like a fire bell than an alarm.

So it was that I watched as everyone in the sanctuary jumped a foot . . . twice. First, when Pastor Beamering shouted, and again when the alarm went off. From my vantage point high in the back of the church, it looked as if some huge hand had grabbed every person in the room by the back of the neck, thrown them first this way and then that, and then dropped them back in their seats.

The effect was astounding. Pastor Beamering went on to preach a powerful sermon on spiritual vigilance, and, with the exception of Mrs. Gullickson complaining about heart palpitations, it turned out to be Jeffery T. Beamering's most splendid Sunday so far. The line to see the pastor was the longest ever, including many people who had never talked to him before. Convinced that he had engineered the whole thing, everyone was talking about what he might do to top it the following week. Their exuberance was so great, there was no way he couldn't take credit for what had happened.

Adding to the mystery was the fact that the microphone had picked up some of Ben's movements behind the organ pipes, and when he was climbing into position during the opening hymn, he slipped on the bars. Mrs. Jacobson later said she thought she heard a swear word, Mr. Johnson thought he heard feedback and bumping in the sound system, and Cheryl Willaby was sure she heard the ticking of a clock. But everyone said they heard, on the hymn right before the fated Scripture reading, an angelic voice, and they all agreed that it must have been coming straight down from the heavens. Given the special visitation that everyone believed had come upon Pastor Beamering that morning, angelic voices seemed strangely appropriate.

Now Ben's father was in a very delicate situation. All week long he kept hearing things like "Great sermon, Pastor" . . . "That one sure woke me up" . . . "Way to wake up the sleeping saints, Reverend." One woman even reported that every morning that week when her alarm clock went off, she immediately thought, "Awake thou that sleepest, and arise from the dead, and Christ will shine on you," and because of this she had enjoyed the most spiritually shining week of her life. There was even an increased turnout for prayer meeting that week.

I didn't know what to think. What had begun as a joking retribution had turned into a contribution, and we had come away clean. Ben had gotten himself down from the scaffolding and hidden in the kitchen before anyone saw him, and no one suspected I was in the tower.

"We did it!" shouted Ben, all out of breath as he biked into our driveway the following Tuesday and skidded into the garage where I was at the workbench getting an early start cutting more balsa two-by-fours for the walls of our houses. "We pulled it off!"

We hadn't seen each other since the big event. Not wanting anyone to start getting any ideas about us, we had decided not to even be seen together on Sunday.

"Yep," I said. "We sure did! I'd say Operation Mercy Canary was a huge success, wouldn't you?"

"Well, not exactly. Sunday was a success, but Operation Mercy Canary has only just begun. Think of it as a trial run."

7

Now There Were Three

Wait a minute. A trial run? Here I was feeling like God had somehow seen fit to work my deviant acts into a blessing, letting me off the hook . . . feeling like I had somehow gotten lucky and could now get back to enjoying the warm, carefree days of summer, and Ben was talking about a trial run?

"How about 'Operation Mercy Canary: Phase One'?" said Ben with his characteristic winning smile.

I tried to manage a smile but couldn't. I hadn't signed up for anything like this. As my desire for safety once again tried to pull back from Ben's thirst for danger, I dug my heels in even harder.

"Ben, look, why don't we just quit while we're ahead. Look

how great everything turned out. No one can get mad at us even if they do find out."

"I know. That's just the point. It turned out too good."

"Well, maybe that's exactly what was supposed to happen."

"What's supposed to happen is what we make happen," he said emphatically, "and so far, it isn't what I want to have happen."

I always had a two-sided reaction to Ben when he talked like this. One side was scared to death, wondering if he was profaning the sacred; the other side wanted to believe that he was fighting for something fundamentally right. On that Tuesday morning following our first (and I hoped last) mercy canary, the scared side was definitely winning.

"I talked to my father yesterday," said Ben. "I think he knows."

"Why? Did he ask you about it?"

"Not exactly. I just think he knows."

"Well, what did he say?" I was growing more exasperated by the second.

"He said that if I had anything to do with the alarm clock going off, he didn't want to know. And then he said that if I had any ideas about doing something like that in the future, he'd ground me and I couldn't play with you anymore."

"See? I told you this was going to happen!"

"Relax, Jonathan. He doesn't mean it."

"What do you mean he doesn't mean it?" I was almost yelling by now.

"What I mean is," Ben was trying to calm me down by controlling his voice, "I think he's bluffing."

Ben was still on his bike, straddling the center bar and leaning over the handlebars, rocking on his feet as he rolled his bike back and forth. I noticed he was still breathing heavily from the ride. Two or three times I had turned my back on him in frustration and continued slicing two-by-fours with a single-edged razor blade. They all had to be exactly the same length to keep the height of the wall even. Most of the pieces I cut during this conversation had to be thrown away.

"How do you know he's bluffing?" I said, with my back to him.

"Here, look at this."

I turned around and Ben handed me a church bulletin he'd pulled from his back pocket. It was from the previous Sunday, except the now infamous Scripture reading from Ephesians 5 had been crossed out and under it was typed a new one, from Ephesians 6. Then I noticed the date was crossed out as well, and typed in next to that was July 6. Next Sunday.

"Where did you get this?" I asked.

"It was taped to a rung of the ladder up to the tower. I found it there Sunday night."

"Somebody knows!"

"Yes, and they want us to continue what we've started."

"Who could it be?"

"That's why I think my father is bluffing. It has to be him. Who else would know the Scripture reading for next week?"

"So you're saying your father knows we did this and he wants us to do it again and he's even giving us the Scripture reference a week ahead of time?"

"That's the way I figure it."

"But why would he tell you not to do anything like this again?"

"He has to protect himself. He can't let on, even to me, that he knows. Probably so if we fall flat on our faces, he can say that he didn't know anything about this."

"Are you sure you haven't been reading too much Sherlock Holmes?" I said. It seemed too bizarre. Yet, maybe Ben was right. That was the problem; Ben was usually right. I wanted all this to be over. But what if we were being asked to make a contribution to the church? Was somebody telling us to go ahead with Ben's plan? Was the bulletin some kind of secret blessing? I decided to at least get my Bible and look up the reference for the following week.

"I already looked it up," Ben said as I returned to the garage. "It's all about fighting battles, and I've been thinking about it for a couple days now."

"Do you have any ideas?" A silly question to ask Ben.

"Tons."

I turned to Ephesians 6 and read out loud: " 'Finally, my brethren, be strong in the Lord, and in the power of his might.

Put on the whole armour of God, that ye may be able to stand against the wiles of the devil. For we wrestle not against flesh and blood, but against principalities, against powers, against the rulers of the darkness of this world, against spiritual wickedness in high places. Wherefore take unto you the whole armour of God, that ye may be able to withstand in the evil day, and having done all, to stand.'

"So what have you been thinking about?" I asked.

"Well, it's talking about a battle, so I thought we could make all kinds of battle sounds. Friday is the Fourth of July, and my dad always gets fireworks. I can easily sneak a few away. I thought maybe a couple cherry bombs, a few firecrackers, and follow it all up with a smoke bomb and a fan to blow it out through the organ pipes. That should do it."

"You've got to be kidding!"

"Do I look like I'm kidding?"

Thus it was that Operation Mercy Canary went into full swing, and for the rest of the summer it was Ben behind the organ pipes (Control Center) and me up in the tower (Command Center). And each Sunday afternoon, like clockwork, the next week's Scripture reading would be taped to the same rung of the tower ladder, typed on the present Sunday's bulletin.

I figured Ben must have been right about his father bluffing because Pastor Beamering never said a word. What we didn't know at first was that we were about to make him famous. All we knew was that everyone was keeping quiet.

Pastor Beamering kept quiet because it was good for him and the church. Whereas most churches slacked off in the summer, Colorado Avenue Standard Christian Church was on the rise. New membership classes were filling up, there were baptisms almost every week, and a general buzz was going on about the place.

My father kept quiet because he had a job.

Ben and I kept quiet because someone was sanctioning our activities by informing us of the Scripture verses each week.

So we spent the rest of the summer playing cars, building suburbia, and setting off alarms all over the Word of God. And we got very good at it.

Some of the alarms were humorous, like the Bob's Big Boy

sign we dropped down on the slide screen for John 4:32: "I have meat to eat that ye know not of"; or the array of rubber-tipped arrows that came flying out from behind the organ pipes on Psalm 91:5: "Thou shalt not be afraid for the terror by night; nor for the arrow that flieth by day." We came up with cymbal crashes on Psalm 150; and for the story of Gideon, Ben blew his brother's trumpet behind the pipes and I blew my father's from the tower. The people thought they were surrounded by Midianites!

Or there was the Sunday when the reading was on the baptism of Jesus, and Ben let a white dove loose in the church. It circled a few times, and just as it was coming in for a landing on top of the organ pipes, a splotch of gray matter landed on Mr. Bickford's bald head in the back row of the choir. The dove perched on the pipes for the entire sermon—until the organ introduction for the final hymn startled it back into the air.

Whether he planned it or not, it seemed to work this way for Ben. Just when it seemed he had gone too far, the situation would redeem itself in ways he could never have controlled. True, the dove came close to disrupting the entire service; but then again, there was nothing quite like singing "Spirit of God, Descend Upon My Heart" while sunlight streamed through stained-glass windows and a white dove circled overhead, looking for a place to land. People talked about it for weeks. Indeed, it seemed the Scripture reading was all people talked about that summer. Never before had the congregation been so enthusiastic about the Bible. They were studying it, talking about it, and, most of all, remembering it. The first thing everyone did when they got the bulletin on Sunday morning was to look up the Scripture passage and try to figure out what might happen.

I always thought one of the most effective Sundays was the one when we actually did nothing. As soon as he discovered that the next week's passage was Matthew 16:1–4, Ben had announced that we would have a vacation that week: "The Pharisees also with the Sadducees came, and tempting desired him that he would shew them a sign from heaven. He answered and said unto them, When it is evening, ye say, It will be fair weather: for the sky is red. And in the morning, It will be foul weather to day: for the sky is red and lowering. O ye hypocrites, ye can discern the face of the sky; but can ye not discern the signs of the times? A wicked and adulterous generation seeketh after a sign; *and there shall no sign be given unto it*, but the sign of the prophet Jonas. And he left them, and departed."

So that Sunday we did nothing. As the passage was read from the pulpit, everyone stared at the organ pipes, waiting for something to happen. But there was no sign. No display. Then Pastor Beamering got into the act by leaving the platform, and the whole congregation just sat there, feeling the lack of the signs and wonders they had gotten used to, and feeling the stinging rebuke of the words of Jesus.

After a few uncomfortable moments, Pastor Beamering returned to deliver a most uncomfortable sermon about the prophet Jonah. Not about Jonah and the whale and Jonah's reluctance to go to Nineveh, but about how upset Jonah was over the fact that God was going to actually save Nineveh. Jonah wanted to predict the city's destruction and then sit back and watch God's judgment fall from heaven.

"This morning," Pastor Beamering exhorted, "we all sat there, like Jonah sat under the withering vine, waiting for something to happen. Like Jonah, some of us can't wait for all the bad guys to get it. We want to stand back and watch the judgment fall. But God is not going to entertain us with the judgment of people for whom He died. God is in the business of saving people, not destroying them. He is longing to fill the God-shaped vacuum in every human soul, and He waits for your invitation."

As the weeks passed and Operation Mercy Canary continued, Pastor Beamering became more and more adept at incorporating our theatrical displays into his sermons—supporting the congregation's belief that all this was planned in advance—and Ben and I managed to keep from being discovered (not that anyone was trying that hard to find us, given the success the church was experiencing).

The organ chamber was behind a locked door, and Ben's master key took care of that handsomely. Most people in the church didn't even know where the door was. It was more a panel than a door, so it was very easy to miss. Also, Ben would leave the scene of the crime at various times, depending on what was going on that particular Sunday. Once we had a close scrape with Bobby Brown when he posted himself in the passageway behind the organ for the whole service. He never even located the panel, but he counted on the fact that whoever was back there had to pass through the passageway at some point. Luckily, I saw him there before church and signaled Ben with Morse code not to leave. When Bobby's parents finally called for him to go home and he walked away scratching his head, I gave Ben the "all clear." Being the last to leave church had its advantages.

We sometimes wondered at the relative ease with which we were able to go about our business. Even encounters with Grizzly were almost nonexistent.

"I think he likes what we're doing," Ben said one day. "Have you noticed how he's been out of our hair ever since the alarm clock went off?"

"I wonder how many people know?" I said. We were eating our typical lunch of peanut-butter-and-jelly sandwiches, potato chips, milk, and Oreo cookies together in our favorite secret hideout, a long row of juniper bushes that lined the playground at my school just down the street from our house. We would crawl in about ten feet, where there was a large, cave-like opening hidden by the thick growth of twisted branches.

"I think a lot of people know, but no one's telling."

"Do you still think it's your dad leaving the bulletin on the ladder each week?" I said, working on unsticking my teeth from a mouthful of peanut butter and Concord grape jelly with a big gulp of milk.

"Funny you should mention it. I was just going to bring that up. I'm beginning to suspect it may be your father."

"*My* father? Why my father?"

"Our fathers are the only people who know about the order of service that far ahead of time. They work on it two weeks in advance. It could just as easily be your father as mine. Maybe your father is trying to keep this whole thing going for the sake of his job," Ben said. He began making lines in the frosting of his Oreo cookie with his teeth. He always scraped the frosting off first and then ate the chocolate part of the cookie separately.

"Maybe we could hide in the tower next Sunday afternoon and see who it is?" I said.

"I thought of that already, but I can't come up with a way we could be away from our parents all afternoon. And on Sunday—"

"We could set it up so that your parents thought you were at my house and my parents thought I was at yours." I surprised myself with that one. I was starting to think like Ben.

"No. That's too risky."

"I know. Why not take a picture?" I was thinking a lot about taking pictures right then since I had gotten my very own Brownie camera a week earlier for my tenth birthday. "I bet we could rig it up so that opening the door would set it off and 'Bingo!' we've got him, whoever it is."

"That's a pretty good idea, Jonathan. You're thinking more like Sherlock Holmes all the time."

The following night at prayer meeting we set it up, which was relatively easy to do. The camera had a shutter-switch that pulled down the side, and by tying a string to it and then threading the string through a series of screw eyes that led it to a spot high up on the door, we got the shutter to click every time the door was opened. Ben had the brilliant idea of using elastic for part of the string so it wouldn't pull the camera off the wall and give the whole operation away. The only problem was whether or not there would be enough light to get a picture, since using a flash was out of the question.

"Maybe we should do a test run first. If it doesn't work, then at least we don't risk having someone discover my camera," I said.

"Yeah, but we don't have enough money for two rolls of film . . . and we have to pay to get them developed."

"You're right. What do you think will happen to my camera if they notice it?"

"Don't worry. No one's going to notice it the way that door squeaks when you open it. They wouldn't do anything to the camera anyway—probably just take the film. We'll just have to wait and see how it comes out. We've got nothing to lose," Ben said.

We did wait, but it was difficult. It seemed like the week would never end. Not only were we anxious to determine the identity of our informant, we also wanted to see if our plan had worked. We kept trying not to get our hopes up too high. As it was, we rode our bikes down to the drugstore on Wednesday even though they told us the pictures probably wouldn't be in until Thursday.

Friday they were ready, and I almost tore the prints trying to get them out of the envelope. The first few, the ones we had taken of each other as we were rigging the camera, were disappointing. You couldn't even tell me from Ben in the dark and the shadows. But when we got to the last picture in the roll, our mouths dropped open.

"It's Grizzly!" we said in unison. Sure enough. The camera had caught the same backlit image we had seen countless times from our darkened hiding places. His arms outstretched holding the door and his unmistakable wiry hair gave him away. We were experts on that silhouette.

"What do you think this means?" I said.

"It means that Grizzly is a lot smarter than we thought," said Ben.

We started back to my house, riding our bikes side by side so we could talk as we pedaled.

"Why do you think he would want to help us?" I said as my loose fender rattled across the cracks in the pavement.

"Maybe he's a prankster at heart," said Ben.

"Maybe he thinks we're good for the church," I said.

"Maybe we should ask him," said Ben.

"You mean let him know we know?"

"Why not?" said Ben, speeding up to race me the rest of the way home. "We could probably use the help." Ben would often race me back to the house, but I noticed he only did it when we were a short distance away—about half a block. And he would always collapse on our front lawn, exhausted from the brief spurt of energy. This particular time was no exception as we both lay panting on the grass in the shade of our Chinese elm tree. Ben always panted faster and heavier than I.

"How will we talk to him?" I asked.

Ben caught his breath. "If he's smart enough to supply us with the information we need every week, he's smart enough to figure out how to communicate with us. He may not be able to hear or speak, but that doesn't mean he can't think!"

That Sunday it actually took some doing to find Grizzly. Our hide-and-seek game with him had been reversed, but we finally managed to corner him in the janitor's closet. He was very frightened at first, and it seemed strange for us to be frightening Grizzly. I wondered if all along he had really been frightened of us rather than after us. Some people are more scary when they are frightened than when they are trying to do the frightening. The only way we got him to calm down was to produce the latest bulletin, point to its updated Scripture entry, and then point to him. He understood immediately and dropped his head as if he had been discovered doing something wrong.

"No," we shook our heads, then spoke slowly, hoping he could read our lips. "It's okay. We like you. We need you. You can help us." Somehow this seemed to get across to him, and he started to settle down. Then he surprised us both by pulling a notepad and pencil from his shirt pocket and writing on it. Neither one of us knew he could do this. The impression around the church was that Grizzly was retarded and illiterate. Ben was right again. Not only could he think, he could communicate.

"I bet he can read our lips," I said later to Ben.

"I'm sure of it," said Ben. "He understood us perfectly."

What he had written was "YOU R DOING GOOD. PEOPLE NEED WAKE UP."

To which we had responded, "We need your help."

That got him excited, and he wrote, "I HELP."

Now there were three of us.

———

"Guess what I have in here?" Ben said early the next week when he arrived at my house. He was holding up a grocery bag rolled closed at the top.

"I haven't got a clue."

"Ashes . . . from our barbecue."

I looked at him blankly. "So?"

"I'm going to blow them all over the choir loft just like you did in your parents' room so we can have the last laugh. I've even got the verse for it . . . something about 'heaping burning coals on their head.' It's in Romans somewhere."

"Are you sure you want to do this? If you're talking about

getting back at your father for embarrassing me, don't bother. I don't really care anymore."

"Well, you don't have to, because I do. I care a whole lot, and I've been waiting for this moment all summer. Remember, that's why we started all this in the first place. And this time it's not going to backfire and turn into something good. I've thought about this a long time, and I'm convinced there is no way anything good can come from blowing ashes all over the choir."

"Don't forget, your dad can turn just about anything into something positive. My dad, on the other hand, will kill me. It will be the end of everything. The choir robes will have to be sent out. It'll be a mess!"

"Don't worry. You're not going to have anything to do with this. I'm going to do this one all by myself."

"No way, Ben. We're in this thing together all the way." I went to my room and got my Bible.

"I think it's in the last part of Romans," Ben said when I got back outside. I found the last chapter and started to work forward.

"Just when are you thinking about pulling this one off?" I said as I scanned the pages. "Aren't we doing the 'wind of the Spirit' this week?"

"Yes. But I'm going to do it soon. Summer's almost over."

"Well, Operation Mercy Canary will be over as soon as you 'heap burning coals' on the choir loft. You can be sure of that!"

"That's fine with me," said Ben. "I don't want this job anymore, anyway. It was just an excuse to get back at my father, and now we've made him famous. Especially after this week."

The coming week was going to be our most ambitious project to date. We were going to illustrate the part in John 3 where Jesus says the Spirit is like the wind and we never know where it comes from or where it's going; we only see its effects. For this we were going to tape colored streamers all up and down the organ pipes from the back side so they couldn't be seen until we turned on a wall of fans that would blow them out and set them flying between the pipes (at least, that's what we hoped would happen).

"Here it is," I said. "It's Romans 12. But, Ben, look at this. It says the opposite of what you want it to. It says *not* to take vengeance on somebody who has wronged you but to return good for evil. That's when you will 'heap burning coals on their heads.' "

"So? We'll just be helping God out a little . . . throwing a few coals on a few heads. Besides, we've been returning good for evil all summer, and it's making me sick. We've been doing way too much good around that church lately. In fact, this Sunday is going to be so good that next week might be a perfect time to spring something truly bad. I'm just not made for this much good."

That week we were incredibly busy getting ready for Sunday. We had to make all sorts of excuses to spend time together at the church, but with our parents' "secret support" that wasn't too difficult. We also had a great deal of help from Grizzly, who was turning out to be an ideal accomplice. As far as everyone in the church was concerned, he was outside the sphere of intelligent communication, so there was no one better suited for keeping our secret. Besides, this project was too big for just the two of us. We needed physical strength and size, both of which Grizzly possessed in abundance. He was over six feet tall and had the biggest hands I had ever seen.

By Wednesday, Grizzly had amassed all the fans he could find and had helped us strap them up to the scaffolding behind the organ pipes.

"I don't think we have enough," Ben said, surveying the take. "Are you sure there aren't any more?"

Grizzly shook his head "Yes" and then wrote, "EVEN TOOK PASTOR'S FAN."

Of course it would turn out to be the week the usual end-of-summer heat wave hit southern California, and by Thursday the church staff was clamoring for the missing fans. Grizzly was called in to try to solve the problem, but he managed to feign total ignorance, confirming everyone's opinion of him. Pastor Beamering finally sent the assistant pastor out to purchase four new fans for the church offices.

"That should do until this heat wave *blows over*," we heard him say to as many people as possible, enjoying his own joke as always.

"Perfect," said Ben. "Four more should give us enough to cover the whole area."

On Saturday we finished by adding the four new fans behind the bottom row of pipes. Unfortunately, because of a wedding that day in the sanctuary, we were unable to test the whole system to our liking, but a small area test earlier in the week had convinced us that the streamers would indeed fly as we planned.

As usual, Ben directed the whole operation. He had very clear ideas about where he wanted each fan, but it wasn't until Sunday morning that I realized there was a reason for this. Just as there was a reason for the inordinate amount of time he spent setting up the system electrically. The fans had to be plugged in a particular way, and had I not known that Ben was generally particular when it came to these kinds of things, I would have suspected something. As it was, I only saw this as his usual meticulous attention to detail. So Grizzly and I simply followed directions.

Sunday morning came with the usual anticipation. I was at Command Center. Ben was up in Control Center, waiting with a mass of tangled extension cords and plugs only he understood. Grizzly was standing by at the foot of the scaffolding in case any problems developed with the fans or the extension cords. Pastor Beamering stepped up for the Scripture reading, John 3:1–8. Everyone had already read it a number of times. Now they were watching as much as listening.

" 'There was a man of the Pharisees, named Nicodemus, a ruler of the Jews: The same came to Jesus by night, and said unto him, Rabbi, we know that thou art a teacher come from God: for no man can do these miracles that thou doest, except God be with him. Jesus answered and said unto him, Verily, verily, I say unto thee, Except a man be born again, he cannot see the kingdom of God. Nicodemus saith unto him, How can a man be born when he is old? can he enter the second time into his mother's womb, and be born? Jesus answered, Verily, verily, I say unto thee, Except a man be born of water and of the Spirit, he cannot enter into the kingdom of God. That which is born of the flesh is flesh; and that which is born of the Spirit is spirit. Marvel not that I said unto thee, Ye must be born again. The wind bloweth where it listeth, and thou hearest the sound thereof, but canst not tell whence it cometh, and wither it goeth: so is every one that is born of the Spirit.' "

As soon as I heard the words, "The wind bloweth," I hit the button on the flashlight and, slowly, a wave of colorful streamers began to appear from behind the organ pipes, lifting their long arms, then dancing and rippling in the mysterious breeze that seemed to come from nowhere. By the time Pastor Beamering finished the passage, the entire twenty-by-forty-foot area of organ pipes above the choir was bathed in shimmering color.

The congregation let out a gasp of pleasure like an audience at a fireworks show, and Milton Owlsley, inspired by the display, moved spontaneously into the familiar introduction to Beethoven's "Ode to Joy." My father quickly passed on the hymn number to Pastor Beamering, who announced it to the congregation, and they all stood and sang along. And when they got to the lyric "hearts unfurled like flowers before thee," well, I thought my ten-year-old heart would burst with the glory and pride of having something to do with it all. This was truly our finest hour. At least right up until they finished singing and the congregation erupted into spontaneous applause (Standard Christians never applauded—at least not in 1958).

But somewhere during the applause some of the streamers stopped streaming, and the ones that kept on waving in the wind of the carefully placed fans spelled out, for just a few seconds, three clearly recognizable letters: BEN.

Murmurs rippled through the congregation as the applause died. Then all was quiet. Pastor Beamering complimented everyone on their splendid singing and went on with the service as if nothing unusual had happened. It was the same reaction we had to Ben's singing of "Jesus Loves Me" in children's church—a kind of trance followed by a group denial. An unspoken resolve that no one was going to discuss this further or even try to figure it out. Just act as if nothing had happened.

8

Ivory Tower

"It's your sister," said Ben. "We've got to do it for your sister."

It was the Monday following Ludwig von Owsley's memorable "Ode to Ben," and Ben was talking about how our plan to heap burning coals on the choir was going to have to wait for at least another week. Something had come up.

For some weeks, while the Scriptures had been dramatically unfolding before everyone's eyes, another development had been unfolding under our watchful surveillance. Ben and I had been following closely the movements of the assistant pastor.

It had all started one Sunday after church when we were in the tower and spotted Pastor Ivory sitting on the fourth row of an empty sanctuary with Meg Alderman, one of my sister's classmates. At first we didn't think much of it and continued with our business, planning a new wiretapping system for bugging church offices from the attic. But then, when I checked the window and saw them still there, I noticed something unusual about the way they were sitting.

"Ben, look," I said, backing away to let him see through the window. "What do you think they're doing down there?"

"Looks like they're talking."

"Isn't that kind of strange—the way he's leaning over with his hands in her lap?" I said.

"Well, now that you mention it—"

For some reason it made me think about the last time I had ever "played doctor" with my sister, Eric Johnson, and Gail Bradshaw, a neighbor of ours about my sister's age who moved away when I was eight. I think I was probably six or seven, and while pretending to tend to Gail's "broken leg," I had touched her bare thigh and something wonderful and horrible and powerful all at the same time had happened inside me—something I didn't understand and had never talked about. Whatever it was, I had decided never to play doctor again. Now something about the way Pastor Ivory was sitting gave me the same feelings all over again.

"Ben, what if they're playing doctor?"

"No," he said, keeping his eyes on the window. "Grown-ups don't play doctor."

"But why are his hands in her lap like that?"

"Maybe he's showing her something in her Bible. It's probably nothing . . . wait a minute. Someone's coming," and he held out his arm to keep me away from the window so he wouldn't miss anything. "Boy, they sure stood up in a hurry. She does seem to have something in her hand. It's a book, but I can't tell if it's a Bible. Now she's straightening her skirt. I don't know," he said, backing away from the window, "but I think we should step up our spying on Virgil Ivory, just in case."

This new information had given us an incentive to finish our bugging system, which amounted to nothing more than long strings tied to the heating vents of various church offices and attached, on the other end, to the bottom of empty tin cans—a primitive listening device, but surprisingly effective when pulled taut and held up to the ear. We had successfully located a command post in the attic that put us on a straight string-pull from each of the office vents.

It was from there that we had discovered, while listening to phone conversations from his office, that Pastor Ivory might be interested in more girls than just Meg Alderman. Twice we heard him talking with junior high girls about keeping secrets.

"Shouldn't we tell somebody about this?" I said after Pastor Ivory's half of a conversation with Julie Flory had buzzed down the line into my tin can.

"Not yet," Ben answered. "We don't have enough information. He's never said anything we can use, and we didn't really see anything from the tower. Sherlock Holmes would not have a case on him."

"But I distinctly heard him say 'Remember our little secret' to Julie Flory, and he said the same thing to Meg. The sound of his voice when he said it still gives me the creeps."

As our investigations progressed, we became increasingly convinced that something creepy was indeed going on with Pastor Ivory. Ben had even come up with a phrase to describe it: "Virgil's on the verge!"

So when Ben brought up the subject of my sister that Monday, it was against the background of these events and impressions. Apparently he had picked up on a conversation the day before between my dad and Pastor Ivory about a committee Virgil was forming to plan social events for the junior high department. My sister was on the committee, and the only time they could meet, he said, was on Thursday nights after youth choir rehearsal.

"And then he told your dad not to worry about getting your sister afterward . . . that he would be happy to bring her home! Do you realize what this means?" Ben said. "It means that Becky is next on Virgil's list."

"But my father's the choir director."

"So? Meg's parents are Sunday-school teachers. That doesn't seem to have stopped him."

"Well, what if we warned Becky about him?" I said, fishing for a solution. "Hey, maybe she could even be the bait for a trap."

"She probably wouldn't believe us. Besides, do you want your sister alone in a car with that creep for even one minute, regardless of the reason?"

"Well . . . no . . . not when you put it that way," I said, feeling suddenly like I had just offered to feed my sister to the lions.

"Boy, Virgil's thought up a nifty one this time," he went on. "Every Thursday night, right under our noses!"

"We've got to do something," I said, as the implications of this arrangement began sinking in. "Maybe we should talk to my mom."

"I don't think so. We've got to break this out into the open all at once in front of the whole church so he hasn't got a chance to defend himself. There's only one way to do that. Go get your Bible."

As I ran inside the house, the implications behind Ben's comments slowly registered with me . . . we would not be heaping burning coals on the choir next Sunday. Ben wanted to bring this thing out into the open in front of the whole church! Had it not been my sister who was involved, I probably would have bucked his plan, but all I could think of at that point was Becky alone with that creepy man, and I was suddenly willing to do anything to stop it. Who would have thought our detective games would lead to this?

How brash our actions must have seemed to many in the church, but to us—and especially to Ben, for I would never have had this boldness apart from him—we were simply doing what we had to do. Whereas other kids looked out at a relatively un-complicated world populated with their peers, Ben was sure that the things that were important to us were just as important to everyone else, regardless of their age or position. And he had the audacity to act out these convictions, whether or not they were welcomed or appropriate or even solicited, and no matter how far they pushed the adult boundaries around childhood behavior. To Ben, his ideas and opinions were as valid and as important as anyone else's, and he assumed they would treat them accordingly. It never occurred to him that being ten made him any less im-portant than anyone else.

Once, Ben revealed to me, he had even sent the Ford Motor Company his own designs for a new car before the covers ever came off the Edsel. He showed me his rough drawings, and I had to admit it was a pretty good-looking car. He called it the Mon-arch. (A name which, incidentally, was used by the Ford Motor Company years later in the Mercury line, and I maintain to this day that Ben was the one who first deposited it in their idea file for possible new names for cars.) Ben took it as a personal affront that his ideas not only were never accepted, but were never even acknowledged. Had he possessed the wherewithal to get himself to Detroit, I am convinced he would have marched right into the appropriate office and demanded a hearing.

That Monday when I returned to our garage with my Bible, Ben started looking through it while I continued cutting the thin sheets of balsa wood that would go over the studs to make the walls for our model houses. We were working at my dad's work-bench, which he let us use, "as long as you clean everything up when you're done."

"I know it's in Luke someplace," Ben mumbled, "but I forget exactly where."

"What's it about?" I asked, holding my tongue just right as I lopped off a four-inch section of a balsa-wood wall.

"Here it is. Luke 8:16 and 17. Listen to this," and Ben read to me as I cut out the frame for the bedroom door of his house. " 'No man, when he hath lighted a candle, covereth it with a vessel, or putteth it under a bed; but setteth it on a candlestick, that they which enter in may see the light. For nothing is secret, that shall not be made manifest; neither any thing hid, that shall not be known and come abroad.' "

"Wow," I said. "How did you find that?"

"I used the concordance. Looked up 'secret.' And guess what else I found? We've come all the way back to the beginning, Jonathan. Remember the first verses we did out of Ephesians?"

" 'Awake thou that sleepest?' "

"Yeah. But remember, right before that it talks about the deeds of darkness? Here. 'For it is a shame even to speak of those things which are done of them in secret.' "

How could I forget the rush of guilt I'd felt that first Sunday in the bell tower, thinking I was doing a shameful thing in secret?

"Well, this is one of those shameful things," Ben went on with conviction. "That's why we can't speak about it. We've got to write it on a big sign so everyone can see it. Pastor Ivory is about to 'come abroad.' "

"What are we going to say?"

Ben methodically reached into his back pocket, unfolded a sheet of paper, and smoothed it out on the workbench. On it was a drawing of the slide screen pulled down the same way we did the Big Boy sign. He had even sketched the edges of the organ pipes that could be seen on either side of the screen. Across it in bold capital letters were the words:

PASTOR IVORY HAS SECRETS
WITH JUNIOR HIGH GIRLS

9

Love, Rebekah

My sister was twelve at the time, but she didn't seem as old as Meg Alderman or Julie Flory, who looked about twenty. It was so unfair. In 1958, when I was ten, most twelve-year-old girls looked twenty, while most twelve-year-old boys looked . . . well . . . twelve. When I get to heaven, I'm going to have a few words with the Creator about adolescence.

Becky was closer to what I thought "twelve" should be, though there were hints of impending womanhood. None of us knew at the time that she was only one year away from almost inexpressible beauty. She already had my mother's Minnesota skin—very white and thin, like a delicate membrane—and her bony features and gangly girlish figure were about to perform a metamorphosis of grace. Once in a while, if you caught her profile just right, framed with a few curls of her fine blond hair escaping her ponytail, you could see it coming.

"What are you guys looking at?"

Absorbed, our heads bent over Ben's drawing, we did not hear her until she was inside the garage. Her question was our only warning. Ben whisked the drawing into his back pocket, and we turned around much too quickly and too nervously not to telegraph the importance of its secrecy.

"So, what have we here?"

"Nothing," I said.

"Certainly looks like something to me," she said, slowly moving sideways, dipping her shoulders and curving her mouth, relishing our predicament. We countered each of her moves in the opposite direction to keep her as far as possible from Ben's pocket.

"You boys haven't gotten hold of a nasty photograph, now

have you?" We moved in a half circle until we had traded places; now she was by the workbench and we were by the door.

"No . . . nothing like that," I said.

"Then, why don't you let me see?"

We were just about to turn and bolt when she lifted a heavy pipe wrench off the wall behind her and held it casually over the delicate balsa-wood frame on the workbench.

"Well?" she taunted, rocking her lanky body back and forth and wagging her bottom lip with overconfidence.

"You wouldn't do that," I said, knowing she would.

"Oh yeah?" she said, raising the wrench a little higher. "One good drop should do it."

"Wait a minute," said Ben, holding up his hands. "We'll show you."

I searched Ben's face for a trace of concern over this forced disclosure, but there was none. Becky, always thorough in her teasing, continued to hold my house hostage while Ben calmly pulled the paper out of his back pocket, unfolded it, and took it over to her at the workbench.

"There . . . see for yourself."

She looked at the paper briefly, then looked up, puzzled. "This is it? What's the big deal?"

"What's the big deal?" I repeated. "You're next. That's the big deal! Virgil is on the verge!"

Then I noticed Ben glaring at me, his face red with anger, and suddenly I realized that his superior sleuthing brain must have engineered a way out of this predicament. Apparently the drawing had not been the only paper in his back pocket. When I looked closer, I saw that Becky was holding a magazine clipping of an Edsel ad. *Sorry, Sherlock,* I thought.

"Will you guys please tell me what this is all about. Just what am I 'next' for?"

"Okay, you might as well know," Ben said, pulling the other piece of paper out of his pocket and smoothing it out on the table. "This is the Scripture illustration for next Sunday."

Becky stared for a moment at the drawing while her wide mouth and eyes grew wider. "What is this, another one of your jokes?"

"It's no joke," said Ben. "It's the truth."

"What do you mean? What secrets?"

"You have to promise, on your honor, that you won't say a word about this until after next Sunday," said Ben. "After next Sunday, everyone will know."

"I'm not promising anything yet. What are you talking about? What has Pastor Ivory done? And how do you know about it?"

"We've seen him touching Meg Alderman," Ben said, "and heard him telling secrets on the phone to Julie Flory."

"And we think you could be next," I concluded. "Now would you please get that thing away from my house!" afraid she was about to go into shock and drop the wrench on my nearly completed living room.

Becky slowly set the wrench down on the table, and her shoulders rolled forward. She began to blush and started fidgeting with the edge of the workbench, making circles with her long slender fingers. One leg pivoted nervously on the ball of its foot as loose curls fell down the side of her face. Suddenly my big sister, the bossy one who always wanted to be in charge, appeared small and helpless. The mere idea of some kind of interest in her on Pastor Ivory's part had made her will visibly flutter, or maybe it was being put in the same camp with Meg Alderman and Julie Flory that weakened her. Whatever caused it, the effect on me was new and awakening. For the first time, I felt a strong urge to protect her and an anger at anyone who might threaten her in any way. If my physical growth could have been activated by my heart at that moment, I would have grown several inches.

"How can you guys be sure about this?" Becky said, biting her lip.

So we told her all the things we had seen and heard from the beginning, including Pastor Ivory's arrangement to bring her home every Thursday night.

"Okay, so even if this stuff is going on, nobody's going to believe you. You're just a couple of kids. Plus, you really haven't caught him doing anything bad."

"Oh yeah? We saw him with Meg alone after church," said Ben. "The guy's a creep, Becky!" He was getting worked up now, and we both tried to calm him down.

"Look," I said, "all we want to do is make sure he won't be

bringing you home on Thursday nights."

"You guys are really sweet to care about me like this, but I think I can take care of myself. I really don't think you should do this. You're messing with someone's life—"

"Yeah . . . someone who's messing with a lot of other people's lives, too," Ben said.

My sister shrugged her shoulders and smiled. She already knew enough about arguing with Ben to know how fruitless it was. "Well, you have my word; I won't tell a soul."

"Thanks, sis," I said.

"No," she said emphatically. "Thank you." And she put her hand on my shoulder and kissed me on the forehead, and everything went crazy inside of me. For a moment, I thought my chest would burst.

"You having any second thoughts about Sunday?" Ben asked after she was gone.

"None."

"Good. We'd better get started on that sign."

———

Ben slept over that night, so we were both at the dinner table when my dad brought up the fated arrangement. "Pastor Ivory says you're on the junior high social committee, Becky," he said, as if to congratulate her.

"Yeah." My sister blushed and looked down at the table.

"He said he'd be glad to bring you home afterward," my dad went on, "which I thought was really nice of him, since your mother and I have to stay for choir rehearsal."

"Yeah . . . sure," Becky said.

"Well, who's going to stay with Jonathan until she gets home?" my mother interjected, slightly annoyed that my dad hadn't considered this. Thursdays were already a logistical mess with youth choir and adult choir back to back. My father directed both, and my sister was in the youth choir and my mom was in the adult choir. Becky always had to get a ride home with a friend so she'd be there in time to take over when my mother went off to her choir practice.

"I forgot about that," said my father. "But don't you think Jonathan is old enough to be on his own for a half hour? I can't imagine Becky's meeting lasting any longer than that."

Yes, but how much longer will it be before good old Virgil actually gets her home? I thought, and I had a feeling Ben and Becky were thinking the same thing.

"Absolutely not," said my mother. "We'll have to get a sitter."

"Maybe this would be a good time to try out the woman down the street you were talking about the other day," said my father.

"I'll call her tomorrow," said my mom. I noticed that she was watching Becky closely. Ever since the subject of Pastor Ivory had come up, my sister had been nervously moving food around her plate. "Rebekah, honey, are you okay?"

"Yeah. I'm just not very hungry right now. Could I be excused?"

"Of course, dear. It's Jonathan's turn to clear the table anyway."

"What's wrong with her?" my father said after Becky was gone.

"I don't know, but as soon as you mentioned that social committee, she seemed upset. Maybe there's someone on it she's having trouble with. I'll talk to her about it."

At that point, I jumped up and began removing the dishes, and Ben started helping me.

"Virgil Ivory's a nice guy," we heard my father say as we carried the dinner plates through the swinging door that separated the kitchen from the dining room. "It was awfully thoughtful of him to offer to bring Becky home."

On the kitchen side of the door, Ben and I rolled our eyes at each other.

"I want to throw up!" whispered Ben. " 'Awfully thoughtful of him,' " he mocked. "Awful thoughts is more like it!"

"Shhh!" I whispered with a finger to my mouth. "Let's not blow this open again. I've already done that once today."

Later on, when we were in bed, I brought it up again. "Sorry for messing up your plan this afternoon. That was some slick move—switching papers on my sister."

"That's all right. It turned out okay. It's probably better that your sister knows. I think she actually appreciates what we're doing."

"I know she does," I said.

"Ben?" I went on.

"Yeah?"

"Do you think it's okay to have feelings for your own sister?"

"I don't know. I've never had a sister."

"What I mean is, when she kissed me today in the garage, I felt . . . well . . . really good inside, and I'm not sure it's okay to feel that way about your own sister."

"She didn't kiss you on the lips or anything."

"No," I said real fast. "I don't know . . . I've just never felt this way before about her. You know, she's usually just a big pain."

After a few moments, Ben said quietly, "I think you're lucky."

My mother came to tuck us in and hear our prayers. For the first time I could remember, I prayed for Becky without any coaxing. My mother pulled the covers up around our chins, squeezed us down into our pillows, and kissed us both good-night. As she turned to go, I saw in her profile a shadow of my sister. *Maybe this feeling is the same as loving my mother,* I thought, and I decided it was good to feel this way.

"Jonathan?" Ben said after she left.

"What?"

"Have you ever heard God talk?" Now it was his turn to disclose some secret in the dark. These were our most intimate times together—with the lights out and only shadows on the wall.

"No."

"You know that voice I told you I heard once . . . someone calling my name? I've been thinking that if there is a God, He could probably do anything He wanted. He could even call out my name."

"I guess so. He called out to Samuel."

"Yeah, I thought about that. Can't you hear Him calling: 'Sam! Sam!' "

Something about Ben playing God and calling out "Sam" struck me funny at the time, especially the way Ben said it. But, of course, ordinary things are often funny late at night when you're in the shadows and you're supposed to be asleep.

"Maybe you should try answering the voice next time."

"I thought about that. What was it Sam said?"

" 'Speak Lord, for thy servant heareth.' " I'd learned that in Sunday school.

"I don't know. I think I'd have to believe in Him first before I'd be able to talk to Him."

"Maybe not. Maybe talking to Him means you believe."

"Do you believe in God?" asked Ben.

"Yeah, I guess so."

"Well, how come you believe in Him if He's never talked to you?"

I had to think about that one for a minute. "I don't know. I just do. I can't tell you why. It's something I feel inside."

As I lay there on my back, staring up at the lines made by the wooden slats of the ceiling, my hands slipped under my pillow. I felt something. A piece of paper.

"Ben, turn on the light." Being on the bottom bunk, he was closest to the switch.

The paper was a note from my sister.

GOOD LUCK, YOU GUYS!
LOVE, REBEKAH

10

Coming Abroad

Well, we never did get to heap burning coals on the choir. After that Sunday morning we were out of the Scripture illustrating business for good. I suppose we should have known that our shocking accusation would mean an end to our freedom behind the organ pipes, but ten-year-old minds never seem to foresee the consequences of their eager imaginations.

It was fortunate for our scheme that Virgil Ivory was the Scripture reader that fateful morning—for two reasons. If Pastor

Beamering had been preparing to read the Scripture, he might have discovered that the passage in the bulletin was not the one he had entered in the bulletin plan and left on his secretary's desk on Thursday to be printed. No, that plan had been intercepted by the watchful eye and hand of Harvey Griswold and changed to our passage: Luke 8:16 and 17. Or, even more likely, Pastor Beamering would not have even checked with the bulletin, but simply read the passage he was prepared to preach on. Virgil, however, was only following the program.

The other reason, of course, was that Pastor Ivory got to preside personally at the reading of his own indictment.

I will never forget the look on his face. He finished reading verse 17. "For nothing is secret, that shall not be made manifest; neither any thing hid, that shall not be known and come abroad." As he finished, closing the Book and chanting in his deep, throaty voice, "May the Lord add His blessing to the reading of His holy Word," the stunned congregation sat looking at the sign that had dropped down behind his head. A few snickers escaped younger members of the congregation who did not understand but saw something humorous about "PASTOR IVORY" and "JUNIOR HIGH GIRLS" being up on a sign together. The rest of the Colorado Avenue Standard Christian Church sat silently aghast, incapable even of the familiar murmur that had come to accompany our Scripture illustrations. And then Virgil, following their gaze, turned and looked at the sign himself, and all color immediately drained from his face. It was as white as the slide screen behind it.

I still wonder how those who believed his denials in the days following (mostly everyone in the congregation) could disregard that obvious look of a guilty man trapped in his sin. Maybe I simply recognized it so readily because that was a look on which I had the inside track. Ten-year-olds are experts on guilty looks, so it was obvious to me.

There is a look you have when you have been falsely accused. It has mostly anger in it. There is a look you have when you have been caught contemplating some evil, maybe even come dangerously close to it, but have not yet succumbed. That look holds some fear, but mostly relief. And then there is a look you have when you have been correctly accused—nailed to the wall—surprised by the truth, with no chance to prepare a fake reaction. And there you have the look of Pastor Ivory.

I remember, too, searching for Meg Alderman, wanting to see her face. I couldn't. She kept staring down at the floor throughout the remainder of Pastor Ivory's amazing plea from the pulpit. I couldn't see Julie Flory's face either; it was bent over and buried in her hands. But I could see Becky's face, because she sat up tall, her shoulders regal and proud. It wore a quiet, firm look of peaceful absolution.

Pastor Beamering, to his credit, somehow managed to keep a stoic expression throughout this whole ordeal. For the initial seconds-that-seemed-like-years, he sat still in his chair to the right of the pulpit, waiting to see what Pastor Ivory would do—and, I'm sure, trying to figure out his own course of action.

Pastor Ivory, in the meantime, was regaining some composure, and the unbelievable events that immediately followed were a testimony to how quickly people can forget that which may have been confirmed by their eyes and their ears, and even their intuition, and yet covered up by what their minds are simply not willing to believe. Small amounts of life began to flow back into his face as he slowly managed a smile. Then he spoke.

"If this statement was true . . . and of course it is not, it would be a titillating example of what, according to this passage . . . will happen to us all." His voice was halting, but reaching for a way out. "Imagine having your worst nightmare . . . thrown on a screen behind you." He was gaining a bit more strength. "Imagine if it was something like this." He was starting to see it. "What would you do?" Now he was grabbing for it. "I realize this is a shocking question, but we wanted to emphasize a moment you would never forget."

I could hardly believe what was happening. The murmurs came back to the congregation, and I could almost hear them thinking: *So it's only another illustration. It's not true. Oh . . . we get it now. Something just to shock us, like they are always doing with the Scripture reading. Well, they may have gone a bit too far this time. But it certainly was effective. Got to hand that to them; it was effective. Boy, were we scared there for a minute.* The murmurs were murmurs of relief.

"What would your sign say?" The smooth voice continued,

now back in control and reveling in its recovery. "Would it be something like this?" and he gestured to the glaring words behind him that were already losing some of their glare in the light of his dazzling rationalization. "What about those secret thoughts you hold in your mind?" That was when I started to feel physically sick inside. " 'Nothing is secret, that shall not be made manifest.' "

Pastor Ivory stepped back briefly to wipe his brow. He had them back. He had them eating out of his hand. He was holding the reins again. Feeling the power.

"Believe me," he went on with his improvised melodrama, "even though I knew this was going to happen, I can't tell you how shocked I was. For one thing, I'm not sure who did this; this is not the message I was expecting, and I question its propriety. But it sure worked, didn't it? How horrible it felt standing here in front of you! And that's just the way we will all have to face our real deeds someday. We've all gotten a little taste of that today. I wish you could have seen what I saw as I looked out at your faces—"

Suddenly a high shrill voice screamed out from behind the organ pipes. It was Ben's last attempt to cry out the truth, muffled in a deacon's hand.

Heads bobbed and the murmur returned, but Pastor Ivory didn't flinch. He leaned into the microphone, stared all around the room with his jaw set, and laid his last card on the table. "Do you want this to happen . . . to you? Then start living right. Live in such a way that no one can put anything on your sign that you would be ashamed of." And then he backed up, wiped his brow once more, and turned and sat down.

Meanwhile, several men in the choir had been trying to get the movie screen to retract, but to no avail. I found out later that Ben, anticipating this, had hidden the crank in our secret compartment in the tower. It had been right next to my face the whole morning.

Had they been able to get the screen back up, I think the service probably would have gone on. But Pastor Beamering simply couldn't continue anything meaningful from the pulpit with PASTOR IVORY HAS SECRETS WITH JUNIOR HIGH GIRLS waving behind him like a giant headline. The deacons tried to get some help with the screen from Mr. Griswold, but no one could find him. Later he was discovered hiding on the first landing of the front stairs to the side balcony, which meant he had faced his own phobia in order to remove himself to a place where he knew no one would ever look for him. Ben had been taken to his father's study to await the inevitable inquisition.

Pastor Beamering somehow managed to close the service with some semblance of grace, leading everyone in all four verses of "Search Me, O God" and sending them out, in a purposeful state of silence and meditation, to contemplate their own lives in relationship to this scripture. Not knowing any of the facts, he could only try to salvage something out of the Word, and something of his own integrity as a pastor, and something of his church service. All of which, combined with the assistant pastor's devilishly brilliant recovery speech, served only to strengthen Virgil Ivory's case. The more Pastor Beamering tried to redeem the situation, the more it looked like it had all been planned. While it had been a bizarre morning, Ben and I had trained this congregation to expect fireworks and doves and streamers from the organ pipes. So why not this? It had all been so brilliantly orchestrated before, many argued, why not this time as well?

Once again things worked against Ben. Not unlike the first alarm clock.

After church, Pastor Beamering held a meeting with Ben and Pastor Ivory. I thought it best to stay out of the way, not knowing how much of our activities Ben would want to reveal, but I quickly got to our bugging devices where I could listen in on the entire meeting.

It was swift and final. Pastor Beamering made sure there were no questions remaining. Ben gave his story of seeing Pastor Ivory and Meg Alderman alone in church and of overhearing him talking about secrets on the phone with Meg and Julie Flory. He even mentioned how Pastor Ivory had "engineered" a way to bring my sister home every Thursday night, alone.

Pastor Ivory solidly defended himself on each of these charges with an air of irritation at having to even be bothered by the obviously exaggerated accusations of a ten-year-old—one who had just disrupted an entire morning service. That last part he said, but the first part was in his voice. He had an answer for everything. He was in the church showing Meg passages in the Scriptures to help her handle the grief of losing her grandmother earlier in the week. (We later found out her grandmother lived in Indiana and Meg had seen her only two times in her whole life.)

"Is that why she was straightening her skirt?" Ben tried to get in a few licks.

"Ben," said his father sternly. "Women and girls always straighten their skirts when they stand up."

"And I suppose they always stand up that fast when someone comes in the room?" He wouldn't let go.

"Virgil?" I heard Pastor Beamering throw him the question.

"I did stand up quickly, Jeff, because I suddenly realized I was alone with her in the sanctuary and somebody might get ideas. I certainly never expected this."

"And what about the 'secrets' with Julie and Meg?"

Pastor Ivory laughed. "That was all about a surprise skit that Meg and Julie and two other students were planning for the junior high meeting on Wednesday night."

Yeah, "our little secret," I thought. That's the way you talk about a surprise skit. But I could hear the way this was going, and I knew Ben was probably thinking the same thing. There was no way we were going to win on this one.

Pastor Beamering, the acting judge in this court, had the final words. He reminded his assistant pastor that a cardinal rule of the ministry was never to counsel women alone. "Try to have someone else around. Remember, we must refrain from every appearance of evil. And while your offer to Becky was kind, it was not worth the questions it might raise, especially now. It's quite obvious, Virgil, that you are going to have to steer clear of any direct contact with junior high girls, at least until this thing cools down." Ben's father paused for a moment. "Also, I do need to add, Virgil, that I did not appreciate the way you talked to Ben just now. He may be only ten years old, but he still has a right to his opinions and his judgments. He thought something was wrong and, however misguided, was trying to make it right."

There was a long pause. Then Pastor Ivory spoke up, haltingly. "You're right, Jeff. I was out of line and I apologize, Ben."

Pastor Beamering then reprimanded Ben for jumping to conclusions before he knew all the evidence. "This bugging and spying you and Jonathan have been up to has now gotten way out of hand. It all has to stop, including the antics behind the organ pipes. It did us all good for a while, but now people are not going to be able to trust what's being done in the pulpit. I'm afraid, Virgil, your bit of fancy footwork this morning is going to hurt us."

"I was only trying to save the service," he said.

You mean save yourself, I thought.

"Well, we're going to save the service. We're going to get back to the pure, unadulterated preaching of the Word of God. That's the only thing that will save this service and this church now. Ben, the pictures you helped paint for us were stimulating and exciting, but they also forced Pastor Ivory and me to stretch the truth to try to incorporate them into the service.

"Tell you what, son. If we ever do this kind of thing again, we'll do it together. Is that a deal?"

"It's a deal," said Ben.

"Then I have nothing more to say. Let's get back to what we're called to do here."

"It's all fine with me," Ben said to me afterward when we talked about it all. "Summer's over anyway. Besides, we accomplished what we set out to do. Becky's never going to have to know what it would be like to ride home alone with Virgil on the verge."

He was right about that.

11

Under the Junipers

"Quick! Get your bike!" said Ben, rolling up on the sidewalk on his Schwinn one Saturday morning in October. "The '59s are in the showroom!"

He was speaking, of course, of the new Edsels. He'd been calling the dealership every week since the first of September to get an update on their arrival.

"Okay, okay, but I have to finish this first."

I was raking the front parkway at the time, ridding it of the Chinese elm leaves that were falling in abundance. It was my regular job on Saturdays to rake the front and back yards, getting them ready for my father to mow. I enjoyed doing the backyard because the sycamore leaves were big and airy. They were easy to gather together, and they made a big, crispy pile that was fun to roll in and easy to pick up. The elm leaves, by contrast, were small and heavy. They could wedge their way sideways between blades of grass and defy the teeth of my rake—it was impossible to get them all—and the pile they made was small and dense and seemed to take forever to pick up because the little heavy, shiny leaves kept slipping through my hands and fingers.

"If you helped me, this would go a lot faster," I said, knowing my appeal was probably futile.

Ben was not a physical person. In the six months I had known him, I had never seen him play any sports. The only truly physical activity we ever did together was bike riding, and we didn't do a lot of that because he tired easily. I never brought this up with him, but I had talked to my mother about it.

"Some children are just born weaker than others," she said. "Ben does seem to have less strength than his older brothers, but he also has a lighter build."

"Do you think there might be something wrong with him?" I had asked.

"I don't think it's anything serious or Mrs. Beamering would have told me. He's probably never going to be a physical person. Some people are just like that. I think that's why he uses his mind so much more than other children. He makes up for his physical weakness by using his head."

"You're doing such a good job with those leaves, I wouldn't want to get in your way," Ben said, using his head.

"I hate these leaves. I can never get them all up—and look, I'm raking so hard, I'm tearing up the grass." I held up a mass of stringy grass roots clumped together and hanging off the end of the bamboo rake like angel hair.

"Someone should come up with a big outdoor vacuum that would just suck up all this stuff."

"Yeah, or blow it away," I said, "now that I'm so famous for that."

"You still get people bugging you about that?"

"All the time. Bobby Brown never lets up."

"Too bad we never got to blow ashes on the choir."

The Pastor Ivory incident had blown away, too. Apparently Meg and Julie had corroborated Virgil's version of the story, and everyone—except us—believed them.

In spite of this, I think in the long run we did the whole church a service. If Pastor Ivory did have a problem in this area, it never surfaced again during the remaining two years he served at our church. Perhaps we helped him face something he had been unwilling to face before. Perhaps we stopped him on the verge. Whatever the truth was, the true message of that Scripture passage came through with a visual power not soon to be forgotten. I know I've never encountered that passage again when I did not see Virgil's face in front of that sign and imagine what mine would read. As disrupting and confusing as it was, it was still our most powerful image.

It also had an effect on Pastor Beamering. The dip in the road the church went through because of this incident took a little of the bounce out of Jeffery Beamering's steps and put a little more reality in his voice.

Still, without Ben behind the organ, playing the scripture

through its pipes, the church returned to its former predictable self. Ben didn't mind; he was happy to be out of business.

All he could think of now was the Edsel car. While I finished the leaves—and he successfully avoided any actual labor—I listened to him go on and on about what we were about to see on the new models. There were no secrets about the changes this year. No covered cars being clandestinely transported across the roads of our nation. No grand unveiling. The new models had already been revealed and reviewed in a number of magazines, and Ben, of course, was an expert on all these critiques.

"*Popular Science* is calling it a much more sensible automobile. They said the first Edsel was overdressed, but this one is played down. Simpler. Less showy. In other words, they've turned it into just another car. They're trying everything to make it sell—even dropping the price—but they're trying the wrong things. They should have stuck with what made it different until enough people caught on. You can't get people to change overnight."

I finished dumping the leaves on the trash pile behind the garage and got permission to bike to the Edsel dealership, which was about a mile and a half away.

"Just be sure and take the back roads and stay off Broadway."

"Okay, Dad."

When we checked out with my mother, she had, as she usually did, a great idea. "Why don't I make you two lunches and you can stop and have a picnic on the way back."

"Yeah!" we said in unison, and soon we were on our way with peanut-butter-and-grape-jelly-sandwich lunches bouncing around in the baskets of our bikes.

The trip took us through a typical cross section of suburban Los Angeles. In only a mile and a half, we actually went through the official districts of three different cities. We lived right on the edge of Eagle Rock. Two blocks away was a more industrial section that was part of Los Angeles County, and then we entered the city of Garfield, where the Edsel dealership was. As long as I have known it, Los Angeles has been like this: one suburb after another, distinguished only by the economic echelon of its inhabitants. Eagle Rock was on the edge of middle class. Garfield was on the other side of the tracks, downward. Its brightest spot was that section of Broadway called "Auto Row" where all the car dealerships were lined up one after the other.

It was the first Saturday the new cars were in the showroom, and there was a steady crowd at the Edsel dealership. Ben was on a first-name basis with most of the salesmen by now, but they brushed us off that day with so many potential customers roaming around.

Ben walked around the first model, the top-of-the-line Corsair, as if he were in a morgue. "Sensible isn't the word," he said finally. "The word is boring."

Ben pulled out a picture of the front of the '58 Edsel that was so familiar now to both of us and held it up so we could do some detailed comparing. He was right. The '58 may have been ugly by some people's standards, but it certainly wasn't boring. The lines around its infamous grille, around the headlights and the edge of the hood, were sharp and clear. By comparison, the front of the '59 looked like they had rounded everything off. The grille still had its characteristic vertical oval, but it was filled in with a metal grid instead of being set off so dramatically by the double chrome lines of the '58. Plus, the oval was no longer standing alone. It was now set inside a horizontal grid that extended the grille across the whole front of the car, filling in and flattening the area from the front edge of the hood to the top of the bumper. Gone were the sunken cheeks that protruded the headlights like beady eyes and gave the oval its pucker. The headlights on the new model had been lowered and set inside the flat horizontal grille, putting the whole front surface of the car on one plane. Gone, too, were the sharp diagonal lines from the top of the oval back down the hood, the ones that echoed the old Model T. There was a small mound there, but softened so much as not to be noticed. That was pretty much what had happened to everything that had been distinctive about the Edsel: softened so as not to be noticed.

"Look at that grille," Ben said remorsefully. "All the suction has gone out of it. Remember those ads about how you could notice an Edsel farther away than any other car? I wonder what they're going to say now?" The grille on the '58 made you think it would suck you right in, like a huge vacuum, if you got too close. The '59 wouldn't suck in a Kleenex.

The back was even worse. The new design was only vaguely

reminiscent of the gull-wing taillights of the '58 model. The "wings" had also been dropped a few inches, and there were three round lights set in each wing that didn't seem to belong at all. The back looked like they'd had three different ideas and decided to use them all.

We didn't stay long. Ben picked up a new car brochure, and we rode our bikes in silence to our private lunch spot for the postmortem. It was an overcast day, and all the way there I wondered if it might rain on us. Even when we reached our destination in the juniper bushes, we were silent for a while except for the crunch of potato chips and the turning of pages in the colorful brochure. Ben kept shaking his head as he read the specifications.

"They took the push-button shifting controls out of the steering-wheel hub, dropped the remote-control trunk lock, the three-stage engine warm-up, and the air springs. Well, the air springs could go; that was a big goof anyway."

"Sounds like they stripped it," I said.

"No, they killed it," Ben said. "Any chance they had of saving this car is over. When you get a new idea and you sink 250 million dollars into it, you have to stick with it regardless of what anybody says. Somebody back in Detroit has got a pretty weak backbone. You don't sink 250 million into an idea only to back off from it after the first year because it didn't catch on fast enough."

I was so tempted to say, "Ben, it doesn't matter. It's only a car," but I didn't, at least not at first. I knew there was some mysterious connection between Ben and the Edsel that I didn't understand. And I didn't understand his preoccupation with the fate of a line of cars, but he was my friend, so what mattered to him mattered to me—at least most of the time.

"It's doomed now. The smaller cars are going to take over. Their chances of building a more daring automobile are gone. Look. It's right there in the brochure," he said, pointing to the glossy pictures lying open on the floor of our fort among the junipers. "You can't go back on that. It's all there in chrome and steel. The only chance for the Edsel was for it to be different. Soon its weirdness would have proven something. Mark my words: Someday they're going to look back at this car and call it a classic. I should have known this would happen."

Suddenly I blurted it out without thinking. "Ben, it's only a car—"

"What do you mean, 'it's only a car?' " Ben interrupted with a look of angry desperation. "It's only my life! What do you think about that?"

We stared at each other for a moment. We had both said too much. I had hurt him by not allowing him to be different, and he had put into words the thing my mind had been nudging at all the time—that somehow when he was talking about the Edsel, he was talking about himself, too. Now we had overstepped that invisible boundary of respect and mystery, and we were both afraid some delicate thread had been broken.

Why did Ben only sing on rare occasions, and why did his voice cast such a spell on people? Who was calling him by name? Was it God? What was Ben's connection to the Edsel? What did it all mean? These were questions I had learned not to explore. Not because Ben was hiding anything, but because he didn't know the answers any more than I did. All we knew was that these feelings were real, and to ask one of these questions was to somehow violate the trust between us.

Ben and I always seemed to be on opposite sides of belief. We were both near it, mind you, but on opposite sides of it. I had passed through belief to the other side: I believed, but wasn't sure why. Though my faith was real, it was often distant from the life I lived and the questions life threw at me. Ben lived behind his belief: He stopped short of faith, wanting to believe but, because of his questions and searching, not yet able to. These two sides pushed and pulled on us—like the conflict we were feeling at that moment—but also kept us together. I think we somehow realized that we each needed what the other had. My belief needed Ben's questions and his demand for truth to make it real; Ben's searching needed the substance of my faith to continue its hope of finding a home. Ben envied me for my ability to believe; I envied him for refusing to accept an answer that failed to connect with the world as we knew it.

I dropped my eyes down to the brochure and stared into the rear end of a '59 Edsel. It really was ugly . . . uglier than before. The '58s were at least proudly ugly, and in that there was a certain attraction. This car was simply ugly and no longer proud of it. This car looked like it wanted to hide somewhere—blend back in with the masses.

"Looks like any other car now, doesn't it?" Ben said, echoing my thoughts.

"Yeah," I said, relieved to be on surer footing, away from the emotional precipice over which we'd been dangling.

"I bet this is the last model. The Edsel won't even see 1960."

For some unexplained reason, a huge lump began forming in my throat and I could not look at Ben. In the silence that followed, I found myself wanting to do the strangest things. I wanted to scream out "No! It's not fair!" I wanted to go door to door and try to get people to buy Edsels. I wanted to go to Detroit and find somebody important and shout in their face, "Why did you do it?" I even thought about getting President Eisenhower to endorse driving Edsels. How about making it the official car of the 1959 Tournament of Roses parade? But a '59 Edsel would look terrible. A white '58 convertible like Ben's would look great draped in garlands of red roses. Put a wreath right around the lemon-sucking grille. That's it! Make everybody fall in love with the 1958 Edsel so they would all go out and buy up the last of them and demand more in such a huge frenzy that the Ford Motor Company would be forced to go back to its earlier design. Ben would love it. I would love it.

A light rain started to fall. It was the first rain since summer, and the wild smell of it hitting the dust and dry weeds of the school playing field mixed with the pungent odor of the little blue juniper cones clustered overhead.

We ate our Oreo cookies in silence as the rain softly settled on the tight, mat-like branches that shielded us from the weather, the world outside, and the future. A car swished by now and then on the growing wetness of the street nearby and then faded into the distance. Slowly, large drops of water began to form on the underside of the branches as the rain found its way down through the thick needles. For a while, we spotted the heaviest drops and caught them in cups we formed with the palms of our hands, watching them make little splashes in the tiny puddles within our clutches. But soon their intrusion overcame us—more drops than we could handle—and cold, heavy beads of water settled in our hair and ran down our foreheads and cheeks. I finally looked at Ben and thought that if you wanted to, it was a good time to cry. No one would know.

12

E-BEN-ezer Scrooge

Christmas in southern California is an anomaly. Windows and evergreens are flocked with pink and blue snow. Strands of Christmas lights grow like vines, up and over anything. Santas sweat, reindeers collapse from heat exhaustion, and palm trees with tiny white twinkling lights wave in warm breezes against the setting sun.

A few Christmases in colder climates go a long way toward curing a native Californian of these strange aberrations. A spotlight on a front door wreath in New England and a candle in each window are all that is necessary to decorate a house that already resembles a Christmas card. Any more than this would spoil the natural Currier and Ives look. Some places are so made for Christmas that they do not capture their full identity until December. That's probably why wreaths often stay on front doors, in colder climates, through March.

Of course I knew nothing of this in December 1958. California was all I'd ever known, and except for an occasional trip into the San Bernardino Mountains, anything white on Christmas was only something to be sung about or sprayed out of a can.

Christmas of '58 was also the last year for heavy, leaded icicles on the Christmas tree. After that the manufacturers went to the plastic ones, and I never got used to them. They're too light. You can't make them drip from the branches. You have to wrap them around the end of a branch to get them to stay, and the slightest movement of air sends them every which way. You can't have icicles growing sideways. This never happened with the old heavy ones. You could fill up a whole branch by simply draping them from trunk to tip, and they would always hang down.

My father would string the lights, he and my mother would hang the ornaments, and then Becky and I would finally get a chance to put on the icicles, strand by strand—never thrown at random. As far as I was concerned, there was nothing more magnificent than our tree fully draped with leaden icicles so that its branches sagged under the weight as if they were truly burdened with winter ice.

I always enjoyed getting ready for Christmas more than I did the actual day. Christmas Day was always a confusion of emotions for me. I wanted to believe in Santa Claus, but I was never quite sure it was all right to do so. My parents seemed ambivalent about crediting Santa with any responsibility for holiday cheer, as though somehow it wasn't honoring to the birth of Jesus. So Becky and I grew up with the idea that Santa was okay up to a point, but no one ever told us where that point was. As a result, I never fully believed the Santa myth and all its related childhood wonder. I say "fully" because I did imagine, I did wonder, I did try to hear sleigh bells outside my window on Christmas Eve. But I always felt a little bit guilty about wanting to believe all that stuff. And just a little bit disappointed on Christmas morning when "Santa" didn't come through with what I really wanted but didn't tell anybody.

Ben wasn't much help when it came to Christmas. He was pretty pessimistic about the whole thing. His struggle with being a preacher's kid kept him from entering into the joy of Jesus' birth, and his distaste for fantasy pretty much did everything else in.

Ben's negative reinforcement threw me deeper into my imagination that Christmas. He was so "humbug" about the whole thing, and the more "humbug" he became, the more I "ho-ho-hoed." Except it wasn't "humbug" Ben said (neither of us had been introduced to Ebenezer Scrooge yet); it was "hogwash."

"Hogwash," he said the first time I brought up the approaching yuletide season. "Christmas is a whole bunch of hogwash."

"Why?"

"Well, for starters, it's a pagan holiday. The Greeks and Romans were having their winter festivals, and the Christians de-cided to get into the act. Who really knows what day Jesus was born anyway? And then there's all that stuff about Santa Claus. We're supposed to believe in flying reindeer?"

"Gee whiz, Ben," said my sister, who had stepped into my room when she heard us talking. "What's your problem?"

"He doesn't like Christmas."

"So I guessed," she said with a sneer. "No presents for you this year."

"I don't want any presents. That's the worst thing about it. All everyone talks about is what they're getting for Christmas. It's so selfish. And have you noticed how nervous everyone is? My parents hardly argue at all, but if they do, you can be sure it will be in the month of December."

"Your parents argue?" I said.

"Sure. Don't yours?"

"No. Never."

"I've heard them argue," said Becky. "In fact, just the other night Mom was getting upset about all the time Dad was going to be gone next month with all the special rehearsals."

"See. What did I tell you?"

"But we can still pretend," Becky said, rushing back to St. Nick's defense. "There's nothing wrong with make-believe."

"I don't like pretending," Ben said.

"Oh yeah?" she said. "You guys pretend all the time with your houses and your cars. What about all those silly lines you have painted all over the sidewalks outside? I suppose those are *real roads*?"

"It's real play," said Ben, unshaken by her attack. "We know these are model cars and that our houses are model houses. We don't try and tell ourselves any of this stuff is real. If I thought it was real, I'd put an ad in the paper and sell my Edsel for two thousand dollars!"

"Well, that's just what I mean!" said my sister, getting more frustrated by the minute. "We can pretend about Santa Claus even when we know it's not true. It's still fun to play. Honestly, Ben. Sometimes you're impossible."

As December twenty-fifth drew closer, I felt a growing desire to get Ben out of his "hogwash" mentality. Two weeks before

Christmas, I brought up the subject in the car on the way to view Christmas lights, one of our favorite family holiday traditions. One night during the Christmas season we would go for a drive and try and find the houses with the most elaborate decorations.

The highlight was always a particular area in Huntington Heights, where the whole neighborhood went in for decorating in a big way. Each year the homeowners got together and came up with a theme for their street, so that the parkway—the strip of grass or ivy between the sidewalk and the street in front of every house—was decorated the same. It might be a cutout of an elf holding a big candle with a red light bulb for a flame. In which case, you would turn down that particular street and see a whole row of elves holding glowing red candles. Huntington Heights had become so famous for this that it would take over an hour to drive through an area only six blocks square. The constant flow of snail's-pace traffic was a kind of inside-out parade where the audience moved slowly down the street while the floats stood still. On the way to Huntington Heights I brought up the subject of Ben's distaste for Christmas.

"You should have invited him to come with us tonight," said my mother. "This drive always does it for me every year."

"Wait until the all-choir Christmas program next week," my father said, trying to help. "That will get him in the spirit."

They clearly did not understand the magnitude of the problem. My sister did, though. "None of the usual things are going to work on Ben. He has a bad case of the grumps."

From the backseat of our '57 Ford, with colored lights dancing off its clean windows and waxed hood, I wondered how much Ben's grumpiness was affecting me. For some reason, the lights didn't seem as bright as I remembered; everything looked a little smaller. Maybe I was getting too old for this. I didn't realize, of course, that I'd reached that age where I was young enough to still be caught by the charm but too old to give in to it, and not old enough yet to play the game.

By now we were inching along with the traffic snaking its way up and down the streets of Huntington Heights. Many of the parkways and decorated houses were the same as the previous year. There were always certain houses that had moving displays—animated reindeer and elves and waving Santas. Some blared Christmas music through loudspeakers. As I got older, I used to wonder what it would be like to live in this neighborhood. I wondered if real estate companies were obliged to tell people who were considering buying a house here that one month out of the year their street was going to turn into an "E" ride in Santaland.

I wasn't the only one who thought the show was a little down that year. My parents said they didn't think it was as spectacular as the year before, and Becky agreed. It was probably for that reason that we were all counting on La Palma Street to make up for our disappointment. La Palma, the last street, was usually the most spectacular. More lights, more moving parts, and more cooperation among the homeowners. On this street they not only coordinated the parkway; they also decorated their homes as a variation on a theme.

We were not disappointed. For when we turned the last corner onto La Palma Street, what awaited us was a block-long display of Charles Dickens's immortal *A Christmas Carol*, complete with the Ghosts of Christmas Past, Present, and Future, as well as the likeness of Ebenezer Scrooge running around in his nightshirt as each revelation unfolded in colorful display. Luckily, my mother was familiar with the story, so she filled in the details for Becky and me. The block seemed to go on for miles as I heard and imagined, for the first time, the great old story that had worked its magic on generations.

"Slow down, Dad," Becky and I kept saying. If there was a space in front of him, my father seemed to feel he was obligated to speed up to fill it for the guy behind him.

When we got to the last few houses, we made such a fuss that we actually got him to stop long enough for us to read the three tombstones sticking up out of the parkway. Two of the tombstones bore the name EBENEZER SCROOGE and told, underneath his name, the story of Scrooge's final visit by the Ghost of Christmas Future.

The last display, however, was an ominous conclusion to an evening of Christmas lights, fun, and merriment, which probably explained why there was a rapidly growing space in front of us that my father was doing his best not to fill. On the lawn was a rendering of an old man in a nightshirt clutching the black robe of a tall, hooded specter whose skeletal hand pointed at the last gravestone, on which was written: "I will honour Christmas in my heart, and try to keep it all the year. I will live in the Past, Present, and the Future. The Spirits of all Three shall strive within me. I will not shut out the lessons that they teach. Oh, tell me I may sponge away the writing on this stone!" The only comfort was the fact that there was no EBENEZER SCROOGE inscribed above the writing on the last tombstone— only a blank space.

At least that's what everyone else said they saw. I couldn't talk about what I saw. For I still to this day do not know how it happened that I saw the name BEN in the blank spot on the last tombstone, right where the BEN in EBENEZER would have been had Scrooge's name been printed there. Whether it was the power of suggestion, or my mind playing tricks on me, or whether I myself was visited by a Ghost of Christmas Future, I do not know, but I know I saw it. Saw it in much the same way as Charles Dickens himself described Scrooge seeing Marley's face in the shadow of his door knocker: "It was not an impenetrable shadow as the other objects in the yard were, but had a dismal light about it, like a bad lobster in a dark cellar."

The next thing I remember was someone behind us honking and my father racing around the corner so fast that we missed the fact that there was yet one more house to see—the last page of the story.

"Oh, look! There's one more house!" was all my mother could get out as the lights and decorations on the last house on the corner flashed by. Most likely it was a scene involving a converted Scrooge celebrating and making merry with his astonished friends and relatives, but we would never know. We sped out of Huntington Heights as if my father had seen a real ghost, but it was only his embarrassment at being honked at and his anger at us for being the cause of it, so that the rest of the evening was spent with a heavy Scrooge-like silence bearing down on all of us in the car. I didn't mind actually. I was too frightened and troubled by what I had seen to want to talk at all.

One thing I was certain of as the lights of Christmas Tree Lane floated by in silence. I had to somehow get myself back to Huntington Heights.

Huntington Heights was ten miles from my house. Uphill. It got its name from the fact that it was in the foothills. I had never thought about riding that far in my life. Ben's house was four miles away, and that took fifteen minutes downhill, forty-five minutes up. At that rate, I figured Huntington Heights was at least two hours away by bike. I wondered if I could even make it.

Then there was the matter of whether or not to take Ben with me. I wanted him to see the story; I wanted to introduce him to Scrooge. It seemed such a fitting rebuke of his present attitude toward Christmas—and one bizarre enough for his taste. But if I thought I might have difficulty riding that far, I knew Ben would; some days the ride to my house about did him in. Besides, I wasn't sure I wanted him to see that tombstone. If I was somehow able to get back to Huntington Heights, would I see it again? Nobody else had seen it. Was it just my imagination? What did it mean? With all these thoughts and emotions tumbling around inside me, I could hardly sleep that night.

The next day, however, my sister's announcement offered me an alternative course of action. At breakfast she brought up the fact that she had an unusual assignment for school. Apparently a movie version of *A Christmas Carol* was going to be shown on television that week, and her English teacher had told the class to watch it and write a report on it before Christmas vacation. I could hardly believe my good fortune.

"Mother, could we have Ben over to watch it with us?" I said excitedly.

"Not so fast. One thing at a time, here. Becky, when is the movie being shown?"

"Well . . . tonight."

"Tonight?" My mother was not very happy to hear this. "How long have you known about this, Rebekah?" It was always "Rebekah" when she was upset.

"About a week."

"A week?" she said. "Why didn't you bring this up sooner?"

"I forgot, Mom. I was going to tell you about it last night when we saw the Christmas lights and all, but then Dad got upset and I didn't think it would be a good time to—"

"A week ago would have been a good time," my mother interrupted emphatically. "As it is, this puts me and your father in a very difficult position. You know we have a rule about no movies in this house. You should have told us about this immediately."

My mother had been pouring a second cup of coffee for herself when Becky started talking about her assignment. My sister and I were eating our breakfast in the small breakfast nook off the kitchen where we ate most of our meals. Now Mother sat down at the table with us, her hands wrapped around her coffee cup.

"Rebekah, I have to talk to your father about this, and you haven't left me much time. If you'd told me last week, I could have given you a note for your teacher about our convictions regarding Hollywood movies and suggested you read the book instead and report on that. When exactly is this assignment due?"

"On Friday," Becky said, her voice dropping down into her cereal bowl where three lonely Cheerios were swelling in a half inch of sugary milk. Today was Tuesday, the 16th of December.

Mother thought for a moment.

I tried to break into the silence. "Mom—"

"Just a minute, Jonathan," she said, then turned back to Becky. "I can't believe the public school would assign you a movie. They must know people have convictions about these things. We're not the only Christian family in town."

My parents had a strict policy about movies. Movies glorified everything we stood against as Christians. People in movies drank and smoked and danced and committed adultery. And then there was the kind of crowd that hung around the movie theater. The clearest way to deal with all this was to simply "refrain from all appearances of evil." We were never to darken the door of a theater. "What if Jesus came back and you were sitting in a movie theater?" was always their clinching argument.

Then came television, and my parents had a real problem on their hands. We got our first TV set in 1952. (I can always remember that because the first thing we watched was the coverage of the Eisenhower/Stevenson election.) But in order to remain consistent with their convictions, my parents wouldn't watch, nor allow us to watch, any movies that were shown on TV. If we couldn't go to a theater and see them, we shouldn't be able to see them at home. I knew a number of church families that made this exception, but my parents were strict about it.

Things had been quiet for a few minutes now while my mother decided what she was going to do. Finally she presented her verdict.

"All right, Becky. I'm going to write a note to your teacher explaining our policy on movies and suggesting that you read the writing of Charles Dickens, a much more rewarding experience anyway, and do your report on that. I'm sure we have *A Christmas Carol* in The Harvard Classics; they have most of the writings of Dickens. You can start tonight."

"But, Mom, that will take so much longer than just watching the movie," my sister whined with her characteristic pout.

"That's not my problem, and it wouldn't have been yours if you had mentioned this assignment when you should have—a week ago."

"Mom," I ventured, "may I say something now?"

"All right, Jonathan, go ahead."

"It's a good story. You told it to us last night. If Becky can read it in a book, why can't she see it in a movie? What's the difference? Why can't we all watch it as a family?"

"Yeah, Mom," said Becky, surprised at my aggressive defense on her behalf. She didn't know I had reasons of my own for this. "The teacher says the movie was made in 1938," she added. "They didn't even know what sin was in 1938."

"I'll have you know, young lady, that society was so decadent in 1938 that it took a world war to bring America to its knees! But that's not the point. The point is that we have a policy here. It's a matter of principle. Besides, this is an opportunity to witness to your class about your convictions."

"Mom," she said, "I witness to them every time there's a dance and it hasn't proved anything. They just think I'm a ding-dong. If it wasn't for Susie, I wouldn't have one friend at school."

Susie was Becky's best friend. She went to a Pentecostal church that was even more legalistic than ours. She couldn't wear lipstick or nylons or Bermuda shorts or even pedal pushers. Susie didn't seem to struggle with these rules as much as my sister and

I did, with the exception that she loved to go behind the garage with Becky and listen to rock 'n' roll being borne on my sister's bright-red transistor radio.

I knew my parents felt a need to conform to the standards of most of the families in the church, especially with my father being on the church staff, but I also knew they never totally bought the whole legalism thing. Otherwise, they would never have given my sister her radio for Christmas. Because Becky and I intuitively sensed the vagueness of this line, we pushed on it as hard and as often as we could.

I could tell, too, that Becky's last comment had hit a vulnerable spot, because my mother didn't give the usual response: "Deep down other kids really do admire you for having convictions," followed by the story about some high school girl somewhere who took a stand against dancing and got ridiculed for it, but when one of her non-Christian friends got in some serious trouble later on, guess who she came to? And guess who had an opportunity to lead her to the Lord? All because she took a stand on dancing. I'm sure it had to have happened somewhere, sometime—although no one was ever specific about where or when.

This time, however, my mother spared us the lecture and the story. Maybe she was finally thinking that a so-called "witness" that alienated you from the very people you were trying to witness to was a bit of a contradiction. Or maybe she was weakening. Maybe she really wanted to see the movie herself. It had been obvious the night before that she loved the Dickens story. She had told us how she had first read it as a child and how it had had a profound effect on her. She had also been very quiet during my father's Scrooge-like performance in the car when he had complained about the "satanic" influences of ghosts in the story, and the fact that Scrooge had experienced a conversion without Christ. "A pagan conversion experience," he had called it. "A Christ-less salvation. It's as bad as calling Christmas 'Xmas,' taking the Christ out of Christmas."

For a moment, it felt like my mother was right on the verge of speaking to us as equals. You could see it in a slight widening of her eyes, but then it was gone.

"I'll go write the note for your teacher," she said. "You two need to finish getting ready for school. Don't forget your secret Santa gifts."

The fact that by seven o'clock that very same night my family and the Beamerings were huddled around their television set watching Reginald Owen as Ebenezer Scrooge is a matter of profound significance in understanding the fickleness of legalistic Christianity. Once the rules become anything other than what is clearly laid out in Scripture—those laws of love and rules of the heart that transcend all cultures and all time—then they become only a matter of someone's interpretation, usually the strongest, most authoritative one. In the hands of such a person, they can be torn down as easily as they were put up. In this case it was the influence of Pastor Beamering that overruled.

From what I picked up from my parents on the way to the Beamerings, it seems that it had all started that morning when my father and Pastor Beamering had a conversation about our encounter with the Scrooge story in Huntington Heights. Apparently before my dad could get out many of his negative comments, Pastor Beamering, in his own bullheaded manner, had dispelled them all with a few "humbugs" of his own.

" 'Humbug' to those who think this story is only secular," my father quoted. " 'Humbug' on anyone who fails to be moved by the joy of being given another chance. This is as close as anyone who doesn't know Jesus can come to expressing what it means to be born again. It's a second chance!"

What could my father say? To top it off, Pastor Beamering had stopped by the choir room later to inform my father that he had just seen in the paper that *A Christmas Carol* was going to be shown that night at seven o'clock on television.

"Why don't you all come over and watch it with us?" said Pastor Beamering. "I'll have Martha fix a dessert, and you can come over right after dinner. Martha and I were just talking last night about how we wanted to get our two families together over the holidays, but our calendar is filling up so fast . . . if we don't do it now, we might not get another opportunity."

I'm sure my father wanted to say something about the no-movie-watching rule, but the Beamering tide was too strong. Besides, he was probably in shock. Apparently the Standard

Christian rules operated on a different standard where Jeffery T. came from.

I could tell by my mother's tacit endorsement of this plan that, as I had guessed, she had wanted to see the movie all along. Needless to say, I was elated. Things couldn't have gone more perfectly. Now Ben was going to have to face a little bit of his sullen spirit on television in the person of Ebenezer Scrooge.

We were all charmed by the movie—well, almost all. I caught my mother crying when Tiny Tim and his father were singing "O Come, All Ye Faithful" in church on Christmas morning and when Tiny Tim's voice rang out in the final scene: "God bless us every one!" For some time afterward that became Pastor Beamering's favorite phrase. He repeated it several times that evening in his usual affirmative voice and even worked it into his sermon the following Sunday.

Though I found tears on some faces and joy on others by the end of the movie, what I found on Ben's face haunted me for a long time. He was stoic through the whole show. In fact, the only thing he appeared to gain from that evening was a new word to capture his anti-Christmas sentiment: "Humbug." That was all he could say when asked what he thought of the movie, and he said it in a way that made it hard to tell if he was kidding. Though everyone else laughed it off as a joke, I knew he was serious.

I knew it wasn't a joke because I had seen Ben's face during the visitation of the Ghost of Christmas Future when his skin went cemetery gray in the pale glow of the television set. While everyone else's face reflected the characteristic blue of the black and white picture tube, Ben's face, drained of all color, was incapable of throwing back anything but a shadow of itself, a shadow remarkably similar to the dismal light I had witnessed glowing in the form of Ben's name on the tombstone in Huntington Heights.

The hoped-for conversion of Ben to a post-visitation Ebenezer Scrooge was nowhere in sight. In its place was something dreadfully worse. What I had formerly regarded as just a nasty little quirk of character—Ben's usual refusal to buy in to the prevailing mood for the mere sake of conformity—turned out to be related, instead, to something real outside himself. It was as though he knew something about his own Christmas future that he wasn't telling anyone, even himself. Something that was working on me as well. Like a premonition of something bad.

My plan had backfired. The story of Ebenezer Scrooge played right up to the Ghost of Christmas Future and stopped there, just as our drive down La Palma Street was ended abruptly by my father's swift exit. Once again, the joy and celebration at the end of the tale went by me like a blur in the window. The dark hooded figure dominated everything. He dimmed Scrooge's conversion and cast his shadow back across all the joys of former Christmases. I went home that night feeling like an Ebenezer who could not be comforted, lost in an unpleasant dream from which he could not awaken.

Hooded figures and tombstones towered in my dreams that night. What was death to a ten-year-old—to anyone, for that matter—but a bad dream from which you hoped to escape? I remembered being in one of those dreams when I was seven. On that occasion I had been in a state of half-sleep most of the night. Next to my bed, in an empty milk carton, lay a dead wren I had shot out of the sky with my BB gun during a vacation visit at my cousin's farm in Minnesota. It had been exciting at first to see the bird drop, felled by the accurate shot of my gun, but that had changed rapidly to feelings of guilt and disgust when I caught up with the helpless creature flapping on the ground. I had only winged it. Then my cousin, an expert in heartless bird-killing, had strangled the poor little thing to death against my desperate pleading. I woke up the next morning expecting to see the little wren as I had seen it in my dreams, hopping around in the milk carton by my bed, pleading to be taken outside and released to the sky where it belonged. I remember looking down at the tiny still body, its eye creased tightly shut. Perhaps it was only sleeping. Maybe it was thirsty. Hoping it had all been a bad dream, I carried the fragile little body into the kitchen and held its limp head up to the faucet so that the water ran over its locked beak. "Drink, little birdie, drink," was all I remember saying. It had been my first direct encounter with the irrevocableness of life and death. Standing there at the kitchen sink, letting water flow over the head of a dead wren. The deed was done. There were no second chances. This was not a vision or a bad dream;

it was a real dead thing I held in my hand. There was nothing
more to do but bury it, which I did with great pomp in a shoe
box with tiny wildflowers adorning its still breast.

After a night bouncing restlessly among images of the Ghost
of Christmas Future, of water running over the beak of a wren,
of Ben's name glowing on a tombstone, and of his face marked
with the same bad-lobster glow, I decided to put away any ideas
of returning to Huntington Heights. The story was no longer
useful to Ben, and whatever I had seen on the tombstone was
something I wanted to forget.

I tried very hard to put it all out of my mind, and for a while
I did a pretty good job of convincing myself that I had only
imagined what I saw there.

13

Young Pascal

Christmas went by quickly, as it always does. Some-
times it seems that Christmas is all anticipation and regret. At first
it seems it will never come, and then suddenly it's over. Actually,
I usually enjoyed the day after Christmas the most, because that's
when you got to play with all your new toys.

I hadn't seen Ben since the night we watched *A Christmas
Carol* at his house. The busy schedules both our families kept
during the holidays also served to keep us apart, so it was great
to hear his voice when I called him on Christmas afternoon to
find out what he'd gotten for Christmas. He invited me to come
over the next day to play with his new toy. For someone who
thought Christmas was all "humbug," he certainly sounded
happy about his gifts.

Ben's new toy, although you could hardly call it that, was a
chemistry/physics set. I had gone through a couple of small
chemistry sets of my own, but they were nothing like this. To

me this looked like a scientist's laboratory. Along with an elaborate lineup of liquids and powdered chemicals, there were two racks of test tubes and a number of odd-shaped glass beakers, one of which was bubbling over a candle.

I hadn't seen Ben this happy since I gave him his Edsel. He had everything set up on a card table in his room, and from the smell of the place when I first got there it was clear that he had already concocted quite a brew. But it was the physics side of this kit that excited him most.

"Look at this! Here's a small car with a spring-loaded lever on top that shoots this ball up in the air. If you keep the car going in a straight line at a steady speed, the ball will travel at the same speed as the car and come right back down in the same spot. There . . . like that!

"And here's a sealed vacuum tube. This is really neat. Look, there's a bell attached inside. It's the same as this one here outside the vacuum. Hear how loud it is? Now, try and ring the one inside the vacuum."

I picked up the tube and shook it, but couldn't hear anything. I could see the clapper hitting the side of the bell, but there was no sound.

"How thick is this glass?" I said.

"Not very thick at all," answered Ben proudly, as though he had created it. "It's not the thickness of the glass that matters; it's the vacuum. Sound doesn't travel in a vacuum. Sound makes pressure waves when it travels, and if there are no molecules to move, there will be no sound. Look, it says it right here in this manual.

"Oh yeah, and listen to this. This one's definitely for you. It's under the section: 'EXPERIMENTS YOU CAN PERFORM WITH WHAT YOU HAVE AROUND THE HOUSE,' " Ben started to read. " 'For this experiment, you will need a Ping-Pong ball and (get this) a vacuum cleaner with the hose attached to the blowing end—' "

"Oh no. I'm not doing that again . . . ever!"

"It says if you set the ball gently at the top of the blowing stream of air, it will stay there. Even if you turn it at an angle, the air stream will hold the ball right out there in midair!"

"Naw, that's impossible. If the air is blowing, the ball will go flying off somewhere."

"It says it won't. I can't wait to try it. But I wanted to wait for you."

"Does it tell you why the ball stays there?"

"Yeah. It tells you everything."

Anything having to do with vacuums intrigued Ben, and I didn't understand why until later. It was all connected: Ben's interest in vacuums, Pastor Beamering's love for Blaise Pascal's "God-shaped vacuum in every human heart," and Pascal's own love of and study of the properties of a vacuum, the study that had inspired his statement on the condition of man. Ben was another young Pascal, working back through the physical experiments from which his father's favorite conclusions had been drawn. Reading it in a book in seminary had been enough for Jeffery T. to jump straight to the spiritual conclusions, but that would never be enough for his son. That was the difference between the two of them. Yet it was a difference that I now believe they both secretly understood. It was that secret understanding I had first seen as a twinge of admiration on Pastor Beamering's face at the dinner table that first Sunday we met when Ben informed him of the true cause of the Edsel's demise. The father knew his son was going to have to prove everything that he himself had come to believe so easily.

Ben had to run all the experiments himself. He couldn't accept the spiritual conclusions until he had touched the physical reality. If Ben had been a disciple, he would have been Thomas. Everyone seems to think Thomas was a doubter, on the unbelieving side of belief. I don't agree. I think Thomas was a prover. He just needed to put the physical stuff together in order to get to the information he needed. And he needed to do it himself, and Jesus was understanding enough to let him do it—to let him touch the wound in His side and the nail prints in His hands.

It's clear to me now that Pastor Beamering knew all this about his son, or at least enough of it to secretly help him understand. I believe he was pulling for Ben all along, and in a way, he was pulling for himself as well. Jeffery Beamering had always believed. He grew up believing. I understand that, because it was the same with me. I never seriously questioned my faith. Such belief is admirable and even enviable to those who have to struggle to believe—and yet, it brings its own vulnerability: *What if? What if* it's not true? *What if* this belief is only a part of my culture? *What if* I accepted it too quickly, too easily? For someone in Pastor Beamering's position, those questions could hardly be allowed. He was in too deep.

So all the questions found their expression in his son. And for that reason, Jeffery T.'s faith was riding in some small way on Ben's experimental discoveries. It was the thing that set Pastor Beamering apart from the other pastors who ruled with impenetrable dogmatism. Jeffery T. allowed his son what he had never allowed himself: the luxury of doubt and the freedom to put truth to the test. I'm convinced this was the reason he had looked the other way while Ben and I played behind the organ pipes.

It was no mere coincidence, then, that on that day after Christmas, while exploring the properties of the vacuum Pascal had discovered over three hundred and fifty years before, Ben and I had our first really important talk about God.

"Did you know that outer space is a vacuum?" said Ben, holding up the vacuum tube with the bell inside. We both stared into it as though we were testing the universe—exploring into the unknown. "If it weren't for gravity and our atmosphere, we'd all be sucked out of here into nothingness."

"Wow. It's a good thing we've got someplace to go to out there instead of being vacuumed up."

"Are you talking about heaven?" said Ben.

"Of course."

"How do you know there really is a heaven? Maybe we'll end up in someone's vacuum bag."

"Oh, come on, Ben. You're just sorry that you don't have Santa to pick on anymore since he went back to the North Pole."

"Just like God went back to heaven?"

"Ben, you don't mean that—" I couldn't even say it.

"That I don't believe in God? Is that what you want to ask?"

"Well . . . yeah, I guess so."

"Of course I believe in God. I just don't know what good it does."

I thought I was relieved, but I wasn't sure. "What do you mean?"

"God is always going to get to do what He wants to do because He's God. Like this vacuum tube here. Look, you turn it on its end and the steel ball and the feather fall at the same speed." He turned another tube on end and, sure enough, both the steel ball and the feather inside fell to the other end side by side.

"Wow, that's pretty neat . . . but I don't get it. What does that have to do with God?"

"God's got us in a big tube where He makes all the rules. Like one of those Christmas globes; you turn it upside down and make it snow on the little Christmas tree inside. Well, God can turn our world upside down and make it snow whenever He wants to, and we don't have anything to say about it. Yeah, I believe in God, but I don't see what difference it makes. Whether you believe in Him or not, He's still going to do what He's going to do anyway.

"For all we know, we might be just a big joke to Him. Maybe He's playing around with us like we play with our model cars and our houses. Maybe we're His toys. Imagine if I could create someone to drive my Edsel and live in my model house. I wouldn't have to do anything to entertain myself but sit back and watch. And if I got bored, I could kick His world upside down with my foot just to see how my little person reacted."

Ben scared me to death when he talked like this. I didn't like him putting himself on God's level, and I especially didn't like the God he was coming up with when he did this. This was pushing my little faith much too far—putting too much of a burden on its young, inexperienced back.

"But why would God send His Son to die on the cross if this was all just a big joke?" I said, attempting to defend the structure of the world I knew. As uncomfortable as it made me, Ben was closer to my real feelings and questions about God than I wanted to admit, even to myself. Inside I guess I was secretly hoping he just might happen upon some answers to the questions I didn't have the nerve to face.

Ben didn't say anything for the longest time. Then, finally, "That's a good question," he said. "That's a really good question. I'm going to have to think about that."

I should have left my little accidental triumph alone. Instead,

I rushed to fill in the awkward space. I was uncomfortable with the feeling of having stumped Ben on any level. He was supposed to be the author of those uncomfortable spaces, not me. I wasn't profound enough.

"If God's playing a joke on us, then maybe He came and died to be a part of the joke so He could have the last laugh."

I started to laugh at my poor joke, but Ben turned on me in instant fury, "Death is nothing to joke about!"

A confused and hurt silence filled the room. For the second time, I was the object of Ben's anger. I hated that look on his face. I fidgeted with the scientific implements, and Ben went back to his manual and began working on another experiment as if nothing had happened. Wherever this anger had come from, it was too deep for me to unravel—and Ben gave no indication of wanting to. So I stepped around the dark hole from which tombstones and hooded figures once again protruded, and finally found a way out when my nervous eye spotted the vacuum tube.

"How did you get the ball and the feather to fall together?" I said weakly.

"I didn't do anything. The feather and the steel ball fall at the same speed because they're in a vacuum, remember? There's no air in there to slow down the feather. It falls just as fast as the heavy steel ball."

"Wow. That's pretty neat," I managed to say in a falsely casual tone.

"Here, watch this," he said as he lit a candle and placed a tall glass tube over it in a determined manner, giving the task his full attention. Our mutual absorption in details gave the illusion that everything was back to normal, but my feelings were raw and chafing from the rub of Ben's emotions. The candle burned for a few seconds, then slowly went out. Ben lit the candle again and placed the tube over it like before; but this time he slid a metal plate down the center of the tube until it was a couple inches over the flame. He held it there as the candle burned on happily.

"How come it keeps burning?" I asked.

"In the first experiment, the heat made the oxygen rise up the tube, where it met with the air in the room pushing down on it; this formed a seal and created a kind of vacuum. The candle then burned up all the oxygen that was left in the vacuum and went out. It suffocated itself."

"So how come this candle is still burning?"

"Because the divider allows the hot air to go up one side of the tube while it pulls cold air down the other side. Look at the candle blowing to one side in there. It's creating its own draft."

Sure enough, the candle looked like it was waving in some mysterious breeze.

We played in Ben's new laboratory for the rest of the day. We blended chemicals that created their own heat. We changed the color of various solutions like magic. We dissolved crystals and formed crystals. We even suspended a Ping-Pong ball in midair from the end of a vacuum cleaner. I made sure Ben had full responsibility for that experiment.

"Amazing!" I said, watching the ball spin in the air as the vacuum blew on it. "What makes it stay there?"

"Hear, listen to this," and he read from the manual: " 'The molecules in the center of the air stream are traveling faster than the ones around the edges which are being slowed down by friction with the still molecules in the air. Because the pressure decreases with higher velocity (Bernoulli's principle)—' "

"What's velocity?"

"Speed. How fast something travels," Ben went on, always impatient with such interruptions. " '. . . the lower pressure in the center of the air stream creates a partial vacuum, thus holding the ball in place.' "

That night I stayed over at Ben's house, so we worked on through the afternoon and evening. I found myself growing fonder and fonder of the glass shapes and rubber tubes and corks and wooden holders and jars of chemical substances that comprised Ben's Christmas gift. It all seemed so significant, this universe of order. Things behaved in predictable ways. You could count on them. And there were reasons for everything. It was all in Ben's manual.

Ben's mom came into his room at various times during the day . . . to bring us a snack of frosted Christmas cookies and milk . . . to see what we were doing . . . to call us to supper . . . to make sure we hadn't blown ourselves up! I liked Ben's mother. She always encouraged us without ever being in our way. She never complained when our ventures into the unknown caused a spot on the rug or a mark on the wall. She made us clean up our messes, but she let us make them.

Mrs. Beamering's favorite passage from the Bible, which she quoted often, was Revelation 3:15 and 16: "I know thy works, that thou art neither cold nor hot: I would thou wert cold or hot. So then because thou art lukewarm, and neither cold nor hot, I will spew thee out of my mouth."

"Whatever you do, don't be lukewarm," she would always say, revealing her origins with a slight Texan drawl.

Ben's greatest fan was his mother. She always said she wanted him—and his brothers—to be one hundred percent at whatever he did. It didn't matter if he was one hundred percent right or one hundred percent wrong, as long as he was one hundred percent *something*. And if she suspected otherwise, she'd say, "Art thou being lukewarm again? O spew thee out of my mouth!" Ben's desire to know the truth about God came from his father, but his desire to know and question anything at all came from his mother.

That night, it was Ben's father who came to tuck us in and hear our prayers. He often did this when I stayed at Ben's house—more often than my father ever did—and I found myself starting to like him in spite of his Howdy-Doody smile and his theatrical voice.

"So what have you two little Einsteins been up to today?" he boomed as he walked into the bedroom and Ben and I scampered back into the beds we were supposed to be in. Our beds at Ben's house amounted to sleeping bags on the floor. Ben had only a single bed in his room, so we would camp out on the floor. We'd hide our flashlights in our sleeping bags and shine them around the room after the lights were out.

"We found out a lot about the vacuum," Ben announced.

"I thought Jonathan already knew all there was to know about vacuuming," his father said, with a grin and a wink in my direction. "Just kidding, Johnny. . . . You mean Pascal's God-shaped vacuum, right?" he said, getting down on his knees and tickling Ben until he laughed.

"No!" Ben said, sitting up and trying to be emphatic. "The tube-shaped vacuum that came with my new physics set."

"Ah yes, and what did you find out about the vacuum?" Pastor Beamering was rocking back on his knees, ready to listen.

"We found out that a bell doesn't ring in a vacuum, that a candle doesn't burn in a vacuum, that a feather and a steel ball fall at the same rate in a vacuum . . . let's see . . . what else did we find out, Jonathan?"

"That a vacuum holds a Ping-Pong ball in the air," I said.

"Oh yes, I forgot about that one," said Ben. "It's Bernoulli's principle."

"Well, I'll have to hear more about that tomorrow. It's time for you two to be asleep. But thanks for the new information. I can definitely make something of a bell that doesn't ring and a candle that doesn't burn in a God-shaped vacuum. Just remember to watch out for that vacuum cleaner, Johnny! Good-night, you two."

"Ben," I said after he'd left, "does your father ever think about anything but sermons?"

"Apparently not."

Ben pulled out his flashlight and cast its beam around the room, then onto the table where his new scientific equipment lay motionless for the first time that day. The tubes and beakers made huge scary shadows dance ominously on the wall like a scene out of Frankenstein's laboratory. Then he flicked the flashlight off, and we silently shared the blackness. There's something wonderfully protective about that time with a friend, staring separately into the darkness before sleep comes. You can say anything and it's completely safe. After a while it seems you don't talk to each other as much as you talk to the dark, and maybe someone hears and maybe someone doesn't. Maybe someone is already asleep. It doesn't seem to matter.

I was wide-awake though when Ben spoke. "If the hole in everybody is God-shaped, what shape do you suppose God is? A circle? A square? How about a trapezoid?"

"I know that one," I said. "I bet God is in the shape of a heart."

And somehow what Ben said next made me feel all warm inside, as if I might have finally offered to him a realization that he did not already possess.

"I bet you're right," said Ben. "God is in the shape of a heart."

14

New Year's Eve

Maybe it was all the strange fumes we'd inhaled that day in Ben's laboratory, but he beat me to sleep for once, and as the silence filled up the darkness, questions filled up my mind. I was still feeling the harsh edge of Ben's anger pressing against me. I didn't understand his sudden outburst when I'd joked about death. Then my mind went back to the time Ben had turned on me under the junipers when I'd criticized him for being too involved in the fate of the Edsel. And what about his reaction to Scrooge's last ghostly visit in the graveyard? What was all this about? Where was it all coming from?

As I thought about it there in the darkness, curled inside my sleeping bag, it became clear to me that death was the common thread. Each thing that had set Ben off was somehow related to death. And I decided then and there that as crazy as his notions might seem, I would take them seriously. He was my friend, and what were friends for if you couldn't trust them to believe you when nobody else would? I would believe Ben and his vague notions about the future. I would not joke about them ever again. As I drifted into sleep, I was thinking about what we could do to help stall the downward spiral of the Edsel.

"Ben, are you awake?" I said as soon as I opened my eyes the next morning. I looked over at his sleeping bag. It was empty. Before I went to look for Ben, I got a piece of paper and started writing so I wouldn't lose my brilliant idea.

Dear Ford Motor Company,
    We think you have made a big mistake. You did not give the original Edsel enough time to catch on before you killed it. The 1958 Edsel is one of the most important cars to come along in the history of cars. It is a car no one will forget. It

takes people a while to catch on to something new and this different.

The 1959 model is not going to convince anyone. It certainly hasn't convinced us, and we've been following the Edsel since the beginning when you had the new cars all covered up in magazines. Even though the 1958 model didn't sell like you wanted it to, it is still a better car than the one you have now.

We have a idea. We think you should admit you made a mistake and go back to the 1958 model. No one has ever done this before. It would get a lot of attention. You could say you are keeping the original design as a classic that should not be forgotten.

Please feel free to use any part of this letter for advertising, or use us as two ten-year-olds who thought up this idea. We take good photographs.

> Sincerely,
> Benjamin Beamering
> Jonathan Liebermann

Ben came in just as I was writing our names. "What are you doing?" he asked.

"Just a minute. I'm almost through . . . there. What do you think?" and I handed him the letter and watched his face as he read. His expression didn't change, but that didn't mean anything.

"This is a great idea, but it's too soon," he said. "They have too much invested in the '59s right now. But if things are still going downhill by summer, who knows?"

"Really? You think we've got a chance?"

"It's worth a try, but not yet. People have to start missing the first Edsel enough, and the sales on the '59s would have to be so bad that they would be desperate for ideas. I think we should keep this letter in my Edsel file until the right time."

"But do you like the letter?" I said.

"It's pretty good, except there are a couple problems."

"Like what?"

"Well, you know where you say, 'you had the new cars all covered up in magazines'? It sounds like the cars were buried in a pile of magazines."

"Okay. What would you say?"

"Something like, 'since the first ads of covered cars appeared in magazines.' "

"Great. I got that down. Anything else?"

"Yeah. The word is 'photogenic.' "

"What word?"

"We don't 'take good photographs'; we're 'photogenic.' If we were 'taking photographs,' we wouldn't be in the picture. That's the only part I don't like, because we're not photogenic. Besides, I hate having my picture taken."

"I know," I said. "But we wouldn't be models or anything. We'd just be typical kids."

"And what does a typical kid look like?"

"Like us," I said, a bit exasperated.

"I'm not typical," said Ben. Well, I had to grant him that. Truer words were never spoken.

It was Saturday morning, the second day after Christmas, and the conversation around the Beamering breakfast table soon centered on New Year's Day and the Tournament of Roses Parade.

The Rose Parade is one event that has stubbornly refused to be captured. The only way to truly appreciate this parade is to see it in person. No picture, radio commentary, or TV camera can convey the magnificence of a float two stories high brimming with the vibrant color and fragrance of over a million flowers.

Anyone who desired an unobstructed view of the Rose Parade either had to purchase a seat in the grandstands near Orange Grove Avenue, or stake their claim on New Year's Eve, anywhere along the five-mile parade route, and join the all-night revelry on the street. Except for the members of the Colorado Avenue Standard Christian Church. On January 1, every year, this parade passed right by the front steps of our church, so someone always saw to it that good seats were made available to members of the church.

The youth pastor was usually the one in charge of reserving the area in front of our church, since the high school students were young and crazy enough to see this guard duty as an all-night party and not a chore. In between shifts the kids could go inside the church to get warm and have something to eat and drink. And for those who were so inclined, there was a volleyball tournament going on most of the night in the gym.

"What's your family doing for New Year's, Jonathan?" asked Mrs. Beamering as she served up hot french toast from the griddle. It was just Ben and his parents and I at the table that morning, since Ben's two brothers had left for junior high winter camp in the San Bernardino Mountains the day after Christmas.

"Oh, not much. We usually have my aunt and uncle over for ham dinner."

"After the Rose Parade, I'm sure," said Ben's father.

"Well . . . if we go."

"You're not sure you're going to the Rose Parade?" he said, turning the log cabin on the syrup bottle upside down and looking longingly at his wife.

"There's another bottle," she said.

"I bet you've been so many times you're tired of it," he continued. "Though I can't imagine anyone being tired of a parade—especially that one."

"I've only been once."

"Once? And it's practically in your backyard? I'm surprised your folks haven't made more use of the reserved seat privilege."

"Well, my parents are usually pretty tired after the Watch Night Service and all."

"New Year's happens only once a year," said Mrs. Beamering, setting a new bottle of syrup in front of her husband. "We can't wait to see the parade. We've heard so much about it. I just love a good parade, and this one is supposed to be the best."

"Oh, it is!" I said. "You can even smell the flowers."

"But you're not going?" Pastor Beamering interjected.

"Well, I'm not sure. My parents haven't really said anything about it either way."

"You're welcome to come with us," Mrs. Beamering said. "You could stay overnight after the service and go with us in the morning."

"Really?" I said as Ben flashed me a smile. "Wow, that would be great!"

"Mom, do you think Jonathan and I could stay out all night with the older kids?"

My heart started pounding. I'd wanted to do this for the past couple years, but my parents didn't think I was old enough.

"What do you think, Jeffery?"

"I don't know. Greg and Sandra are going to have their hands full as it is. I don't think there would be adequate supervision."

"Why don't we stay out with them too?" said Mrs. Beamering matter-of-factly. "It would be fun."

"Are you sure you want to do that, Martha?"

Ben's head and mine were flipping back and forth between Mr. and Mrs. Beamering, following this exchange with rapt attention.

"Well, then, I'm game," said Ben's father, wiping the syrup off his shiny lips, and Ben and I both let out a yell at the same time.

After breakfast, Ben went straight to his Edsel file and started flipping through his large collection of newspaper and magazine clippings.

"Here it is," he finally said, and pulled out a page of newspaper photos. He pointed to a picture of a white convertible draped with roses. The caption read: "Over 5,000 roses decorate the open convertible in which Mayor Seth Wilson of Pasadena and the city's First Lady, Mrs. Wilson, ride. Mayor Wilson wears the white suit and hat and the red tie of the organization."

"That's from last year," said Ben.

The rose garland draped around the car began at the front grille, opened into a V across the hood, fell down around the sides, and came up into another V that closed across the back of the convertible and cascaded down the middle of the trunk. Rose petals in a bed of greenery spelled out "MAYOR OF PASADENA" on the side of the front door, and the mayor and his wife were waving from the backseat.

"Where did you get this picture?" I said. "You weren't even here last year."

"At the Tournament of Roses archives. It's only a few blocks from here. They've got everything there—pictures all the way back to the first parade seventy years ago. This picture was in a free brochure about last year's parade. Don't you notice anything . . . about the car?"

I hadn't even paid attention to the car yet. It was difficult to identify because it was a complete profile buried under all the roses. It shared a page with pictures of similarly draped cars that were easier to identify because they were photographed from a front angle. The president of the parade was in a '58 Oldsmobile convertible; the Grand Marshal and his wife were waving from the back of a high-finned '58 Cadillac convertible.

"Wait a minute," I said as I noticed the widening stripe down the side of the back fin-less fender on the mayor's car. Then I saw the little scoop under the headlight that made it protrude.

"It's an Edsel!"

"You're darned right it's an Edsel," said Ben. "Good old Seth Wilson is my kind of guy."

"Well that means there probably won't be an Edsel in the parade this year. I don't think Seth would put himself in the backseat of one of those ugly '59s."

"It probably depends on how big an Edsel fan he is. I'm sure dealers offer these cars for the parade. That's a lot of free publicity. I bet Seth has any car in the world to choose from."

"It's just like your car, Ben—a white convertible with a gold stripe."

"Yep. A white Citation convertible."

"Boy, it sure looks good with all those roses on it." It was just how I had imagined it.

"I've got an idea," I said. "Let's decorate your Edsel for the Rose Parade."

So Ben and I spent the rest of the day making our imaginations come true on the plastic hood and trunk of his white convertible Edsel. If it was going to be authentic, we decided, we had to use real plants as they did in the real parade. This took some doing and some help from Ben's mom, who suggested we use sprigs of parsley for the greenery. For the roses, we used some of the red-violet azaleas blooming in the Beamerings' garden. The needles inside their blossoms made a perfect tiny red bud. I worked on the garland and Ben worked on the "MAYOR OF PASADENA" sign. Mrs. Beamering was so impressed with the authenticity of the finished product that she insisted on using it as a centerpiece on the dinner table.

When my parents came to pick me up, the Beamerings convinced them to stay for dinner. By the time we all sat down around the table with the decorated car as a focal point, it did seem a little like a real Rose Parade, where the beauty had to be enjoyed immediately and not taken for granted. Another day and the garlands on Ben's car would wilt and die. That's the other part of the Rose Parade that makes it so special. You feel the flowers are living for the moment—even living for you.

"It's not an actual parade, but it's close," said Mrs. Beamering.

"It *is* a parade," said Ben as soon as Pastor Beamering finished praying over the meal, "right down the center of the table."

I'm positive that our work on Ben's car contributed to everyone's growing excitement about the Rose Parade. Even my parents decided to go all the way and stay out all night on New Year's Eve and join the fun at the church.

That was the year my excitement for New Year's surpassed even Christmas. Usually New Year's was an afterthought—a kind of farewell to the departing holidays. Television coverage of the various college bowl games was edging toward the saturation point it enjoys today. New Year's Day was, more than anything, an excuse to be lazy, at least for the men. For the wives it was only another special meal to prepare, though never as elaborate as Christmas. New Year's Day was cold ham, cold turkey left over from Christmas, homemade eggnog, various salads—prepared by my mother and my aunt—and football on TV in and around a host of table games.

Games were the highlight of the day for my invalid uncle, confined to a wheelchair since childhood from a bout with polio. My Uncle Wally was a shriveled man who looked far older than his years, and in terms of what he had to battle as a child, he must have earned that look. When it came to games, however, this stubbornness only made him meaner and more determined to win. Most adults tired of games quickly. My uncle was relentless. The only part about New Year's Day I ever looked forward to was playing table games with Uncle Wally.

But New Year's 1959 was different. I'm sure my uncle didn't like it at all that his favorite playing partner was sound asleep most of the afternoon, paying the price of the all-night party on Colorado Avenue. For those who brave the street, the all-night party sometimes overshadows the parade itself. Not because it is any better, but because the warm sun on your face the next morning makes it hard to fight the groggy results of a sleepless night.

Actually, it would have been hard for anything to beat the night Ben and I had celebrating New Year's on the parade route. As far as we were concerned, the continuous train of cars that rolled slowly by all night long was a pre-parade that came close to overshadowing the real one. There was no letup of traffic until around six in the morning, when they finally closed off the street. Up until then it was a bumper-to-bumper party: hot rods and cool coupes; souped-up varieties of '55 and '56 Chevys and Fords; low riders, mags, cherry-red paint jobs; Harleys; even regular passenger cars filled with families celebrating the New Year on wheels; and accompanying it all, the constant background rumble and deep-throated purr of glass-packed mufflers. It was a made-for-California experience: a drive-in party on a street that for one night a year turned into the ultimate cruise. People hung out windows, sat on hoods, blew party whistles, but mostly blew their horns all night long.

The '50s was the last decade you could readily tell the make of a car. A Buick was a Buick; a DeSoto was a DeSoto. Cars had personalities, and even though each make had different models, they all bore the family resemblance in some way.

To pass the time, Ben and I played a game called "Spot-A-Car Auto Bingo." It was a game our family often played on long trips, but I had objected to my mother bringing it that night. I was afraid Ben would think it was corny. To my surprise, he loved it. Auto Bingo consisted of a number of cards designating makes and colors of cars you had to spot. When you did, you marked it on a grid until you got a bingo horizontally, vertically, or diagonally. Fords and Chevrolets always filled up first, so you were usually stuck trying to find a blue Packard or a two-toned Nash or a black Hudson. Since the game was made before the Edsel, we decided that any Edsel could fill a free spot anywhere. Not content to sit and wait for the designated cars to pass, however, Ben kept running up and down the street to find a car before I did.

"Where's Ben?" his mother would say.

"He's looking for a red Studebaker," I'd say. And just when

we were starting to get worried, Ben would show up a little out of breath.

"Bingo! I found an Edsel!"

"Ben, I don't want you wandering off anymore," his mother would say. "You stay put and let the cars come to you." But the cars were coming too slowly for Ben, and though he tried to stay put, he would unconsciously start drifting up the line of traffic, much like a person gets pulled away from a spot on the beach by a drifting tide. I would look and he'd be right there, and then I would look and he'd be gone.

"Honestly, where has that boy gone to now? Jeffery . . . Ben's wandered off again," and Pastor Beamering would march off and return a few minutes later with Ben up on his shoulders, smiling and waving his winning Auto Bingo card.

"There's a pink Edsel station wagon up there. It'll be here in about ten minutes. It's a beauty!"

"Well, that will do me a lot of good. You already have bingo." As a result of Ben's wandering ways, I never won one game.

"It's just too much of a temptation," said Mrs. Beamering finally. "If you can't stay put, you'll have to stop playing that game." Which we did at about three in the morning.

"What now?" Ben asked like a playful puppy who'd just had his ball taken away.

"How about we get some sleep?"

"Not on your life. We didn't come here to sleep. Look at that parade of cars right in front of us. I bet we could find all the new '59s in there somewhere. That's what we could do. Let's see how many different new cars we can find."

So we made a list and spent the next two hours marking down every '59 car we spotted. In the course of two hours we saw several new Fords, Chevrolets, Oldsmobiles, Buicks, one Mercury, a couple Plymouths, and a Dodge.

"No Cadillacs," I said. "I wanted to see a Cadillac up close."

"If you had a new Cadillac, would you drive it down this street?" said Ben. "I saw someone throwing a bottle about a block up."

"Does that explain why we haven't seen even one new '59 Edsel?"

"I wish it did, but it probably doesn't. Still . . . we haven't seen a new Chrysler yet either."

"Or a Lincoln," I added. "What cars do you suppose the bigwigs will be driving?"

"Well, the Grand Marshal will be in a Cadillac. He always is. And the president will be in a Buick or an Oldsmobile. And the mayor? Who knows? According to the program, it's going to be in an open convertible—"

" '. . . decorated with over 5,000 roses,' " I completed. "It says the same thing it said last year. And good old Seth will have on 'the white suit and hat and the red tie of the organization,' " I continued reading from the program my parents had bought from a vendor. "They must use the same paragraph every year."

"He'll probably stay with the Ford Motor Company," Ben said, thinking out loud, "but that would leave him only the Mercury. A Lincoln would upstage the president's Buick or Olds. It's going to be a Mercury. Bet you anything. The Edsel was perfect for him last year, but you won't see him in one now."

Ben wanted to place bets on what cars the president and the mayor would be driving, but I resisted. I had always been taught that any kind of betting was a sin. Becky and I couldn't even say "I bet you so and so will happen" without drawing a condemning look from one of our parents.

"Oh, come on," said Ben, zipping open his sleeping bag and starting to climb in, much to my tired body's relief. "A nickel says the president will be in a Buick and a nickel says Seth will be riding in a Mercury."

"I'll take an Oldsmobile for the president and an Edsel for the mayor," I said, feeling like I was committing a mortal sin. "It's just for fun, right?"

"Just for fun."

"Are you going to sleep?" I asked hopefully.

"Of course not," said Ben, reaching for some hot chocolate from his mother. "I'm just getting warmed-up."

The last thing I remembered was the warm feeling of hot chocolate on my insides and the heavy feeling that the darkness was starting to lift from the sky and I still hadn't slept. Soon the heaviness overcame me.

15

On the Blue Line

I half awoke to the sight of Ben in my face and the sound of distant drumming. The early sun was warm and thick on my skin, and my sleeping bag—even on the hard asphalt of Colorado Avenue—felt like a feather bed. Ben was shaking me, telling me the parade was coming. I didn't care about the parade; I only wanted to sleep. Then Pastor Beamering's big wide grin was filling my vision.

"Wake up, Jonathan!" he shouted, his pastoral pipes aimed mercilessly at point-blank range. "You're blocking someone's seat!"

I sat up to find that I was in the center of a huge crowd of people. In the brief hour and a half I had been asleep, the parade goers for whom we had braved the night had arrived with their folding chairs, their thermoses, their programs, and their high spirits. It felt like the whole church had just turned up in my bedroom.

The street was buzzing with activity, but not like the noisy cars of the night before. This was the buzz of voices, and the excitement in the air slowly seeped into my tired bones. I climbed out of my sleeping bag, and Becky handed me a cup of orange juice. The few feet of space I'd just vacated by merely sitting up was already filled with a folding chair.

A few people were still making their way along the street, burdened with lawn chairs, coolers, and blankets. An occasional vendor came by with souvenirs, and every few minutes a motorcycle policeman would race down the middle of the street to scare the last walkers back into the crowd. Then a police car came slowly down the center of the street and I thought it was the beginning of the parade—until I heard the loudspeaker on his car telling everyone to make sure they got behind the blue line.

At least our all-night vigil had earned us a spot on the blue line, the closest you could get to the coming attraction. I could hear the drums of the first band, and I pulled my feet in until I could see all the blue of the six-inch blue line. It was the first day of a new year, and something big and loud and wonderful was coming down the street, right in front of my feet. Suddenly I no longer resented the people who had interrupted my sleep, because I knew that these mere spectators could never feel what I felt. This was my little spot on the street; I had paid all night for this. No matter how good their seats were, they would never know what it was like to wake up on the blue line with the sun on your face and the 70th Annual Tournament of Roses Parade coming down the street.

It began with a long line of motorcycle police motoring down the blue line on both sides of the street. They passed so close to me I could hear the leather seats crackle against their crisp uniforms. They didn't stop for anything. You knew if your toe was on the line, they would run over it; at any rate, it wasn't worth a challenge. Then came banners and a band and a couple of floats, and then the three parade dignitaries in their new cars—just what Ben and I were waiting for. Ben was the first to spot the Cadillac that carried the Grand Marshal, but I beat him to the other two. My father had a pair of binoculars, and I got him to lift me up on his shoulders.

"It's an Oldsmobile!" I shouted at Ben. "The president's in an Oldsmobile! You owe me a nickel!" and it was lucky that I was straddling my father's head because just as I said that I lost my balance and involuntarily boxed his ears with my legs trying to save myself from falling. That meant my father did not hear what I said to Ben, or he would have been very angry at me— not only for betting in the first place but for shouting about the wager in the hearing of a large representation of our church congregation.

But because he didn't hear that first part, he didn't recognize the second part as a bet when I shouted, "Make that a dime! It's an Edsel! Holy cow, Ben, it's a '58 Edsel!" I climbed down excitedly, handed my bewildered father the binoculars, and squeezed back to the blue line next to Ben.

"You're kidding," he greeted me. "Not a '58 Edsel. It can't be."

"It is!" I assured him, and as soon as the president's car passed by, we could see, just over the mayor's banner that preceded him, the familiar horse-collar grille and the sunken cheeks of a beautifully ugly 1958 Edsel.

"It's the same car he drove last year!" said Ben, looking as though he'd seen a ghost. "No one's ever done that in this parade before. They always drive new cars. This is a New Year's parade, for heaven's sake. This is 1959 . . . and he's driving a 1958 car?"

The car passed by us in slow motion. I had never seen an Edsel look so proud. It was all white and gleaming. The roses were draped across the hood, so you could see the classic diagonal indentation that gave the front of the car such clean lines. The heavy chrome sparkled in the sunlight, and the deep buttery red of the roses seemed ready to melt. In the backseat, waving, were Mayor Seth Wilson and his wife.

Suddenly Ben did what you were never supposed to do: He ran into the street. He picked up a rose that had fallen off an earlier float and ran toward the mayor's car. Ben's father started to get up to stop him, but Mrs. Beamering grabbed his arm and gave him a look that stopped him instead. Ben, meanwhile, ran up to the Edsel, handed the mayor's wife the rose, exchanged a few words, and then ran back before a tournament official could stop him.

"What did you say to them?" I said as Ben resumed his place next to me and we watched the gull-wing taillights glide away.

" 'Happy New Year.' "

"That's it? That's all you said?"

"Yep."

"Well . . . what did they say?"

Ben gave me that how-can-you-be-so-stupid? look. "They said 'Happy New Year' back."

"Didn't you say something about the car?"

"No . . . that will come later."

Later? What was he up to now? I looked at Ben as he stared

out at the Odd Fellows float passing by, a 1959 version of space travel. I knew that look: he wasn't looking at the float; he was looking through it while his mind worked. After two more floats, a band, and a Spanish equestrian unit, I finally found out what Ben was thinking.

"We're going to write him a letter," he said.

"Who? Seth?"

"Yep," said Ben. "And we're going to send him your letter too."

"My Ford Motor Company letter? Why send it to *him*?"

"So he can send it for us. It will carry more weight coming from him—the mayor of Pasadena—the man who dared to drive a year-old car in a New Year's parade." And then he turned to me so I would get the full weight of this next statement. "Don't you see? He did the very thing you are suggesting. He brought the '58 Edsel back—in front of a national audience, no less. He must have a reason for this. We have to find out why."

The parade went by for what seemed like a day. It was one of the few times I can remember getting my fill of a good thing. Just when you started to feel sad that the parade might be over, it delighted you with more. By the time five million people surged into the street after the last float, I was ready to go home. Actually, by then I was almost asleep.

"Can Ben come home with us and stay over?" I asked my mother sleepily as we made our way through the press of the crowd.

"I don't know why not . . . if it's all right with Martha."

"It's all right with me," said Ben's mother, lugging a large picnic basket and a couple blankets. Everyone had an armload. "But you're having guests, aren't you, Ann?"

"Just family. It will be no problem. You know we love having Ben."

So Ben got to meet my Uncle Wally, and the two of them hit it off immediately. They played games all afternoon, facing off with equal intensity. I slept most of the afternoon, waking up long enough to eat supper and sit around in a foggy state of consciousness until bedtime.

"Your uncle's a lot of fun," Ben said as we were getting ready for bed.

"Well, you sure made his day."

"Seth Wilson made my day," said Ben, climbing into the bottom bunk.

"Shall we write that letter tomorrow?" I said, yawning. I didn't hear Ben's answer to my question as I drifted off, vaguely wondering how he could keep going so energetically on so little sleep.

———

The next morning I awoke to the sound of Ben hunting and pecking away on my parents' black Royal typewriter.

"What are you doing?" I said sleepily, rubbing my eyes.

"I'm finishing our letter to the mayor."

"Finishing? When did you start it?"

"Last night after you fell asleep. Here, what do you think of this?" and he started reading:

Dear Mayor Wilson:

Yesterday my friend Jonathan and I attended the Tournament of Roses Parade. I was the one who gave you a rose just past Loma Alta Boulevard. That was me, Benjamin Beamering.

We want to congratulate you on your excellent taste in automobiles. We believe that the 1958 Edsel is one of the finest cars on the road today and we figure you must feel the same way since you dared to drive one in a New Year's Day parade even when it was a year old.

We are trying to get the Ford Motor Company to bring back the 1958 Edsel. We think it is a much better car than the one they introduced as a poor excuse for a 1959 model. Would you please help us by sending our letter on to them? It would get more attention coming from you. If you choose not to send the letter on, please return it since it is the only copy we have.

Thank you for your help in this matter.

Sincerely,
Benjamin Beamering
Jonathan Liebermann

"I thought you made a carbon copy of that letter to the Ford Motor Company."

"I did, but I don't want him to know that. This way, we should hear back from him. Even if he doesn't do anything, at least he should have the courtesy to send the letter back. Otherwise we would have no way of knowing if our letter to the Ford Motor Company was sent. If the mayor doesn't come through for us, we will still send the letter ourselves."

By that afternoon our letter to the mayor would be signed and in the mail. And by that afternoon also, the front page of the *Pasadena Star-News* would give us a pretty good indication that our letter would get immediate attention when it arrived at the mayor's office.

The January 2, 1959, edition of the *Star-News* was a particularly eventful one for me. Not only did it contain information pertinent to our fledgling save-the-Edsel campaign, but it was also the first day I delivered that very edition as a rookie newsboy. However, if Ben hadn't mentioned the paper at breakfast that morning, I might have missed that appointment.

"You get the *Pasadena Star-News,* don't you?" said Ben immediately after we had prayed over our breakfast of pancakes and bacon. My father's prayer had been short due to the fact that his pancakes were already on his plate and he liked them hot. The Scripture reading from *Daily Light* had been slipped in neatly just before the cakes came off the griddle. My parents had this timing down pat.

"Yes, we do," said my father, whose presence with us was uncharacteristic for a Friday morning. Since Christmas and New Year's fell on Thursday that year, Pastor Beamering, inspired, I think, by the conversion of Ebenezer Scrooge, had given the church staff both Fridays off—a nice holiday bonus.

"When does it come?" asked Ben.

"It's an evening paper," said my mother. "It usually arrives anywhere between three and six o'clock. It depends on when the newsboy gets around to it."

"You mean ex-newsboy," Becky interjected. "Marvin quit last week, remember? Boy, is he a creep! I can't believe Mrs. Fields put me right in front of him in class. He's always catching flies and torturing them while I—"

"Wait a minute—" My mother put her hand on Becky's shoulder, interrupting the acceleration of my sister's dramatic performance. "Jonathan, aren't you supposed to start that trial run on your paper route soon?"

"Yeah, the day after New Year's."

Everyone stopped eating and stared at me until I figured out why.

"Oh my gosh. That's today!"

"Wow. How can you be so smart?" (Becky, of course.)

"You start delivering the *Pasadena Star-News* today?" said Ben excitedly. "That means we'll get it sooner than anybody!"

"Why so much interest in the *Star-News*, Ben?" asked my father.

"I want to see if they say anything about the mayor riding in a 1958 Edsel in the parade yesterday," Ben said, then turned to me again. "You didn't tell me you were going to be delivering the *Star-News*."

"I forgot all about it. It's only a two-week trial. I may not like it."

"You'll like it. My brothers both had paper routes when we lived in Texas. It's a lot of fun throwing papers at houses. I'll help you with it. Besides, it will fit perfectly into our plan. Anything that will involve us with the city of Pasadena right now will help our plan."

"And what plan is that?" asked Becky.

I looked at Ben, my eyes asking him silently, *How do we explain this to anyone else?*—something we hadn't even spoken about directly to each other. In fact, I was surprised Ben had brought up the subject so freely.

"Our plan to bring back the 1958 Edsel," he said without hesitation. Becky rolled her eyes, but otherwise nobody made any comments or asked any more questions. I'm not sure why. Perhaps my parents didn't want to dampen our spirits, figuring time and reality would leaven our enthusiasm. So instead of questioning us about the nature of our strange campaign, my father changed the subject by reaching across the table and pointing with a puzzled look to a faint blue spot on Becky's nose where she had permanently ground asphalt into it on a fall off her bicycle some five years earlier.

"What's that on your nose?" he said.

Now we all stared at *him* in amazement.

"Darling, her nose has been like that for the last five years, since she fell off her bike in Minnesota. Walter, you need to spend more time at home."

Ben and I excused ourselves from the table as soon as we were done eating and went over our letter to the mayor one more time. Then we both signed it and rode our bikes down to the post office to mail it. Ben was concerned that if we waited for the postman to pick it up at our house, it might take longer to get there.

"He's still got to take it to the post office anyway, and it won't get there till the end of his route. We can't afford to waste a day. Got to get to Seth while his memory is still fresh." So we had the letter there by ten o'clock and spent the rest of the morning and early afternoon working on our houses and waiting for the *Star-News* dealer.

Our housing construction had been almost at a standstill since school started. During the last two weeks of summer, with our Scripture-illustrating days at an end, we had managed to get walls up over all the studs, inside and out. Presently we were working on the windows, and making the tiny frames out of thin strips of balsa wood required a great deal of patience. It seemed like we spent most of our time picking dried glue and wood fragments off our fingers. At first we had tried to make the windows so they could actually slide up and down, but that hadn't worked. We did manage to make the upper half set outside the lower half, however, just like the windows in real houses.

The next big decision we faced was whether to make the roofs removable or to attach them permanently. I wanted to be able to take the roof off and see the detail of all the rooms in the house, but Ben didn't like that idea at all. "These aren't doll-houses, for goodness' sake!" For Ben, it was enough to look in through the windows and see that there were real rooms inside. "We're in construction, not interior design. You can have Becky furnish your house if you want to show off the inside, but I'm putting my roof on permanently," he'd said, ending the discussion.

Midafternoon we heard a car drive up in front of the house—one of those glass-packed muffler jobs you could hear approaching a block away, swallowing and burping air and carbon monoxide as it slowed down to meet our driveway. Ben and I walked around from the garage to find a cherry-red, low-riding '55 Chevrolet with spinner wheels and flames on the side pulling in our driveway and onto our front lawn. A teenager wearing a white T-shirt with rolled-up sleeves and an Elvis haircut stepped out, leaving the door open to a blaring radio, and sauntered around to his trunk where he pulled out a bundle of newspapers.

"One of you guys Johnny Liebermann?" he said over the "Dum, dum do dum dooby do" of the radio, dropping the bundle and lighting a cigarette from a pack that he rolled back into his T-shirt sleeve, revealing a thin but muscular upper arm with a dragon tattoo. He wore blue jeans, white socks, and black loafers, and his pompadour of black hair shone with grease.

"I am."

"Here," he said, handing me a manila envelope, his cigarette wobbling on his lip as he talked. "Everything you'll need for this route. It's a real cinch. Only forty-eight customers, but you'll get more. Ever had a paper route before?"

"No."

"You ten years old, kid?" he asked, squinting against the smoke.

"Yeah," I said.

"Got a good sturdy bike?"

"Yeah."

"Go get it. I'll show you how to carry papers."

I ran back to the garage, and while I was getting my bike out, my father came out, looking agitated.

"Is that the newspaper dealer?"

"Uh huh."

"What's his car doing on our front lawn? Hasn't he ever heard of driveways?"

"I don't know, Dad. That's where he wanted to park, I guess."

My father watched me roll my bike down the driveway, then went back into the house. By the time I got to the front yard, Ben was in the backseat of the Chevy, inspecting the white tuck-and-roll seat covers, and Becky was in the front seat, singing along with "Why must I be-ee a teen-a-ger in love" and feeling the fuzzy dice hanging from the rearview mirror.

That was when my mother steamed out the front door and ordered Ben and Becky out of the car.

"It's okay, lady!" the newspaper dealer yelled. "They asked me."

"Well, it's not okay with me!" she shouted sternly. "Is it possible for you to show my son how to start a paper route without playing that thing so loud?"

"Oh, sure. No problem." He went over to his car, turned off the radio, and slammed the doors shut as if this was a familiar confrontation for him. Then he turned and extended his hand to my mother. "Hi, I'm Tony Gomez," he said. "I'll be Johnny's dealer. You must be Mrs. Liebermann."

"I am," she said as she shook his hand. "And his name is Jonathan."

"Cool."

"And I'm Becky," said my sister, bouncing her ponytail and trying hard to make her twelve years stretch as far as she could.

My mother spoke before Tony could even respond. "Run along inside, young lady. This is Jonathan's business, not yours."

"But Mother, can't I—"

"No. This is not a party. Jonathan is starting his first business, and this all needs to be taken seriously." She seemed to be saying this for everyone's benefit—Tony's included. "Now, Mr. Gomez, is there anything you need from me?"

"Everything is explained pretty good in the papers I give Johnn—uh—Jonathan. There's a form you need to sign since he's under twelve, but you can get that back to me later."

"Fine. Well, you all have work to do, don't you? Oh, and in the future, Mr. Gomez, would you please be kind enough to use our driveway for your car?"

"Sure, ma'am. Be happy to."

My mother went back into the house, and Tony backed his car onto the driveway, the muffler rumbling. As he turned off the ignition and got out again, he noticed Ben trying unsuccessfully to pull a paper out of the stack, bound tightly with wire.

"You need a pair of these," Tony said, pulling a pair of wire cutters out of his back pocket.

"That's some mother you have, Johnny," he said, snipping the wire and popping open the bundle.

"Yeah. Well, she's not always like that."

"I've never seen her like that," said Ben.

"It's me," said Tony. "Most parents don't dig me. I bring out the worst in parents. I don't mind, though. I'm used to it."

"Wow, look at this!" Ben had been glancing over the front page and was pointing to a headline in the lower right-hand corner: "Mayor Snubs' New Car."

"A whole article on it!"

Ben and I were both looking at the front page in amazement when Tony spoke up. "Hey look, man, you don't read these things; you just deliver 'em. Here, get folding," and he threw me a box of red rubber bands.

Ben retired to the front porch with a paper, while the closest I got to the coveted article was to snap rubber bands over it. It was a large paper. Larger than normal for a Friday, according to Tony, because this was a special post-parade issue. Usually Friday papers were only twenty-four pages and you could fold them in fourths. This one had to be folded in thirds.

Ben, meanwhile, had finished the article, and I could tell by his famous devilish grin that the news was good. Really good. I resented him for going ahead and reading without me, but I resented more the fact that he wasn't helping me fold. Tony wasn't helping me either. He was going over my route and telling me all the things I needed to know about delivering papers.

"Every day you get three extra papers. In case you lose any along the way."

"How would I do that?"

He shrugged his shoulders. "Throw it on a roof . . . lose it in a bush . . . drop it in a puddle. . . . Anyway, when you're done, deliver the extras as a free paper to the same house for a few days. Then stop by and ask if they want to subscribe. It works. And the more customers you get, the more money it means for the both of us."

Tony was big on new customers, but I wasn't too sure how successful I was going to be at selling or delivering. Even with him rumbling along next to me that first day, like a pace car in the Indy 500, I broke two geranium plants, put one paper on a roof, and made a cat jump three feet when the paper landed on the driveway in front of him. He never saw it coming.

Tony pointed to each house and yelled "Driveway!" or "Porch!" or "Lawn!" depending on where the owner wanted it delivered. I had to move fast to keep up with him.

"Any questions?" he said out the window of his car after I sent the last paper sliding down a long driveway on Seamour Street.

"Yeah. Isn't this just a trial? When do I really start?"

"You start now. Papers come at 3:00 in the afternoon and at 4:30 in the morning on Sundays. Got to have them out by 6:00 either way. You did good, kid. Get us some more customers," and he rumbled off up Seamour Street, laying down a little strip of rubber each time he shifted gears.

"Some car, huh?" I said to Ben, who had labored along behind me on his bike.

"Yeah," he said, panting. "So what do you think?"

"I liked it. Did you see that cat jump?"

"Yeah! I thought he'd never come down."

The route ended six blocks from my house, but it was downhill all the way back, so we coasted side by side. I decided I liked delivering newspapers, and Ben said he would help me with collections and getting new customers. "As long as I get a percentage of the houses I sell," he said, always the businessman.

I tried to get him to tell me about the article on the way back, but he said he wanted me to hear it straight from the paper. So he read it aloud to me as I put away my bike and washed my hands, blackened with the newsprint of the world. He followed me around as he read, from the garage to the bathroom and past my father who was taking a nap in the living room.

Mayor Seth Wilson surprised the 1959 Tournament of Roses Committee, the Emerson Edsel dealership of Pasadena, and a number of observant parade goers ("That would be us, of course," interjected Ben.) when he chose to ride in this year's parade in a 1958 Edsel instead of a new 1959 car. It was the first time in the 70-year history of this parade that a dignitary did not ride in a new car.

No one was more surprised than Orel Humphrey, owner and general manager of Emerson Edsel, whose historic establishment on Fair Oaks Blvd. (formerly Emerson Ford) has been providing a new convertible for the acting mayor to ride in for over 25 years. According to Mr. Humphrey, Mayor Wilson turned down his offer of a new Edsel convertible in favor of his own personal 1958 Edsel, the car he rode in the Tournament of Roses Parade last year.

The issue created a notable controversy between the mayor and the Tournament Director, Frank Milner. "This not only breaks an important long-standing tradition, it flies in the face of the spirit of this parade, which is a celebration of the new year," Mr. Milner told the *Star-News* earlier this week when it became clear the mayor was going to insist on riding in his own car. "Even an older classic car that would reflect our great history would make more sense than this. A '58 Edsel is nothing more than a used car now."

Mr. Humphrey was less critical. "Mr. Wilson bought his car from us after riding in it in last year's parade and simply chose it over the newer model. As far as I'm concerned, it's his business what he wants to do. We can't help it if Mayor Wilson happens to like his '58 Edsel."

Riffs between the mayor and local committee members are certainly nothing new. The mayor has a reputation for being a man who thinks for himself and does not kowtow to political agendas or special interest groups.

"Those who are having a hard time living with an uncompromising Mayor Wilson should remember it was that same trait that made him such an attractive candidate a year and a half ago," said Mr. Humphrey, a strong supporter of the mayor despite his snubbing of the new car. "Those who made their bed when they put Wilson in there have got to learn to lie in it." Humphrey, who seemed amused over this incident, seemed happy enough it was still an Edsel in the parade. ("And listen to this!" Ben said.) Apparently sales are indicating that Mayor Wilson is not the only person who prefers the original Edsel to the new one.

Ben paused so we could savor the sound of those words. "I can't believe this," I said.
"Wait. There's more."

Although the mayor himself was unavailable for comment, his office, aware of the controversy and Mr. Milner's comments, dispatched a news release to the *Star-News* just prior to the parade in which he stated, "Those who disagree with my decision to enjoy this great parade with Mrs. Wilson from the backseat of my own car need to realize I am not only exercising my prerogative as the mayor of this great city, I am exercising my freedom of choice as an American citizen. Mr. Milner seems to favor either a new car or a classic car as worthy of this parade. To that I wish to say that I believe the 1958 Edsel will, in time, be recognized as the American classic that it truly is."

Ben read that last sentence in reverent tones.

Hearing this amazing confirmation of our own values and feelings from the lips of the mayor and the front page of the newspaper sent my thoughts and emotions into overdrive. In fact, it was more than a confirmation of our plans; it was a vindication.

"Where's Becky?" I said. "I want her to see this."

Then I remembered our letter to the mayor.

"Ben! Our letter's already in the mail!" I shouted.

"I know," he smiled, and said with controlled confidence, "We're going to hear from the mayor."

16

The Pontiac

Ben stayed over the entire weekend, even Saturday night, which was a first for us. He'd often slept over on a weeknight during summer or on a Friday during school, but with the typical Sunday being the busiest day of the week for both our families, our parents preferred to have us in our own beds on Saturday night. However, this was not a typical Sunday; it was my first Sunday morning as a newspaper boy, and Ben and I convinced our parents that I needed his help to pull it off. My parents didn't need much convincing. They were happy that I had someone to accompany me that early in the morning, and my father was especially grateful that it wasn't going to have to be him.

Ben and I got up at 4:30. Later I found out I could get up as late as 5:00 and still get all the papers folded and delivered by 6:00, but on my first Sunday I wanted to be sure I had plenty of time.

Waking up that early is not a chore when you're ten years old. I loved the excitement and anticipation of opening my eyes in the darkness, in possession of a secret reason for getting out of bed before the sun and most other people. Usually it was to go fishing, leave on an automobile trip, or open presents on Christmas morning. Today, however, anticipation and excitement blended with a feeling of importance: I had a secret assignment; I had to get the news out.

I already liked the smell of fresh newsprint, the sound of rubber bands snapping over folded papers, and the look of the newspaper saddlebags stuffed with important information and hanging full and heavy under my handlebars. *Pasadena Star-News* stood out in bold, black Gothic letters on the new, white canvas bags.

Sunday was the biggest paper of the week, and I soon learned I couldn't carry all the papers at one time. It would require two trips.

"This paper route is a great idea," said Ben as I loaded the saddlebags for the first run. "You should keep it."

"I will, if you'll help me."

"Of course I'll help you."

At 5:10 when we set out on the first leg, it was still pitch dark. Ben didn't have a light on his bike, but I had solved that the night before by installing Becky's light on his bike. Both Becky and I had generator lights, which were head lamps connected to a small bottle-shaped generator that was spring-loaded so it pressed up against the front tire and generated power as the wheel turned against it. The generator didn't fit quite as well on Ben's bike as it did on Becky's, but we figured it would work okay for one morning. Later he could get his own.

"Just think of how all these people are depending on you, Jonathan," Ben said as we rounded the first corner and headed for the beginning of my route. He was riding just behind me, carrying on his commentary in a volume that would have embarrassed me if I'd thought anyone was awake to hear it. "They'll wake up in a few hours, put on their bathrobe and slippers, and the news of the world will be waiting for them at the end of their driveway. All because of you, Jonathan . . . 'All the news that's fit to print.' Did you know that's what it says on every *New York Times* newspaper?"

"No, I didn't," I said as we rounded the second corner and I pulled out the first paper like a gun out of its holster. It was so heavy it almost slipped out of my grasp.

"You'll notice they don't print that on top of the *Star-News*. That's because it's full of stuff that's not fit to print . . . except for anything they want to print about Mayor Wilson," said Ben from behind me. "Seth is fit to print."

"How did you know that about *The New York Times?*" I asked. "Wait a minute . . . the library, right?"

"Yep."

Slap! went the first heavy paper on the driveway of 308 Del Mar Avenue. In the silence of the morning, I thought it would wake the dead.

"Seth is fit to print," I repeated like an "Amen" back to Ben.

There were no cars on the road, no sounds except the ones we were making: the flick of our pedals, the rattle of metal over bumps in the road, the high-pitched whine of generators rubbing against front wheels, and the slap and slide of the big Sunday paper landing on concrete and echoing through the silence of early morning.

"Can I throw one?" Ben asked.

"Sure. Here. Try 321 across the street—the one with the Ford in the driveway."

Since I had only run the route twice—with the Friday and Saturday evening papers—I still had to stop often and check the street numbers on the card Tony had given me just to be sure. Checking the card was made more difficult by the fact that my generator light only worked when the bike was moving, so I had to hold the card down by my light and focus on it with one eye while I watched where I was going with the other, or I had to stop directly under a street lamp.

"Remember to throw it in the driveway," I called out after Ben. Though the folding and lugging of these big papers was more time-consuming than the weekday editions, the ease of delivery made up for it. Tony didn't want Sunday papers delivered anywhere but on driveways, because the noise of a big thud on the front porch or an errant slap against a front door might wake a sleeping customer.

"How about under the Ford?"

"Ben!"

"Relax. It's just barely under the back bumper. They'll find it. Here, give me another one. Where do you want this?"

"Well . . . next one on that side is . . . 325," I said, almost running into a parked car while trying to read the card.

As far as moving cars, we saw only three that morning, which made us more daring about riding in the middle of the street, or slanting back and forth across it with ease.

"Where to next?" Ben would ask, and I would stop and check the card while he circled in the street with a fat paper resting on his handlebars, waiting for its designated driveway.

As a bike rider, Ben—never a natural athlete—was always a bit shaky. This hadn't really bothered me before, but now it made me nervous. Especially when he wobbled up next to me, trying to guide his bike with one hand while reaching to pull a paper out of my bag with the other. I held my breath a few times, but the first leg went without a hitch.

"Let me have more papers this time," Ben said, back at our house, as I was loading up for the second run. "In fact, why don't I fill your schoolbag and strap it over my shoulder. I bet I could fit five or six papers in there—enough for one side of a block. Then I could take a side and you could take a side."

I went with the idea because it meant he wouldn't be fishing newspapers out of my bag on the move anymore. I didn't realize that it also meant he would be going up and down sidewalks, jarring his bike over the cracks that had formed from expanding tree roots, as well as bumping on and off uneven concrete driveways.

"I have an idea," said Ben as we were just about to start up Live Oak Street. "Let's race. Give me all the numbers on the right side, and we'll see who finishes the block first."

"Okay." I got out my card and picked out the numbers. "You're on the even side, so you take 312, 324, 332, and 336. Can you remember that?"

"Sure . . . 12, 24, 32, and 36 . . . hike! Give me four papers. Okay, here I go!"

What a rat. He didn't even give me time to check all my numbers. I had to jump on my bike and try to hold the card down close to my generator light while I kept riding.

Slap! went Ben's 312.

Slap! went 324.

Slap! went my 317 as I raced along, reading and throwing.

Slap! Slap! Slap! 325, 329, and 333.

Suddenly I was at the end of the block and there were no more slaps. I looked back and there was no more Ben. Nothing but an eerie silence.

"Ben?" I called out cautiously.

I crossed over to his side of the street and started coasting back slowly. I could hear only the ticking of my bike. Then in the faint light of a streetlamp I saw the wheel of his bike, on its side, sticking out from behind a parked car.

"Ben!" I shouted as I pedaled up beside it. No Ben. Just his bike with a gaping hole in the twisted spokes of the front wheel.

"Ben! Where are you?"

"Over here," came a muffled voice from the other side of the car. I jumped off my bike, ran around the car, and there was Ben sitting on the ground, leaning back against a tree and holding his face. Blood was running down his arm and dripping off his elbow.

"Ben! What happened?"

"I don't know . . . it happened so fast . . . suddenly I was smack up against the back of that station wagon." He sounded like he had a mouthful of marbles.

"Here let me see," and I moved his hand away. It didn't look good at all. His lip was split open and there was a lot of blood. There was also a gash over his eye.

"Oh, my gosh!" I said.

"I think I jutht thpit out a tooth," he said with a lisp.

"Ben, you stay right here and don't move. I'm going for help."

"No, I'm okay. I'll just ride back to your house. You have to finish your route . . . got to get the news out."

I glanced back at his mangled bike. "You're not going to get anywhere on that! I'll find a telephone and call my dad. Don't move!" All that blood was really scaring me.

I ran up to the nearest house and rang the doorbell and pounded on the door even though I heard it ring inside. The number on the porch was 332. I rang again and heard someone moving inside. Then the porch light flicked on and a woman opened the door.

"Mercy! What happened to you, laddie? You look like you've seen a ghost."

"I'm sorry to bother you, but my friend's had a terrible accident and . . . do you think I could borrow your phone?"

"Of course you can," she said, noticing Ben's blood on my shirt where I had wiped my hand. "Come right in." As she led me quickly to the kitchen she said, "St. Eustace must have led you here. I'm a nurse. Where's your friend?"

"He's out front."

She pointed to the phone, grabbed a towel from a rack next to the stove, and rushed out the front door, muttering to saint somebody. I called my father and told him what had happened.

"Why don't you come on home and we'll have a look at him."

"We can't. His bike won't work."

"How far are you? Can you walk?" he said.

"Dad, he's bleeding all over the street!"

"Oh, my. I'll be right there. What's the address?"

When I got back out to Ben, the woman had him lying on his back. She was cradling his head with one hand while she held the towel to his mouth with the other.

"This boy needs to get to the hospital right away," she said. "Is someone comin'?"

"Yes, my dad's on his way. Is he going to be all right? Can you tell how bad it is?"

"Believe me, I've seen a lot worse, laddie."

I stood there looking at Ben, looking so out of place in the arms of this total stranger.

"Well, I found out this is Benjamin here," she said. "And what's your name, laddie?"

"Jonathan . . . Jonathan Liebermann."

"I suppose one of you is the new paper boy."

"I am," I said.

Suddenly Ben started trying to wiggle out of her grasp, but she clamped down harder. "Now listen here, Benjamin, you'll do as I say!" she said.

"Ma'am, I—I think he needs to breathe!" I said. His face was reddening as his eyes widened.

She loosened her grip, and Ben gasped and started coughing and choking into the towel she had stuffed in his mouth. "That'll mean he's probably got a broken nose to go along with the two teeth he lost."

I started praying for my father's quick arrival, not only to get Ben to the hospital, but to save him from suffocation.

"So you'll be bringin' my paper to me now?" she asked casually, while Ben writhed under her with eyes that seemed to be telling me to do something about setting him free. She only let him up for air when his face got real red. "Well, I know you'll do better than the last laddie. Seems like we played hide-and-seek every day with my paper. I never knew where 'twas going to turn up next. You sure someone's comin'?"

I nodded my head, and then she recited what I first thought was a song, then a verse, and finally realized was a prayer.

"Anthony, St. Anthony, please come 'round," she muttered. "Something is lost and can't be found." Within a breath of her completing this little ditty twice, I heard the familiar V–8 engine of my dad's Ford Fairlane purring through the quiet morning.

"Works every time," she said, lifting Ben up into a sitting position as my father drove in the driveway.

"All right, I'll be gettin' in the backseat with Benjamin here," she said as my father started around the side of the car. She tried to get up while still cradling Ben's head, but fell back awkwardly, unbalanced by Ben's weight. My father stepped over to help her up, while I ran to her other side and helped with Ben. Through all of this, she never loosened her hold on Ben's face.

"That's very kind of you, ma'am," said my father, "but I'm sure I can take it from here. Uh . . . why don't you let me have a look at his face? I can have him to his parents in ten minutes. I'm sure he'll be all right—"

"He won't be all right if we don't get him to the hospital straight away! Believe me, I know what I'm doing. I'm a nurse.

Now help me get him into this car!"

Ben fainted clean away as soon as we got him up on his feet.

"This boy's lost a lot of blood," the woman said. "We can't afford to have him be losin' any more." She and my father lifted him into the backseat.

"St. Mary's is the closest," she said, settling in the back beside Ben, once more cradling his head.

I jumped into the front, only to have my father jump on me. "Jonathan . . . your paper route!"

"But Dad—"

"Finish your route and go home. I'll call from the hospital. Go on now!"

I shut the door and watched helplessly as they sped off with Ben out cold in the backseat and a huge sinking feeling inside of me. I looked down at the paper still in the woman's driveway where Ben had delivered it. I looked at a trail of blood turning black on the asphalt and a large spot that had soaked into the dirt near the tree. I felt something sticky on my hands. Then I looked at Ben's bike and my eyes welled with tears. This whole thing was my fault. The head-lamp generator had worked loose from all the bumps and slipped down into the spokes of the front wheel. It was tangled so tightly that I couldn't remove it.

I lifted the front of the bike and rolled it on its back wheel, dragging the chain that had popped off during the impact. I pulled it around to the side of the woman's house, crying all the way, and then went back to the front yard and sat down with my head in my hands. "God, please help him to be all right. Please." It was all I could say.

I looked up and tried to reconstruct what must have happened. Ben had delivered the paper, so he must have been riding back down off the sidewalk into the street. Sure enough, there was about a two-inch drop from the driveway to the road. That had probably been the final blow in a series of bumps that jarred the generator loose so that it slipped off the rim and into the spokes, jamming the front wheel and slamming Ben into the back of the Pontiac station wagon that was parked on the street.

In spite of everything I was feeling, when I saw it was a Pontiac, something actually tried to laugh inside me. Ben hated Pontiacs. He thought they were ugly and heavy. He even said that you should never run into one, because "you're the only one who's going to get hurt." *I don't think this was quite what he had in mind when he said that,* I thought.

I stood up and picked up my bike, its proud saddlebags sagging with the few remaining papers. Only two and a half blocks to go. Before I left, I glanced at my card and found Live Oak Street, number 332. Fitzpatrick, Mary K. *I hope she lets him breathe,* I thought, remembering my last view of Ben's unconscious face.

The darkness was starting to lift from the sky, but the heaviness would not lift from my heart. Ben would be all right, I told myself. Ben had to be all right.

"Please, God, help him to be all right," I said out loud as I got on my bike to finish what was left of my paper route.

17

Molly Fitzpatrick

That afternoon, when I finally got to go see Ben in the hospital, I was all ready with a line about meeting Pontiacs head-on. He beat me to the punch.

"This is what happens," he said, pointing to his face, "when you run into a Pontiac."

I managed a little laugh. "That was going to be my joke."

"Well, you'll have to leave the jokes to me, because I never laugh at my own jokes, and it hurts when I laugh."

I could see why. His face was a mess. His upper lip was the size of a golf ball, and his nose looked like the rear end of a Studebaker. There was a cut over his eye with several stitches, and he was black and blue from between his eyes to the bottom of his lip.

"You look great," I said. "So that old lady let you breathe after all?"

"You mean Mrs. Fitzpatrick?"

"Yes. Mary K. Fitzpatrick. She's one of my customers."

"Well, according to the doctor, I wouldn't be here if it wasn't for Mary K. Fitzpatrick. She did the right thing: stopped the bleeding. She knew everybody in here and took me right to a doctor. She was pushing people out of the way. She's nice, too. She stayed around most of the morning."

She had also gotten me in to see Ben. Kids didn't have visiting rights except for immediate family, but Mary K. Fitzpatrick, though she was retired, still carried a lot of weight around St. Mary's Hospital.

"Ben," I said, biting my upper lip, "this whole thing was my fault. I knew that generator didn't fit right."

"I suppose life is your fault, too. While you're at it, why don't you blame yourself for that?"

"But this never would have happened—"

"Listen, Jonathan, you better get over this kind of thinking if you plan on being my friend. There's a lot more to life than what happened and who caused it.

"By the way," he said after a few moments of silence in which I was trying to figure out his last statement. "What did happen?"

"You don't remember?"

"I remember delivering the paper and heading back out to the street. That's all."

"The generator slipped down and got hung in the spokes. It jammed the front wheel, and you went right over the top into the Pontiac. Too bad it was a station wagon. If it had been a regular car, I think you could have at least gotten your hands out in front of your face."

"And broken an arm or something? No thanks. I'm glad it was my nose I broke. I don't have to use that for anything except breathing, and I can do that with my mouth . . . ouch!"

"What?"

"I said 'mouth' too loud and hurt my lip."

"Does it hurt a lot?"

"Only when I talk."

"I'd better go then."

"No, tell me about my bike."

"Well, your front wheel is completely ruined, but I'll get you a new one as soon as I get paid for my first month."

"Don't worry about that. You'll just have to bike to my house for a while. By the way, what about 336 Live Oak? Did you deliver their paper? I never finished my side of the street."

"Oh no! I forgot all about them! I didn't start delivering again until the next block. Darn. I missed 336."

"You should go see them. Make sure they get their paper."

That was Ben. Lying in bed in the hospital with stitches and a broken nose, and he was still worried about whether or not someone got their Sunday paper.

Just then Ben's family entered the room along with my mother.

"Say, Ben," said Peter, "you look like you just ran into a truck."

"Almost," Ben said. "It was a Pontiac." Then he turned his head to look at his father. "Dad, can I go home now?"

"No, son. The doctor wants to keep you here overnight so you can get plenty of rest and they can make sure everything's all right."

"But, Dad, I can rest at home better than I can here. They keep waking me up all the time to give me pills or stick me with something. I don't like this place."

"I know, but it's just for tonight. Your mother will keep you company. Before you know it, you'll be right back up on that bike again."

Obviously Pastor Beamering hadn't seen Ben's bike yet.

"Can I stay with him too, Mother?" I said.

"No, Jonathan. There's no place for you to sleep. Besides, you have school tomorrow."

"I could sleep in a chair . . . I don't care. Mrs. Beamering's going to be here. Please, Mother—" I tried my most pleading look, "please?"

It must have worked on Mrs. Beamering, because I saw her give my mother a look that said it was all right with her. I knew if it was the other way around and I was the one in the hospital bed, Mrs. Beamering would have let Ben stay. She always seemed more willing to try something new, especially with us kids. Her tendency was to say "Yes" to our ideas and then think about them later, whereas my mother would usually say "No" and only occasionally reconsider. Today was no exception.

"No. Absolutely not," said my mother. "And I don't want to discuss it anymore." Which usually meant just that.

As soon as I got home I went right to my delivery bags and counted the leftover papers. Four. I'd been so worried that morning that I hadn't even thought about delivering the three extras as free papers. If I had, I'd have realized there was an extra one. I had finished the route as fast as possible and raced home, thinking I was going to be able to join Ben immediately at the hospital. Instead, when my father returned, which was not long after I did, he told us Ben was going to be okay and we were all going to church as usual. Mrs. Beamering was already with him at the hospital, and there was nothing for us to do but be in the way.

Be in the way? How could a best friend be in the way? It didn't make sense to me, but I had no choice.

That was a horrible Sunday morning—not only being in church without Ben, but knowing that he was lying in a hospital bed. Why did church go on just as if nothing had happened? How could Pastor Beamering get up there and smile his winning smile when his son was in the hospital. Every time I closed my eyes to pray, I could see the bicycle wheel jamming and Ben flying full speed like a battering ram into the back of that car. They should have canceled church. That's how I felt about it.

I decided to walk up to Live Oak Street, deliver the newspaper, and then stop and pick up the remains of Ben's bike. The Johnsons at 336 were not home, so I left the paper on their porch and walked to Mrs. Fitzpatrick's house. Ben's blood on the street now looked like splotches of dirty oil, but it still gave me a sick feeling to see it there where it didn't belong. His bike was right where I'd left it, leaning up against a trellis of roses at the side of the house. By the time I had wheeled it to the front, Mrs. Fitzpatrick was out on the porch waiting for me.

"I saw the bicycle and I knew you'd be comin' back. I'm just about to have my afternoon tea. Won't you come in?" She led me through her living room, past a statue of a woman in a blue robe holding a child, and into her kitchen where I could hear water boiling. Though her house was warm and inviting, it was confusing to me as well.

I had noticed the statue of the woman that morning when I used the phone. Something in the kind face reminded me of my mother. But there were candles around it, and that made me think it might be an idol. I'd heard about idols in Sunday school when we studied stories from the Old Testament, but I had never seen one.

Then, in the kitchen, above the breakfast table where she invited me to sit, was the strangest picture of Jesus I had ever seen. He was standing with his arms outstretched, and He had an enormous red heart in the middle of His chest; it was all wrapped with thorns that were making it bleed. Something about that heart gave me the creeps.

"That's the Sacred Heart of Jesus. Anyone who displays the Sacred Heart in their home, sudden death will never happen to them," Mrs. Fitzpatrick said as she poured hot water into a flowered teapot.

"Molly" was what she said I could call her. "Fitzpatrick is a mouthful," she added, lifting a small cake out of a flowered tin bread box on the counter.

"So did you ever get the Johnsons their paper?" she asked.

"Yeah, I just dropped it off. How did you know they didn't get their paper?"

"Oh, I know everything about this block, laddie. I walk to Mass every morning at a quarter to eight, and keep track of the neighborhood along the way. When the Johnsons asked me if I'd gotten my paper this morning, I told them what happened. Don't you worry now; they're very understanding. I doubt they'll even register a complaint."

Tony had warned me that if I failed to make a delivery, I would hear about it the next day by way of a pink slip with the word ERROR printed down the side. It would not be good for me to be getting a pink slip after only three days on the job. I hoped Mrs. Fitzpatrick was right about the Johnsons.

Suddenly I saw a pink slip with the word ERROR printed down the side and my name on it. Tony was handing me the slip as Ben lay in the street with an enlarged heart wrapped in thorns.

"Are you all right?" Molly asked.

"Yeah," I said, shaking my head. I normally didn't have nightmares in the middle of the day. "I'm just tired, I guess."

"I'm not surprised. You've been through a lot today. Here, have a piece of cake."

"Ben's accident was my fault," I blurted out.

"Oh? How's that?"

"I didn't tighten the generator light down on his bike as well as I should have."

"Well, things like that happen. That's something you'll be learnin' from in the future. But remember, laddie, there be bigger forces at work in life than just our mistakes."

"Yeah, that's kind of what Ben says too."

Molly Fitzpatrick was sort of ugly in a nice way. She had lots of brittle orange hair pulled back into a tight bun, and her face and arms looked rough and red, like she had a rash. She told me she was Irish. I figured that must be why she had an accent and why her sentences sounded more like questions than statements.

"Where do you live, Jonathan?"

"A couple blocks over on Sequoia."

"Might you be livin' in that yellow house with all the pretty flowers down the side of the driveway?"

"Yes. Those are my dad's prize chrysanthemums."

"I thought I'd seen you there before. And Benjamin . . . now where does he live?"

"He lives over in Pasadena."

"How is it you two know each other?"

"We go to the same church. His father is the pastor; my father is the choir director."

"Well, isn't that nice. And what church would that be?"

"Colorado Avenue Standard Christian Church—in Pasadena."

"Wait a minute now . . . Colorado Avenue Standard Christian Church," she repeated slowly. "Might that be the church that was shootin' off fireworks and settin' off alarms and the like during Sunday service?"

"Uh . . . yes, it was," I said in a mild state of shock. I had no idea we had become famous outside our own circle.

"The paper did a story on it in the religion section a few months ago."

I resisted the temptation to tell her that it was Ben and I who were responsible for this activity, not knowing what she felt about it.

"I didn't know we were in the paper," I said.

"Oh yes. I found it quite amusing myself. You see, laddie, I don't think God takes us half as seriously as we take ourselves sometimes. Whoever was behind all those flyin' doves and streamers and such . . . well, let's just say my hat's off to 'em. I've been trying to talk our own Father Michael into making some changes. Anything that will shake people up and make them think is fine by me."

"It was us," I said.

"What's that?"

"It was us doing that . . . Ben and me."

"You don't say! You boys? Just the two of you?"

I nodded my head vigorously.

"You pulled all those tricks on your parish?"

"Yep," I said, a bit taken aback. "But we're not going to perish for it, are we?"

"No, no, laddie," she said, laughing. "I meant your church. We call our church a parish. You and Benjamin should come to our church and wake us up sometime. Heaven knows, we could use a few good surprises."

"Oh, I don't think my parents would want me to come to your church."

"Why wouldn't they?"

"Be—because you're a Catholic . . . aren't you?"

"Yes. And we aren't supposed to be goin' to your churches either. But it wouldn't surprise me a bit if we didn't both know the same Jesus—born o' the Virgin Mary, died on the cross for our sins, rose again from the grave . . . sound familiar?"

"Yes, it does."

"Here, have another piece of cake. You made quick work of that first one."

The cake and the warm sugary tea were beginning to perk me up.

"Now, let's talk about Benjamin." Something in the way she said it made me sit up. "I spent the morning at the hospital with him, and I never believe in keepin' anyone in the dark. How much do you know?"

"I know he has a broken nose," I said, a bit confused, "and he's missing two teeth and has a big cut over his eye."

"Yes. His cut and bruises should heal in a few days. They'll have to put in a retainer to fix his teeth and maybe do a bit o' reconstructive work. But there's something else I think you should know about."

"What?" I asked.

"Benjamin has a heart murmur, which means they will have to watch him very closely to guard against any infection. That's why he's staying in the hospital tonight . . . just to be safe."

"What's a heart murmur?" I asked, thinking again of an enlarged heart with thorns wrapped around it.

"It's usually caused by a small hole in the inner wall of the heart. When the doctor listens to the heartbeat through his stethoscope, it makes a different sound."

"A hole in his heart? Did the accident cause it?" I asked with a terrible chill of guilt.

"Oh no, laddie. He was born with it. But fortunately, God makes hearts stronger than they have to be, so they can make up for things like this," she said. "Would you like some more tea—another piece of cake?"

"No, thanks. I better get home. My mother is going to start wondering where I am."

"Now listen, Jonathan, you stop by and see me again. Any time. Bring Benjamin when he's better."

"I will," I said. Then, "Can I ask you one more question?"

"Certainly . . . as many questions as you like, laddie." She raised a penciled eyebrow, and the wrinkles on her face waited in a question mark.

"Do you think Ben knows . . . I mean, about the hole?"

"Oh yes. I talked to him about it. He's known for quite a while now."

"Oh," I said.

I thanked Molly Fitzpatrick for the tea and the cake and for saving Ben's life. Then I went out and picked up his mutilated bike and pulled it home to the slow ticking of the back wheel.

All I could think of was Ben in the hospital with a banged-up face and a hole in his heart.

18

"As We Know It. . ."

Everything about Mayor Seth Wilson's office was official, from the seal of the city of Pasadena on the wall and the backs of the black wooden chairs, to the 70th Annual Tournament of Roses commemorative plaque that graced the polished woodwork where it hung, to the fresh long-stemmed red rose on the mayor's desk—a year-round tradition he himself had established, given the profound importance that particular species of horticulture continually bestowed upon the life-flow of the city. All of this officialdom was about to be brought to the immediate aid of our save-the-Edsel campaign, for the mayor had indeed gotten our letter, and now he wanted to see us.

It had happened so fast—too fast for Ben's face—but we couldn't afford to wait. Actually it was the mayor who couldn't afford to wait.

Seth Wilson was still getting heat from Frank Milner for driving a year-old car in the Rose Parade, and he didn't like it. In fact, our letter had landed on the desk of the mayor's public relations man the same day Milner was quoted in the *Star-News* as saying: "Perhaps it's appropriate that Mr. Wilson would be driving a year-old car in the Rose Parade since that is about how long it takes his office to respond to a phone call."

So when his eyes lighted on our letter, the PR guy must have seen a golden opportunity to strike back. Perfect! Two young boys echoing the mayor's sentiments. Endear them to the public, and make the mayor a hero. A scriptwriter couldn't have come up with a better story.

Even though Ben had put his return address on the letter, the call had come to our house. With Ben still in the hospital and his mother spending most of her time there with him, the mayor's office couldn't get an answer at the Beamering residence. Luckily, Ben had written the letter on church stationery—thinking it would make the letter more official—so they had tracked me instead, probably figuring that Benjamin Beamering and Jonathan Liebermann must be the sons of the Jeffery T. Beamering and Walter K. Liebermann imprinted on the letterhead of the Colorado Avenue Standard Christian Church.

My mother received the call on the Monday afternoon after the accident. I was out on the front lawn folding my papers at the time—four folds, only twenty-four pages.

"Jonathan," she called through the screen door, "there's someone on the phone for you. He says he's from the office of the mayor of Pasadena?"

"Really? Oh, wow!"

"Wait a minute. Not so fast. You're not touching that phone until you wash that black stuff off your hands—and until you tell me what's going on."

"It's about the Edsel the mayor drove in the parade," I told her excitedly as I ran to the kitchen to wash my hands. "Ben and I wrote him a letter about it."

"Well . . . here then, see what he wants."

"Hello?"

"Hello," said the voice on the telephone. "Is this Jonathan Liebermann?"

"Yes, it is."

"Jonathan, this is Bob Appleby from the mayor's office in Pasadena, and we received the letter you and . . . let's see here . . . Benjamin Beamering . . . the letter you two sent to the mayor dated last Friday."

"Yes?"

"Jonathan, the mayor would like to arrange for you and Benjamin to come to his office at your earliest convenience—hopefully tomorrow after school. We realize you may need to discuss this with your parents, but Mayor Wilson wanted you to know he is very interested in your proposal and would like to speak to you personally. If transportation is a problem, we would be happy to provide that for you."

My heart had started racing—so much so that I couldn't even speak.

"Jonathan?"

"Yes . . . I'm here . . . I think you'd better talk to my mom."

And then my mother had gotten on the phone and listened to Mr. Appleby explain what was going on while I ran to my parents' bedroom to listen in on the extension. I picked up the other phone just in time to hear her say: "The problem is, Mr. Appleby, Ben is presently in the hospital recuperating from an accident he had yesterday."

"Oh, I'm sorry to hear that. What happened?"

"He took a nasty spill off his bike while he was helping my son with his paper route."

"Your son has a paper route? What paper does he deliver?"

"The *Star-News.*"

"This is getting better all the time."

"I beg your pardon," my mother said.

"Excuse me, Mrs. Liebermann, I'm just thinking out loud. Jonathan being a newsboy for the *Star-News* will be a great asset to our story."

"You're going to do a story on the boys?"

"Well, yes, Mrs. Liebermann. It seems that your son and his friend and the mayor all see eye to eye on the 1958 Edsel that has been giving Mayor Wilson such trouble lately. I'll be frank with you. The boys' letter gives us an opportunity to do a light-hearted story on the subject that we feel will greatly enhance the mayor's image and hopefully take the heat off this issue. We assure you, it will all be handled in good taste. We would want you present, of course, for the interview."

"Well . . . I don't see any problem other than Ben's health. He is supposed to be coming home from the hospital tonight. As to whether he can see you tomorrow, however . . . well, I can't answer that. You'll have to speak with his parents."

"That's fine. I'll contact the Beamerings. How is Ben, by the way? Any broken bones?"

"He broke his nose and lost two teeth," I said, jumping into the conversation on the extension.

"Wow, he must have hit the ground pretty hard."

"No. He hit a Pontiac."

"Oh, dear. How's the car? Ha, ha, just kidding. Well, you

take care of your buddy Ben—okay, Jonathan?—and hopefully we'll see you tomorrow."

"Okay."

"I'll get back with you, Mrs. Liebermann, as soon as I find out something definite from the Beamerings. If you need to reach me, I'll be in my office until about 5:30 today. I hope to have all the arrangements made by then." Then he gave her the number and said goodbye.

"Yahoo!" I shouted as I hung up the phone in the bedroom.

"Now don't get your hopes up," my mother said when I met her in the kitchen. "We have no idea how Ben is."

"Believe me, Mother, when he hears about this, he'll be just fine."

"Well, we'll see," she said. "Now run along and finish your paper route."

"Can't I call Ben now?"

"No, finish your paper route first. I'm sure we'll hear from Ben soon enough," she said. "How did this all come about, anyway? You said you and Ben wrote a letter to the mayor?"

"Yeah. Want to see it?"

I ran and got the copy, then watched as a smile formed on her face while she read it.

"You two are really something, you know that?" she said, shaking her head in amazement. "You do realize, however, that the mayor has other reasons for this than bringing back the Edsel car, don't you? He's a politician, and they're all the same."

"But we're still getting what we want. That's okay, isn't it?"

"Well, I'm not sure it's always okay, but it's definitely politics. Come on now. You've got to get back to your papers. It's almost four o'clock. We'll work this out when you get back."

As I headed outside to resume my folding job, the phone rang again. Figuring it was probably Ben or Mrs. Beamering, I stopped in the front hallway to listen.

"Hi, Martha. I expected it would be you. How's Ben?"

"Oh, that's good news."

"Yes."

"Yes, he called here too. This is really something, isn't it? What are we going to do with these two kids, anyway? Now they're into municipal politics."

"No, no, no. It's all your fault. Jonathan was a nice normal kid before Ben came along!" She laughed. "Well, what do you think?"

"Frankly, I'm a little worried about it. I'm afraid they're only going to get their hopes up over nothing."

"You think so? Well, it sure has made history with Jonathan. But aren't you concerned about them being used?"

"Believe it or not, that's just what Jonathan said. What are you teaching my son, Martha? Pretty soon these two are going to run for office, I tell you."

"Right, right . . . and carry all forty-eight states, too!"

"You really think he'll be okay? What about his face?"

"Oh no." She started laughing loudly at this point. "Oh, Martha, did he say that? Gracious, where did you get this boy?"

And whatever Ben's mom said to that made my mother almost come apart at the seams.

"No, you're right. I don't think we have to worry about God spewing either one of these two out of His mouth. Not the way they're going."

"Okay."

"No, don't you worry about it. I can take them. I want to go anyway. I want to be sure they aren't misrepresented in any of this."

"Great. I'll be there. Glad to hear Ben's doing better. Give him our love."

"Okay."

Before she hung up, I slipped out the front door and attacked the remainder of unfolded newspapers with glee. It was going to happen. It was truly going to happen. We were going to meet the mayor.

———

When we were ushered into Mayor Wilson's office the next day, it was immediately obvious that there was more at stake here than the future of the Edsel. There was Mr. Appleby, a camera crew, people from the newspaper, and a couple of city councilmen. The mayor himself wasn't present when we first arrived, so we talked informally with Mr. Appleby while the photographers shot some pictures.

Ben was a sight. He had put a bandage on the cut over his eye even though he didn't need one. He said he wanted to make sure people knew that his face was the result of an injury and not a permanent condition. I have to say, though, that Ben's swollen nose actually improved the proportional makeup of his face. It seemed to push his ears back more where they belonged.

When the mayor finally showed up, there was a round of formal introductions and a flurry of photographs. Then, to our relief, Mayor Wilson shooed everyone out of his office except Ben and me and my mother and Mr. Appleby. Seth Wilson was a take-charge sort of person, and he wasted no time getting down to business.

"I apologize for all this hullabaloo," he said. "You know, a lot of people think I'm only doing this for political reasons, but I have to tell you I share a genuine interest in the Edsel car. What many people don't realize, especially Mr. Milner, is that I am a stockholder in the Ford Motor Company. Have been for years."

The mayor was a powerful orator, and he soon had us all enthralled and swiveling in our chairs as he paced the floor and delivered a lecture of carefully measured words. Indeed, most of those words appeared the following evening in the paper, proving that our meeting had been set up as a platform for his agenda. But not the political one my mother had expected. And not the "lighthearted" image-builder Mr. Appleby had anticipated. It wasn't even a personal squabble with Mr. Milner—who, in fact, wasn't mentioned once in the article. No, Mayor Wilson's agenda was, after all, believe it or not, the Edsel. Well, actually it was the Edsel's "window on American business . . . as we know it." The 1958 Edsel was Mayor Wilson's soapbox.

"I sweated over this car, boys—sweated over the first complete line of cars under a new name in a decade, and I believe the 1958 Edsel is the last hope for American business as we know it. The Edsel is a 250-million-dollar experiment that, if it fails, may very well usher out the heyday of American economic superiority in the world as we know it. Already we are watching the growing success of the Volkswagen, built by the Germans and commissioned by Adolf Hitler himself, and mark my words: I predict we are going to see the rise of Japanese production, the likes of which history has never known, in the next two decades.

"You see, boys . . . Mrs. Liebermann . . . there is much more at stake here than just a uniquely designed car. There is the future of American business as we know it." (We all came very close to mouthing "as we know it" with him.)

"Yes, I drove this car in the parade because I want the American public to buy this car . . . to love this car . . . to recognize this car for what it is: the most truly American, truly unique design to come down the pike in twenty years. If this car goes down, business in America as we know it goes down with it."

I'm not sure whether Ben found a spokesman in Mayor Wilson, or whether Mayor Wilson found a spokesman in Ben, but the truth of the matter was, they found each other that day—like two people who had been mysteriously singing the same song for some time. And something powerful happened in that room that left me out, but not in a sad way. Something was provided for Ben that I could never provide—something that sanctioned his character . . . that made Ben official.

"Ben and Jonathan, I like what you said about the 1959 Edsel being . . . how did they say it, Bob?"

"Uh . . . let's see . . . 'a poor excuse for a 1959 model,' " he quoted from our letter.

"That's it. That's exactly right. As a stockholder I told them this over and over again. You've got to keep this car unique. People are going to catch on, but it's bound to take time. There's never been anything more American than this car. Whatever happens to the future of the Edsel, the 1958 model—the first model—will always be a classic. You boys recognize that.

"I mentioned that to Edith when you brought us a rose in the parade and told me how much you liked my car. 'Now there goes a fine young lad,' I said, 'with a fine taste in automobiles,' " he said, smiling at Ben and sitting on the edge of his solid mahogany desk that was swept clean of everything but a blotter and a set of pens. Leaning over to Ben, he clasped his hands and said, "And here you are in my office. I'm honored. And I want you both to know I have already forwarded your letter to Richard E. Krafve, vice-president and general manager of Ford's Edsel Division. But more than that, because of your willingness to be here today, I intend to use this story for a major media push, not only in our local paper here, but in papers around the country who we have already contacted.

"Yes, I drove a 1958 Edsel in the 1959 Tournament of Roses Parade," he continued, pacing again behind his desk, "and thanks to you two, a whole lot of folks in this country are going to know about it. Tell me, gentlemen . . . ma'am . . . do I have your permission to publish in the newspaper the letter you wrote to the Ford Motor Company, as well as the one you sent to me?"

"Yes," said Ben without wavering. "Permission granted."

"Thank you very much. Now, what are we going to do about that face?"

"Not much we can do I guess."

"I understand this happened while you were delivering the newspaper. You're a newspaper boy?"

"No. That's Jonathan," Ben said, pointing to me. "He's the paper boy. I was only helping."

"Well, I certainly hope you will be like new before long. So, Jonathan, you deliver the *Star-News*?"

"Yes, sir."

"Splendid. That will help get us excellent billing in tomorrow's paper. Well, boys, it looks like we're in business. Welcome aboard!" And he leaned over his desk and extended a big hand and a big smile to each of us. "And thank you too, Mrs. Liebermann, for coming. I assure you these boys will be well represented, wherever we publish this. I will personally see to that."

"I have every confidence you will," said my mother, caught somewhere between pride and disbelief.

Like most Californians in the 1950s, Seth was from somewhere else, and he still reflected remnants of his Texas heritage. Everything he did—his talk, his walk, his gestures—was big and slow. He had a presence that filled the whole room. When Seth Wilson walked in, the room was instantly crowded. The wide-brimmed white hat that was a part of the traditional Rose Parade garb for all mayors of Pasadena on January 1 hung on a hat rack next to his door. It had become a daily signature in Seth's wardrobe.

"Now, I've been doing all the talking," he said, finally sitting down in his leather armchair and pulling it up to the desk. "I told you why I'm interested in the 1958 Edsel. Now you tell me what your interest is."

I looked at Ben, knowing he was altogether prepared for this moment. Following the precedent set by Mayor Wilson, Ben stood up and prepared to speak. His presence swelled, like his nose, and the room got suddenly crowded again.

The first thing he did was reach into the small paper sack he had been clutching in his lap and pull out his model car. He set it carefully on the mayor's large, clean desk.

"This is my own 1958 Edsel, Mr. Mayor. It was given to me by my best friend, Jonathan Liebermann, for my tenth birthday," said Ben. "He worked hard for it and endured some embarrassing situations in order to get it for me. I love this car, and I brought it with me today because I want you to have it." I had tried to conceal my pride as Ben spoke. Now I tried to conceal my surprise. "I want you to have this car because I want you to remember that your struggle to save the Edsel is mine too. You know more about why your struggle is important than I do, but that shouldn't make mine any less important."

Ben was pacing the room now, and we were all—including Seth Wilson—watching him as intently as we had watched the mayor. His words were coming out just as measured as the mayor's.

"As far as the real Edsel is concerned," Ben said, "I must say I love it and hate it at the same time. Love it because not everyone likes it. It's a car that stands out in a crowd—a car that only certain people can love. I want everyone to like the Edsel, but I'd somehow be disappointed if they all did. Do you know what I mean?"

The mayor nodded vigorously, as if Ben's comments had taken him to a place he understood completely. There was a look of concerned wonder on his face, and his eyes gripped Ben.

"We love this car," said Ben, "but we also hate this car. We hate it, Mayor Wilson, because of what we fear. You fear the fall of American business, and I don't know anything about that. I fear it because the Edsel's failure somehow represents the end of something for me, something I don't know yet, something that will alter life . . . as *I* know it."

The connection between the mayor and Ben had cast a spell

over us that not even Ben's pun could break. The lack of response, in fact, made the silence even more pregnant. Everyone sat frozen until the mayor spoke, his eyes never leaving Ben nor losing their intensity.

"We will fight this anyway, won't we, Ben? Even if it looks like it's a lost cause."

"Yessir," said Ben, still locked in his gaze. "And if we lose?"

And then the mayor said a most amazing thing.

"I have a feeling I may . . . but you won't."

19

Turning the Other Nose

"Well!" The mayor clapped his hands together and stood up. "Gentlemen . . . ma'am . . . we have work to do," and he walked around to the front of his desk and picked up Ben's car. He examined it closely, turning it in his hands.

"You've got some mileage on this baby, don't you? Looks like at least fifty or sixty thousand to me," he said with a twinkle, and then his expression turned earnest. "I am deeply honored that you would trust me with something so important, Ben. Will you do the same for me?"

He went to a display case along the wall of his office and produced a car of his own—a model of a 1958 Edsel convertible similar to Ben's in size, but made almost entirely of metal. It had greater detail than any of our cars, and this particular one had written on the sides in royal red letters: "Tournament of Roses Official Car."

"Here. I want you to have this. It's been in my display case now for over a year so it has hardly any miles on it. It's ready to run. Consider yours a trade-in on this."

Ben reached out and took the car, and his face somehow managed to radiate pleasure even through its painful appearance.

Suddenly we were on my bedroom floor and I was watching again as Ben laid eyes on his birthday present for the first time. He eyed it from every angle and then set it on the mayor's desk where he could see it at road level and roll it back and forth. The mayor studied Ben's reaction with obvious pleasure.

"Wow! I've never seen one like this before!"

"It's a limited edition model. Here, look at this," and the mayor swung both doors wide open and lifted the hood.

"Wow, look, Jonathan! The doors open! I've always wished our cars would do that. And an engine, too!"

With the exchange complete, Mayor Wilson made it clear that it was time to wrap up our little meeting. He ushered us briskly toward the door, shaking our hands and thanking us one more time as we filed by.

"Be sure and check the paper tomorrow—well, I guess you will, Jonathan, since you'll be delivering it. Your story will be there. And thank you again, Mrs. Liebermann, for bringing the boys. I want you both to know that you are welcome any time in my office—oh, and I almost forgot. Bob . . . the keys."

And Mr. Appleby produced from his briefcase two official keys to the city of Pasadena, which the mayor handed to us with appropriate pomp.

"These give you carte blanche to our museums and special services—and they ensure you a reservation in the VIP grand-stands for next year's Rose Parade. If the Edsels are still coming off the line by then, you can bet I'll be in my '58 one more time, even if it costs me my election."

"Thank you anyway," said Ben, almost brashly, as we received our keys to the city, "but we'd rather stay out all night and hold a place for ourselves on the blue line. That's the only way to really see the parade."

"I understand completely," said the mayor, unaffected by the tone of Ben's remark. "I'd do the same thing if I wasn't riding in it."

The mayor's office was on the third floor of a building with no elevator, so Mr. Appleby escorted us downstairs through a concrete stairwell, our footsteps echoing off the hard walls. Before we left, he took us to his first-floor office where he had my mother fill out forms for each of us about our background, where we were born, how many brothers and sisters we had, what our dads did for a living—any information that would be needed for a story about us. He seemed nervous, and on the way home, as we tried to reconstruct our experience in the mayor's office line by line, we all figured it was because the mayor had also surprised him at the meeting. Appleby only wanted to take the heat off the mayor and get back at Mr. Milner in the papers. He could probably care less about the Edsel and the future of American business stuff; in fact, my mother said, he might even think it could hurt Wilson's reelection chances. The mayor, however, saw a bigger picture, and we all agreed—including my mother—that we were very taken by him.

"That was one of the highlights of my life so far," said Ben.

" 'As we know it!' " I added. I couldn't resist.

The following day the front page of the *Star-News* carried a picture of Ben and me and Mayor Wilson. In the picture I was shaking hands with the mayor while Ben clutched the paper sack that held his Edsel model. Though Ben's swollen face and bandage somewhat hid the fact, you could still see the unmistakable squint that I had seen in that first picture in the church bulletin. Ben still didn't trust cameras.

The article, however, made me extremely uncomfortable. I didn't even know how to approach Ben after reading it. The headline said it all: "Mayor Champions Star-News Carrier in Fight for Edsel."

The whole thing was written from *my* perspective, as if I were the main character, and the name of the newspaper appeared in just about every other sentence. It didn't, of course, mention the fact that I had only been delivering the paper for four days on a trial basis. You would have thought I was some kind of newsboy hero. It didn't say much about Ben at all, except that it made a big deal about his broken nose. Apparently the writer of the article thought that Ben slamming into the back of a Pontiac was a clever twist after all the talk about the Edsel, so he'd used it as a concluding anecdote. Of course the last part of a story is the first thing everybody remembers.

Luckily Ben saved me from having to bring up the subject. He called me right after school.

"I know all about it," he said.

"What?"

"The article. I know it's all about you and that the only thing I seem to know how to do is run into a Pontiac with my face."

"How did you know? I haven't even gotten my papers folded yet. Your delivery boy must be awfully fast!"

"No, I haven't seen the article yet. The mayor called me this morning to explain. He said he had to go with the story the way they wrote it in order to get the article on the front page. He thought I'd understand, but he wanted to call me anyway and prepare me for it. That was very nice of him, don't you think?"

"Do you understand?"

"Of course. It's all politics. The newspaper gets to promote themselves for free on the front page. The important thing is the Edsel got the exposure. That's all we wanted anyway. This wasn't for us; it was for the Edsel, remember?"

"Yeah, I guess you're right." I felt better that Ben was taking this so well, but I still thought what they'd done was unfair.

After the next day at school, I felt even worse. Far from being a hero for appearing on the front page of the paper, I was much closer to being the laughingstock of the school. All day long I got comments like:

"Hey, there's Johnny Edsel!"

"Hey, Johnny, don't you know a lemon when you see one?"

"You mean you like those funny lookin' cars?"

"Go suck a lemon; then your mouth will look like the front of an Edsel!"

"I know this guy who has an Edsel. His dad won it at a raffle. Now they can't give it away. They can't even sell it for enough money to buy a real car."

But the one that really got me was: "Too bad your friend didn't run into an Edsel. It might have improved his looks!"

Now I had never been in a fight before in my life, but that wisecrack cocked my arm right back without even thinking. Unfortunately I never did get to extend it because my inexperience got me punched first. Right in the nose. As I ran to the nurse's office with blood on my shirt, I was hoping my nose was broken—just like Ben's. Alas, it was only a nosebleed.

I made the most of it, though. I let the blood dry on my nose, and I had the nurse call my mother to come take me home from school. I enjoyed the fuss my mother made over me. While she was fixing my favorite lunch of hard-boiled eggs in a white sauce over toast with the yolk sprinkled on top, I called Ben to tell him about my nose, but he was already back in school. That's when I started feeling bad about making such a big deal about it. By the time my face turned black and blue (actually, it looked much worse than it felt) and I realized I really could get some mileage out of this, I felt like a real phony. It never even hurt very much.

Since I was home from school for the rest of the day anyway, I decided to put my remorse to work on an idea that had been brewing in my mind ever since we left the mayor's office. I thought the mayor needed more of an explanation about why we were trying to save the Edsel than Ben had given him. It took me almost as long to find the right words as it did to find the letters for those words on the typewriter at my father's desk, but I managed to finish it before my paper route so I could drop it in a mailbox on the way.

Dear Mayor Wilson:

There's something you should know about my friend Ben Beamering and the Edsel car. Ben has gotten the idea that his life is somehow connected to what happens to the Edsel. The problem is that so far a lot of Ben's ideas have been right, and now I just found out from Mrs. Fitzpatrick that Ben has a hole in his heart. That's why you have to do everything you possibly can to get people to buy Edsels just in case Ben is right again. This is one time I hope he is wrong.

Yours truly,
Jonathan Liebermann

P.S. Don't let anybody know about this letter. Especially Ben. No one else would understand and Ben and I never talk about this.

As soon as I mailed this letter to the mayor, I began wondering if I'd done the right thing. Had I said too much? Would I be hearing from him? Would he do anything about it? My first indication that he might came on the following Sunday.

———

I didn't see Ben again until that Sunday, but my nose still looked pretty bad. Ben's face was healing—he even had two new front teeth set in a retainer—so we met somewhere in the middle as the blue-nose twins. Ben thought the whole thing was pretty funny.

"Why didn't you at least hit the guy?" he said.

"I never got a chance."

"Some defender of my honor you are!"

"Well, at least I tried."

Ben hadn't had half the problems I had over the newspaper article when he went back to school—or even over his accident—because he was already considered a weirdo. His identification with the Edsel was right in line with his firmly established station as an outcast from fifth-grade society. None of this fazed Ben in the least. Peer pressure was never even on his agenda.

Ben and I were up in the bell tower after church. We had been going up there again for a number of weeks, not to pull any pranks, but to hide and seek in our own world. The tower had become both our lookout on the world and our city of refuge, where our private worlds came together and came true. It was a place of definitions and dreams and measurements of a much bigger world, and it was now protected by none other than Grizzly, who kept an eye on the door whenever we were up there.

Ironically, we had just been talking about the mayor and wondering when we might hear from him again (I was wondering the most) when Ben exclaimed, "Oh, my gosh! He's here!"

"Who's here?"

"The mayor! He must have come to church this morning. Look!"

Ben had been peering through the slats in the vent that afforded us a clear view outside to the front steps of the church. He moved away so I could see, and, sure enough, there was the mayor's white hat throwing off the bright morning sunshine.

"Well, I'll be—"

"And he's wearing the white suit and hat—"

"—and the red tie of the organization," we both said at the same time.

"And look at Mrs. Wilson," said Ben, looking over my

shoulder. "She's still wearing white too. Maybe it's their uniform. Why do you suppose he's here?"

"I don't know," I said, wondering if it had something to do with my letter.

"Look," said Ben. "He's talking to your dad." And then we both noticed my father looking around the crowd out in front of the church, obviously searching for someone.

"I bet he's looking for us. Let's go!"

We clamored down the ladder and out into the narthex, where we immediately slowed our pace to casual nonchalance.

"Oh, there they are," we heard my father say. "Jonathan! Ben! There's someone here to see you."

"Well, you're looking a lot better," the mayor said, bending down and greeting Ben with a handshake, "but what happened to you?" he said to me. "Aren't you getting a little carried away with this friendship? You don't have to share broken noses, you know."

"It's not broken. I got into a fight."

"He was defending my honor," said Ben.

"And the honor of the Edsel," I added.

"Did this have anything to do with the story in the paper?" asked the mayor.

"Some smart aleck in my class said that if Ben had run into an Edsel, it might have improved his looks."

"Well, now," said the mayor, "that's worth getting punched in the nose over. I wouldn't have let that guy get away with that either. If you look like this, I can't imagine what he looks like."

I didn't say anything. Ben didn't say anything. So we all imagined that I had plastered the other guy. It was nice, if only for a moment, to think I had landed that punch. And while standing there proudly next to Ben and the mayor, I began to believe I had.

My father, however, probably worried about the spiritual implications of fighting and not too happy with the mayor's encouragement of such a thing, decided right then and there to defend the Word of God over anyone's honor, including my nose. "What about 'turning the other cheek'?" he said.

There was a brief moment of silence while we all felt the awkwardness of the question.

"It wasn't his cheek, Mr. Liebermann," said the mayor. "It was his nose. Does the Good Book ever say anything about turning the other nose?"

Ben laughed, but I tried to keep a straight face, knowing it was my father's comment that was on the line. And I breathed a silent sigh of relief when my father finally laughed too.

Actually, though, that's the way most adults in our church operated. They didn't argue about the Bible. It seemed to be enough just to quote the Scriptures—as if the actual words carried some magical power that would stop people in their tracks. They memorized the Scriptures and learned how to say them at the right time, and if they got the right one at the right time, it was always the last word. Anyone who questioned the meaning of the Scriptures, or who joked about them as the mayor had done, was considered a potential enemy of the faith. Learn the Word, believe the Word, say the Word; that was it.

This was why our summer antics behind the organ pipes had been so good for the Colorado Avenue Standard Christian Church: They forced people to think about the words and what they meant. But those Sunday morning moments of life and joy were long gone now, and most of the congregation were already tightening their grip on the old ideas of spirituality.

The mayor quickly bridged the tension by introducing his wife to us. She was a pleasant-faced, white-haired lady who smiled from under her aqua-blue hat. We each shook her white-gloved hand.

"Seth has told me so much about you two. I never have understood his fascination with the Edsel, but I guess you boys do. It's not an easy thing to get my husband's attention as you have."

"Mr. Liebermann," said the mayor, diplomatically using the voice he had used with us in his office, "Edith and I are looking to join a church, and we'd like to investigate yours further. How would we go about that?"

"Well," said my father nervously, "let me introduce you to our pastor, Pastor Beamering—uh . . . Ben's father."

"Would you please excuse us," the mayor said to Ben and me, making us feel very important, while my father was already on his way to where Jeffery T. was shaking hands with members of our congregation.

A small group, who recognized the mayor, had positioned themselves around us. They were too sophisticated to gawk, but they had arranged themselves and their conversations in our vicinity so they could overhear what he was saying and steal a few glances. We knew this because as soon as my father spoke about introducing the mayor to Ben's father, a path formed between us and the pastor. And when he said in a loud voice, "Jeffery, I'd like you to meet the Honorable and Mrs. Mayor Seth Wilson," there was a temporary suspension of all conversation and all eyes turned in their direction.

"How do you do," said the mayor, beating Pastor Beamering to the punch and ignoring the surrounding attention. "You must be Ben's father."

"Why yes, what a privilege—uh—to meet you."

"The privilege is mine," said the mayor. "That's some son you have there."

"Why thank you, sir. Yes, he's a fine boy."

"Fine taste in cars, too."

"What was that? . . . Oh, yes . . . the Edsel."

"You know, Reverend, in all my days I've never seen such a bright young man, and when I heard he was the son of a preacher, well . . . I decided I had to come hear his father preach, and I must say, you sure know how to deliver a sermon."

"Why thank you, Mr. Mayor." Pastor Beamering's usual confidence was returning. ("Don't you ever spring an introduction like that on me again without proper warning," I heard him say later to my father.)

"Please call me Seth," the mayor said, "and this is my wife, Edith." They all shook hands and said how pleased they were to meet each other. The little crowd on the steps was still quiet, hovering in suspended animation.

"By all means, call me Jeff," said Pastor Beamering, picking up on the mayor's cue. "We can dispense with titles, can't we? After all, this is the kingdom of God."

"Well, I wouldn't know about that, but it's a mighty fine church, and Mrs. Wilson and I here are interested in joining." A murmur of surprise swept over the little audience, and once again Pastor Beamering was at a momentary loss for words.

"What a coincidence!" he said after a brief pause. "We just

happen to be starting a new members' class this week. I could contact you tomorrow with all the information."

"Splendid," said the mayor. "By the way, Pastor, what kind of car do you drive?"

"A Ford," he said. "Why?"

"Have you ever thought about driving an Edsel?"

"Not really. They're a little outside my price range."

"You should look again. There are a wide range of models, and the least expensive are only a few hundred dollars more than a new Ford. You should look into it."

"Well, I'm not really in the market for a new—"

"You should look into it," the mayor said, squeezing Pastor Beamering's hand extra hard as they said goodbye.

"Uh . . . maybe I could . . . yes," Pastor Beamering was, uncharacteristically, stumbling again.

"Good. You owe it to yourself. Trust me."

That conversation, and the wink he gave me when he shook hands with Ben and me again, convinced me that Mayor Seth Wilson had indeed gotten my letter.

"What membership class?" my father said to Jeffery T. while we watched from the steps as the mayor and his wife got into their Edsel and drove off.

"The one I planned on the spot," Ben's father answered as the gull-winged taillights floated out of sight. "The Hicksons and Masons are ready for one anyway. I just stepped up the schedule by a few weeks. The mayor joining our church is worth calling a membership class any day."

20

Sycamore 5–2905

"You might want to call and cheer up your friend," my mother told me as I slapped my schoolbooks down on the dining room table Monday afternoon. "Ben's been home all day with the flu."

"The flu? Boy, is he getting all the hard luck." I went straight to the refrigerator to get myself a tall glass of cold milk while my mother gave me a disapproving look and her clockwork response.

"Luck is for gambling," she said. In our family "luck" was a totally secular term that denied the existence of God. Luck had no regard for God's will. Then she quickly smiled and added, "Hey, where's my kiss?"

"Oh, sorry, I forgot." She was sitting at the breakfast table, and I went over and kissed her, holding a bottle of milk in one hand and a glass in the other.

"Yes, it's definitely a testing time for Ben," she said.

"For me too," I said.

I poured my milk and then proceeded to consume a handful of chocolate chip cookies from the fresh batch cooling on the kitchen counter. I especially liked this time right after school because I got my mother all to myself. Becky usually came home at least half an hour behind me.

"Jonathan, you're still blaming yourself for Ben's accident, aren't you?"

"I can't help it, Mother. I knew the generator wasn't on tight enough."

"How many times have we been over this? You've got to let it go. It was an accident. You can't keep carrying this around. What does the verse say again? One more time: Romans 8:28—"

"Mother, I know the verse, but it doesn't help."

" 'And we know that—' . . . come on, say it with me." And we said it together—my mother's voice ringing with positiveness and hope, mine dragging behind with resignation and weariness: " '—all things work together for good to them that love God, to them who are called according to his purpose. Romans 8:28.' "

"But—"

"No 'buts,' Jonathan. Remember what we said? It's either true or it's not. There are no exceptions. It doesn't say: 'God will work everything together for good to those who love him, except when Jonathan Liebermann neglects to tighten down the generator on Ben Beamering's bike in 1959.' "

"Yeah, I understand that, but—"

"Jonathan, do you love God?"

I nodded.

"Well, then, the promise applies to you. It's settled. Now let it go."

I brushed the cookie crumbs from my hands into the kitchen sink and rinsed my empty glass under the faucet. Then jumping up to sit in my favorite place on the counter next to the sink, I looked out the little bay window and saw my sister starting home from the school playground with a group of her girlfriends.

"Mother, what if something really bad had happened?" I said, looking out at the sky, overcast with a lid of clouds that never rained. "Let's just say something happened to Ben and it was my fault and he never got better? How would God work something good out of that?"

"Are you asking me, what if Ben were to die?" my mother said as she came over and stood next to me.

"Well . . . just suppose."

"Jonathan, that's something you don't even need to think about. Ben is going to be just fine."

"I know, but just suppose."

"One thing you're forgetting, Jonathan, is that it's God's good He's talking about here. You might be confusing His good with what you think is good for you."

"You mean it might be God's good for someone to die?"

"Of course it can be God's good for someone to die. Where do we go when we die?"

"We go to heaven."

"Wouldn't that be good for God? Isn't that where He wants us all to be, anyway—in heaven with Him?"

I was getting her point, but I didn't like it.

"What you're thinking is that God's good might not be what you want," she said. "That's it, isn't it?"

"Well, it hardly seems fair that God would get Ben and I wouldn't."

"Whoa now, just a minute! What are you talking about? Who said anything about God taking Ben away from you? You're getting way ahead of yourself, now." And then she stepped up close and took my face in her soft hands and said, "Hey, listen to me. Ben got banged up a little. He's getting better every day. Our bodies are made to heal up after accidents like this. Ben's going to be just fine." And she gave me a big hug.

"Now, why don't you go give him a call, and then you'd better hit the papers." And she smiled that wide-open smile that blew into my heart like the big clean sky over a Minnesota corn-field, and all the dark clouds that had accumulated in my mind sailed off into the blue.

"Okay, Mom." I hugged her back, then jumped down off the counter and dialed Ben's number. I had it memorized. Sycamore 5–2905.

"Hello, this is the Beamerings'."

"Hi, Mrs. Beamering. Can I talk to Ben?"

"He's sleeping right now, Jonathan."

"Okay. How's he doing."

"He's better. He was running a temperature this morning, so I kept him home from school. Must be a touch of the flu that's going around."

"Maybe I'll call him when I get back from my paper route."

"That'll be fine, Jonathan. I'll tell him you called when he wakes up."

"Thanks, Mrs. Beamering. Goodbye."

At that moment Becky came in, slamming the front door behind her. "Hi," she said rather coldly as she passed me on her way to the kitchen and the refrigerator. I followed her. If I'd been smart, I would have kept on walking—right out the back door. An older sister in a snit was nothing to mess around with.

"You don't know how awful it is having an Edsel salesman for a brother, Mom," Becky complained as she began concocting her own version of the after-school snack: a bowl of broken-up graham crackers with milk on top—an instant soggy mess. "I just wish he'd drop this thing with the Edsel, whatever it is. First I can't go to dances, and now my brother's on the front page of the newspaper trying to save a dumb car. My friends are begin-ning to think our family's nuts or something."

"Now just a minute," said my mother. "Don't go bringing up the dancing again. We've been over that enough. Plus, you have plenty of friends at church."

"Even they are starting to wonder about Ben and Jonathan,"

Becky said. "Those two are always keeping to themselves—hiding out somewhere—and then they make this big appearance when the mayor comes. And it's all over a stupid car! I don't get it."

"I'm not sure I understand either, but Jonathan is your brother and you need to stand behind him when no one else will. You two have always supported each other. He's not stupid, Becky. Neither is Ben. In fact, Ben is one of the brightest little boys I know."

"Yeah, but do you mean on this planet?"

"Jonathan, can you shed some light on the subject for your sister?"

I'd been leaning against the back door, staring at the floor, during this entire conversation. There was so much I wanted to say—so much waiting to spill out from the inside. About the really important things Ben and I had been doing behind the scenes. About the fate of the Edsel. About the oddity of the Edsel and how it looked like Ben's face. About my fears for Ben. But there was no way I could explain it to anyone. I didn't even know what it all meant myself.

"No," I said.

Becky sighed in exasperation. "See, Mom? You can't talk any sense into him. I swear, he and Ben have gone off the deep end this time."

"Come on outside, Rebekah," my mother said, apparently realizing this conversation was going nowhere. "Help me take the clothes off the line. It looks like we might be getting some rain before the day's out."

That day, and for many days hence, my paper route provided a timely escape. The rhythmic folding, stacking, packing, and slap-sliding of newspapers on concrete became a language all its own, speaking to me of responsibility and importance (the news must get out), while certain headlines stuck in my mind like a kind of unwritten journal—corresponding events that held no connection for anyone but me, marking the days. My daily appointment with the news also meant that for at least an hour a day I was alone in a world outside my usual sphere.

My route took me down streets and into neighborhoods previously foreign to me. With each day, I was cutting down my delivery time, leaving me free to explore and still return without being missed or questioned as to my whereabouts. To the west and south I discovered stores and industry. To the east were more modest neighborhoods like ours on Sequoia Street. And northward, where the streets widened and the houses and yards grew more spacious, I found the home of Lisa Day.

Lisa was one of my fifth-grade classmates and the most beautiful girl I had ever laid eyes on. Not that I'd even had a passing conversation with her. But then you didn't need to talk with Lisa Day to appreciate her; you only needed to look. To actually talk with her would have placed me right in the middle of a whole lot of feelings I didn't understand, or want to. I wanted only to circle those feelings, to be close to them and cherish the fact that I had them. So every few days I would gather the courage to ride down her street and circle the block like some planetary moon.

That afternoon I orbited half a dozen times, feeling the gravitational ache in my heart, before I turned back home via Live Oak Street.

Live Oak presented another kind of ache—the cold, sharp pain of a face slamming against an immovable object, the nauseating smell of fresh blood, the taste of it in your mouth. I knew that taste now, after being hit in the face myself. I don't know why I returned so often to the place where Ben met the Pontiac. Maybe it was like a criminal returning to the scene of his crime. The similarities were certainly there. For despite the noble attempts of my mother and Ben to exonerate me, I still thought of his accident as my fault.

I'd seen Molly Fitzpatrick only once during the week after the accident. She'd been outside in the yard one afternoon when I came by with her paper, and we'd started talking about Ben. Then, looking down the driveway, I caught a glimpse of what looked like an old classic car in her garage, and when I asked her about it, she proudly took me back and showed me a black 1939 Lincoln Zephyr in cherished condition. She told me it had been a prized possession of her "dearly departed Patrick, who's been gone from me now ten years this March the 13th." The car hadn't been driven since his death, she said. "It's in good running condition, though. I have a nephew who hopes to get this car from me someday. He comes over once a month and cares for it like it was his baby."

"You don't drive at all?" I couldn't imagine anyone in southern California not driving.

"Oh, mercy no, I don't even have a license," she said. "Too much responsibility."

Afterward, on my way home, I had started feeling a bit guilty about my encounter with Molly. My parents hadn't been very happy about my lengthy stay at her house the day that Ben got hurt. It had been such a traumatic day to begin with, and then they couldn't find me for over an hour while I was having tea in Molly's kitchen. Being missing from home would have been bad enough without adding Molly's Catholic influence. Especially when my mother heard me say St. Anthony's prayer for finding lost articles. You'd think she would have been happy that she almost immediately found the car keys she'd been looking for all day, but instead she was terrified. Finding her keys, especially at that moment created nothing but a dilemma for her. For a child who believes in God, prayer is a simple matter of faith. For an adult with my mother's misgivings, there were a host of unknowns.

"I never want you to pray that prayer again" was her clear instruction. "Jesus is the only one you ever need to be praying to. And I don't want you spending any more time with that Mrs. Fitzpatrick."

"But, Mother, she cares about Ben, and she knows a lot about his problems. She used to be a nurse."

"What problems are you talking about?" she asked.

"His accident," I said. For some reason I didn't want to tell her about the hole in Ben's heart. "She knows all about how to take care of him."

"Yes, and so do the people at the hospital, Jonathan. I agree she's a very nice lady, and you can certainly be friendly to her. I just don't want you over there at her house, that's all," she said in her do-what-I-say-and-don't-ask-questions voice. "And as far as Ben is concerned, you've got to remember that as much as she may care about him, she is not the doctor."

"But Mrs. Beamering said that Ben's regular doctor was on vacation and that having Molly there made her feel a lot better."

"Who's Molly?"

"That's what Mrs. Fitzpatrick asked me to call her."

"Now see? That's exactly what I'm talking about. It's not right for a woman over sixty to be having a ten-year-old call her by her nickname."

"Why?"

"It's just not done, that's all."

That conversation with my mother had been enough to make me hurry past Molly's house when I made my delivery, hoping she wouldn't come out. Today, however, she caught me returning to the scene of the crime on my way home. I was straddling my bike on the sidewalk, three feet from the tree I had found Ben leaning against just a week and a day earlier, when she opened the front door and came out to pick up her paper.

"How's Ben?" she asked.

"Oh, hi . . . he's fine I guess."

"Well, I've missed you, Johnny." Something about the way she said the nickname—one I hated from anyone else—with her Irish roll made it seem all right. It sounded more like "Junny" when she said it.

"Yeah, I've missed you too," and I really had. I had missed talking about Ben to someone who understood. Hearing about the hole in Ben's heart had turned out to be more of a relief than an alarm. I had always suspected something was wrong—the way he got tired so quickly and all—and putting a name to that something had alleviated at least some of my fears. But it was a knowledge I had decided to keep to myself. I hadn't even let Ben know that I knew.

"I bet you two have had a busy week now that you're celebrities."

"No one at my school thinks I'm a celebrity."

"I'd like to be knowin' the last time any one of them was on the front page of the newspaper with the mayor."

Where was she when I got punched in the nose? I thought.

"I had no idea you two were so interested in cars or I would have shown you the Lincoln earlier. Maybe you can bring Ben over to see it too. I don't care much about cars myself. I just keep the Lincoln because dear Patrick loved it so. It's like havin' a bit o' him around here." She stared off into the distance as if she saw something she recognized. "I'll never get rid of that car as long as I live.

"So how's everything?" she asked, returning from her memories. "What's the latest on Benjamin? When was the last time you saw the little rascal?"

"Yesterday in church. He looked great. And I talked to him this afternoo—" and then I caught myself. "I forgot. I haven't talked to him yet today. He was home all day with the flu."

"The flu?" she asked, showing a little concern. "What kind of flu? Sore throat? Stomach flu?"

"I don't know," I said. "His mother said she kept him home because he had a fever."

She stood there for a moment and fed that look of concern.

"Johnny, you know his phone number, don't you?" I nodded. "Come inside with me. I want to give Mrs. Beamering a call."

"Why? Is something wrong?"

"I hope not. I just want to ask her a few questions."

I got off my bike and followed her into the house. She had the receiver in her hand by the time I got in the front door.

"Sycamore 5–2905," I said, and heard her finger circle the dial seven times.

"Hello, Mrs. Beamering? . . . This is Mary K. Fitzpatrick, the nurse that helped—"

"Yes! Just fine, thank you. Mrs. Beamering—"

"Oh, certainly. 'Martha' it is then. Martha, Johnny stopped by this afternoon . . . in fact, he's here lookin' at me right now, and he mentioned that Benjamin was home today ill. I don't mean to be nosey, but I am a little concerned after becoming familiar with his history. Jonathan says he has a fever. How high?"

"There may be. Does he have any other symptoms, Martha?"

"Uh huh."

"And you reported that to your doctor?"

"And what did he say?"

"He did?"

"Would you say that Benjamin has been getting steadily better then, since his accident? There haven't been any setbacks?"

"Yes, and what was that?"

"You what?"

"You got that done where?"

"In emergency?"

"And what did your doctor say?"

To herself, under her breath, she muttered, "On vacation . . . saints preserve us—"

"No, nothing. Did they give him penicillin then?"

"Do you know how much?"

"Well, that will be important to find out."

"Yes. Something could be very wrong. Children with hearts like his are very susceptible to infections. All right, Martha, I want you to listen to what I tell you now. I know I'm no doctor, but I have been a nurse for over thirty-five years, and I have seen more of these illnesses than ever I wanted to. Now I pray that I'm wrong, but if I'm right, then timing is critical. Are you hearin' me?"

"Good. This is what you must do. I want you to take Benjamin to St. Mary's straightaway. Now, it's half-past four. Good. Dr. Penrose will still be on duty. I want you to go to the third floor nurses' station and ask for Mary Brown. She's the head nurse. I will call ahead right now and have everything arranged for you properly."

"Yes."

"Yes, that's right."

"Well, yes, there is a chance of that, and in that case you'll see one of the other doctors. It's just that Dr. Penrose is the best. If for some reason you end up with someone who has not heard the details from me, just tell them about everything: his heart defect, the accident, the infected stitches, and the fever. Anyone puttin' all these symptoms together will see a cause for concern. And what you want is a cardiologist to do a complete checkup."

"Well, you're quite welcome."

"Oh yes, it's Atlantic 7–6623. Feel free to call me if you have any questions at all."

A light rain had begun to fall. I could hear it building on the roof of Molly's small single-story house. It grew right along with the seriousness in her voice.

"It's not good, is it?" I said after she hung up the phone.

"No, it's not, Jonathan," she said. She was the first adult I'd known who didn't pretend. "Then again, it could be nothing . . .

I have to make some phone calls now. Why don't you come have a seat here next to me."

I sat stunned as she made a flurry of calls to nurses and doctors. When she hung up the phone for the last time and let out a long sigh, my eyes started to fill with tears.

"Why is this so serious?" I asked. "Doesn't he just have the flu?"

"For someone with Ben's heart condition, any illness is serious. You must take every precaution. I'm not convinced that has been happening in this case. Did you know that they went back into the hospital last Friday to get that cut over his eye cleaned out because it got infected?" she asked me.

"No. I never heard anything about that," I said, and then I paused. "That's the bad part, huh?"

"Yes, laddie. That's the bad part."

"What do you think will happen?"

"They'll start with a number of tests. If they find an infection, they'll give him lots of medicine. God willing, it may only be the flu, after all."

"And what if it's not? What else could it be?"

"Well, Johnny, it could be an infected heart. Certain bacteria sometimes get in the bloodstream and attach right where the hole in the heart is. Used to be almost certain death in children Ben's age, but now, with so many antibiotics, they can stop it more often than not. Let's just pray it's only the flu."

"I've never prayed for anybody to have the flu before," I thought out loud.

"This is probably the only time you ever will," she said. "Would you like some tea and cake?"

"No, thanks. I better go. My parents will be looking for me," I said.

I rode home as fast as I could, setting my face straight into the driving rain that completely soaked my hair, clothes, canvas bag, and the three copies of leftover news that no one would receive free on Monday, January 12, 1959.

21

Back in Business

I didn't get to see Ben in the hospital until Wednesday after I'd finished my paper route. My mother took me there, and Mrs. Beamering got me in to see Ben.

"Don't you just hate hospitals?" I said first thing.

"I hate everything right now, so I can't tell if I hate hospitals in particular."

"Here. I brought you something from the front page of the *Star-News* today that might cheer you up. How's this for a headline: 'Doctor Tells What He Knows About Noses'?"

"Very clever. What does he know?"

" 'It's amazing what Ralph Riggs knows about noses,' " I read from the front page. " 'Dr. Riggs, of Louisiana State University, got onto the subject while addressing a seminar on nose surgery yesterday at the College of Medical Evangelists.' "

"Medical evangelists?" said Ben. "What are they doing, preaching to noses?"

"Yeah, and we should get this guy in here to preach to yours, 'cause it really needs to get saved!" I said. "Now pay attention to this part, Ben: 'A man that really knows noses knows that surgery to change the appearance of the nose can have severe psychological effects—' "

"Wait a minute," said Ben. "How does he know he knows noses?"

"Because he knows his own nose," I said.

"But does his own nose know what my nose knows?" That one got me laughing. "And if he knows his own nose," Ben went on, brightening, "he knows noses know when they're being too nosey!"

"Aaaak!" I cried. "Stop! I can't take any more."

It was good to see his familiar trick smile again. It hadn't been a good day. Ben had been in the hospital since Monday night. The tests had not turned up any sign of bacterial infection, so on Tuesday everyone was encouraged; Ben's temperature had returned to normal and he was feeling fine. But late Tuesday night the fever hit again, and by Wednesday morning it was up to 103.

"Is that the best you could find on the front page?"

"Yep," I said, holding it up, "unless you want to hear about Ike's make-or-break fiscal year ahead."

"No thanks," said Ben. "I don't want to hear about anybody's year ahead."

"Hey, here's one about two bandits in New York who thought they were making off with a whole bunch of money when all they had was a custard pie," I said.

For the remainder of that week I visited Ben in the afternoon after delivering my papers, and each day I tried to look for humorous stories like the one about the pie bandits and the nose evangelists—things that would make Ben laugh. Sometimes they backfired on me. Like the time I read an ad about the last chance to buy a copy of the *Star-News* New Year's Rose Parade Souvenir Edition, to which Ben replied: "Yeah. Last chance to see Mayor Seth Wilson in an Edsel in the Rose Parade."

The happiest I saw him that week was on Saturday.

Aside from the fever, which remained fairly high but could be controlled somewhat by aspirin, he was not in a lot of pain. If you asked him where it hurt, he would say, "My butt. I think they're running out of places to stick me."

What they were sticking him with, I found out later, were large doses of penicillin and a host of other antibiotics, hoping to hit the strain of bacterial infection in Ben's bloodstream that so far had eluded both blood tests and medication.

But on Saturday, the glint was back in his eye in spite of his fever. Ben Beamering was back to his old tricks.

"You've got to do something very important for me tomorrow," he said.

"What's that?"

"There's going to be a baptism service before my dad preaches."

"So?"

"You know those silly waders he wears when he's baptizing people so he doesn't have to get wet?"

"No. I thought he wore a robe."

"He does wear a robe, but underneath it he wears these fishing waders—heavy rubber boots that go all the way up to his chest. Fishermen wear them when they want to stand in the water all day."

"How do they stay up?"

"Suspenders."

"Wait a minute. I know what you're talking about. I've seen those things in the baptismal room. I've always wondered what they were for."

"They keep him dry when he's baptizing people so he can switch back into his suit faster for the rest of the service. But it's not right. Imagine John the Baptist baptizing Jesus in fishing waders! We can't let him get away with baptizing people without getting wet himself. That's downright hippo-crazy."

"What?"

"Hippo-crazy. That's the way I remember that word. It's really 'hypocrisy,' but 'hippo-crazy' is how you look doing what you tell other people not to do—or in this case, you're not doing what you expect of everyone else. Can you imagine what would happen if the people who were being baptized were wearing those things? I don't think God would even count it as an official baptism. How could you be officially baptized without getting officially wet? It's no different for him. If the people are going to get wet, then he's got to get wet too. That's the way it has to be. Something's got to be done, and I think I've finally figured it out."

"Okay. What's your idea?" I was all ears now.

"I knew you'd do it for me."

"Wait a minute. I haven't even heard the idea yet."

"This is a cinch," said Ben. "It will be the easiest prank we've ever pulled."

"Let me guess: You want me to steal the waders before the service."

"I thought of that, but this is even better: You're going to poke holes in them so they'll fill up with water while he's in the pool. It's better than hiding them. For all we know, he may have an extra pair of those things around somewhere we don't know about. This way he'll be completely surprised. He won't even know what's happening until it's too late. I know my father. He will never let on that anything's wrong. He'll just stand there and carry on as if nothing unusual is happening while the water rises in his boots. It's the perfect plan."

"What do you think he'll do?"

"I don't know. But you'll have to remember every detail so you can tell me. I hate to miss it," he said. "My father's wading boots slowly filling up with water and there's nothing he can do about it. You have to do this for me, Jonathan. This is the best. This is better than heaping burning coals on the choir."

How could I turn him down?

"What will I use to make the holes?"

"So you'll do it?" he said excitedly, and the brightness on his face that very moment was all the convincing I needed. It was so great to see him this happy.

"I know!" I said, starting to show my own excitement. "My parents have an old ice pick. I know right where it is in the drawer in the kitchen."

"Perfect!"

"How many holes should I make?"

"Two."

"Only two holes?"

"Yep. One right above each heel will do the trick."

"But the water won't go up very far then, will it? Won't it just get his feet wet? Don't we have to poke holes all the way up the waders to get the water to come up that high?"

"Nope. Only one hole in each foot. Here, watch this." And he reached under the covers and produced a doctor's rubber glove he had somehow managed to confiscate. He picked up a pencil from his bedside table and made a small hole on the side of one of the fingers, near the tip. Then he held up the pencil in one hand and said, "This is my dad's leg," and the finger of the glove in the other, "and this is one leg of his waders." Placing the pencil inside the finger, he plunged it down into the glass of water sitting on the table. We watched as the water level inside the rubber finger slowly rose up around the pencil leg until it was equal to the level in the glass.

"It's a vacuum," he announced emphatically. "There's more pressure outside the boot than there is inside it. Once the hole is there, the water is forced in until it equalizes the pressure. It's almost exactly like one of the experiments I did with my physics set."

I looked at him in amazement as he beamed his triumphant smile.

"We've been much too quiet around that church lately," he said. "Time for Operation Mercy Canary to strike again!"

22

All Wet

"I can't wait to try out our new choir robes today," said my father when we were about halfway to church the next day.

"Which way are you going to have them wear the stoles?" my mother asked.

"The green side. The green contrasts better with the gold robes, don't you think?"

"Oh yes, definitely. The white side washes out the gold. I think it makes the robes look dirty, even though they're brand-new."

"I do too. I can't imagine when we would ever want to wear the white side out."

"Maybe after the congregation has seen green for a long time they will welcome a change. But remember, Walter, you haven't seen the choir yet in the loft with them all wearing the new robes. You've only been looking at one robe at a time, up close. The colors might take on a whole different quality in the choir loft."

"That's a good point, dear. I'll have to test the combinations out this week in choir practice. I could have done it last week if they'd gotten there when they were supposed to."

"Oh, Becky—" My mother suddenly changed the subject. "Did you end up setting a place for Joshua?"

"Yes, Mother."

"Good, because he's coming after all. And you didn't set one for Mrs. Beamering, did you?"

"No, Mother, you told me not to."

"I can't believe Martha is able to stay at that hospital around the clock. I've never heard of them allowing such a thing."

"I think it has a lot to do with Martha," said my father, motioning to someone that they could turn in front of him. "Have you heard her talking to doctors and nurses in that hospital?"

"You mean like she's in charge?" answered my mother. "Well . . . she is. She believes that the doctors and nurses are working for her, not the other way around, and I have to admit, that's the way it should be. But I'd never have the mettle she has when she speaks to them. She's really got them hopping."

"Too bad she'll miss the mayor's baptism. I've heard there might even be members of the press there today. The new robes arrived just in time."

"What? The mayor's being baptized?" I asked from the backseat of the car. My father's comment had poked me as sharply as the ice pick in my pocket was poking my side. "I thought you had to go through a whole bunch of classes and stuff first."

"You do, unless of course you're Seth Wilson."

"How does Jeffery even know the mayor is a Christian?" asked my mother. "Isn't this happening a little fast?"

"Oh my, didn't I tell you?" said my absentminded father. "Mayor Wilson became a Christian this week. He prayed with Jeffery in his office on Friday."

"Walter!" said my mother, sounding happy and frustrated at the same time. "I can't believe you didn't tell us this sooner. After we've met him and been in his office? Why . . . this is wonderful news."

Yeah, just great, I thought. I was about to let the baptismal waters of the Colorado Avenue Standard Christian Church seep into the pastor's waders while he baptized the newly converted mayor of the city of Pasadena on camera. Why did these things always get so complicated at the last minute?

"Isn't that great news, Jonathan?" my mother said, turning around in the front seat so she could see me.

"Yes." I managed a smile.

"I wonder if Ben knows?" she said, facing forward again. "Ben should have been the first to know."

"He didn't say anything about it yesterday when I saw him," I said. "Why should he have been the first to know?"

"Well, it's all because of him," she answered. "The mayor wouldn't even have cared about our church if it hadn't been for Ben and his crazy attachment to Edsels. Honestly, those two make quite a pair."

"Which two?" said my sister sarcastically. "Ben and the Edsel?"

"Ben and the mayor," corrected my mother emphatically. "And you watch your attitude, young lady."

"It's more than the Edsel, Ann," said my father as he turned up the last street toward the church. "Jeffery told me that when the mayor found out we were the church that was so creatively illustrating the Scriptures last summer, and that Ben was behind that too, he was convinced this was the place for him."

"Wait a minute," said Becky, risking one more shot. "Did the mayor accept Jesus or Ben into his heart?"

"Rebekah!" said my mother. "This is nothing to joke about. And the truth is, it doesn't matter what brought him to the church; what matters is that he came and became a Christian. And here he is getting baptized in our church! My stars, I can't believe it."

I couldn't believe it either. My mother reminding us how similar Ben and the mayor were helped me relax again about the ice pick in my pocket. If something unusual or outlandish happened on the mayor's baptismal day, he would probably consider it a great honor.

Ben had been right again. This was the easiest prank we ever pulled. I found the door to the baptismal room wide open and no one there—and I immediately located the waders. They were hanging in a changing area marked "PASTOR." Three other changing areas were each marked "CONVERT." There were lots of other signs in the room as well. One said: "PLEASE

WEAR BATHING SUIT UNDER ROBE" and another read: "FOR THOSE WITHOUT BATHING SUITS." Under that one were two bins marked "MEN" and "WOMEN" containing clean underwear of various sizes. Next to the bins was a clothes hamper marked "SOILED LAUNDRY."

I drove the ice pick all the way into the back of each wader boot. There was a crease just above the heels where the rubber folded over from its weight and it concealed the holes completely.

That was all there was to it. No timing, no signals, no need to account for our absence. All I had to do now was sit in my usual place in the service and watch the drama unfold.

In the wake of the Pastor Ivory incident, my father had been thrust into a more prominent role in the morning service. Though Virgil had apparently been vindicated by his explanations and the statements of others involved, he had, at least for the present, lost a certain amount of credibility. So more and more, Pastor Beamering had had my father pick up the duties of "host" on Sunday morning. He handled the announcements, led the congregational hymns, read the scripture, and sometimes did the pastoral prayer, all in addition to his duties with the choir.

Surprisingly, my father had become a sort of reluctant success at this. As quiet and unaware as he could be sometimes, my father never failed to come alive when you put him in front of a group of people. He didn't have Pastor Ivory's suave casualness; instead, he had something much better—a kindness and genuineness that made almost everyone like him and trust him.

On Sunday, January 18, 1959, when the morning paper I had delivered some six hours earlier announced that Soviet Deputy Premier Anastas I. Mikoyan, in the heat of a Cold War, would cut his U.S. trip short by three days and return to Moscow on Tuesday, my father got up in the pulpit of our church to pray. It was an emotional prayer.

Most of the people in the congregation were unaware of the nature and extent of Ben's medical problems, and though this was certainly a time to pray fervently, it was not a time to go into great detail. So what my father did was to inform everyone that "Our pastor's son, Ben, is gravely ill in the hospital with a high fever due to unknown causes" and that he and the family were in need of their prayers and their support, which my father then gave, on behalf of everyone, through a very moving prayer that brought out many tissues.

I sat through all this with a growing lump in my throat, not unlike the one I'd had when I held on to my offering money so I could buy Ben his first Edsel. Ben's joy over the wader prank had overshadowed everything else, and in the excitement and anticipation I had forgotten how sick he was. Somehow, it had been like old times; we were at it again together and I was holding the flashlight. Even though I had carried out the dirty work alone, Ben had conceived and directed it. But suddenly, in the midst of the tears being shed on his behalf, it seemed inappropriate.

Of course, none of these thoughts could alter what was about to happen. The deed was already done. As soon as my father finished praying, Pastor Beamering came out to introduce those who were about to be baptized, his robe brushing the toes of his secretly perforated black rubber boots.

There were three people being baptized that day and, as was his custom, Pastor Beamering conducted a brief, informal interview with each and had them give their testimonies. This was done from the platform before the actual baptism since the baptistery was set up in the wall behind the choir loft in between the banks of organ pipes and there was no means of amplification from there. Of course Pastor Beamering's pipes were quite adequate to reach the whole church and beyond without any assistance, but that was not the case for most timid believers on the brink of baptism.

Pastor Beamering left the mayor for last. And though he may have given the mayor preferential treatment with his hasty membership and baptism, Jeffery T., to his credit, treated the man like any other member of the congregation from the platform. Seth Wilson was simply a man who did not waste time once he made up his mind about things, and Pastor Beamering did not see any reason why he shouldn't accommodate this aspect of the man's character. After all, the membership class had only been stepped up by two weeks, and the baptism had been on the calendar for a year. Nor was Jeffery T. one to deny the political benefits of the mayor's new interest in his church.

These were certainly evident that morning, with a marked rise in attendance. Not that this event had been publicized (I had looked for signs of it in the *Star-News* and found none), but there was always the grapevine. Just as there was the press contingency, whom Pastor Beamering had relegated to the balcony and denied the use of flashbulbs. You could still hear the cameras clicking, however, as Mayor Wilson gave his personal testimony.

"I've been slowly coming to a faith in Christ for some time now, Pastor, but I've been quiet about it because of my political aspirations. It was actually through your son, who stood in my office recently over something he believed in, that I began to see my own faith as something to stand up for. As you know, I am vocal and forthright about most things" (a comment which brought a polite ripple of laughter from the congregation), "so why not be forthright about my faith in Jesus Christ?"

"And your reason for wanting to be baptized today?" Pastor Beamering asked in interview style.

"Well, I was baptized as a child. I was sprinkled actually, with a little water on my head," and here he wiggled his fingers on top of his white hair. "Now that I've made my stand with Christ, I really want to be baptized for good. A little sprinkling just ain't gonna do it for me. I want to get *all wet*."

At this point the congregation applauded. Perhaps it was the mayor's gift of oratory, or perhaps it was the presence of the press and the cameras that spurred them on; but whatever it was, it loosened the tension everyone had been feeling since my dad's prayer for Ben gripped them. All I could think of, however, was that Mayor Wilson wasn't the only one who was going to get all wet.

After the interviews and testimonies, Pastor Beamering led the three baptismal candidates off the platform while the organ played softly. Moments later he appeared in the baptistery. That part had always seemed eerie to me: to watch the pastor leave the room and suddenly reappear halfway up the wall in a pool of water, like one of those colored Sunday school pictures of Jesus' transfiguration. It always reminded me of one of our favorite family jokes that started when a member of our church, a contractor, had come to our house to help my father with a roofing project. His first name was Palmer, and because he was always called in when my father's handyman expertise had reached an impasse, he had come to be known around our house as Super Palmer, the caped carpenter who once again saved the day. And he had truly lived up to that name the day he jumped onto the roof from a ladder outside our breakfast room window. Just as Becky cried, "Look! It's a bird! It's a plane! It's . . . Super Palmer!" all we could see through the window were his legs leaving the ladder and taking to the sky.

I always expected to see Super Jeffery take to the sky as he finished the last baptism—one more step up from his perch on the wall. This Sunday, however, Super Jeffery wasn't taking off anywhere.

"Seth Wilson, I baptize you in the name of the Father, and the Son, and the Holy Ghost," and down went the mayor. Once again, uncharacteristic of our church, there was applause as the mayor came up out of the water and hugged Jeffery T. No one had ever hugged Pastor Beamering in the baptistery before, and it took him and everyone by surprise and delight. As the mayor mounted the steps and left the pool and Milton Owlsley began to play the usual meditative transition on the organ, to give the pastor extra time to change back into his suit, Jeffery Beamering followed, but only to the first step. At that point he seemed to have difficulty getting out of the water. He tried it again, but some invisible force was pulling him back. After the third try failed, he returned to the center of the baptismal pool and faced the congregation with his hands folded in front of him and a rather strained look on his face.

My father, who had faced forward after the last baptism so he could resume his duties, went ahead with the congregational hymn, "Standing on the Promises," which must have put no small strain on the eardrums of Pastor Beamering, perched as he was between two banks of organ pipes. I knew how loud that organ could be from back there.

When the pastor did not reappear on the platform by the end of the last stanza of the hymn, my father resorted to the tried-and-true stopgap: He had the congregation sing the first verse again. And when that time was used up and there was still no Pastor Beamering, my father launched into a filibuster about how Standard Christians had somehow gotten into the bad habit of leaving out the second verse of so many great hymns in the interest of time, and how that was such a shame since so much had gone into every word of each one of these hymns, and how would we feel if we had written a poem and someone else took out a verse just because they thought the poem was too long, and how we should all stand together and sing the second verse of this great hymn, and how we should then finish up with the last verse one more time, and "Milton, while we're at it, why don't we take it up one step on the last verse, pull out all the stops on the organ, and let's raise the rafters of this church!"

Meanwhile, the congregation slowly began to catch on to what was happening, and an undercurrent of controlled amusement began to leak out in a snicker or two.

Right before we went into the much-neglected second verse of "Standing on the Promises," Pastor Beamering tried to stop my father. He held up his hand and started to speak, but since Milton couldn't see the baptistery from the organ console, his opening chord totally drowned out Jeffery T. All you could hear was the organ introduction to "Standing on the Promises," and all you could see was Pastor Beamering holding up his hand and forming a silent "Walter!" with his mouth.

That brought an immediate response from the congregation, causing most of us to laugh our way through the second verse. But when we came to the last verse and Milton pulled out all the stops, a moment he always relished anyway, Pastor Beamering had no choice but to put both hands over his ears and wait it out while Milton, enraptured in the glory of full throttle, played it out all the way to the resounding AMEN!

When Milton finally pulled his hands up off the organ keys after the final note—something he always did with a flourish—there was nothing left to compete with the uncontrolled laughter that filled the sanctuary, leaving my poor father utterly bewildered. I can only imagine what must have been going through his head. *Was it something I said? Is my fly open? No, that can't be it; I'm wearing a robe. What is it?* And then, after a number of people pointed to the wall behind him, he finally turned around and saw Pastor Beamering standing in the baptismal pool. Of course, by now he too was laughing.

"Walter," Jeffery T. said quickly and compassionately, trying hard to get control of himself and diminish my father's embarrassment, "never again shall we ever omit the second stanza of a hymn," a comment that brought more laughter and applause.

There was no doubt about it: Ben was back. Disarming the congregation, upsetting the status quo, and laying bare genuine human feelings and emotions.

As the laughter gradually died and my father sat down, shaking his head, Pastor Beamering stood still in the baptistery waiting to speak. He smiled and let the silence return until it felt slightly uncomfortable. Once again, our plan to thwart the service was about to backfire into something positive.

"While you have been singing," Jeffery T. began, loud and clear to the last row even without a microphone, "I have been standing up here trying to think of a graceful way out of this situation. There is none. I've been trying to come up with a way to make you think this was all planned, but unfortunately that came into conflict with Walter's attempts to do the same thing. The truth of the matter is, neither one of us knows what is going on. All I know is, I can't move." Murmurs rippled across the congregation.

"Most of you don't know this, but when I perform baptisms I wear a pair of wading boots that come all the way up to here under this robe." (He indicated the spot with his hand.) "They're the kind fishermen wear so they can fish from the middle of a stream. I do this because it enables me to keep dry and change more quickly back into my suit for the remainder of the service.

"Well, this morning, for some unknown reason, these things have filled up entirely with water" (some gasps and laughter), "making it impossible for me to get out of the pool because of the weight of all the water in my boots. This means I cannot get to my notes for the sermon I prepared for you this morning, but that is just as well, for I fear I could not give it to you anyway. Or if I could, my heart would not be in it, for my heart is only one place this morning and that is with my son, Benjamin, in the hospital" (sudden silence).

"Those of you who have been with us since I took over the pastorate of this church last March know that one of my favorite sermon images is the God-shaped vacuum in every human heart. What you don't know is that from birth Ben has had a real physical vacuum in his heart—a real hole in his real heart. The problems he has presently are related to this. It appears he has contracted an infection, and the doctors are having difficulty treating it. And just this morning they told us that Ben's heart condition has already deteriorated so much in his fight with this disease that there is a good chance he will not live to see another Sunday." (That last sentence seemed to suck the very air out of the room . . . out of me.)

"I am telling you this because you are our family and we need you. I am telling you this because I want you to pray. We believe God can heal. I am telling you this because if God chooses not to heal, and He has the sovereign right to do so, there is something I want you to know now, while there's still hope—while I can speak more freely. Otherwise I may not be able to speak of this for some time."

He paused here for a moment to gather words—to gather courage—and I was glad he did. I needed this moment to breathe. I needed it to find something to hold on to. Molly had prepared me for the seriousness of the disease facing Ben, and Ben's own strange comments and my premonitions had hinted at something ominous; but this was the first time the thought that my friend might die had hit me straight on.

"Actually, it's quite ironic. Ben has been trying to get me out of these waders for some time now, and I can't help but think that even in his present condition, he may have had something to do with this. Actually . . . I saw him this morning, and he did have that look on his face that he gets when he's up to something."

Then, as he rubbed his chin and grimaced, I noticed for the first time on his face the traces of Ben's smirk.

"Maybe that look on his face this morning was all because he knew that soon my waders were going to be filling up with water."

A kind of crying laughter leaked out from the room. And then he froze me to my chair by saying, "And, Jonathan Liebermann, I'm going to have your father check you after church for any sign of sharp objects on your person!" Somehow I managed a smile because he was smiling too.

"I wish you all could have seen Ben this morning," he continued in a wistful tone. "He had a look on his face I have never seen there before. It was a look of great peace and unexplainable joy. I think most of you who know Ben know that these are not things found typically on his face.

"No, Ben's joy this morning was more than the anticipation of another prank. It was because something had happened to him that we all long for—something saints have lived and died for without ever finding—and Ben received it last night at the ripe old age of ten.

"Ben heard from God."

His voice caught in his throat as he said this, and a reverent silence filled up a long pause.

What is he talking about? I thought. I hadn't seen this on Ben's face. Besides, it was hard to imagine anything like peace and joy in the general vicinity of Ben's face. But then again I hadn't seen him this morning. Maybe something *had* happened last night. Suddenly I remembered that bedtime conversation months before when Ben had told me about hearing someone call his name. Maybe it had happened again, and maybe he had heard the message this time.

"I do not know what he heard or what he saw," Pastor Beamering continued from his watery pulpit, "but I can tell you that it doesn't really matter to us. What matters is that it was enough to give Ben courage to go on—courage to face whatever lies ahead for him. And I also know that I gained great courage this morning from merely seeing his face, for if one has not had a vision of God, it is like the thing itself to look upon the face of someone else who has.

"Suddenly I realized I was staring at my own son whom I love, and he was staring off somewhere I could not even see— looking over some huge abyss that strikes mortal fear into all of our hearts, and yet there he was at peace. I cannot explain adequately what it was like, except that suddenly, at that moment in my mind and heart, all theology and practical living and the steps we try and reduce the Christian life to were reduced even further—to their simplest form: There is a God, and He loves us each individually by name, and He wants to be with us . . . . and to have us with Him."

There was one last, long pause here and it was welcomed.

Unlike the other silences, this was a full, rich silence—full of knowing and pondering the profound and real place of faith we had been brought to.

"I have not had a vision of God myself. I stand before you once a week without the benefit of miraculous signs and wonders. I am a pilgrim like you. If I look like I've got it all together—like I'm somehow skirting over the life you have to trudge through—then there is something wrong, either with the impression I am giving or with your impression of me.

"And while Ben has visions of God in the hospital, I stand here before you in four feet of water both inside and outside my boots. I'm going to wrap this up quickly because . . . quite frankly, it's getting cold in here." And then he smiled. "I bet you wish all my sermons were this brief.

"Not only are we going to sing all the stanzas of our hymns from now on, Walter" (and he smiled at my father, who had turned around and caught his eye), "but you can be sure that as certain as I stand here before you this morning—or I suppose I should say wade before you—I am never going to baptize in these things again. From now on, no matter how long it takes for me to get back into my suit, I intend to get 'ALL WET.' " And there was something in the natural theater of his voice and the echo of Mayor Wilson's moment that triggered the applause meter of the congregation once again. This time it was a corporate release of emotion.

When the response finally died down and silence returned, Pastor Beamering motioned with his hands and said, "Please rise for the benediction." And as he stretched his arms out from his place high up on the wall, I thought for a moment that it really was Super Jeffery up there.

Finally, he did something strange and wonderful. He dropped his hands into the water and then brought them up cupped, so that the water rained slowly off his hands and arms and splashed back into the pool all the way through the benediction. And I could have sworn that standing there in my pew, hearing the words and the water fall, I was getting all wet.

23

1939 Lincoln Zephyr

"So how long did he stay up there?" asked Ben later on that day after I had detailed the morning's events.

"I'm not sure. My dad went up right away and pulled the curtain on the baptistery, but your father never showed up out front after the service. For all I know, he might still be up there."

"No, he's not. He's been here with me at the hospital since church. But it's so disappointing," he said a bit too dramatically to be very convincing. "Every time I try and mess things up, it always turns out good. I wonder what would happen if I ever tried to do something good for a change. I'd probably mess it up for everybody. Hey! Maybe that's what I should do!"

"You'll do nothing but rest and take it easy," said the nurse who had come in to check his temperature. "Now don't go letting this young man here get you all riled up. You're looking better today. Let's keep it that way."

He did seem to look a little better, and his fever had been down for twenty-four hours. Maybe the deadly bacteria had finally met its match somewhere in the barrage of drugs they'd been throwing at it.

"I don't know," I continued when she was gone. "Our message about Pastor Ivory made a pretty big mess of things."

"Yeah, but that message was true. It was really the right thing to do. It was the most right thing we did all summer. We didn't mess up anything; the mess was already there. All I want, for just once in my life, is to make a success of doing the wrong thing."

Ben had a lot of visitors that day. Not all of them got to see him. I wondered if some of them only wanted to see the face that had seen the vision. I kept looking at that face myself and saw no evidence of any change other than a return of some of his spunk. It certainly wasn't my idea of the face of someone who had just heard from God. I guess I thought being closer to God should make you more angelic—more sweet, perhaps. If Ben really had seen God, it had only made him more Ben.

I felt like walking out and telling everyone in the waiting room, *Hey, you might as well go home. It's just Ben—like he always was.*

"Anything interesting on the front page today?" he asked.

"Seth Wilson's on it."

"Really?"

"Yep." And I produced Sunday's front page with a picture of Mayor Wilson and a man named Ray O. Woods over the headline "Two City Fathers Seek Reelection" and a subtitle "Primary Election Looms."

"Read it to me," Ben said.

" 'Seth Wilson and Ray O. Woods, two members of the Pasadena Board of City Directors, yesterday announced their candidacy for reelection in the March primary vote. Long active in civic affairs in Pasadena, Wilson is a past president of the Pasadena Optimist Club—' "

"That makes sense," Ben interjected.

" '—and the Overland Club and has held board positions in the Tournament of Roses and the Boys and Girls Clubs of Pasadena. He is also a member of the Masons and the University Club. "Pasadena has always enjoyed good, clean city government, and it is my desire to perpetuate this high standard which my colleagues and I have tried to maintain," Wilson, 66, a longtime classic-auto enthusiast, declared.' "

"What do you suppose a 'classic-auto enthusiast' is?" I said. "Do you think he collects classics?"

"Or maybe he fixes them up," said Ben. "Hey, maybe that's it!"

"What?"

"Maybe that's why he likes Edsels so much. He realizes all the money he can make fixing them."

"What do you mean?" I asked. Ben started to pull something out from under his pillow just as the nurse he affectionately called "Attila the Hun" came back in the room.

"Time's up," she announced, and one did not argue with the

Hun. As she ran me out of the room, we ran right into the next visitor—none other than the mayor himself.

"Jonathan! How wonderful to see you!" He greeted me and shook my hand as if I were the president of a company or something. "This is ideal. I was hoping I'd be able to see both of you together. Let's go see Ben." He took my hand to draw me into the room with him, but we had only taken a step when the mayor came nose to nose with Attila.

"Not so fast, you two. Only one at a time, and you've already been in," she said, wagging her finger at me.

"Excuse me, ma'am, but I don't believe we've met."

"Sarah Baumgartner," she said. "I'm the nurse in charge here."

"Miss Baumgartner, I'm Seth Wilson, and I happen to be the mayor in charge of this city. Now, my friend and I would like to visit with the patient for a few minutes, if you would please—"

They stared each other down for a few seconds while Sarah weighed the consequences. She was still weighing them as we walked right past her into the room.

"Ben!" the mayor boomed. "You're looking chipper today."

"Mr. Wilson! Hello! We were just reading about you in the paper."

"Tell me, how are you feeling, Ben?"

"Oh, not too good, but better than yesterday."

"Yes, that's what we hear. Good news. Good news, indeed."

"I see you made it past Attila the Hun," said Ben.

"Oh, that's what you call her? Very appropriate. But she's just doing her job," he said with a bit of a chuckle, then continued in his commanding tone. "Ben, I must tell you, your father was brilliant this morning. You two make a great team."

I wasn't sure what team he was talking about. I'd never thought about Ben and his father as a team.

"Jonathan and I were just talking about that," said Ben. "I keep trying to mess it up, and it keeps turning out good."

That made me think of my mother's favorite "all things work together" verse—the one she kept trying to drum into my head.

"You mess things up in the right way, Ben. You make people think about what they do, especially your father. And you know what? Your father is going to be one heckuva—I mean—one great pastor because of it. He already is."

Ben's only reply to that was a "Harrumph" and his usual twisted-up expression.

"Now, I want you to hear something I received in the mail last week. Here, Jonathan. Why don't you read this out loud for us?" He handed me a letter and stepped over to the other side of the bed so I could face both of them. That in itself was a sight. Mayor Wilson standing behind Ben with a look of great expectancy, and Ben lying in bed with his I-won't-believe-it-till-I-see-it look.

"It says 'To the Honorable Mayor Seth Wilson,' " I said, and began reading.

> I am writing you in response to your letter and the letter of Ben Beamering and Jonathan Liebermann, who must be two exceptionally fine young men. All of us here at the Ford Motor Company, and especially those in what we fondly call the "E" car division, want to tell you how much we appreciate their letter and your loyal support of the Edsel car.
>
> Though sales continue to be lower than anticipated, we remain confident that America is waking up to the quality and value of owning and operating the new Edsel. It is important to note that none of us here in Detroit, or anywhere else for that matter, could have foreseen that our new line of cars would be introduced at a time of economic recession, when virtually all automobile sales in this country are low. Like other car manufacturers, we are confident that our sound economy will soon rebound and the wise tastes of the American public will once again focus on our fine line of cars.
>
> We are proud of both our '58 and '59 models. The changes you mentioned in the '59 model came from extensive consumer research. In fact, there has never been a car in history more connected to the direct needs and wishes of the American people than the Edsel. The Edsel was and continues to be the car America wants.
>
> Please consider this letter a personal invitation from me to all three of you and your families to come tour our spacious "E" car facilities here in Detroit and take an exclusive test drive on our demanding "E" car test track.
>
> Thank you for helping us make the Edsel a classic for

generations to come. It is people like you that make us proud
to be in the business of making fine cars.

Sincerely,
Richard E. Krafve
Vice-President and General Manager
"E" Car Division
The Ford Motor Company

"Wow! How about that?" I said, looking at a proud Mayor
Wilson. He had been beaming the whole time I read, but Ben's
face remained expressionless.

"I'm going to see to it that this gets printed in as many newspapers as possible," said the mayor.

"You better not. Here, may I see that?" Ben said.

As he looked over the letter, a familiar scowl formed on his
face.

"Humbug! I've never seen more lies on one page in my life."

The smiles on our faces froze in a facade of empty hopeful-
ness.

"What are you talking about?" asked Mayor Wilson.

"First of all, the Edsel is not connected to the 'needs and
wishes of the American people.' It was maybe five years ago
when they did their study, but that was five years ago. Now
people are going to smaller, more economical cars. Look at this
on the bottom of the stationery: 'They'll know you've arrived
when you drive up in an Edsel.' They're way behind the times.
Prestige isn't popular anymore. People want value and economy.
Most people today see the Edsel as a chrome-laden albatross.
They can't sell to the American people this way. People are
smarter than this. They don't even know their market."

The mayor and I exchanged glances of alarm. This kind of
emotional binge couldn't be good for Ben's heart. But he had
taken us so by surprise that we could do nothing but stand there
in disbelief. Ben was on a roll.

"They've got to be hoping we don't take them up on this
invitation and come to Detroit, because then we'd discover that
there are no 'spacious "E" car facilities' to be seen anywhere.
They make Edsels on standard Ford and Mercury assembly lines,
where workers have to squeeze one Edsel in between 60 Mer-
curys and put a whole different set of parts on it without even

getting paid for it. No wonder they hate this car in Detroit.

"Here, it's all in here if you want to read it for yourself," and he threw a current issue of *Consumer Reports* at the foot of the bed. The mayor tried to slow him down, but got run over.

"Did you know that in order to have 75 cars for reporters to drive back to their local dealerships as a publicity stunt in 1957 when the Edsel first came out, it took them two months to fix that many cars? That's right—fix! They had to *repair* cars coming off the new-car assembly line, and of the 75 cars they started with, they only ended up with 68 that would run. They tore up the other seven for spare parts! And get this. They had a $10,000 repair bill on each car! Imagine that? A repair bill on a new car before you can even get it out of the factory—and a bill that's over three times the sticker price! And what's this about 'the car America wants'? Come on, we're not that dumb. If America wants it, why isn't America buying it?"

"What's going on in here?" said Miss Baumgartner, rushing into the room.

During this tirade, Ben had been growing more and more agitated until, at the very end, he was actually screaming. As his voice got higher, his breath got shorter. Mayor Wilson and I had tried to get him to stop, or at least slow down, but to no avail. He was still yelling and gasping about "quality" when the Hun physically pushed us out of the room. We went willingly. It was obvious that our presence at that moment wasn't helping anything.

"You better not print that letter unless you want to show Mr. Krafve up as the liar he is!" was the last we heard as the door closed behind us.

The mayor and I stood there stunned outside Ben's room. I stared at the *Consumer Reports* magazine I had managed to grab on the way out. "The Edsel: Doomed From the Start" was printed across the top.

Just then Mrs. Beamering, who had been taking a break while I visited with Ben, walked up to us from the waiting room down the hall.

"My goodness. Why the long faces?"

"Have you seen this?" I said, handing her the magazine.

"No," she said, smiling at the mayor. "What is it?" And then she saw the title and the smile vanished from her face. "Oh no. Has Ben seen this?"

"Yes, that's the problem. He's furious—almost out of control."

Mrs. Beamering looked at our faces more closely, thrust the magazine at me, and bounded into Ben's room. We could hear Nurse Baumgartner's protesting voice ordering her out, covered by the protesting voice of Mrs. Beamering ordering herself in, and then the door closed on their muffled arguing.

Silence again gripped the mayor and me as we walked slowly down the hall to the waiting room where my mother was sitting and talking with Mrs. Wilson. Once again we had to explain our drawn faces.

"Oh, my," said my mother. "I hope he's okay. He was so much better today."

"Yeah . . . 'was' is right," I said.

"Now, now," said Mayor Wilson optimistically, "he'll be all right. He just got a little upset. I'd be upset too if even half of the things he said are true. Here, may I see that magazine?"

"I'm so sorry," said Mrs. Wilson as her husband began scanning the article. "Ann and I were just talking about how providential it was that this strange car had brought us all together."

"How do you suppose he even got ahold of this magazine?" said my mother.

I looked around at all the magazines on the tables. "Probably from in here."

"But Ben isn't supposed to be wandering around the hospital. They have strict rules about him being in his bed."

"Mother. Since when have rules meant anything to Ben?"

"This is very damaging stuff for the Edsel and the Ford Motor Company," said the mayor, looking up from the magazine. "Somebody in Detroit is going to hear from me about this." He started pacing the floor. "Ben was right about this letter, and I have half a mind to print it anyway, just to show up that scoundrel Krafve. I never did like him anyway. I've never seen any ad campaign full of more air, and I *like* this car."

"Seth," said Mrs. Wilson, "let's not get going again about the Ford Motor Company. This is not the time or the place."

"You're absolutely right, my dear. I apologize for getting carried away . . . almost as bad as Ben, I suppose," he said, directing his remarks in my mother's direction, who was ready and eager to change the subject.

"I didn't get to speak to you this morning, but I wanted to congratulate you on your baptism today," she said. "Your words were a blessing to so many people."

"Thank you, Mrs. Liebermann. You don't know what an encouragement these boys have been to me. Why, they've made me see the value of my childhood again. We should never be too old for the things that really matter. Coming out for my faith—even for this car—may cost me my next campaign, but I don't care," he said. "Do you know, I was almost too old to cry? But this morning I . . . I . . ."

My mother jumped in to help him. "I don't know of anyone who could have sat through that service this morning with dry eyes."

"Well, let me tell you, Mrs. Liebermann, a few weeks ago I could have. I got to where nothing mattered but my political gain. These boys have given me back my humanity . . . and my faith."

He had just breathed a long sigh when Mrs. Beamering came into the waiting room.

"He's going to be fine," she said. "He just got a little worked up, and they've given him something to calm him down. The doctor has requested no more visitors for the day, however."

"Yes, of course. That's understandable," said the mayor. "I'm so sorry—"

"There's nothing to be sorry about. You had no idea he'd seen that article. Besides, these are all Ben's own feelings and they are very important to him. None of you are responsible for that. We can't tell Ben to stop feeling just because his feelings may not be good for his health. If God wants him hot or cold, like he's always been, then everyone else is going to have to learn to take him that way too, including the doctors and nurses around here."

I came home from school the next day to find that Ben's condition had worsened in the night. His fever was still down, but there was something about a lot of water in his lungs. As my mother told me this, she looked like she'd been crying.

"I'll have my papers done in half an hour," I told her, "and then we can go right away."

"I'm afraid not, Jonathan."

"What?"

"I'm sorry, but they've said he cannot have any more visitors until he improves. He's in critical condition, honey."

"Did you talk to Mrs. Beamering? Did she say I couldn't come?" She was the only one I would take a "no" from in this matter, since she virtually ran the hospital in Ben's case.

"No, Jonathan. It's not necessary to bother her. This is hospital policy," she said. "It's for Ben's good. We've just got to let the doctors and the hospital and the Lord take control now."

Yeah. A lot of good they'd done so far. If it hadn't been for Molly, they wouldn't even have known what Ben's problem was. And as far as the Lord was concerned, well, I figured He was on my side. Ben needed me. Ben needed me there. The Lord would be for that. I knew my mother was only doing what she thought was right, but I had to do what I thought was right too.

That afternoon I rifled the papers down every driveway. I didn't even look to see where they landed. The whole thing took a record twenty-five minutes, from folding to the final house. Then I headed straight back to Molly's. I skidded in her driveway, slammed my bike against the fence, and pounded on her back door.

"What is it, laddie? Is it Benjamin?"

"Yes," I panted. "My mother says he's in critical condition. Molly, what's really wrong with him? Yesterday in church his father said he might die. Is he really going to die?"

Molly put her arm around my shoulder and drew me down beside her on the sofa in her living room.

"Yes, Johnny. He might," she said, and then went on to explain exactly what was wrong with Ben.

He had a ventricular septal defect, she said. A VSD. That was the proper medical description for a hole in the membrane that separated the right and left sides of Ben's heart. It was something you were born with, and the seriousness of this defect depended entirely on the size of the hole.

Small VSDs often closed on their own and never posed any

noticeable problems, and some people even lived fairly normal lives with medium-sized VSDs that never closed. For children with small to medium-sized defects, like Ben's, they just had to wait and see.

"The heart is a muscular pump," said Molly. "It sends tired blood to the lungs from one side and rejuvenated blood to the body from the other. But when there's a hole between these sides, it can create a cross-flow and the blood can go to the wrong place."

In essence, Molly said, Ben's heart simply had to work harder than normal hearts in order to get the job done.

What was causing the problem now, however, was the infection.

Children with septal defects were particularly vulnerable to acute bacterial endocarditis, an infection of the heart. Something about the nature of a hole in the heart encourages the bacteria to take hold there, inflame the tissues, and multiply. Before the advent of antibiotics, children who contracted this disease survived only three days to three weeks. By 1958, many cases of endocarditis could be cured with large doses of penicillin and a growing battery of newer antibiotics coming out on the market. In Ben's case, however, so far the bacteria had resisted everything they'd tried.

Last Friday, when his condition worsened, they had first heard what they called a "new murmur" from his heart, meaning it was indeed inflamed with bacteria attaching itself there and creating a different second sound from his normal heartbeat.

I didn't understand everything Molly told me, but I understood enough to know it was serious.

"I've got to see him. He needs me. I've got to be there," I said. I wanted to burst into tears, but I made myself keep talking. "Nobody will listen to me. I've got to see him."

"Go get in the car," Molly said. "I'll be right there as soon as I find the keys," and off she went muttering St. Anthony's prayer.

I went out and opened the wide wooden swinging doors to her garage and got inside the beautiful old Lincoln Zephyr. The seats were gray velvet and there was real wood on the dashboard. It had a musty, oily smell that reminded me of my grandfather's garage in Minnesota. I fought with tears. As long as I kept moving and talking, the black figure couldn't touch me, but when I stopped, it was as if I was being choked.

"Now don't you worry," Molly said as she opened the driver's door and settled behind the wheel. "We'll get you right to him."

It wasn't until she backed up like a shot out of the garage and came within an inch of the side of the house that I remembered Molly wasn't supposed to be driving. It was a minor miracle that we got to the hospital in one piece. If California drivers weren't so defensive, we never would have made it because Molly certainly wasn't looking out for anybody but herself. Point it and step on it and don't stop until you get there. That was Molly's philosophy on her first day at the wheel. And all the while we were bouncing along, she spoke to me as casually and calmly as if we were sitting in her living room.

"I can't guarantee that everything's going to be all right when we get there."

If we get there, I thought.

"I never have been one to give people false hopes. But I can promise you that I will get you to Ben," she said.

At the hospital Molly made one stop to get the information she needed and then took me straight to Ben's room. To my surprise, he was in the same place he had been the day before. His mother was standing in the hallway just outside the door.

"Jonathan," she said with a smile when she saw us. "I'm so glad you're here. He's been asking for you all afternoon. I've been so busy I didn't think to call. Mrs. Fitzpatrick! How good to see you again. Where's your mother, Jonathan?"

"She said Ben was in critical condition and I couldn't come," I said. "But I had to come, so . . . Molly drove me here. My mother's going to be angry, but—"

"Don't you worry about a thing, honey. You go in there and see Ben. I'll handle your mother."

I ran into the room. Ben was propped up in his usual position.

"Hey, how's it going?" he said.

"Good," I managed to say, though it sounded a little funny when I said it. Suddenly everything slowed down and became like it always was when Ben and I were together.

"Get the news out?"

"Yep. Did it in 25 minutes flat today."

"Did you bring me the front page?"

"Oh no, I forgot. I was in too much of a hurry. I can't even remember anything on the front page. Must not have been anything important."

"How'd you get here?"

"Mrs. Fitzpatrick brought me. I'm lucky to be alive. She doesn't know how to drive; she doesn't even have a license. You should see this car she has, Ben. It's a 1939 Lincoln Zephyr in mint condition."

"No kidding? That's a Ford car—one of the best they ever made. How come she brought you?"

"My mother didn't want me to come. She said you couldn't have any visitors. She's gonna have a fit when she finds out. Besides, she doesn't like me spending time with Mrs. Fitzpatrick."

"Why?"

"I don't know. I guess because she's Catholic. And she prays to all these saints like St. Anthony."

"Did you know there's a St. Genevieve?" said Ben. "She's the patron saint of fevers and she also saved Paris from Attila the Hun."

"You could sure use some help from her!"

"That's what I thought. Hey, you know what, they're giving me this stuff that makes me pee every five minutes," he said.

"Yeah? How do you do that? I didn't think they let you out of bed anymore."

"They don't. Look at this." And he pulled back the covers to show me a tube attached to his penis. "How about that? I bet you wish you had one of these."

"I already got one."

"No, the tube, dummy." And we both laughed. I laughed so much I couldn't stop for a while. It felt so good to be laughing with Ben—to know he was there with me and able to laugh.

Just then Attila came in.

"Now, now. No fun allowed," she said, but I could see a bit of a twinkle in her eyes. "I do need to have this nice-looking young man to myself for a while, though, so we can run some tests. You may see him again in an hour."

"Can you stay?" Ben asked as I started for the door.

"Yes," I said, knowing that there was nothing and no one who could get me to move from that hospital.

"So the nurse kicked you out, did she?" said Mrs. Beamering, barely looking up from her magazine as I walked into the waiting room.

"Yeah. She said I could see him again in an hour."

"Yes," she said. "They're running some more tests." And then, without looking up from her magazine, she began to cry. It was a soft, sobbing kind of cry, and she reached out and pulled me to her and leaned her head against my chest. "You're such a good friend to him," she said, and she squeezed me real hard when she said this.

"Mrs. Beamering, can I stay here with you?" I said while she got a Kleenex from her purse and tried to straighten out her face.

"Why, of course you can, Jonathan." Her voice was broken and wet from crying.

"I mean . . . not just now, but tonight . . . tomorrow maybe?"

"Well, that's up to your mother and father. It's certainly all right with me. You can sleep on the couch in here when you get tired. I'm sure Ben would love to have you around."

"Where's Mrs. Fitzpatrick?" I asked.

"She had to go back home. She said she was expecting company."

I thought of her nephew and the car.

"Yeah. She doesn't like having that car out any more than necessary. You should see her drive the thing. I thought I was going to end up getting here in an ambulance. What are you looking at?"

She stopped turning pages and looked right at me with tired red eyes. "Jonathan, I've gone through every magazine in here probably a dozen times, and if you asked me to tell you what was in any one of them, I couldn't tell you a thing. I'm just giving my eyes a place to look for a while that doesn't remind me of a hospital."

"Oh," I said. "What did my mother say?"

"Your mother wasn't home. I'll try again in a few minutes."

"That won't be necessary," said a familiar voice behind us.

"Mom!" I said, turning around and running toward her. "Mother, I'm—"

"It's all right, Jonathan," she said, putting her hand lightly over my mouth. She went over and hugged Mrs. Beamering. "How is he, Martha?"

"Well, he's holding on. That's about all we can say."

"What's this about 'critical condition'? When I called, the hospital said he'd been moved."

"Oh, that must have been earlier this afternoon. They were going to move him, but then he suddenly improved. It's been like that all day. Up and down, up and down." She looked knowingly at my mother and me and added with a smile, "I think I'll go look in on him."

As soon as she was out of the room, we both started to talk at the same time. My mother prevailed.

"It's all right, Jonathan. I'm just glad you're safe. I was worried that I'd find you here in a bed next to Ben. That's not the way I want you visiting him."

"I'm sorry for—"

"No, no. You let me talk. I'm the one who needs to be sorry. I got caught up in the rules. You were following your heart, Jonathan, and that's important, too. I pushed you into disobeying me. Don't worry about it. You made a good choice. I'm just glad you're safe." She pulled me to her and kissed my forehead, and we sat there while she held me close. In the comfort and security of her arms, I felt the tears forming in my eyes. She pulled her face back to look at me and lifted my chin.

"Are you mad about me going with Mrs. Fitzpatrick?" I asked.

"No. She called me and explained what happened," she said, wiping my eyes. "Maybe I have some things to learn too, you know."

"Good," I sniffled. "Then you won't mind if I stay with Ben tonight?"

"If you what?" she said, backing away even farther and making me think she wasn't ready to learn quite that much, that fast.

"I want to stay here with Ben. Mrs. Beamering said it was okay."

"Yes, I'm sure it's all right with Mrs. Beamering," she said, sounding slightly angry. Then she squeezed me real tight again, rocked back and forth, and let out a soft, exasperated sound. "Yes, Jonathan. You can stay . . . and I'll stay with you."

"Gee thanks, Mom," and I hugged her back as hard as I could.

"Mrs. Fitzpatrick told you how sick Ben really is, didn't she?" my mother said.

"Yes," I said. After a few moments I said, "Mom, do you think Ben knows?"

"I don't know," she said.

Truth of the matter was, of course, Ben did know. Ben had known all about his heart since he was seven. In fact, Ben knew more about his problem than his parents. He knew what the chances of survival were, and the possible complications including bacterial endocarditis. You see, Ben knew all about books and libraries and *Nelson's Textbook of Pediatrics*. Ben knew, better than anyone, that of all the places affected by the properties of a vacuum, one of the places where those properties didn't work as well as they should was his own leaky heart.

24

A Bucket for Mrs. Beamering

Spending the night in the hospital wasn't anything like I thought it was going to be. For one thing, I hardly got to see Ben at all. For another, the couch that Mrs. Beamering said I could sleep on wasn't as comfortable as it looked. Since they always seemed to be kicking visitors out of rooms or not letting them in, I figured maybe they put uncomfortable furniture in the waiting rooms so you wouldn't hang around there either.

"That's what most of the rules are for around here," I heard

Mrs. Beamering say to my mother. "They just want to keep people out of their hair as much as possible. Most people never question anything a doctor or nurse says. That's why I dislike hospitals so much. People become so passive—people who should know better. They walk around like ghosts. People lose their dignity here before they ever lose their life."

Between Ben and Mrs. Beamering, this hospital staff had just about all they could handle. On one hand they had Mrs. Beamering virtually throwing the visiting policy out the window, and on the other they had Ben giving doctors and nurses instructions on how to treat his disease.

"If it's a staph infection, you better be giving me more than just penicillin" . . . "How come they haven't gotten a cardiologist in here to see me yet?" . . . "Wait a minute! What is that stuff? Digoxin? Never heard of it. What does it do? Is this a new antibiotic? Am I a test case? I'm not a laboratory rat, you know. Somebody get me a medical dictionary! Where's my mother? *I demand to know what that stuff is that you're putting into my body!*" And before the nurses could even get near him, they had to get a doctor up to Ben's room to give him a detailed description of the procedure and an explanation of exactly why this prescription had been decided upon. Ben always wanted to know all the options.

Once he got so heated that they had to call in an anesthesiologist to sedate him; he was endangering himself by getting so worked up. Ben, however, was convinced that they put him under so they could do what they wanted without having to explain it to him.

"They just wanted to make me give up like everybody else in here," he told me afterward. I was in the room when he came to. I watched his eyes pop open, get their bearings, and then immediately fill with anger as he remembered what had happened.

"Don't you ever do that to me again!" he said for anyone's benefit who might have been in the room at the time, and he repeated it to every person in a white coat who walked into his room that day, whether they had already heard it or not.

"This is not a prison, you know," Ben told me. "I don't have to do everything they say if I don't want to. These guys walk around here like wardens. They use their knowledge to scare people into doing what they want. That's what a hospital does. They make people feel small and helpless. Well, I may be small, but I'm not helpless. Besides, everything these guys know is in a book somewhere, and I can read the same book! After that, it's only a guess. That's what it finally comes down to—an educated guess."

This kind of confrontation had been going on ever since Ben had been admitted. (A word he hated, by the way. " 'Admitted'—sounds like I've been 'committed.' ") By Monday night, however, he was much quieter. Mainly because he was much worse.

Most of the night seemed like a dream. I fell asleep to nightmares and awoke to nightmarish reality so many times that afterward I had difficulty distinguishing them from each other in my memory. It was a lot like the night I spent with the little wren lying dead in the milk carton by my bed.

I did remember being awakened by the rushing sound of men and machines running down the hallway. My head was in my mother's lap, and I sat up and listened. There was a lot of rapid talking coming from the hallway in the direction of Ben's room. I started to awaken my mother, but she was in a deep sleep with her head leaning back on the couch. I decided to let her sleep and see for myself what was going on.

To my dismay, but not to my surprise, it was all coming from Ben's room, and I stood in the doorway and watched as four or five people in white coats worked around him. I had no idea what they were doing except that they did it quickly and furiously. It seemed as if they were mad at him—grabbing and throwing things at him. At one point, they hit him, driving him down into the bed. They did this two or three times. I would have yelled for them to stop, but Ben's parents were right there, and I knew that if what they were doing was wrong, they would be yelling. They weren't. They were standing off to the side. Mrs. Beamering had her hands to her mouth, looking uncharacteristically helpless while Pastor Beamering had one arm around her.

I may have even tried to yell, but just like in a dream, I couldn't tell if any sound was coming out. I couldn't tell if I was even in the picture. Through this whole terrifying scene I felt like an invisible spectator, like the ghost of Ebenezer Scrooge wandering through the mists, looking down on what was and what might be.

It wasn't until the fury subsided and some of the white coats backed away from the bed that Mrs. Beamering came over and touched my face, pulling me to her side and wrapping her arms around me, and I began to think this all might really be happening. Ben's father came over too, and the three of us filled up the doorway.

"Is he dead?" I said, a little surprised that the words actually came out and I could hear them.

"No, Jonathan. Looks like he pulled through this one. It was close . . . too close."

One of the doctors came over then and motioned us out into the hallway.

"I'd like to speak to the two of you—" and then he glanced down at me, "alone."

Mrs. Beamering looked him straight in the eye and said sternly, "I am already as alone as I ever want to be." Her hold on me tightened as she said this. "You will speak to all three of us."

"Very well, then . . . I'm afraid it's only a matter of time. The infection is actually now under control, but his heart has taken a beating and the defect has sustained more permanent damage. This was actually a mild heart attack he just experienced. There may be more. We have to also consider the possibility of embolism—a stroke. He has a good deal of water in his lungs, which explains his shortness of breath. We're giving him something for this, but very honestly, it's like trying to bail water out of a sinking boat. We simply don't have enough buckets or enough time. The hole is too big."

Mrs. Beamering received this news with her head up. Her eyes filled, and her head started shaking. After a few long seconds of painful silence, she said, in a very calm and determined voice that grew louder with each word, "Well, then, get me a bucket. NOW!"

"Martha," Pastor Beamering said, his voice rich with a tenderness I had never heard from him.

Up until that moment, he had seemed weighed down—unable to move. But his wife's response woke something in him. He turned to the doctor and said urgently, "Well, you heard her. Go get my wife a bucket!" And the doctor, the one who normally held people in a suspended state of incapacitation, scurried off in search of something with which to bail out the life of Ben Beamering.

And when Pastor Beamering affirmed her command, Mrs. Beamering suddenly lost her hold of me and crumpled into his arms, weeping loudly. Just then my mother appeared in the doorway of the waiting room, and I ran to her, seeking other arms to hold me.

"Mother . . . Ben is dying."

"Oh, honey," she said, walking me back to the horrible brown couch in the waiting room where she held me tightly for a long time, stroking my forehead and running her soft fingertips through my hair. Her warm comfort cradled my troubled heart. Then, from a special place where only mothers draw their strength, she pulled a song—a hymn she used to sing as a lullaby to Becky and me—and she sang it softly and rocked me gently back and forth in her arms.

> Sometimes on the mount where the stars shine so bright
> God leads His dear children along.
> Sometimes in the valley in darkest of night
> God leads His dear children along.

I'd heard this hymn so many times. I knew all the words. But I never knew what they meant until that night.

> Some through the waters; some through the flood.
> Some through the fire, but all through the blood.
> Some through great sorrow, but God gives a song
> In the night season, and all the day long.

The night season . . . that night felt like a season.

She didn't sing the last verse. Maybe she was hoping she wouldn't need to sing it so soon. I knew better, and I heard it in my heart as she went to humming the tune:

> Away from the mire and away from the clay,
> God leads His dear children along.

Away up in glory—Eternity's Day,
God leads His dear children along.

After some time, while she was still rocking me gently, I heard her mutter under her breath, probably thinking I had fallen asleep, "I don't think it was a good idea for you to be here."

"Mother," I said, "I don't think death is a good idea."

25

Saint Benjamin

The next morning when my mother and I returned to the waiting room to resume our vigil after a rare breakfast out with my father, the noise and bustle that had subsided during the night was back in force. Actually it was breakfast "out" for him but not for us, since we ate downstairs in the hospital cafeteria. My parents tried to get me to go out to a restaurant—even bribed me with my favorite pancake house—but I refused to leave the hospital.

Back up on Ben's floor, bells and buzzers and leather heels on hard linoleum and rolling carts rattling their medicine bottles down crowded hallways were the sounds of daytime returning to the hospital. Even the waiting room exchanged its nocturnal ghostly silence for the friendly conversations of a steady stream of visitors.

All this activity gave the illusion of being out of danger. If Ben had made it through the long sinister night, he could certainly weather the day. Partly because of a lack of sleep and partly because of this false sense of safe passage, I found myself dozing off into a dreamless sleep.

I didn't get to see Ben again until about eleven o'clock that morning when Mrs. Beamering came and hurried me from the waiting room to a new room in another wing where they had moved him after his ordeal in the night. Mrs. Beamering had gotten pretty good at learning how to sandwich me in between nurses' rounds and doctors' examinations.

"Hi," I said, unable to couple it with the usual "How are you?" when the obvious answer lay before me.

"Hi," said Ben weakly. "What are you doing here? Why aren't you in school?"

"Becky went to school. Joshua and Peter went to school. I figured that was enough people at school for one day when you're in here."

"How did you ever get your mother to let you miss a day of school without being sick?"

"I had her talk to your mom," I said, looking around the room. It was newer and better equipped than the old one, and Ben had tubes and clips attached all over him. Looking at him, I felt a growing ache inside. It seemed like every tube and wire attached to his body was sucking away a part of him, leaving behind something that bore a vague resemblance to Ben, but wasn't him at all.

"You look like an overloaded wall socket at Christmastime," I said.

"And if they try and plug one more cord into me, I swear, I'm gonna blow a fuse."

"That was the longest night of my life," I said. "Longer than waiting for the Rose Parade."

"Don't worry, you won't be needing to wait much longer."

I felt a sharp pain inside when he said this, and a strong desire to stand and fight, but I held back. Something was different.

"They can hook me up to as many machines as they want, but it won't matter."

It was his face that was different. Something I had not seen there before. A smile. Not the usual kind of smile people get, with the corners of their mouth turned up and all. Nor was it the kind of smile I was accustomed to seeing on Ben's face—his sinister smile—the look Pastor Beamering said he got when he was "up to something."

The closest I can get to describing it is the look people get the moment someone whispers a secret in their ear. Their eyes are looking off somewhere, or maybe darting around randomly, but they are listening very carefully. There's a bit of a startle and even a silent giggle in this look, because it tickles to have someone whisper in your ear. It's also a look that is suspended, because you can't have a big reaction when someone is whispering in your ear; you have to remain as quiet as possible lest you miss an important word of the secret.

"Jonathan," he whispered, and motioned me close to his lips. Was it because he was running out of strength or because he was trying to listen at the same time?

I leaned my elbows on his bed so I was right up next to him. His voice was like a wisp of air. "You were right. It was God calling me."

"I thought so. What did He say?" I whispered at about the same level.

"He's expecting me."

"Anything else?"

"He's expecting me to go out with a bang."

"How are you going to do that?" I said.

"I'm not sure. That part's up to you."

"Me?" I said, startled.

"Yeah. I can't do it anymore. It has to be you."

"What are you talking about, Ben?"

"I don't know, but I know there's one more laugh. It's a big one. And I know I can't do it from here, so it has to be you." He coughed and wheezed and then continued even more softly. "You did great with the waders."

"Yeah, but that was easy. Besides, you told me what to do."

"This will be easy too, once you know what it is."

I didn't want to know what it was. I didn't want to pull another prank without Ben. I put my hands over my ears and started speaking very loudly. "No! No! Stop talking like this. You're not going anywhere, Ben! You're staying right here with me!"

"Wait a minute, wait a minute, calm down, please!" said a nurse coming in the room—not any nurse we had seen before. She looked at me and suddenly became very angry. "What are you doing here? This is not visiting hours, and even if it was, you can't visit this patient without an adult present. Now you get out of here right now!" Obviously this particular nurse had not yet had the privilege of encountering Ben's mother, who, fortunately, entered the room at precisely that moment.

"Excuse me, this young man is with me," said Mrs. Beamering, "and I will not have anyone speaking to him in such a manner."

"Well, it makes no difference, because I'm ordering you both out of this room right now. This patient cannot tolerate the kind of display that just went on in here!"

"You mean like the one you're putting on right now?" said Ben's mother, very controlled, as if she had something else on her mind and was giving this conversation about half her attention.

The nurse's mouth dropped open and she began turning red. "Mrs.—"

"Beamering. The name is Martha Beamering," Ben's mother said in a kind voice and offered the nurse her hand. When the woman failed to acknowledge the handshake, Mrs. Beamering said, still in a soft but firm voice, "Look, Miss Armstrong, I pay for this hospital, I pay for this room, and I pay for you, and unless you have some specific medical task that you are instructed to perform in here right now, you may leave."

The nurse glowered at her and stormed out of the room.

"I love it when you do that," whispered Ben.

"How did you know her name?" I asked.

"They all wear name tags."

"I could have told you that," said Ben weakly, still in full command of his know-it-all expression.

"Now, do you two have anything you would like to discuss with me?"

"No, Mom," said Ben. "Everythi—" He started coughing and wheezing and gasping for air. Mrs. Beamering immediately pushed the call button, and the same stern-faced nurse came back in.

"He needs oxygen," said Ben's mother, and Miss Armstrong went right to work, though using every moment she could to cast an I-told-you-so look in Mrs. Beamering's direction.

Ben's lung capacity was decreasing, and it had become fairly routine for him to need a fresh shot of oxygen. It was a procedure serious enough to require my leaving the room, however, and I returned to the waiting room with a new conflict of feelings going on inside me.

My mother tried to probe those feelings over lunch in the hospital snack shop, but I couldn't sort them out. I was happy and sad and angry all at once. Happy over Ben talking about God in a positive way for the first time in his life. Sad and angry over what that revelation might cost me personally.

A full stomach and the overly warm waiting room soon buried my confusion under a heavy cloak of sleep until my mother woke me in the middle of the afternoon.

"Ben wants to see you," she said, sounding urgent.

I hated sleeping in the afternoon, mainly because I hated the lethargic where-am-I feeling that came with waking up. Today was no exception, and I walked into Ben's hospital room in a fog.

Ben was propped up in his usual position, looking drawn and pale. Was this it? Was this the dreaded thing? I leaned in close so I could hear him.

"It's three o'clock," he whispered.

I stared at him for a few seconds. He kept looking at me as if this information was supposed to mean something.

"So?" I said.

"Three o'clock," he repeated. "Time to get the news out."

"Oh my gosh! My paper route! I forgot all about it."

Time and life had gotten lost inside the hospital. I had been there almost twenty-four hours, awake most of the night, asleep most of the day. Getting the news out was the furthest thing from my mind.

"Maybe I could get one of your brothers to do it," I muttered. "My dad might do it."

What I couldn't tell Ben was that I was afraid if I left him— left the hospital for any period of time—he would leave me. Somehow I thought that if I was there, I could keep him right there with me. Even after my mother and I had returned that morning from breakfast, I had raced back to his room, sure that something horrible had happened. It had. Someone had misplaced his Edsel, the one the mayor had given him—the one thing he kept by his bed at all times. One of the nurses had inadvertently sent it to the dishwasher on his breakfast tray, and they had to retrieve it from the kitchen.

"No," Ben whispered. "You have to do it yourself. It's your responsibility. Besides, you have to read me the front page. You forgot about it yesterday."

"I'll get my mother to buy a paper downstairs."

"Jonathan, you don't understand, do you?" and I felt one of his lectures coming on. I wanted to tell him to save his precious breath, but I didn't. "You can't stay here with me. You can't go with me, either. You're not being hot or cold right now. You're just wandering around here looking like God already spewed you out of His mouth." Then he motioned me closer to him, and I leaned over and put my ear right up to his face. His whisper was like a shout. "Jonathan, I'm the one who's sick. You have to get the news out! It's your job."

My mother couldn't believe she had forgotten about the paper route too. She said something about the loss of time one experiences in a hospital and took me home, then went on to the church to pick up my father.

All the while I folded and delivered my papers, I kept thinking about what Ben had been telling me and fighting a major war inside. Mostly I just wanted to feel sorry for myself and be comforted. I wanted to immobilize myself, and here was Ben, the very person I wanted to grieve over, giving me an assignment—telling me I had to complete his vision. It seemed like the joke to be played was on me.

When I got to Molly's house, I caught a glimpse of her down the driveway working on her trellis of roses. I turned up the driveway and approached so fast that I startled her. She dropped the box she was holding, and the dead roses she'd picked off the trellis sprayed all over the driveway. I apologized and started picking them up.

"How's Benjamin?" she asked.

"Well enough to remind me about my paper route."

"Hmm. That sounds like the lad."

"Molly," I said, fingering the feathery, light-brown petals, "when people are going to die, do they know?"

"Most of the time," she said. "Especially if they've had time to think about it."

"Do they see visions and hear from God and stuff?"

"Now that would depend on how well they've heard from Him most of their life. Has Benjamin been hearin' from God?"

"He says he has."

"Well, then, laddie, haven't you been telling me yourself that Benjamin is usually right about things?"

"Yes," I said, handing her the box.

"So why would you go doubtin' him now?"

"Thanks, Molly," I said as I hopped on my bike and headed home. She hadn't said anything that would refute or change what Ben had said, but somehow I felt better about it.

By the time my mother and father and Becky and I got back to the hospital that evening, Pastor and Mrs. Beamering and Ben's brothers were all there. While they visited with Ben, I stayed in the background with the front page of the *Star-News* folded and bulging in my back pocket. I did this on purpose in order to try something Ben and I had talked about earlier. I would hide in the closet in his room until everyone left. That way, I could slip in and out of sight without being detected and we could spend more time together. It worked perfectly, since there were enough people milling around that I was not noticed or missed.

And thus it happened that from the wardrobe closet in Ben's hospital room I heard what turned out to be everyone's last words with him—everyone except Mr. and Mrs. Beamering's and my own. There was really nothing significant about these words except that they were each so right. My mother quoted a scripture verse. Peter and Joshua both joked with their younger brother. Becky kissed him through a nose full of sniffles. I knew that because Ben said, after a moment of silence, "Yuck! Wipe your nose off next time!" and everyone laughed. My father, though, was the very best of all, filling up the empty space of his moment with exactly the right thing—the thing he could do best. He started singing the doxology, and everyone joined him, all huddled around Ben's bed. I even sang from the closet.

Ben's eyes were still wet when I came out into the room after everyone was gone.

"Rehearsal," he whispered. "That was rehearsal for when I get to sing with these guys," and he pointed to a large blue book on the table by his bed. It was a book of patron saints, like the one I had seen at Molly's house. "Pull it out. I want to show you."

"Where did you get this?" I asked, opening it on his bed.

"Mrs. Fitzpatrick loaned it to me."

"So this is how you found out about Atilla the Hun, huh? What do your parents think about this?"

"My dad isn't sure, but my mom thinks it's great. She's been reading a lot of it to me. Some of it seems superstitious, like the patron saint of snakebites, but I like hearing about their lives. A lot of these people died for what they believed." He paused to catch his breath. "Read me page 62. I love page 62."

I opened the book to page 62. "St. Apollonia?"

"Yeah. Read to me about St. Apollonia."

" 'Apollonia, Martyr, A.D. 249,' " I read. " 'St. Dionysius of Alexandria wrote to Fabius, Bishop of Antioch, an account of the persecution of the Christians by the heathen populace of Alexandria in the last year of the reign of the Emperor Philip. The first victim of their rage was a venerable old man named Metras or Metrius, whom they tried to compel to utter blasphemies against God. When he refused, they beat him, thrust splinters of reeds into his eyes, and stoned him to death. The next person they seized was a Christian woman, called Quinta, whom they carried to one of their temples to force her to worship the idol. She addressed their false god with words of scorn which so exasperated the people that they dragged her by the heels over the cobbles, scourged and then stoned her. By this time the rioters were at the height of their fury. The Christians offered no resistance but betook themselves to flight, abandoning their goods without complaint because their hearts had no ties upon the earth. Their constancy was so general that St. Dionysius knew of none who had renounced Christ.' "

I was just getting to the part about Apollonia when we heard someone coming. I ducked back in the closet for a five-minute nurse check.

"It's working," Ben said of our plan when the coast was clear. "Great. Now go on about St. Apollonia."

" 'Apollonia, an aged deaconess, was seized. With blows in the face they knocked out all her teeth, and then, kindling a great fire outside the city, they threatened to cast her into it unless she uttered certain impious words. She begged for a moment's delay, as if to consider the proposal; then, to convince her persecutors that her sacrifice was perfectly voluntary, she no sooner found herself free than she leaped into the flames of her own accord.' "

"How about that?" said Ben. "Bet you can't wait to meet her, huh?"

"Is that why she's the patron saint of toothaches—because she got her teeth knocked out? If that's the case, then you could be the patron saint of broken noses."

"Jonathan, I am a saint," Ben said.

He motioned for the book and began flipping through its pages, as if refilling his mind with the contents he had already read.

"You think it's okay to read a book about Catholics?" I said.

"Jonathan, in 249 A.D. these were the only Christians around. You either believed or you didn't. It's the same now, don't you think?"

All I could think of right then was how Molly really did believe in Christ and how Ben was a saint.

"Have you got the news?" he asked, suddenly changing the subject.

I pulled the paper from my back pocket and reluctantly unfolded the front page of the *Star-News* for Tuesday, January 20, 1959. The headlines were not good. There was a lost boy for whom hopes were fading, a critically ill governor of Alaska who had a 50–50 chance of survival, and the Midwest was bracing itself against heavy storms and blizzards headed their way. None of these met with any reaction from either one of us. There was nothing to say about the obvious.

I saved the smallest headline for last, figuring we could use some humor, braced as we were against our own storm. It was a tiny article, only four lines long, about United Nations Secretary General, Dag Hammarskjold, leaving New York's Idlewild Airport that day for a five-day vacation in Nassau, Bahamas. The headline read simply "Dag Vacationing," but as a small headline in smudgy newsprint, it looked more like "Dog Vacationing." Ben and I enjoyed a good laugh, imagining a beagle in sunglasses and Bermuda shorts taking off for the Bahamas.

"There you are!" said my mother as I returned to the waiting room, just when I figured they would be wondering about me. "We've been looking all over for you."

There was one headline I didn't read. I couldn't. Every word of it, as well as its brief accompanying article, was too painful.

Atlas Satellite Nearing End
SAN DIEGO—AP—The Atlas satellite was reported today to have become erratic as it neared the end of its orbiting of the earth.

Tom Hemphill, voluntary tracker for the Smithsonian Astrophysical Conservatory, said the Atlas should plunge into a blazing end in the earth's atmosphere tonight or tomorrow. Its erratic behavior, however, made it difficult to figure where it will be at any given time.

26

Headlines

On the day Ben died a bitter snowstorm buried the Midwest killing twelve people, tornadoes ripped through six southern states, President Eisenhower warned Russia that the United States "simply won't be pushed around," a heart attack ended the fabulous career of Hollywood producer Cecil B. deMille, the governor of Alaska still hovered near death, and a fiery comet spotted in the Pacific somewhere before dawn was thought to be the fall of America's giant Atlas satellite. On Wednesday, January 21, 1959, the front page of the *Star-News* told the whole story.

But I didn't know any of this at 2:30 that morning when I snuck into Ben's room and found everyone asleep. It would be twelve hours before that news would be printed and ready to deliver.

The hospital was quiet in an eerie sort of way. It seemed like everyone was either gone or asleep. Even the usual presence of doctors and nurses was not evident, although it had been that ominous rushing sound of men and machines that had awakened me. Fearing another crisis, I ran out into the hall, only to discover the moving menace floating down the hallway in the opposite direction of Ben's room. I looked back at my mother, still asleep in the waiting room. With everything so quiet and empty, I could slip into Ben's room unnoticed.

Everyone there was asleep, too. Mr. and Mrs. Beamering slumped uncomfortably in their chairs over by the window, and Ben's eyes were closed, his breathing short and labored. It was as if an angel of sleep had passed over our little group and touched everyone but me.

I walked up to Ben's bed and stood there for a while watching him sleep. I had the strongest urge to be as close to him as possible. Lifting up the covers, I crawled in next to him and closed my eyes. Once I was beside him, a peace filled me, and I wanted this moment to last forever. Then, with my eyes still closed, I felt Ben reach over and shake my shoulder gently.

"Jonathan," he said very softly, not because he was trying not to awaken his parents, but because it was as loud as he could speak.

"Yes?" I pulled myself up on one arm to be even with him in his propped-up state. His face was a pale, colorless moon and his thin, delicate lips had a bluish tint.

"Why didn't you read to me about the Atlas satellite?"

"How did you know about that?"

"You showed me the paper, dummy. It was in the column right next to the vacationing dog."

"Oh."

We lay there listening to the silence. The only sounds were a fan on some medical equipment in the room and Mr. Beamering snoring lightly. There was a sense of expectancy in the room, as though everything really had stopped for this moment, waiting for something.

"You know the song 'Jesus Loves Me'?" Ben said, breaking the stillness. "I can sing it now . . . except that I can't get enough breath to sing. Would you sing it for me?"

"Right now?" I said, looking over at Ben's sleeping parents.

"No, there's not enough time now. Sing it sometime for me for everyone in the church the original way—the way it was written."

"What do you mean, there's not enough time?"

I watched his eyes look toward the clock on the wall. "It's three o'clock," he said. "Time to get the news out."

I looked away from his face, toward the clock, and saw that it was indeed three o'clock. Then I looked back at Ben. His eyes were closed, and his head had fallen back on the pillow.

"It's only three o'clock in the morning, Ben. It's not afternoon yet," I said. Suddenly I heard a whine from one of the machines.

"Ben?" I took his limp hand in mine, shaking it lightly.

"Ben?" I said a little louder as a whirl of activity gathered around me.

"Ben!" I shouted, and what I took to be a dark, hooded figure pulled me from the bed and swept me out of the room. It was an attendant, grabbing me along with the sheet off Ben's bed in such haste that the sheet engulfed me in darkness.

"Ben!"

27

The Last Prank

I'm convinced that in the history of the *Pasadena Star-News* there has never been, nor ever will be, a more dedicated paper boy than I was for the next two days. I delivered the news with military precision at exactly three o'clock, every fold, every landing accurate. Delivering the *Star-News* was all I could do. It was the closest I could get to Ben.

On Wednesday and Thursday I was already sitting on the front porch at 11:00 in the morning, waiting for Tony to show up in his red Chevy at 2:30. Becky tried to talk to me, my mother tried incessantly, and once my father even got mad. I ignored them all, refusing to be comforted. I was convinced that no one could understand what I was feeling—no one could possibly have a reason to grieve like me.

I did find some comfort in having Ben's Edsel with me—the one the mayor had given him. Mrs. Beamering had given it to me before I left the hospital the last time. For those first few days after his death, that car never left my side, even when I delivered the paper.

Then, on Thursday afternoon, I remembered the tower. It was the one place I wanted to go. So on Thursday evening, when I finally uttered words at supper, you would have thought the Lord had returned. I only asked if I could go with my father to choir practice, but he seemed overjoyed to oblige.

As soon as we arrived at the church I went in search of Grizzly. He was in the basement putting away Christmas decorations. When he saw me, he tightened his lips and then began to cry. I ran to him as fast as I could, and we held each other for a long time. Then we guided each other over to the stairs and sat down together on the bottom step.

Grizzly was the perfect companion for me at that moment of my life. I don't know what I would have done without him. He couldn't speak; he couldn't hear; he could only sit next to me and understand, and those were the two things—and the only two things—I really wanted right then.

We sat there together, staring at the ground, at each other once in a while, and off into the dark catacombs of the basement. We sniffled and wiped our eyes and let out long deep sighs. Once I cried uncontrollably—the first time I had truly cried since Ben's death. I knew if I cried at home someone would come and put their arms around me and tell me things—things that were probably true, but that I did not want to hear. I did not want to be comforted; I only wanted companionship in my sorrow. Grizzly gave me the comfort of mutual tears.

We sat there until I began to realize choir practice was well under way and there was little time to lose.

First, I informed Grizzly of my plan. I made the sign for the tower, then pointed to myself and walked up an imaginary ladder with my fingers; then I made the sleep sign, laying my head over on my hands. He repeated the gestures, and I nodded my head in confirmation. Then I pointed at him and straightened my back and crossed my arms and made a mean face. His eyes lit up with delight.

Then he took me by the hand and led me to the door of the tower, pointed at me, and then up; then he turned and stood with his back to the door and his arms folded in front of him, looking every bit like the Grizzly for which we had named him. When I nodded vigorously, he pulled out his pad and wrote "HOW LONG?" on it. I crossed out the "HOW" and the question mark and added an "A" above "LONG" and "TIME" below it. He nodded his head and motioned for me to wait right there and he would be back.

Minutes later he returned with two pillows and two blankets. He handed one of each to me and unlocked the door to the tower. Before I entered, he put his own pillow and blanket down on the floor next to the door to assure me he would be staying there with me. I hugged him, turned, and started up the stairs, feeling free for the first time in days.

At the landing, I looked out through the little window and was surprised to see my father's back. He was standing only a few rows from the window in the middle of the balcony.

"Okay, together now, everybody turn your stoles over to the white side . . . okay, hold it for a minute. Now back to the green . . . that's it," he said, clasping his hands together. He was checking to see how the new choir robes looked from there. I remembered the conversation he and my mother had had in the car on the way to church and then realized that conversation had taken place only four days before. It felt like a year had gone by since then.

"Thank you very much, choir, for an excellent rehearsal. I'll see you all on Sunday morning. Don't forget to take home the 'Gloria'—those of you who are unfamiliar with it. We begin work on that next week, and I'd like us all to have a head start."

"Sectionals!" I could hear someone shouting from the choir as my father cupped his ear.

"Oh yes, thank you, Ira. Remember, twenty minutes early next week for sectionals. Thanks very much, everybody! Good job tonight!"

I set about arranging a small bed for myself on the landing. There was just enough room to lie down. Then I checked our provisions. They were meager, but hunger was the last thing on my mind. Sleep was foremost, and somehow I felt that here in this safe place, close to memories of Ben, I would finally be able to sleep.

Next I lay down and tested my bed. It was the best little bed in the whole world, I thought right then. It was a private bed, a stairway away from everyone. I surveyed the tiny closet of a room with my flashlight as I lay there, noticing the notches in the wood, the notes we had tacked here and there, the nails and nooks and crannies in the walls that had turned into other things in Ben's and my imagination. In that place, at that time, I did not feel his loss. I felt, in fact, as if I had found him again, and I felt again the peace I had known lying next to him in the hospital just before he died.

Suddenly I heard my father's voice coming up through the floor.

"Jonathan! Jonathan, are you up there? . . . Mr. Griswold, you must move."

A smile slowly formed on my face. I imagined that it looked a lot like Ben's old smile.

"Jonathan, I know how you feel, but you can't run away forever."

Oh yeah? I thought. For right then and there, I felt like I could.

"Harvey, can you make him come down?"

And then it was quiet again. Every few minutes I got up and checked on our car through the slatted vent at the front of the tower. My father was probably calling my mother from his office, trying to figure out what to do. I wondered if he would call the Beamerings. Mrs. Beamering would understand what I was doing. Perhaps even Mr. Beamering would, and suddenly I realized how much Ben's father had changed.

Whoever my father talked to must have convinced him of something, because I soon heard his voice again coming up through the stairwell in the tower.

"Jonathan, Harvey will take good care of you. If you need anything, you can always give us a call. There's food and juice in the refrigerator in the kitchen. . . . I love you, son."

It was quiet again until I heard a car start. I got to the vent just in time to see him drive off. After that I crawled back into my blanket and fell into a deep and peaceful sleep.

In the morning I awoke surrounded by memories. Thin slats of sunlight streamed in through the vent, and I watched the dust dance in the sunbeams. I remembered the rays of Ben's flashlight playing on the organ pipes. I saw doves fly and fireworks fill the church with smoke. I imagined Ben still behind the pipes, or across from me in the tower, or listening in on a conversation through the vents of one of the church offices. Over and over again, I imagined him coming up the stairs, announcing, "I've got an idea!"

I thought of our houses, still incomplete. They would stay that way. I had no desire to finish them without him. I thought of our cars and the Edsel I had bought him and felt proud that it now stood on display in the office of the mayor of Pasadena. I took the car that the mayor had given to Ben and rolled it back and forth across the blanket, watching the slatted light make rippling lines across it and its pronouncement: "Official Tournament of Roses Car."

I had brought one other thing home from the hospital. It was a piece of paper I had discovered in my hand after being pulled out of Ben's bed. It was all rolled up and limp, as though he had held it in his hand for a long time. He must have slipped it to me when we were lying together side by side, though I didn't remember it.

I found out later that Ben had, in fact, clasped this piece of paper in his hand for days. His mother told me that it got to be a bone of contention with the nurses because he would not let it go for any reason, even in his sleep. I didn't know that at the time. All I knew was that Ben had entrusted it to me. On one side was a hospital breakfast menu, and on the other he had written:

Saturday, January 17, 1959
There is a God-shaped vacuum in the heart of Ben.
There is a Ben-shaped vacuum in the heart of God.

January 17 was the day before the baptism. This treasure was

Ben's record of the vision his father spoke of from the baptismal pool.

I tacked it to the wall of the tower in a prominent place.

This was Ben's own revelation. His odd shape, the horse-collar grille of his mouth, his sunken cheeks, the taillights of his ears curved inward, the gears of his mind that shifted from buttons in the steering column of his inner direction, the engine that ran with a fatal flaw, doomed from the start—this was all a part of the shape of Ben, and this was all loved by God and given a purpose on earth and in heaven. Ben was official.

Though provisions were available throughout my vigil, I did not eat much, for by Friday night the loss began to settle in. I'm not sure whether it was knowing Ben's body was lying open for viewing in a silent room somewhere nearby, or whether the simple effects of time were wearing on me, but the replay of my memories no longer satisfied my hunger for the real Ben. By Friday night, I had played the record so many times that it was already worn and scratched, and that night the nightmare of the wren in the milk carton came back, except it was Ben in a gray coffin beside my bed. More than once in my dreams I pulled his limp body up to the faucet and let the water run over his blue lips. "Drink, Ben . . . drink!" I said over and over before I would wake up alone in the tower. Twice during the night I woke Grizzly and had him sit up with me.

At eight o'clock Saturday morning they brought in the casket. They placed it right in front of the church with two large sprays of flowers on either end. Its small size emphasized his untimely death. It made me wish they had put him in an adult-sized coffin, for though his years were few, his life had adult-sized consequences. Besides, I decided, death was very adult.

I stood up in the tower and stared down at the lonely box for a long time. When I buried the little bird, I had put some flowers in its shoe-box coffin. Maybe I should send Ben away with something. I thought of the note, but he had given that to me. Besides, the note was a message for the living, not the dead. Then I thought of the Edsel the mayor had given him. That seemed appropriate. The Edsel was going to die; the writing was on the wall. The '58 Edsel was already dead, and that's the one we liked anyway. It seemed right that it should go along with

Ben as a symbol for both of them. They were both classic designs.

It was around 8:45 when Grizzly and I went down to the coffin. As we approached it, I felt a growing sense of rage building inside me. That gray box looked so heavy—so impenetrable. I had subsisted on memories for the last three days. Suddenly I realized there would be no new ones, and the old ones were no longer satisfying my appetite for life with Ben. By the time I reached the casket I was ready to pound on it, which I did but found no relief. Finally I cried out something I had been thinking about all morning—something Ben had said in the hospital that stuck with me.

"Well, you finally got your wish, Ben. You made a success of doing the wrong thing, after all. You died. THAT WAS THE WRONG THING TO DO!" and I wept with my face in my forearm on the hard gray surface.

After the tears dried up, I stood there gathering courage. How would I get the car in there with him? It meant I had to open the casket. I wondered if it was locked.

To my surprise, the lid split in half at the middle and opened easily. I stared in shock. I looked at Grizzly, and he was equally surprised.

Who was this? Was it Ben? It was his ears, definitely, and his fine hair and broken nose, but something wasn't right. This was not Ben.

Grizzly pointed at his own mouth and then, putting his fingers on either corner of his lips, he pushed them up into a fake, non-Grizzly-like smile.

That was it! It was the smile. They had Ben smiling the kind of sick, sweet smile that had never once found its way on his face in life. Whatever they had done was something that the muscles of Ben's face were incapable of doing on their own. This was the face of a child that most mothers would love, with the exception of Mrs. Beamering, and I wondered how it had gotten by her. Perhaps she was too overcome with grief to notice, or perhaps by then she didn't care. Well, I had noticed, and so had Grizzly.

In his attempt to show me what was wrong, Grizzly gave me an idea—a sinister, diabolical, Ben-shaped idea. Once again, Grizzly pushed up the corners of his mouth into a smile, shook his head "No," and then placed his large hand over his entire face, gripped it, and twisted it all up, and then removed his hand, freezing his face in that twisted-up position, and nodded his head slowly up and down. I couldn't help but laugh. I stood there right next to Ben's body and laughed, and then I started wondering if we could do that to Ben's face.

At first I couldn't believe I was thinking of doing this. It was wrong. It was desecrating. It was downright creepy! But once in, I could not get the thought out of my mind. This look was wrong too. This man-made look that had found its way to the face of my best friend was the real desecration. It was a betrayal of Ben's own God-given character. If he was supposed to go fill up a Ben-shaped place in the heart of God with this face, he would wander eternity looking for it.

Suddenly I knew: this was it. This was my mission. This was the one last prank Ben had instructed me to carry out. He'd said I would know when I found it, and he was right.

The more I looked at him, the more I realized he would be mad at me if I didn't do something. This face was the work of someone who didn't know Ben. It was a bogus face. Even if they had worked from a photograph, they had betrayed the truth, because I knew what every photograph of Ben looked like—from the very first one I had seen in the church bulletin to the very last one on the front of the *Star-News*.

Suddenly it was as if I was hearing Ben say, "Let's do it." And without bothering to think about it any further, I said out loud, "This one's for you, Ben." And I reached my hands into the coffin, grabbed his face, and twisted with all my might.

It was awful. The rubbery skin resisted my grasp, and its waxy surface slipped under my fingers. I wanted to run, but it was too late. I tightened my grip and squeezed harder, then pulled my hands back, turned around, and slid down the side of the coffin to the floor, staring at the makeup on my hands.

What have I done? I thought. What came over me? What would become of me when they found out? Maybe there's a way we could lock this thing so they'd never be able to open it again. I can't believe I did this.

Just then Grizzly shook me and pulled me up to look at the results of my wrestling. I stared at Ben's face in another kind of shock this time. Then Grizzly and I looked at each other in amazement.

"It's Ben!" I said out loud. "I can't believe it. It's him!" Grizzly nodded in agreement, reading my lips.

Actually, the change was relatively minor. I had been expecting living skin, soft and pliable. I didn't know that when someone had been embalmed, the fluids under the skin coagulated and hardened almost like rubber. In the process of trying to change the face, I had wiped off the makeup, leaving more of the real face of Ben Beamering.

Just then we heard the door of the church office close. Someone was here! I quickly placed the Edsel in next to the body and closed the coffin lid. Grizzly and I just made it out the back of the sanctuary before Pastor Beamering walked in the side door.

Back up in the tower, I looked at my hands covered with makeup and came close to throwing up. I tried wiping them on the blanket, but it seemed like my hands would never come clean.

I looked out the little window and saw Pastor Beamering standing in front of the coffin. He had his shirt sleeves rolled up and his hands stretched out on it, leaning over, praying or crying. When his shoulders shook, I knew he was crying.

Suddenly, to my utter horror, he lifted the lid of the coffin. He looked inside, then turned and looked around the room as if searching for someone, and then looked back at the coffin. When he looked around the room, I could see his face, and it had a wounded look. I imagined him surveying the damage and wondering if the mortuary could repair it. I wondered how long I could stay in the tower. Grizzly couldn't guard me for the rest of my life. They would never forgive me for this.

Once again his shoulders began to shake, and they were still shaking when he put the lid down. But when he turned to leave, it seemed like he had a smile on his face. Had something snapped inside him? Or had he, too, seen the real Ben?

At about 10:30 the first mourners started arriving. I heard the car doors slam, and I watched through the vent as each family made their way to the steps of the church. I watched them smile and try to say pleasant things to one another. I watched the smiles disappear as they mounted the steps to the church. For the next half hour it was motors revving and car doors slamming and high heels clicking on the sidewalk.

At five minutes to eleven, a hearse drove up and parked directly in front of the church, with a limousine behind it. The two drivers, in black suits, got out and stood by their cars. I had the strongest desire to see what the inside of those cars looked like, especially the limousine.

Then I moved across to the other window as Milton Owlsley started playing Beethoven's "Ode to Joy." My father read some scripture, and then two people got up and said something, but not loudly enough to make it through the little window in the tower. I didn't care. This was the only part of the service that didn't make sense. Neither of these people were people Ben would have even been remotely interested in hearing from. One was the children's church substitute who played the accordion, and the other was the deacon who had pulled Ben off the organ scaffolding.

Pastor Beamering then stood up and asked for "a time of silent prayer." No sooner did he say this than a woman dressed in black with a black shawl over her head moved swiftly out into the center aisle, knelt, and made the sign of the cross. Then she walked down to the closed casket, where she knelt and made the sign of the cross again and began to pray. Had she waited a few moments before coming down, many people would have missed this, having their heads bowed and eyes closed in proper Standard Christian mode. Unfortunately these Standard Christians were not quick enough to go into their prayer mode before Molly Fitzpatrick went into hers.

Next came a long uncomfortable silence while Molly knelt alone at the casket, praying fervently, oblivious to the tension that was mounting in the room.

After a long time, which didn't appear to bother Pastor Beamering at all, a woman and a girl got up and knelt next to Molly. I could hardly believe my eyes. It was my mother and Becky. Three-fourths of the congregational heads rose when they did this to see who it was, for these heads were not bowed in prayer; they were only at half-mast, scanning the tops of the heads in front of them in search of the next thing that might happen. Then a man went forward. Then a woman. Then an entire family. That began a trickle of folks coming forward until nearly half the congregation was down front on their knees. Pastor Beamering was one of them. He went over to where Mrs. Beamering was sitting, and together they walked over and knelt among their congregation near the coffin.

If Ben could only see this, I thought. Half the congregation and his father and mother on their knees around him, while he lay inside his little gray box with a smirk on his face.

It was during this time, many children later said, that they heard, from somewhere up and behind them, a voice unlike Ben's, but one that reminded them of him, since it was singing the only song Ben ever sang.

Finally Pastor Beamering stood up beside the casket, like a general amid a fallen army, and the people began to return to their seats. Molly was the last to go.

"Thank you, Mrs. Fitzpatrick, for leading us in prayer," Pastor Beamering said. "Most of you don't know this, but Mary K. Fitzpatrick is a retired nurse who has been of invaluable assistance to us since Ben's accident, for no real reason other than her loving concern and the fact that she was the one who got the knock on the door at 5:30 in the morning three Sundays ago. Has it only been that long?" he said, looking at his wife.

"I wasn't going to speak at all this morning, but I've had second thoughts. Something happened earlier today that changed my mind.

"Last night, as is our usual custom here at the Colorado Avenue Standard Christian Church, we had a small private viewing for family and close friends at the mortuary. It was an extremely difficult and sad occasion for me. Though Ben lay so peacefully with such a happy smile on his face, there was nothing but agony in our hearts.

"This morning I came to the church early, and as God would have it, I decided to risk one more look at my son, knowing I would not see the body this morning as a part of our service. I think I wanted to be totally alone with him to say goodbye one last time.

"When I looked at Ben's face this morning, however, it seemed to me that something had changed. It's hard to see through heavy tears, but the Ben I saw last night was a much sweeter, nicer Ben than the one lying here this morning. The more I looked at him, the more I was convinced that this was not just my tears. Something or someone, it matters not, had altered Ben's face since last night. The sweet smile was gone. In its place was a grimace—a sort of twisted-up face."

At this point, he stepped over closer to the gray pill-shaped box and laid one hand on it. I held my breath.

"Now, as you might imagine, my first reaction was outrage—that such a thing could happen seemed like a desecration of something sacred. But as I stood there and looked at his face, many things came to mind which changed my thinking.

"First, I realized that the sacred part of Ben is gone from here. There is nothing sacred about this shell of a body. It is only a temporary housing for the eternal soul, no longer useful in its purpose since that soul has gone to be with its Creator."

He pulled out a handkerchief and wiped his eyes. He seemed to move in slow motion.

"Then suddenly I realized that I was looking at something very familiar. I was looking at Ben's real face." He replaced his handkerchief in his pocket and turned and held out his hands, gesturing as he spoke. "The smiling face in the mortuary last night was probably what we always wished Ben was like. But it was not the way he was. Was I going to remember him the way I always wanted him to be or the way he was? Actually, the smile was the real twist on the face of Ben. Our twist. It wasn't Ben. Never was."

Now he moved away from the coffin and talked as he walked, leaning into the first row of pews and even coming up the aisle a few steps. It seemed as if he had just realized there were people there and they had suddenly triggered his automatic calling to preach. Suddenly his message was bigger than his grief.

"God made Ben this way, and we had better not mess with it, because something tells me that God wants Ben back just the way He made him. In fact, Ben's probably smirking up there right now at all of us, and most certainly at me.

"Whoever or whatever did this to Ben's face did us all a favor. For had we sent him away with that sweet little smile, who he was and what he stood for would have been that much easier to dismiss. We could have all shed a tear and then gone back to our lives unaltered.

"Come on now, think back with me and remember." Here he twirled around and startled everyone with the strength of his voice.

"This is the face that first WOKE US UP around here and made the light of Christ shine on us. This is the face that made doves and arrows fly through the air, reminding us of spiritual warfare and of our freedom in Christ. This is the face that unearthed a need for forgiveness among us and made us all face ourselves as well, for you cannot remove a speck from your brother's eye without dealing with the beam in your own. And this is the face that set our hearts flying in praise like streamers from the organ.

"That's the way I want you to remember Ben—not with a happy face, smiling in the sweet by and by, but with that tart little face that will forever be smirking at our neat, orderly, comfortable spirituality.

"That face that will remind us that we all have questions and doubts and we should voice them. That face that says what it means and means what it says. That face that will keep us honest and, at the right time, keep us laughing.

"For in the end, that is the greatest thing Ben gave us. He made us laugh. And though there is certainly a time and a place for crying this morning, I know that Ben would also want us laughing. In fact, I think, in the end, it is Ben who has had the last laugh on us all."

And with that final word, Pastor Beamering walked over and sat down next to his wife, and she reached out and held him close. Then my father got up and led the congregation in a hymn and then invited all who wished to remember Ben's face to come view the casket following the benediction.

"And for those of you who are planning on following us to the cemetery," he said, "you will need to plan accordingly, because Mayor Seth Wilson has arranged for a police escort and a five-mile ride down the entire Tournament of Roses Parade route on Colorado Avenue—as his memorial to Ben." My mouth dropped open, and I froze as my father continued, "And, Jonathan, if you can hear me, you have a personal invitation from the mayor to ride with him in the lead car. He is eager for you to join him."

I didn't hear the benediction as I stepped across to the other side of the tower. Sure enough. There, lined up in front of the hearse, was the mayor's Edsel, top down, draped with garlands of red roses, glistening in the sun.

"Yes, I'll go," I said to Mayor Wilson who was waiting for me at the foot of the stairs. "As long as Grizzly gets to ride too."

"Absolutely," beamed the mayor.

And as the uniformed officers in the mayor's police escort kicked their motorcycles into a low rumble and Grizzly and I climbed into the backseat of Ben's favorite car, it seemed entirely appropriate that Ben's funeral would end with a parade.

Acknowledgments

All the headlines from the *Pasadena Star-News* are actual headlines as dated, except for the ones directly related to characters in the story. Also, the mayor of Pasadena really did ride in a new Edsel in the 1958 Tournament of Roses Parade. I have a picture to prove it, courtesy of Dan McLaughlin, Pasadena Public Library.

I would like to thank my friend Dr. Rod Byron, with whom I played cars as a boy, for both his medical knowledge and his childhood memories; Dr. Jones Stewart for getting me into the Los Angeles County Medical Association Library; Dr. Ira Walstrom for "a second opinion"; Elizabeth Thaymer for her knowledge of colorful Catholics and for loaning me her book on patron saints; Nancy Nicholson for locating the Pascal quotation and for second opinions on Catholicism; my father for unearthing two weeks' worth of *Star-News* headlines from the Pasadena Public Library and for his valuable insights into the properties of a vacuum and other applicable physics experiments; Kathleen Cunningham for her ever-available encouragement and critique; Judith Markham for editing the manuscript; Carol and Gary Johnson of Bethany House Publishers for a platform for my writing; and, most important, Marti Fischer for constantly breathing life into these characters and their story.

Four books provided valuable information for this story: Jan Deutsch's *Selling the People's Cadillac: The Edsel and Corporate Responsibility* (New Haven and London: Yale University Press, 1976); Robert Lacey's *Ford: The Men and the Machine* (Boston: Little, Brown and Company, 1986); Michael Walsh's *Butler's Lives of Patron Saints* (San Francisco: Harper & Row, 1987); and Os Guinness's excellent anthology of the writings of Blaise Pascal,

The Mind on Fire (Portland, Oregon: Multnomah Press, 1989).

Final acknowledgment goes to the young boy who, unknowingly, inspired the character of Ben by a mere look on his face on the morning of his father's inaugural sermon in a certain Baptist church in Florida. I have subsequently learned, from one who knows him, that he and Ben actually have a lot in common. I wish him a long life full of the questions that keep everyone around him thinking, and wondering, and guessing.

THE
SAINTS'
AND
ANGELS'
SONG

See that you do not look down on one of these little ones. For I tell you that their angels in heaven always see the face of my Father in heaven.

—THE GOSPEL OF MATTHEW

Our Jane has climbed the golden stair
And passed the jasper gates;
Henceforth she will have wings to wear,
Instead of roller skates.

—*Harper's Weekly,* 1980

Contents

Summer 1959

The roof went easily; it was not properly braced. The walls were surprisingly strong under my foot, however. It seemed, for a second, that I could almost stand on them. But the balsa wood two-by-fours were simply not strong enough for my eleven-year-old weight and they quickly gave in with a loud "Crunch!" I stepped back and surveyed the path of destruction that cut a swath through the entryway, half the kitchen, and most of the living room. And then, my cheeks hot with rage, I jumped and stomped on the rest of my cherished model house with both feet. There was a loud protest of crackling and popping and flying beams, but the tiny timbers were no match for my anger. In an instant it was leveled—a year of painstaking and loving attention to every detail, gone in seconds. I jumped and jumped until the pounding of my tennis shoes returned no sound but empty thuds.

The car was next. I knew it would be harder because it was made of metal, but at least the wheels would break off and perhaps the doors would bend so they would no longer work. I was just about to jump when my mother ran into the room.

"Jonathan! What are you doing? Oh my!" She whisked the car up off the floor, setting the wheels spinning in the air.

"Enough!" she said. "This has got to stop. You can't get rid of your memories of Ben this way."

I wanted to cry but no tears would come.

She reached out to try and hold me, but I turned and left the room without speaking.

1

The Bunker

The house where I grew up in Eagle Rock, California, was only a forty-five minute drive from Huntington Beach. I know that now, but to a thirteen-year-old in 1961 it might as well have been Naples, Florida, or the French Riviera we went to in the summer, because that was how far away Huntington Beach seemed to me then. It was a world away from the small neighborhood streets of Eagle Rock with their curbs and sidewalks and driveways that bumped under the wheels of my bike with methodic regularity.

My life at that time consisted of repeatedly traversing three well-worn paths. I walked up and down the block to and from my eighth grade classroom at Washington Elementary; I zig-zagged my bike daily over the 3.3 mile maze that was my paper route; and at least a half dozen times a week I rode along on the ten-minute drive to our church in Pasadena in the family car. The only variation on that last theme was whether my father would take San Marino Avenue or Santa Anita Boulevard to get to church. "Let's take Santa Anita today!" he would say with an air of excitement that made you think we were about to embark on a hot-air balloon trip around the world. "That sounds like a good idea, dear!" my mother would say.

I was convinced that our '57 Ford had probably worn a groove in the pavement between our house and the Colorado Avenue Standard Christian Church in Pasadena where my father was the choir director. In fact, the blue and white Fairlane could probably drive to church and back on its own.

That's why I could hardly contain myself as I sat in the back-seat of the Wendorfs' silver Thunderbird watching the orange groves slowly give way to the encroaching motels, gas stations, and hamburger stands of Beach Boulevard as we inched our way in heavy summer-vacation traffic toward the Pacific Ocean. This was one week in my year that seemed like a whole year in and of itself.

For the last two years, Huntington Beach had become a symbol of freedom and adventure, beyond the bounds of my neighborhood streets and the control of parents and church. Two summers ago, Matt Wendorf had chosen me to be his guest for a week at Huntington Beach, where his parents rented the same apartment for two weeks every summer and Matt was allowed to invite a friend for the first seven days. I don't know why he chose me in particular—we were not the best of friends, except for this week together—but he did. This was the third summer he had invited me.

"Doggone this traffic!" said Mr. Wendorf. But I didn't mind. There was too much to see. As far as I was concerned, we couldn't drive slowly enough to take it all in. It seemed to me that every wood-paneled Ford ever made between 1950 and 1952 had found its way to Beach Boulevard with a surfboard or two on top or one sticking out the rear window. Occasionally a greaser on a big Harley Davidson would rumble in between lanes of traffic, invoking a similar "doggoning" from Mr. Wendorf.

If I received a punch in my side from Matt, it was because there was probably a pretty girl somewhere in sight. And thus inspired, Matt would break into a strain of "Itsy Bitsy, Teenie Weenie, Yellow Polka-Dot Bikini" as Mrs. Wendorf kept objecting from the front seat: "Matthew! That's not an appropriate song for a Christian young man to be singing!"

"Aw, leave him alone, Bernice," Mr. Wendorf would say. "Let the kid have some fun." Proving, of course, that Mr. Wendorf truly wished he was the one who could have some fun, something it appeared he hadn't had in a long time, if ever.

Mr. and Mrs. Wendorf were always disagreeing about how much fun Matt should or should not be allowed to have, along with mostly everything else that had to do with raising him. This made for an environment where Matt could pretty much get away with anything, as he had become a master at pitting his parents against each other.

Matt's father was a gruff man who seemed to belong to my

grandfather's generation. His rather large nose resembled a road map of broken veins that had lost their sense of direction. He had a mean face and a demeanor to go with it that could occasionally sparkle with wit. But his deadpan humor made it hard to tell whether he was serious or joking; he had the same look on his face either way. Consequently, I never knew when to laugh or shut up, so I generally kept my mouth closed when he spoke.

Mrs. Wendorf had a personality about the consistency of Jell-O. Shake it and it would wiggle; push on it and it would cave in entirely.

Matt was adopted and made no bones about it. He spoke of his parents in a rather distant way, often calling them by their first names. In their presence he gave them the courtesy of "Mom" and "Dad," but when we were away from them, it was always "Leonard" and "Bernice." It seemed odd hearing someone refer to his parents by their first names. I had never heard anyone else do that before. Also, Matt spoke of them the way I might speak about my grandparents, although that became understandable when I realized they were old enough to be just that.

As we got closer to the beach, my excitement was tempered by a growing apprehension. Of all the adventures I had experienced in the last two summers at Huntington Beach, the most prominent in my memory was being kissed by a girl named Margaret on the last day of my visit the previous year. Matt didn't know about it. I knew if I told him, I would never hear the end of it, and whatever was right about it—and I wasn't sure at the time if there was anything, but at least whatever *might* have been right about it—would undoubtedly have been ruined by Matthew Wendorf. Matt seemed to think about nothing but girls and how close you could get to them, which for him was never very close at all.

So there was no one to tell about the kiss, which probably made it a bigger deal in my mind than it was. I knew this, and I tried not to think about it so much, but the more I tried not to, the more I thought about it, until the kiss filled up all I could remember about being in Huntington Beach the year before, even though it had happened in the last few hours before I left. And the closer we got to the beach, the more it grew in my mind.

Questions kept flooding my mind. *Will she be there again this year? Will she remember kissing me?* And, most importantly: *What will I do when I see her?*

I had actually come surprisingly close to not even coming with the Wendorfs because of this, except that I started thinking about bodysurfing and getting a tan and hanging out with Matt and being able to do whatever I wanted, and my good sense had finally won over.

"Hit the road, Jack, and don't you come back no more, no more, no more, no more—" Matt had grown tired of being harassed over teenie weenie bikinis and changed the song. You hardly needed a radio around him. He was a walking jukebox, always up on the latest Top Ten. He said he wanted to be a DJ some day. Happy for a distraction from my apprehension, I joined him, and we started singing and bouncing in rhythm in the backseat, "Hit the road, Jack, and don't you come back no more. . . ."

That song, and repeated versions of it, took us the rest of the way to the apartment only two blocks from the beach. As soon as Mr. Wendorf had pulled into the alley behind the apartment and stopped the car, Matt and I climbed out of the backseat and headed straight for the sand.

"Not so fast, you two," shouted Mr. Wendorf. "You've got a whole week for that. Help us unload this stuff."

A whole week! I thought as I wrestled a big Wendorf suitcase up the pink stairs to the second-floor apartment. Right then, the whole week seemed pretty much like the rest of my life.

Matt and I ran around the apartment checking all the rooms to make sure they were just as we had left them the year before and ended up out on the upper deck. From there you could see the coastline all the way from the Huntington pier, south, to the weird World War II bunker that rose out of the sand to the north like an ancient ruin.

Mr. Wendorf told us that lots of these bunkers had been built along the coastline during the war to protect California from a Japanese attack. The war was over before this particular one was ever completed, and all that remained was an empty shell—the relic of a fear that never materialized. It made for an ideal place to play, though at times it felt eerie being there and imagining guns and ammunition piled up around you and bombs falling overhead. The whole idea of a California beach being a target of war meant nothing to me. The only thing I knew about World War II was that the "Japs" were the bad guys, featured mostly in jokes about Kamikaze pilots. What did mean something, however, was the fact that the bunker was where Margaret had kissed me.

We had been playing hide-and-seek when it happened. Matt was "it," and Margaret and I had both ended up hiding in the bunker. Then, without any warning at all, she just up and kissed me, right on the lips. It came out of nowhere and was over just as quickly.

Now, as I stood on the deck, the smell of sea breezes and sight of the coastline freshened my memories of Margaret. She wasn't what I would call pretty, but she had a cute smile and a sassy way about her that was kind of attractive. That sassy part could be a little bossy sometimes, like my older sister. But Margaret was fun, too. She was a tomboy and had played with Matt and me most every day the past two summers. She and her family were always there for the whole summer, so she knew all the great places—like the bunker, the abandoned lighthouse, the old pier that was half washed away, and where to buy the best snow cones in town. She even taught us how to bodysurf and how to play gin rummy. I never would have learned how to play gin from any of my Christian friends, since Christians weren't supposed to play cards. I wasn't sure why. Something evil about the pictures I think.

That's what had bothered me about kissing Margaret, though, apart from the fact that I had never been kissed before except by my mother and my sister (on the forehead, of course). Margaret wasn't a Christian, at least I didn't think she was, and I was always told never to be unequally yoked with unbelievers. I wasn't sure exactly what "unequally yoked" meant, but I had an idea kissing might have something to do with it. Suddenly I realized that I didn't really like Margaret. I *liked* her, but not in a kissing sort of way. It's just that a whole year to think about that one kiss had thrown everything about her into a different light. Now, closer to all these memories, it seemed clearer to me, and I decided, right then and there, that any more kissing ideas were definitely out. I wasn't even very excited about seeing her any-more. Matt broke in on my thoughts.

"Let's hit the beach!" he said, and we spent the rest of the afternoon diving in the surf like seals set free from captivity, re-membering how to ride the waves and roll on our bellies and backs in the sun. For a while, I forgot all about Margaret.

"You boys did it again!" said Bernice after we had our show-ers late in the afternoon. "No suntan lotion on your first day out. You should have your heads examined."

She was right, but neither one of us would admit it. It was great to get out of the shower and feel clean and hot all over. I looked at my red chest in the mirror and imagined it the color of bronze.

"Mom, we need some money for soda pop."

"There's plenty of pop in the refrigerator, dear."

"But it's not the kind we want. May I just have some money?"

Matt got a handful of change from his mother, and we made our way out the alley to Ocean Avenue. There was a liquor store two blocks down from the apartment where we always got a six-pack of Vernor's ginger ale and a bag of pretzels. Matt was the one who introduced me to Vernor's, and because of that I always associate it with the beach. Vernor's had at least twice the ginger flavor of other ginger ales, and because of that we always imag-ined we were drinking something stronger than mere soda pop. I'm sure we could have found Vernor's at the local supermarket near my home, but I never even asked for it. That would have spoiled everything. Vernor's was for the deck of Matt's Huntington Beach apartment, where we sat drinking and eating pretzels and playing gin rummy as the sun set over the Pacific. It's the way we spent every night at the beach.

Getting ginger ale at a liquor store added to the mystique and adventure. I never would have entered a liquor store at home. As far as my parents were concerned, a liquor store qualified as a den of iniquity. Once when my family was on vacation, my fa-ther had to go into a liquor store to make a phone call because our car had broken down and it was the only pay phone in town. He complained for the next day and a half about how dirty he felt in there. I have to admit, I felt a little dirty in there with

Matt, but that merely added to the feeling of recklessness that was an important part of this whole vacation experience—drinking Vernor's and played cards and carousing on the beach.

And talking about girls, which Matt could do to excess.

"Wow, look at the beauties out tonight," he said on the way back to the apartment, sporting his one-track mind. "Two weeks to enjoy the view." Upon saying that, he rushed up behind three high school girls ahead of us and began swinging his hips, mimicking their walk, until I wanted to find a hole to hide in.

"Hey, come on. Have a little fun," he said, walking back to me and noticing my displeasure. "I know, let's see if we can find any teenie weenie bikinis."

There actually were not many bikinis to be seen. The song was out and the magazines were full of models wearing them, but not many girls had the nerve to wear one in public.

"No, let's go back to your deck and play cards," I countered.

"I wonder if Margaret will be wearing a bikini this year."

I chose to completely ignore that comment.

"Come on," said Matt, "you can't tell me you never thought about Margaret in a bikini."

Now if I had spoken the first thought that came into my head, I would have said something about Margaret not having anything to put in a bikini yet, but I kept that comment to myself and told Matt that the thought had never crossed my mind, which of course was a lie.

"We didn't see her at the beach today," he went on. "Maybe she's not here. She's always at the beach."

"I saw someone that looked a little like her," I said, "but she was much older and she was hanging out with a bunch of high school guys. It almost made me wonder if she had an older sister."

"Well, she *is* older than us," Matt said, and with that I realized I didn't know how old Margaret was. I didn't even know her last name.

"How do you know she's older?"

"I just know."

"How much older do you think she is?"

"She'd be fifteen now."

"Fifteen? How do you know that?"

"She told me she was fourteen last year."

A knot formed in my throat. I had no idea she was that old. *Fifteen?* My *sister* was fifteen! Suddenly I thought of the changes that had recently rendered Becky a different person. My mother explained it by saying that her daughter had jumped from twelve to eighteen in the course of a year and never stopped once along the way. If anything close to this had happened to Margaret in her fifteenth year, it would render new meaning to the thought of her in a bikini. This must have been what Matt was thinking of. But the more I thought about this the more scared I became, especially about being kissed by someone as old as my sister. Maybe Matt was right. Maybe Margaret wasn't here at all, or if she was, she probably wouldn't want to have anything to do with us anymore. That's the way Becky would be if she were here. I began hoping that Margaret wasn't in Huntington Beach, and as I fell asleep later that night, I couldn't get a certain thought out of my mind. *What if the older girl I had seen was actually her?*

The next two days went by at a lazy pace. The first half of the week always seemed to go on forever as we surfed and sunned and played in the bunker, then settled back each evening at twilight with a six-pack of Vernor's and playing cards on the deck of the beach house apartment. We were creatures of habit, Matt and I, and I loved this habit.

By the third day I had decided that Margaret must not be hanging around Huntington Beach at all this year. I hadn't even seen the older girl who looked like her. So by the fourth day I had pretty much dismissed both my hopes and fears about our meeting. That's why it was a huge surprise when, on the fifth day of summer vacation, I came in wet from the water and found a beautiful girl sitting on my towel. When she saw me coming, she stood up and looked nervously around her.

"Hi, Jonathan," she said, biting her lip. "I'm sorry to have been ignoring you. Look . . . I can't talk right now, but . . . here."

She handed me a folded piece of paper, and for an instant we both held on to it. I knew the exact distance between our fingertips without looking. Then her face broke into a quick smile and she turned and walked up the beach.

Matt came up behind me, dripping and panting. "Who was *that?*" he said as we both watched her gracefully navigate the uneven sand. At that moment she turned and gave a cute little wave with a cupped hand.

I couldn't speak. She was not wearing a bikini, but she could have if she had wanted to.

"You were *talking* to her?"

I only nodded. *She knew me. She knew my name. She sounded like Margaret; she didn't look like Margaret.*

"Wow," Matt managed, his mouth hanging open and his eyes as big as saucers.

"Wow," I echoed. We both stared as she joined up with a group of high school kids and disappeared up the beach.

"What did she give you? Is it a note? What does it say?"

We sat down and I unfolded the piece of paper and read it out loud: "Meet me at noon tomorrow in the bunker. Signed, Margaret."

Matt fell over backwards, flat out on his towel.

"Pinch me. I'm dreaming."

"It can't be," I said. "That wasn't Margaret. That was someone posing as Margaret."

"Of course it was Margaret," said Matt. "She gave you the note. Did she say anything?"

"Something about being sorry about ignoring us . . . but I can't believe it was her."

"It was her," said Matt, "and we're gonna meet her tomorrow! Think of that! Wow, what a babe she turned into!"

"I'm not going," I said matter-of-factly.

"What?" he said, sitting back up suddenly like a surfboard stuck in the sand.

"I'm not going," I repeated.

"Why? What's wrong with you? Are you crazy or something?"

"What do you suppose she wants to meet us in the bunker for? She's so much older now. Didn't you see those guys she's running around with?"

"Yeah, but she ran around with us for the last two years. She probably just wants to see us again. Come on, Jonathan. I'm going, even if you're not. I wouldn't miss this for anything."

"Well, okay," I said. The prospect of Matt and Margaret alone in the bunker didn't set well with me. Especially *this* Margaret, whoever she was.

"Now you're talking," said Matt.

It didn't take long for all my fantasies about that kiss to return. The anticipation of meeting this new Margaret had given them substance. Matt was right; we had been an inseparable threesome the last two years. But I was the one she had kissed. At least I didn't think she'd kissed Matt. No, he would have told me. Probably would have stopped everyone on the street and told them too!

After my shower that night I noticed my chest. All the red had already turned bronze, and my hair was lighter and more shiny—bleached from the saltwater and the sun. We had our usual date with Vernor's and pretzels, and the colors of the sunset seemed exceptionally deep that evening as they reflected off the walls and objects on the deck—even Matt's round face, though it was hard to find anything deep about that. All talk, of course, had to do with Margaret.

"Why do you suppose she wants to meet us?" Matt kept repeating.

You mean meet me, I kept thinking.

Though I wanted to talk about Margaret—she was all I could think about—I realized, as I washed a pretzel down with a swig of ginger ale, that it wasn't Matt I wanted to talk to. Somebody, but not Matt. The more Matt and I talked about Margaret, the more I found myself wanting to keep my feelings to myself. Matt had a way of turning everything about girls into something ugly.

"Hey, come on, Matt," I finally said, "it's just Margaret. We played with her all last year, remember? You're talking like she's suddenly some kind of sex goddess or something."

"Yeah," said Matt, chugging a lug of ginger ale and wiping his lips. "That's just the point. She's turned into one, but she's still just Margaret to us. Imagine what we could get away with."

"Matt, cut it out! Don't talk like that! I like Margaret and I don't just want to get away with something."

"Hey," said Matt, "don't get so sensitive. Can't you take a joke?"

"This is nothing to joke about."

I started wishing that I wasn't meeting Margaret with Matt, but then I remembered that he was all talk and no action when it came to girls. It was probably a good thing, since I was still scared about meeting her to begin with, and would be even more scared about meeting her alone.

Those fears came out in my dreams that night. I dreamed that my sister, Becky, was telling me to look out for older girls, and then I saw Margaret, bigger than life, squeezing a bug-eyed Matthew in her huge hands. He was wiggling and screaming for help. That's when I woke up.

The next morning Matt and I were at the bunker by 11:30. It was an exceptionally hot day, but the bunker was always ten to fifteen degrees cooler than the outside. They called them the Bolsa Chica bunkers (there are actually two of them, but the other, smaller one was farther up the coast), and I always thought that was an odd name. It reminded me of the balsa wood model of a house I made once with a friend and how I regretted smashing it later after he died.

The bunker consisted of a long, wide central hallway that ran parallel to the coastline, with entrances from the north and the south. Off the hallway were the barracks and rooms for storing ammunition and supplies. The hallway was long enough to seem like a tunnel, especially if you were in the middle of it. From there, a small rectangle of light was barely visible at either end. It was such a strange and private place, with rooms that we imagined were living quarters for the soldiers and places to store ammunition. The walls must have been at least six feet thick and the ceiling was more than twice that.

"Boy, you could live through anything in here," Matt said, his voice much quieter than usual. It was the same thing he said almost every time we walked into the bunker.

We always got quiet when we first walked in—almost like walking into church. The bunker shut out the sounds of the people on the beach. All you could hear was the faint crashing of the surf.

Talking in the bunker was a little like talking in a tube. Our voices echoed, and Matt and I liked to get on either end of the long hallway and whisper to each other. The dark calm of this place reminded me of a bell tower in our church where I used to sneak away from everybody, especially adults. It was a special place I shared once with a friend, but I had not been up there for a long time.

All similarities with church stopped with the walls. They were covered with writing, pictures, sayings of every kind, and people's names, like "Ralph was here," or "Tom loves Sally." Matt especially liked the more colorful entries, and reading the wall together became a contest each year to see who could find the grossest thing. I always looked for dates because people often put the date next to their name.

"Here's one from 1952," my voice echoed down the tube.

"What's it say?"

" 'Go Ike.' "

"Now *that's* exciting," exaggerated Matt. "Boy, you should see this picture over here." He turned his head sideways. "This guy can draw! What I want to know is: How do you even get your body to do that?"

I didn't want to know. That was the part I didn't like about the bunkers. There were things on the walls that made me want to see them, and then wish I hadn't once I had. Things I found out that I would rather not have known.

"Sooner or later we're gonna have to know about this stuff," Matt would say. "Might as well know about it now. Sure not going to hear about it from Leonard and Bernice."

He was right about that. I knew I wouldn't hear anything about sex from my parents either. We never talked about it at home. I had actually received the bulk of my sex education from the walls of the bunker in the last two years. I figured a lot out from the pictures. I once had a friend I could talk to about these things, but not Matt. He turned anything about sex into a bad joke, like the writings on the wall.

Each summer Matt, Margaret, and I had followed the progress of this graffiti, like time-traveling archaeologists studying what would be the future "cave art" of a lost generation. Each year the writing toward the ends of the tunnel grew more dense as people filled up every available space. Those who wanted more room to spread out their messages and works of art used the area farther in, where there were more open spaces, probably because the light was so dim.

Margaret had even figured out how much the writing moved every year. She measured it from each end with her steps, and based on the average movement over the years she had been there, she calculated that the whole tunnel would be filled up by 1965.

To make her calculations, she had to take into account a small area in the dark, dead center of the tunnel that was filling up much more slowly, but gradually working its way out from the center. These people must have taken the trouble to bring a flashlight in order to put their messages in the belly of the bunker, for whatever reason.

"They probably didn't want anybody to read what they wrote," Matt had said last year.

"But these are the ones that are the most worth reading," I said.

"I know," said Margaret. "These are the people who have something important to say, and they don't want just anybody looking at it. They want you to have to put out some effort to get to it."

We all had agreed that her explanation was the most reasonable. This graffiti was less likely to be seen, so these were probably the more private people. There were hardly any dirty pictures in the middle. People with those interests seemed to be the type who wanted to be sure they had more of an audience.

This time, Matt and I got to the bunker early, partly to be sure and not miss Margaret, and partly to check out the new entries in the center of the hallway. Matt had the flashlight.

"Shine it over here," I said.

There was considerably more writing than I remembered from the year before. A good deal of it was political, having to do with President Kennedy's election and his first year in office.

"What was the Bay of Pigs, anyway?" I said as we surveyed the wall by flashlight.

"It was a whole bunch of people having a big party on the beach and 'pigging out' on lots of food!" said Matt.

I should have expected something like that from him.

"Wait a minute. What was that? Shine the light back over

here." I had seen something as Matt panned the flashlight.

When the light came back, I saw it again. There, right in the middle of the middle, were the words: "Ben was here."

"Hold it right there," I said.

"What are you looking at?"

" 'Ben was here.' "

"So? So was Ralph and Tom and Marvin and Susan . . . come on over here, I saw something really boss—"

"No-no, wait! Let me look at this a little more."

"What is it, Jonathan? What's the big deal? There have probably been a whole bunch of Bens who have been here in the last fifteen years. What's so special about this one?"

"It's just that there's something about the handwriting. If I didn't know he was dead, I'd say that was Ben Beamering's writing for sure. He always made his *B*'s like that. Look how the middle line that cuts it in half doesn't come all the way in to the vertical one."

"Yeah. Looks like a nice set of—"

"Matt! Can't you ever think of anything else? . . . And look at the *N*. It's backwards. The diagonal line goes from bottom to top instead of top to bottom. It was always strange to me that he would make *N*'s like that when he was so smart. He made that same *N* in front of the whole church once. Remember?"

"Jonathan, if Ben Beamering was here, he would have had to have written this at least three summers ago. How come you haven't seen it until now? It's just a coincidence . . . some other Ben with the same way of writing his name."

"Maybe, but I don't think so. I'd know this writing anywhere. This is the writing of Ben Beamering. Maybe Margaret will know something about this."

"Speaking of Margaret, it's after twelve. We'd better head back to the entrance."

We went to the south entrance of the bunker and waited in the shade just inside the opening. Ironic, how in finding the writing on the wall, I had run into the one thing capable of getting my mind off Margaret, the one thing that would put this meeting in perspective. I began to imagine what Ben would say if he were here. Then I realized he probably wouldn't even be here in the first place. He would think this was pretty ridiculous:

two thirteen-year-old boys waiting to meet a fifteen-going-on-eighteen-year-old girl in a place they used to play. What were we expecting? That she would play war with us in the bunker?

I started to feel kind of stupid. And when Matt pointed out that it was 12:30 and we'd probably been stood up, I felt even more stupid.

"Look," Matt said right then, "someone's coming!"

Sure enough, someone was walking briskly toward the bunker. Someone in a sundress. Someone, who, as she got closer, made me wonder if my pounding heart could be heard outside my chest. There was something about the way she walked that made me wish Margaret would never get here. I'd be content just to watch her walk.

"Hi, you guys, I'm glad you're still here."

"Hi," we both said, in a kind of daze.

"What are you doing?"

"Nothing much," I said. It was obvious that Matt and I had not given one thought to what we would do when Margaret arrived. We just stood there awkwardly, not knowing what to do with ourselves.

Margaret did a twirl and sidestepped into the bunker, looking at the writing on the walls.

"There's a lot more this year, isn't there?" she said brightly.

"Yeah," said Matt.

"There's hardly any more room left right here at the entrance," I said, surprised that my voice sounded so high. It had been much lower for the last few months, but right then, when I needed it the most, my future, grown-up voice eluded me completely. It made me not want to speak at all, but I did anyway. "They're going to have to start writing on top of each other." *Did that make sense?* I wondered.

"They're already doing that at the other end," Margaret said, confirming, to my relief, that it did.

"Have you guys been to the middle yet?"

"No. I . . . I mean, yes," I said nervously. My new voice was trying to make a comeback, but the old one would not let go, making them both bounce uncontrollably between each other. I did not remember ever being more completely and thoroughly embarrassed in my life.

"Well, let's go see," she said, grabbing us both by the hand. This was nothing new. The three of us had held hands before inside the bunker because of the dark. But this was different. My hand felt wet and clammy inside hers as she led the way.

Somehow I had the presence of mind to remember Ben. "I want you to see something," I said when we got near the middle. My voice was finally starting to settle down. "Matt, can you find the one about Ben?"

"Do you remember seeing this before?" I asked Margaret as Matt trained the light on the spot.

"I don't think so," she said. "And I'd remember it, with that backwards *N*."

I prayed that Matt would keep his mouth shut about the cleavage on the *B*. He did. In fact his mouth hardly opened the whole time we were with Margaret. Or maybe it never closed. I would never know because we were in the dark most of the time.

"Here, hand me the flashlight," she said, and she walked closer to the inscription, studying it with great care. "This is strange. I can't figure out what was used to write this. It doesn't seem to be paint or chalk. It looks like some kind of stain. Why are you so interested in this?"

"I—we—had a friend named Ben who wrote his name just like this, but it would have to be almost three years old or more if he wrote it, and yet we've never seen it here before."

"What happened to your friend? Did he move?"

"No, he—" and I couldn't finish. The question caught me by surprise, even though I was starting to be able to talk about Ben more freely. It had been two and a half years since he died, and for much of that time I could not speak of it out loud to anyone. Now, suddenly, it felt like I had swallowed my tongue.

"He died," Matt finished the answer for me.

"Oh!" Margaret sounded as if someone had knocked the wind out of her. "I'm so sorry!" Suddenly I felt her arms around me, and I forgot all about how beautiful she was and how old she was and even how much I was in love with her. All I wanted to do was cry. Something about the warmth of her arms filled me with peace. It was a secure peace—a sense that it was all right to cry—a sense of being completely understood, and though I fought it for a moment, I finally gave in and cried. I cried what seemed like two and a half years' worth of tears. I was out of control, but I felt safe. All the while, Margaret just held on to me.

And then, for some strange reason, I started to laugh. Just a little at first, and then more, until Margaret and Matt joined me. There we were, sitting in a triangle in the center of the Bolsa Chica bunker, laughing. Laughing about crying.

Margaret had turned off the flashlight, and I was glad. Now I could know and remember what it was like really being with her, without being confused by all the changes she had gone through. There in the dark, hearing only our voices and seeing the occasional silhouette of a face in the rectangle of light at the end of the tunnel, we talked. We talked mostly about the things we had done the last two summers and how much fun we'd had. I managed to talk a little bit about Ben, and Margaret talked about what it was like to be in high school.

Finally she got a more serious tone in her voice, and we knew something was coming.

"This will probably be the last time I'll see you both. I'm going to be moving to New York at the beginning of next summer. It's been hard because I've wanted to see you more this summer, but, well . . . things are a lot different now."

"We understand," Matt jumped right in, surprising me.

"It's just that I have a whole year ahead of me with these new friends and I want to make the most of it. It's probably weak of me not to stand up to them, but I just don't think they would understand—" Now she was the one who couldn't finish.

It was Matt again who tried to make a bridge. "You don't think they would understand you running around with a couple of pip-squeaks like us, right?" And the way his voice jumped when he said "pip" made us all laugh again.

"It's okay," Matt said, and his voice suddenly had a quality I had never heard there before. "We will always remember you."

I felt soft thin fingers feel for my hand and hold on tight once they found it.

"And I'll always remember you. Both of you."

Suddenly the rectangle of light behind Margaret's face disappeared as she kissed me. Then I heard another kiss, and we stood up and headed back toward the entrance. As soon as we reached the edge of the darkness, she let go of our hands and disappeared into the burning light of day, never looking back.

2

Shore Break

Matt and I stood there for the longest time squinting into the blinding light. I don't know what he was feeling, but I felt terribly empty, as if someone had just given me a gift only to rip it from my hands like some cruel joke. I wanted to be older in the worst way. I wanted to run after Margaret. I wanted her to come back.

"Let's hit the surf," Matt said, finally, and as soon as he said it, I knew that was what I really wanted to do right then.

"Yeah," I said. "Hit the surf."

We swam for hours, bodysurfing in the best waves of the week. They were short, fast, exhilarating breaks, the kind that were easy to catch and easy to stay in front of, once you caught them. The only problem was, they were breaking right on the shore. You could catch a perfect wave and then suddenly wish you hadn't. Looking down from the top of a five-foot swell that is about to slam you down into inches of water is what I call an "uh-oh" experience.

We soon learned how to pull out of the really nasty waves at the last minute and ride in a little behind the curl, using the churning foam as a cushion. Matt found some success somersaulting down under the waves as they broke, though once he started his somersault a little too late and scraped his back on the ocean floor. By the end of the day we were calling them Kamikaze waves.

We were gluttons for punishment. Though battered around, we kept going back for more. It seemed as if the waves were pounding on my emotions until there was no feeling left. The surf was treacherous, and yet we could handle ourselves in it. Dangerous, but predictable, unlike girls.

Matt was the first to notice the sun getting low in the sky, but we decided to stay until we couldn't see each other anymore in the darkness. We always did that at least one night during vacation, and tonight seemed like the perfect time. Besides, we were running out of nights.

I love bodysurfing at sunset. Most people have left the water by then, and you feel like you have the whole ocean to yourself. The waves start to soften as they pick up the tint of the golden sky, and the cooler air makes the water seem warmer.

Mrs. Wendorf joined Mr. Wendorf on the sand just as the round edge of the sun dropped below the horizon. It was Leonard who loved the beach, not Bernice. He was almost always out there in a Hawaiian shirt and a stringy straw hat, sitting in his favorite beach chair and doing crossword puzzles from a book. As we swam into the evening, they were the only people on the beach. They looked so odd sitting there: Mrs. Wendorf, all black and white, the black from her swimsuit and the dye in her hair in stark contrast to the pearly white skin over the bumpy fatty tissue on her legs; and Mr. Wendorf, all brown with sun-beaten, rhinoceros-like skin hanging from his bony legs.

At dusk they waved us in and Matt shouted, "We're coming," which meant we would be swimming for another half hour, at least. You could tell the two of them were arguing about something as they shook the sand from their towels and folded up their chairs and made their way off the beach. I imagined it was probably Leonard overruling Bernice's objections to leaving us out in the water at such an hour.

Matt was just a faint shadow in the darkness now, and the only part of the water I could see was the white foam. I had to guess when the waves were breaking, since there was no foam until after the curl. Twice I got a mouthful of saltwater, looking back for a wave that broke in my face before I could see it. I was tired and wanted to go in, but I was determined not to be the first to say it. We were tough guys out there, Matt and I, and it made me feel strong to be winning a battle against the surf and the night.

After the two mouthfuls of saltwater, I finally learned to recognize an approaching wave from the pattern of sounds. There were a few slaps inside a wave as it rose, but the telling sign was a second or two of deathly calm right before it broke. That little discovery gave me new energy.

"This is a blast, isn't it?" I called to Matt just before I ducked under a swell.

I was good for a few more rides, especially since the rides themselves were improving, as an uncharacteristically large set of waves moved in. I could tell because of the growing amounts of white water after each break and the fact that we were being pulled farther out into deeper, wider water. I was feeling more for the bottom now as we had to go farther out to get in the throw of the wave. Though they were menacing, these waves were the best of the day. We were finally getting away from the shore break.

"I got a swell ride on that one!" I shouted as I dove back in from a long, sustained ride. "These are boss!" No way was I going to quit now. In my excitement, it had not yet occurred to me that Matt was not acknowledging any of my comments.

The waves picked up their intensity. There was a slap, a whoosh, then an awful dead silence, and I realized I was a sitting duck for a wipeout. Time only to grab a breath before a huge wave cracked on top of me, sending my arms and legs tumbling inside its churning fury. When I finally righted myself and opened my eyes, there was white foam everywhere, reflecting what was left of the dim light in the sky. Round circles, where the foam was melting back into the dark water, gave the appearance of a huge blanket of floating Swiss cheese. Hundreds of thousands of tiny bubbles kept bursting, making a high-pitched sizzling sound as the ocean sucked itself back to crash again.

"Boy, did I get wiped out on that one," I said. "Matt?" I suddenly realized it had been three or four waves since I'd heard anything from him.

"Matt?" I repeated.

When I got no response, panic slammed into my chest as I tightened with fear. Where was he?

"Matt!" I shouted, and the anger in my voice let him know this was no time for joking, if that's what he had in mind.

The only sound I heard was a slap, then the silent seconds

before another wall of water rose high over my head and clapped in on itself with a huge cracking sound. I came up from under that wave screaming Matt's name and thrashing about in the foamy translucent fizz.

The ocean seemed impossibly vast. If he was under the water, he could be anywhere. Or maybe he'd already gone back to shore. I looked toward the land and could see only the lights of Huntington Beach. Another wave hit me from behind, knocking me over and under. I came up frustrated and crying.

"Matt! Matt!" My voice was in shreds. Suddenly I thought I heard a voice say, "*Behind you*," and I turned and moved as fast as I could in a straight line directly behind me.

"Matt, is that you?" I yelled.

Just then my leg struck something under the foamy water. It was Matt. I grabbed and got his hair first. I had to grope for any handhold I could find because the surf was sucking him back out. Next I got a hand under one armpit and held on as another wave snapped and crackled overhead, and then, in the dead spot before the crash, the swell of the wave lifted him back toward me and I got a good lock around his waist as we went churning under. At least we were being driven closer to shore. Coming up, I had a better footing and quickly dragged him out of the water and onto the dry sand.

Out of helplessness and utter panic I started shaking him and pounding on his chest. "Come on, Matt . . . wake up!" I even slapped him in the face, but when my knee accidentally jabbed him in the stomach, water flew out of his mouth and he wheezed, coughed, rolled over, and threw up. Something vile was hanging out of his nose, so I got him a towel and fell back in the sand, exhausted but relieved. Matt wiped his face and fell back as well, and for a while we both lay there gasping and panting.

"Not a word of this to Leonard or Bernice," was the first thing he said. "Not a word to anybody, okay?"

"Sure," I said halfheartedly. I had just saved his life and he didn't want to tell anybody? I wanted to tell the whole world. Besides, my mind was full of questions. How did it happen? What was the last thing he remembered? What was the voice? Was it him?

"What happened anyway?" I asked.

"Forget it," he said, and that was the end of it. Matt didn't want to talk at all.

"Come on, let's get back before they come looking for us." He stood up and started walking, wobbling on his legs. He took two steps and then he bent over and threw up again, followed by what sounded like a sneeze and a cough at the same time.

"Are you okay?"

"I'll be fine," he said.

When we got back to the apartment, Matt made a beeline to the shower before Leonard or Bernice could see him. I went to the shower in the second bathroom and let the hot water run in my face. There in the shower I realized how alone I felt, how lonely. I wanted to talk to someone—I wanted a friend. Was this what it meant to grow up and be tough? Almost drown and not talk about it?

Matt was still in the shower when I entered the kitchen in dry shorts with a towel over my shoulder and started munching on some potato chips Mrs. Wendorf had set out for us.

"Hasn't that boy been in the water long enough already today?" asked Leonard as Matt's shower ran on and on.

"The warm water feels great," I said.

"I'll bet it does," said Mrs. Wendorf. "Was it cold out there?"

"Actually it was colder when we got out. Look at my hands—they're like prunes." The skin on the inside of my fingers was white and wrinkled. We had been in the water for hours.

It took every ounce of control in me not to tell Mr. and Mrs. Wendorf what had happened out there, but I realized that if I did, it would probably be the end of Matt's vacation in the water.

"Oh, my gracious sakes alive, what happened to my little dumplin'?" exclaimed Mrs. Wendorf, running over to Matt when he finally came into the kitchen. He was sporting a scrape and a huge bump on his forehead that I had not seen in the darkness. "Are you all right, dear?"

"Oh, come on, Ma, don't drool on me. I'm fine. I just bumped my head on the bottom, that's all."

"Maybe it'll knock some sense into him," said Mr. Wendorf.

"Now, now, Leonard," said Mrs. Wendorf, wrapping her arms around Matt. "He's a very sensible, smart boy." Matt looked like he was being squeezed by an octopus. He rolled his eyes and waited it out.

"Here," she said in her thickest baby-talk voice, "let me take a look at our precious little forehead."

"It's *my* forehead, and it's fine, Ma. Don't worry about it."

"Nonsense, this is what mothers are for. Goodness me! Shouldn't we do something about this?" she said.

"I know just the trick," said Leonard, talking to his book.

"What's that, dear?"

"Take it off at the neck."

"Leonard! This is no time for jokes."

"Who's joking?"

"Look, Ma, I just want to go sit outside, okay?"

"Well, you be careful. You're the only son I've got."

Matt grabbed the chips and a couple of Cokes, and we sat out on the deck with wet hair that we kept shaking because of the water in our ears. The saltwater's blurring effect on my eyes turned the lights on the coastline into tiny stars. It was a warm, still night, and I suddenly felt strong and proud. What a day it had been! I had been kissed by Margaret and had been a hero all in one day. I felt a new kind of camaraderie with Matt in spite of the silence between us. The silence was starting to feel different to me—sort of grown-up and manly. We didn't need to talk about this. We had faced the elements and won. What I did for Matt, he would do for me in the same situation. That went without saying.

"We can get Vernor's and pretzels one more time tomorrow night," said Matt, covering for his exhaustion. The bump on his head made him look like a cyclops. I picked up the deck of cards and shuffled them, wishing he hadn't brought up the "one more time" remark. I did not want there to be only one more day to my visit.

My thoughts turned to Margaret and the loss of my first love on the same day I found out I even had one. *This is just great,* I thought. *I got to find out that Margaret really did care for me just in time to see her go.* I couldn't decide whether to feel good or bad about this. At least I had been important to her—important enough for her to leave her friends and come meet us in the bunker. Important enough to kiss.

"I wonder what Margaret's doing right now," I said, looking out at the crescent of starry lights that followed the coastline north, interrupted only by the dark outline of the Bolsa Chica bunker.

"Probably out with some high school guy."

"You would have to say that."

"Did she kiss you too?" Matt asked. Why did he have to keep bursting my bubble? In my memories of Margaret, there was no one there but the two of us.

"Yeah, just a peck on the cheek," I lied. It had been on the lips, or as close as she could get to them in the dark. Of course, since it was dark, a case could have been made for the accidental nature of her finding them at all—that she had, in fact, only intended to kiss me on the cheek—but I never entertained that possibility except as a cover in front of Matt.

"Me too," Matt said, and I wondered if he was lying as well. I hoped not. If I couldn't see Margaret again, I wanted my memories of her to remain special only to me. I didn't like the idea of sharing them with anyone, especially Matt with his "wonder what we could get away with" kind of girl-talk.

In that regard, however, I had to admit that there was something different about Matt since our meeting with Margaret. The fact that she had kissed him should have kept him foaming at the mouth all afternoon, when, in fact, it seemed to have the opposite effect. It had quieted him down, almost as though he, too, was guarding those moments.

We played only a couple games of gin rummy on the deck that night. We ate the TV dinners that Bernice brought out for us and decided to go to bed early. I was glad Matt brought it up, because I was tired. I couldn't imagine how he must feel. I would think it would take a lot out of you to almost die, and yet he didn't seem to show it. Even the bump on his head would have brought more than a few complaints if it had happened to me. But, then, Matt never did show how he really felt about things.

It was such a nice night that we decided to sleep out on the deck. Lying there in my sleeping bag, staring up at the stars and hearing the constant pounding of the waves made me relive the fresh memories of our experiences in the water. I started thinking about how it had all happened—the impossibility of my even finding Matt in the water, and then how I somehow got him breathing again. It made me shudder just to think of it. And the voice . . . where had *that* come from?

Matt must have been thinking the same thing.

"Jonathan?" he said, checking to see if I was awake.

"Yes?"

"I was scared."

That was it. That was all he ever said about it. I tried to say I was scared too, but I had swallowed my tongue again.

My last day at the beach got off to an early start when Matt woke me up a few minutes before eight. It was still early enough for the air to be crisp out on the deck, but the sun was already reaching through it to touch my face. For beach bums like us, eight o'clock was early. We usually rolled out of the sack around nine or ten. Matt seemed somewhat agitated, though, so I forced myself to sit up, letting the sleeping bag fall off my shoulders. The deck around us was still wet with dew, and I felt like the dry fleece Gideon put out to try and avoid facing the Midian army.

"Guess what I just realized," Matt said.

"What?" I said sleepily, nodding at the cyclops.

"We left Leonard's flashlight in the bunker."

"Oh no."

"Yeah. And it would have to be the good one with five batteries. He'll kill me. Come on. If no one found it last night, we can get there before anyone else does this morning."

I wondered if Matt had seen himself in the mirror yet. He looked worse than the night before. The bump had swollen, and one eye was black and blue. I followed him upstairs to get a pair of trunks and came back down stepping into them along the way. That was all we ever wore at the beach—swim trunks and T-shirts—and often, especially toward the end of the week when our tans were showing, we did away with the T-shirts. I had two pairs of trunks so I could switch, when necessary, into dry ones.

Mr. and Mrs. Wendorf were having breakfast in the little nook off the kitchen, and Leonard's face was buried in the newspaper.

"My, we're up early this morning, aren't we?"

"Yes, we aaaare," Matt echoed his mother's singsongy voice.

Sometimes I couldn't believe what they let him get away with. If I had mocked my mother like that, I would have had a mouthful of soap and the four walls of my room to stare at for the rest of the morning.

"Oh, poor baby, look at your face! Does it hurt, dumplin'?"

"Only when I laugh."

Matt went straight to the drawer in the kitchen where his father put the household tools that he brought to the apartment.

"What are you doing in my tool drawer?" Mr. Wendorf said without lowering the paper.

"I need the flashlight again."

"You mean you put it back where it belonged? Things are looking up with this boy, Bernice."

"Aren't you going to have something to eat before you go out?" asked his mother, looking concerned.

"We'll be right back."

Matt didn't have to worry about his father noticing he had a different flashlight. Mr. Wendorf's face, as usual, never showed itself.

Being on the beach early in the morning made me wish we had gotten up earlier more often. It was a lot like the beach at sunset, with deep colors and hardly anyone around. The ocean was glassy and the sand looked like it had never been walked on. The only people visible were a few surfers taking long, slow rides on the even waves.

"I bet we could do that," I said as we headed toward the bunker. It felt strange to have the sand feel cold to my feet.

"It's a lot harder than it looks," said Matt.

"How do you know? Have you tried it?"

"Last year, after you left."

So that's what Matt did the second week of his vacation.

"Are you going to try again this year?"

"I don't know. I didn't like it very much. I could never stand up."

"What are you going to do if the flashlight's not there?" I said when the opening to the bunker was only a few yards away.

"I'll have to tell Leonard before he finds out. Then Bernice will persuade him to go easy on me for telling the truth. That's usually the way it works."

Inside the bunker, we went to what we thought was the middle and searched the floor with the second flashlight, but found nothing.

"Are you sure we're in the right spot?" I said.

"Sure we are, the writing about Ben was right over—" Matt trained the flashlight beam where he was expecting to see "Ben was here" and illuminated a typical smattering of graffiti. The spot of light jumped rapidly around, searching for the writing that had been so obvious the day before. "Hey, wait a minute. Where did it go?"

"Maybe we're at another part of the wall," I suggested.

"No, this is the center. It starts over here," he found one end of the writing with the flashlight beam and swung it across to the other, "and ends over there."

"Could this be a patch of writing that we missed and it really isn't the middle?" We both stared down the length of the tunnel each way and found the small rectangles of light at the openings to be about the same size.

"Let's walk the whole way just to be sure," said Matt, starting down the corridor with his flashlight.

"Wait a minute," I said after going only a few steps. "What was that? I just kicked something."

Matt trained his beam down at my feet and caught a long silver cylinder in the light.

"It's the flashlight!" he said thankfully, picking it up and testing it. "And it still works!"

"Now that we have two flashlights," I said, still preoccupied with the missing writing, "we should be able to find that writing about Ben."

We decided to split up. Starting at each end, we worked our way inside, checking the wall every inch of the way. By the time we met at the middle, it was obvious that whatever we had seen the day before was no longer there.

"You remember seeing it, don't you?" I said, checking out my sanity.

Matt didn't seem too concerned. "Of course. We all saw it. But look at that 'Go U.C.L.A.' over there. Those brush strokes are big enough to have covered it up. Do you remember seeing that yesterday?"

"No."

"Neither do I," said Matt. "I bet that's what happened. Someone covered it up. We know someone was here because of where we found the flashlight. That wasn't where I left it."

It did seem like a plausible explanation, but I was saddened that it was gone. The writing had been like encountering Ben again—something I hadn't allowed my mind to do in over a year. It had brought out my tears, and I had been looking forward to seeing "Ben was here" again to see if the resemblance to Ben's writing was just a crazy idea or something that would confirm itself by another look.

"I can't believe that someone found Leonard's flashlight and didn't take it," said Matt as we sat leaning against the wall very near the spot where we had sat with Margaret the day before. "This is an expensive flashlight. Five batteries and a beam like a searchlight."

"I know. Somebody was pretty honest. Would you have taken it?"

"Finders, keepers," said Matt, imitating Bernice's singsongy voice.

"Hey, look at that," he said, training his flashlight on the wall opposite us, where it said "Jesus saves."

"I've seen that a whole bunch of times," I said, unimpressed.

"But look what someone wrote under it."

" 'He must make more than I do,' " I read out loud, and we both laughed.

That sacrilegious comment made me think of Ben again.

"I just know that was Ben's handwriting."

"But why didn't we see it last year?"

Matt was right. We had studied these walls carefully every summer. Margaret had measured the growth of graffiti. We had even written down our favorite sayings. We had covered every inch of these walls.

"You're right," I said with a sigh. Still, it puzzled me.

"Come on, let's go get some breakfast and hit the water," Matt said. "This is your last day here."

"Are you okay to swim?" I asked.

"Sure. Just no more somersaults for a while."

3

Sticky Business

The Beamerings lived on a quiet, tree-lined street in an older part of Pasadena. There the streets were wider, the trees bigger, and the curbs higher than where I lived in Eagle Rock. The trees were so big that the whole street was in the shade.

We used to have trees like that on our street, but they had all been cut down early that year to stop the spread of what was called Dutch elm disease, which I never understood, because they were Chinese elm trees. All those great, climbable trees had been replaced by little spineless saplings that had to be wired to green stakes in the ground in order to stay up. It was the saddest thing to ride up and down our street and feel the sky where once there had been a cool, green canopy. Riding up the Beamerings' street reminded me of what my street once was.

In the last three years the Beamering home had turned into a haven for me, a sort of home away from home. I liked to be there because I was comfortable there. With two high school boys in the house there was always something going on. Mr. Beamering (the Reverend Jeffery T.) was the pastor of our church, so there always seemed to be all kinds of traffic in and out the door. I could do anything i wanted at the Beamering home. I could join in and be a part of what was happening, I could just hang around, or I could crawl off somewhere by myself. Whichever I chose, no one would ask any questions.

Once, not long after Ben died, I stayed in his room so long I missed dinner and fell asleep on his bed. The next morning when I showed up for breakfast, everyone treated me as if I were a normal part of the family.

Occasionally Mr. Beamering would start into a speech on my

behalf, but Mrs. Beamering would give him a certain look or walk by and lay a hand on his shoulder and he'd stop. But that's to be expected from someone who is used to making speeches, being a pastor and all.

The "somewhere" I would crawl away to was usually Ben's room. I'd spent a lot of time in that room with Ben, so it felt like it was almost my room too. Ben was the Beamerings' youngest son who had died nearly three years earlier, and he and I had been best friends, spending lots of time at each other's houses. I wondered if the Beamerings liked having me around because I reminded them of him.

They had kept his room pretty much the way it was before he died, except they did put away the physics/chemistry set he loved to do experiments on, and they gave away some of his books to the church library. But they kept his files. I know it's unusual for a ten-year-old to keep any files, but there was little that was usual about Ben. I never tired of going over his files. It was like being with him again.

He kept a file full of floor plans for homes cut out of various *Better Homes and Gardens* magazines. These we had used to develop the model houses he and I built in scale with our model cars. He kept a file on the Tournament of Roses parade in Pasadena, one on the Mayor of Pasadena who was Seth Wilson at the time, one on the Ford Motor Company, and the largest file of all was on the Edsel car. All these files were related to his save-the-Edsel campaign.

Ben had had an obsession with the Edsel that proved to be right. He got the crazy idea that if the Edsel died, so would he. He may have preceded the car by a few months, but the Edsel, as an idea, was already dead and gone by the time Ben got fatally ill. Nobody knew that better than he. This connection was so strong in my mind that even to this day I make the Edsel responsible for Ben's death. The last Edsel came off the line on November 23, 1959. I even clipped the article about it out of *Newsweek* and put it as the final entry in Ben's file, just to complete the story. I needed to complete the story myself, though Ben would never be gone from me.

There was also a medical file where he kept the results of his research on the particular heart condition that he'd had from birth: a septal defect, which is the medical term for a hole in the membrane of the heart.

There was a period of time when I didn't go into Ben's room at all. That was when I was mad. I was still angry, but nothing like that first year. I was mad that God got Ben and I didn't. I was mad that Ben handled dying so well but nobody seemed to think about me. According to Ben himself, he had gone to fill up a "Ben-shaped vacuum in the heart of God," or so he wrote in his final message that he slipped into my hand in the hospital. Well, that was probably fine for him. It was the fact that he had to leave a Ben-shaped hole in my heart to do it that I didn't like. He might have made God happy, but he didn't make me happy at all. That's when I got so mad I smashed my model house that we had built together. If I could have gotten to Ben's house then, I would have smashed it too, but Mrs. Beamering hid it from me, and I am glad that she did. I have his house now at home in my attic.

Seeing the writing on the wall of the bunker, though, had been like hearing again from that vacuum in my heart. I had actually gotten to where I was fairly indifferent about Ben, trying to forget him and doing a pretty good job of it. I was becoming more and more popular with the youth group at church, something Ben and I had never considered important since we kept mostly to ourselves. In school, I played after-school sports the last semester and I was looking forward to going out for flag football in the fall. The eighth grade of grammar school was like the senior class of high school—top dog. Never before had I been anybody at school. Then there was summer vacation, and a week at the beach with Matt, and Margaret to occupy my mind.

Then, suddenly, "Ben was here" had come as a less-than-subtle reminder of my past. Yes, Ben was here in a big way, and no matter how much I tried to ignore it, I would never get away from his influence in my life.

I had not been to the Beamerings' house for almost a month. A week of that was due to my vacation with Matt, but the other three weeks were indicative of the avoidance I was trying to engineer—a getting on with my life that many, especially my mother, had encouraged me to do. But after reading the writing on the wall, I had to find out if there was any connection between Ben and Huntington Beach. Had it only been my imagination?

It wouldn't be the first time I was fooled by writing on the wall. Once, even before I knew he was ill, I had imagined I saw Ben's name on an empty tombstone in a neighborhood display of Charles Dickens' immortal *Christmas Carol*. It was right where the "BEN" in "EBENEZER" would have been had the name not been erased at Mr. Scrooge's request by the Ghost of Christmas Future. No one in my family saw anything on the stone, but to me the word had glowed with a strange light of its own, similar to the writing in the bunker.

I was hard-pressed to excuse this new sighting as only a figment of my imagination. Ben was the farthest thing from my mind with Margaret around. At any rate, I was hoping a visit to Ben's house just might turn up something.

As usual, I came flying down their driveway and skidded to a halt with my bike ending up on its side by the back door. Mrs. Beamering heard me right away through the screen door and welcomed me as if she were expecting me.

"Jonathan, you're just in time!" She was at the back door by the time I got there, trying unsuccessfully to open it with her elbows. The back wheel on my Schwinn was still spinning and ticking.

"Come on in," she said, and I turned the knob easily from the outside and stepped in. Her hands were both out in front of her, covered with cookie dough, so I got a bony elbow hug.

"As you can see, I'm in the middle of baking," she said and went back to spooning balls of chocolate chip cookie dough out of a huge yellow bowl and pushing them off the spoon onto a cookie sheet with her fingers. "My two helpers have characteristically vanished as soon as there were jobs to be done."

"May I help?"

"Sure. In a minute that buzzer is going to go off and I will have to stop what I'm doing and take a tray out of the oven, so you can take over for me at this job. It's sticky business, but it's fun because"—she lifted a dough-caked finger to her mouth and took a long, slow lick, raising her eyebrows as she did—"you get to do that!"

Eager to partake of the fringe benefits, I went to the sink and started washing my hands. The buzzer went off just then and Mrs. Beamering stole my spot under the water and washed off her doughy hands, leaving the water running for me to finish. She put on an oven mitt, pulled out a hot tray of plump, steaming cookies, and flicked off the buzzer with her elbow, while at the same time closing the oven door with her hip.

"Not the best day to be baking," she said, wiping her forehead and setting the hot tray down on the counter, "but I couldn't resist getting ahead. With this new freezer, I can bake enough cookies to last until Thanksgiving."

From the looks of it, I thought she might have a shot at Christmas.

"Freezers are such a great invention. Now I can get all my baking for weeks over with in one day. And I like that because I hate to bake!"

I stood there not quite sure what to do. I'd seen my mother do this hundreds of times, but I was never invited to participate, except, of course, for licking the bowl and the beaters on the Mix Master.

"Just drop a dab at a time on that cookie sheet over there—a couple inches apart to give them room to flatten."

I started spooning out cookie dough and was soon absorbed in trying to control the sticky stuff. This was a lot harder than it looked. I kept transferring little wads of dough from finger to finger, unable to get them to fall off, and when they finally did, I could never make them land where I wanted them to. Mrs. Beamering's trays looked like the stars on the American flag, all lined up in rows. My tray looked like the flag was waving in the wind and all the stars were falling off, but she didn't seem to mind.

"So how's your summer going?" she said, not to break the silence, but to truly find out. That was another thing about being at the Beamerings': you didn't fear the silence there. When you talked, it wasn't because there was dead air to fill up, but because you had something to say.

"Great," I said. "I just got back from a week at the beach."

"How nice. But your father wasn't on vacation this week, was he?"

"No. It was just me. I got invited to spend a week with Matt

Wendorf. His parents rent an apartment in Huntington Beach every year."

Mrs. Beamering slid her spatula under a hot cookie and stared off somewhere for a moment. Then she laughed privately at whatever it was she saw there.

"Oh . . . I'm sorry," she said, "I was just remembering a funny story about Ben at Huntington Beach."

Ben was at Huntington Beach?

"He never told me about going to the beach," I said, trying to be casual about my surprise at discovering this connection so quickly. "When was that?"

Ben and I had been inseparable during the summer of '58—Ben's only summer in southern California. I wondered how this could have slipped past me.

"We were there for a weekend with one of the families at the church. Actually, I think you were out of town at the time. I remember because Ben was so disappointed that you couldn't go with us."

My initial reaction was to be a little put out that Ben never told me anything about this.

"Did he like the beach?" I asked, hoping to find out some other piece of pertinent information.

"Not really," she said, and I wasn't surprised. Ben was not a physical person. "He was pretty bored actually. The sun burned him and the water was too cold, so he spent most of his time indoors reading. A couple of times he went exploring along the beach."

"Exploring? What did he explore?"

"That's what I was laughing about. He found some old bomb shelter and spent most of his time in the Huntington Beach Public Library studying up on World War II, trying to find out about it, I suppose. Doesn't that sound like Ben? We go to the beach for vacation so Ben can research the last major war!"

"Yes," I said. "That sounds exactly like Ben."

Mrs. Beamering and I didn't talk about Ben much, but when we did, it was a little like bodysurfing on a shore break. You'd get excited about catching a wave and then suddenly worry about the crash.

"So what did you do at the beach?" she said quickly.

"Well, we spent most of the time in the water."

"You certainly look like it. That's a handsome tan you've got there, young man. Have I told you how good-looking you are? I bet you have to fight the girls off with a stick."

I knew I was blushing but I didn't mind. Mrs. Beamering often talked like this to me and it made me feel great. I did mind it, though, when Peter and Joshua barged in the kitchen from the living room and started cracking jokes about my being Captain Kangaroo putting on a cooking demonstration in the kitchen.

"And in just a minute we're going to get to see Beanie and Cecil here put on a cleaning-up demonstration in the kitchen," said Mrs. Beamering, evening the score. "And slow down on those cookies. You two are eating them faster than I can bake them."

Joshua was only two years older than me, Peter, four years older, but they both seemed like they had arrived at manhood. Their voices were low, their shoulders were broad, and they walked with an air of confidence that made me feel as if I had a lot of catching up to do.

Peter, though older, was more slight of build. He was the musician and the charmer, like his father. Joshua was the athlete, and his bulk made him look as old as his brother. He had already made the JV football team at Pasadena High. He was the trickster and reminded me more of Ben.

"Here, Jonathan, hand me that tray," said Mrs. Beamering, popping it into the oven and setting the timer. "There. That's the last one," she said as she removed her apron. "We'll leave this mess to these two smart gentlemen and go sit in the next room for a minute."

I washed up quickly and walked by the brothers with my shoulders back. "See ya, Beanie. Bye, Cecil," I said.

"So long, Captain," said Joshua.

"I want to show you something," Mrs. Beamering said as soon as we got on the other side of the swinging door that separated the kitchen from the rest of the house. I followed her into Ben's room, where she set down a plate of the freshly baked cookies and a glass of milk, then pulled out his file drawer and began thumbing through the worn tabs.

"Have you seen this one?" she said, pulling out a file labeled "World War II."

"No," I said. Somehow, in all the times I had gone through Ben's files, I had managed to miss this one.

She thumbed through the papers looking for something. Most of the files had clippings from newspapers and magazines. This one was mostly all notes, probably taken from the library that weekend. Finally she found what she was looking for. It was a clipping from a newspaper that Ben had pasted onto a regular sheet of paper.

"How about this?" she said, handing me the article.

"Nope. Never saw that," I said, because I would have immediately recognized it. It was a picture of the entrance to the main Bolsa Chica bunker—our bunker. Mrs. Beamering left to answer the phone that was ringing, and I sat down slowly on Ben's bed, picked up a cookie, and started to read.

"Built in 1944 by the Army Corps of Engineers, the 600-foot by 175-foot bunker—along with a smaller one nearby—was part of an elaborate defense system planned to protect the California coast from a Japanese attack during World War II. The bunker, designed to hold large gun emplacements at either end, contained huge storage areas for live ammunition as well as a latrine and sleeping quarters for its intended crew.

"Before the facility could be armed and the finishing touches put in place, however, the war ended. For the last few years, the huge empty bunkers have stood as almost irresistible challenges to hordes of local teenagers bent on defying the rules of their elders to enter a place of privacy, darkness, and calm." That last part Ben had underlined.

The article went on to talk about the graffiti on the walls of the bunker and compared it to the drawings in the ancient pyramids or American Indian cave art. "Generations from now archaeologists will probably study these walls in much the same way as they study primitive cave art today."

The title of the article was "Modern Hieroglyphics."

I put the clipping back in the folder and put the folder away. Mrs. Beamering was still on the phone when I passed back through the kitchen on the way out. I told her, in and around her side of the phone conversation, that I had to leave in order to get home in time for my paper route. She waved good-bye and I went out the back door to the accompaniment of the Captain Kangaroo song, courtesy of Joshua and Peter.

Now I knew that Ben *was* there. But what did it mean?

I rode home from the Beamerings feeling a little like cookie dough. That was partly due to the fact that a good deal of it was sitting uncomfortably in my stomach, but mostly because I felt as if I were going through a Mix Master myself. I missed Ben so much that I wanted to find out all I could about him—things that had managed to escape my attention when he was alive. But the more I found out, the more it demanded of me.

I had been doing just fine until I saw that writing in the bunker. Now, in my memory, Ben was doing the same thing to me that he had done in life. He was confusing me—messing everything up. I started wishing I had never seen the writing on the wall, because now I had to figure out what it meant. I started wishing everything about Ben would go away. He had always demanded something difficult from me—something I had never done before—and now he was worming his way back in and doing it again. Then I felt awful for ever even thinking that I was glad to be rid of him. It was all so sticky and unmanageable, like cookie dough you couldn't shake off your fingers.

"Ben was here," said the writing, and for me that could only mean that Ben was back.

4

American Flyer

The Sunday after Matt came back from the beach, Pastor Beamering spoke on angels, and I got a crazy idea in my head. What if an angel left the message in the bunker? What if it wasn't Ben at all, but Ben's angel? One of the verses Mr. Beamering quoted was about how children have their own angels in heaven who are continually beholding the face of God. Well, who's to say that a child who has gone to heaven couldn't, in the same manner, have a few angels down here, on their behalf, beholding *our* faces? It would be just like Ben to send a few of his angels down here just to keep me guessing.

That's what he was always doing when he was here. He kept the whole church guessing for a summer when we were ten. It's hard to even imagine now how we got away with it, but every Sunday Ben and I (it was his idea) had illustrated the Scripture reading with some kind of display. From the little window in the defunct bell tower in the back of the church I would signal Ben, who would be hiding behind the organ pipes, ready to launch some kind of visual volley on the congregation at the appropriate time in the Scripture reading.

I still can't read Scripture without imagining what Ben would do with it. Even that morning as Mr. Beamering was reading verses on angels, I saw Ben's devilish grin cooking up something.

" 'Are they not all ministering spirits, sent forth to minister for them who shall be heirs of salvation?' " Pastor Beamering read from Hebrews 1:14.

"This is great, Jonathan," I imagined him saying. "We could set up something like a storefront window—a wig store. And we could hang a black wig under the sign 'Hairs of Sin' and a blond one under 'Hairs of Salvation.' "

Maybe that's why I lit on the angel theory for the writing in the bunker. Ben got my imagination going in the first place, and it hasn't stopped since. Besides, the angel theory at least explained why we hadn't noticed the message on previous summers. It would also explain how it could be new writing but still look like Ben's. One of Ben's angels would no doubt be perfectly capable of duplicating Ben's particular handwriting style.

"I bet it was hard for a perfect angel to make that *N* backwards, though," said Matt when I shared my idea with him after church. He was back from his holiday and not at all bothered by my suggestion of angelic activity in the bunker. On the contrary, he took it one step further.

"If there was any angel in that bunker, it was Margaret," he said as we talked in the church parking lot.

"Yeah," I remembered wistfully, thinking about her beautiful face and figure. "She was an angel, all right. Just like Bobby Vinton sang: 'Teen angel, teen angel, will you be mine—' "

"No, that's not what I mean," he cut off my solo. "And besides, it was Mark Dinning, not Bobby Vinton." Then he looked around to make sure no one could overhear his next statement, which came out in an embarrassed sort of half-whisper. "I mean . . . what if *Margaret* was the angel—a real one?"

That question hung in the air, and I could only give him a puzzled look. Tough guy Matt talking about being with a real angel was almost laughable.

"Look, I know this seems screwy, but I honestly can't figure it out any other way."

"Figure out what?" I said.

"Jonathan . . . I saw Margaret the day after you left."

"So?"

"What I mean is, I think I saw the *real* Margaret. She was nothing like the girl who was with us in the bunker. She was running around with a couple junior high twerps, just like Margaret would do, and she ignored me completely." His eyes were getting wider as he explained this to me, like he still couldn't believe it.

"Wait a minute! Are you trying to say that the Margaret we saw in the bunker wasn't Margaret?"

"That's what I'm saying."

"How do you know this other girl was Margaret?"

"I just know. If you would have been there, you would have known too. When you know somebody as well as we know Margaret, you know who they are when you see them."

I couldn't argue with him on that, especially after being so confused by whoever it was we met at the beach. Plus, Matt spent one more week with her than I did every summer. He should know.

"Look, the girl I saw and talked to after you left was Margaret, and she hasn't changed that much. Nothing like the beautiful babe we met in the bunker. She made that girl seem like . . ." and we both said it together, "an angel." And then he leaned in even closer to shield this last piece of evidence. "I know it was Margaret because she was like she always was—flat as a pancake!"

Now this was a shock. I was supposed to believe that an angel—a well-formed angel, at that—had appeared to me in a bunker in the guise of a girl I thought I knew . . . and kissed me in the dark?

I started shaking my head and turning away in disbelief, when Matt put his hand on my shoulder and said, "Wait. There's more."

I couldn't imagine how there could be. This was enough to keep me going for weeks.

"Can you picture Margaret—or whoever it was we saw in the bunker—can you picture her face?"

"Sure," I said. How many times since then had I thought about that face?

"So can I. Can you remember what she looked like when she threw her head back and laughed?"

"Yes," I said, and laughter bubbled inside me just thinking about it. "I can remember everything."

"And you remember the expressions on her face?"

"Yeah."

"The dimples?"

"Well, now that you mention it, yes. She had dimples—long ones off the edges of her mouth, right?"

Matt nodded his head.

"Jonathan . . . do you ever remember noticing any of these things about Margaret?"

"Well, no, but . . . I see what you mean. I just thought she grew up and we didn't. Couldn't that still be it?"

"That's what I thought too—until I saw the real Margaret and realized one more thing. It took me so long to think of this. And you haven't thought about it yet, or else you'd be as freaked-out about it as I am."

"Come on, Matt, get to it. What's the 64,000-dollar question?"

"It's worth a lot more than that." He leaned in so we were almost nose to nose. "How do you suppose we know all this stuff about the girl we saw in the bunker when we were *in the dark the whole time?*"

I felt like I had been hit by a brick. I slowly sat down on the low cement wall that separated the sidewalk from the parking lot.

All I could do for a while was stare off at the traffic on Colorado Avenue. Even as I sat there on the wall, I could see her eyes dancing before me as vividly as the cars that were passing by. I could see light flying from her hair. I could see her dimpled smile as she talked to us.

"We saw her face in the light when she first showed up," I said, searching for explanations. "We could just be remembering that, couldn't we?"

"Yeah, for two seconds!" Matt obviously had had time to consider all the initial rationalizations. "Enough to remember all this stuff? Jonathan, I can see her talking to me in the bunker right now, but I didn't see her then. It's like something that only happened in my memory. It's weird!"

I could see her too. It was just as he said. Somehow we were seeing Margaret some other way than we normally saw people— or perhaps some other way than we saw *normal* people—if, in fact, the Margaret we'd seen in the bunker wasn't normal.

"Wow," I finally managed to say.

"You can say that again."

"Wow!" I said it again. "So you think she really was an angel?"

"How else can you explain all this?"

"But wait a minute. If you saw Margaret—the real Margaret—after I left, where was she for the whole week I was there?"

"She was avoiding us for the same reason that the other Margaret said she was. It's just that she was nasty about it. She grew up, got new friends . . . all that kind of thing."

"How was she nasty about it?"

"Well, I wouldn't have even seen her if I hadn't almost bumped into her in the water. 'Margaret?' I said, and she turned around and looked at me and I'm sure she recognized me, but she was with two other older girls who asked her who I was, and she said she didn't know and told me to bug off. Those were her exact words: 'Bug off, you little twerp.' Can you believe that? After all the time we've spent together?"

"Why that little creep," I said. "That is like something she would do, though."

"I know," said Matt. "That's why I think I'm right about this.

It's more like Margaret to insult us than to be nice to us. Jonathan, I think we've been with an angel."

Instinctively I put my hand up to the corner of my lip. "More than that . . . we've been kissed by an angel."

"Yeah," Matt said, his eyes about to pop out of his head. "Mark Dinning move over, we got the *real* teen angel!"

"You know, Jonathan," Matt said after a few moments of stunned silence, "I bet your screwy friend Ben had something to do with this."

"Ben?"

"If you and I have got angels in heaven, why couldn't he have a few down here?"

"This is creepy," I said, "but I've been thinking the exact same thing. That would explain the writing too. Ben would never miss an opportunity to leave his mark."

"What is with you guys?" It was my sister coming to get me. "You look like you've just seen a ghost or something."

I gave Matt a knowing glance and said, "Well, we have, kind of."

"What?" she said.

"Never mind."

"Come on, Jonathan. Dad's waiting."

"I'll see you tonight, Matt, okay?"

"Oh—I won't be here tonight. Gotta go with my parents somewhere."

"Okay. Well, I'll see you around. Say hello to Leonard and Bernice for me," I said to him as Becky and I walked away.

"Are you guys getting to be good buds or something?" Becky asked as we headed to the car. I didn't really think of Matt as a buddy, but now, suddenly, we shared a pretty big secret. I wanted to talk to someone else about this but I wasn't sure who.

As Becky and I hopped in the backseat, I couldn't help but picture Ben in heaven orchestrating angels the way he had orchestrated our pranks at church. It suited him perfectly. The only difference being, now he was behind a cloud instead of behind the organ pipes, and he had much more powerful helpers to do his dirty work than he'd ever had with me.

"Aw, come on, St. Peter," I imagined Ben's current angel saying in heaven, "do I have to get Ben Beamering again? Can't I have somebody normal and boring for a while? Did you hear what he pulled the other day? The last angel had to be a fifteen-year-old dream girl in a bathing suit for one of his friends, for heaven's sake. Are you sure this kid's been checked out properly? I mean . . . does the Boss know about this?"

"What's so funny?" asked my sister.

"Oh nothing," I said. "Just thinking about angels."

"That was quite a fascinating sermon this morning, wasn't it?" my mother said.

"It's a touchy subject," said my father. "I admire Jeffery for tackling it."

"Are there really angels all around us right now?" my sister asked.

"I'm not sure they are around us all the time, dear," said my mother, "but the Scriptures say they are real."

"I liked his point about the fact that Jesus talked about angels much more than we do," said my father. "That says a lot right there. I mean, He should know!"

"I wonder if they're around our car right now," said Becky, "one on each fender?"

Just then my father had to swerve slightly to avoid a pickup truck turning into traffic.

"Way to go, right front fender angel!" he said, chuckling.

"I don't think you should joke about this, Walter," my mother said. "What do you think, Jonathan?" She must have noticed my smug silence.

"Angels are real," I said with a confidence that surprised everyone.

"There, see?" said my mother, looking disapprovingly at my father, who wiped the remaining trace of a smile off his face as he felt her eyes on him.

"I wasn't saying they weren't real, Ann. I was just having a little fun. There probably *are* angels on each fender. Maybe even an extra one on the hood when *you* drive."

"Walter!"

"How about when I get my learner's permit next month?" said Becky.

"A host!" said my father.

"A heavenly host!" said my mother, giving up and joining in the fun.

"And a personal appearance by Gabriel himself," I said, leaning over to my sister, who pushed me away playfully.

"When *are* you going to take me out driving, Daddy? You promised."

"Soon."

"Why not this afternoon, dear," said my mother. "Take her out to the racetrack. There's lots of room in the parking lot."

"She'll need all the room she can get," I said.

"Oh, shut up . . . can we, Daddy?"

"I suppose . . . but after my nap."

Sunday afternoons were lazy times around our house, especially if we didn't have company, which was the case that day. There was a flurry of activity centered around dinner and clean-up afterwards, but then everyone usually settled in with a section of the Sunday paper and an eventual snooze. I would often fall prey to the heaviness of a generous meal in the middle of the day and the natural tendency of my body to make up for waking itself at 5:00 A.M. to deliver the paper.

This particular Sunday, however, my sister kept the house animated, not wanting anyone to sleep through her opportunity to take the wheel of our Ford Fairlane. At the prodding of my mother, my father reluctantly arose from his big comfortable chair in the living room and took Becky to the racetrack for her first driving lesson. I could have gone with them, but I thought my chances for survival were better at home. Besides, I wanted to spend time with my electric train project upstairs.

Actually, "upstairs" is misleading. It really was "upladder." Like most middle-class homes in California in the '60s, ours was a simple single-level house. It was small, with two bedrooms and what amounted to a third—mine—in an enclosed back porch. "Upstairs," for my purposes, was an attic with enough crawl space to maneuver a permanent setup for my electric trains.

The only access to the attic was through my sister's closet— an inconvenience for me and a severe invasion of her privacy, in her estimation. Most difficult were the times when I was already up there and she came home with a friend and I would drop in on them, literally, unannounced. Though at the time I lacked

any real sympathy for her, I admit that it might have been somewhat difficult for my sister to have to explain the sudden appearance of her little brother coming out of her closet door. When I
had friends over, the conflict compounded.

"Why don't you cut a hole through his own ceiling, Daddy?"
she said, more than once.

"Becky, I've told you a hundred times," my father would say,
"you can't get to the attic through the ceiling in Jonathan's room.
You only end up on the roof."

"Well, then, put his stupid train on the roof!"

Our family was famous for indirect reasoning. Anything but
straight to the point, especially when straight to the point went
by way of a conflict—and what we had here was a bona fide
conflict. I had to pass through my sister's space to get to my own.

We were probably the first generation of children with the
physical luxury that could lead to this kind of problem, which
probably led to my father's inability to help us face it. His general
method of dealing with such a situation was to shoot down all
possible solutions and leave us to somehow grapple with it ourselves.

My sister and I actually did a pretty good job resolving this
particular problem on our own. We started with a few ground
rules. If her door was closed, I had to knock to obtain permission
to pass, and I always had to call down before I descended to make
sure she was prepared for my sudden appearance in her closet. If
she wasn't home, I had free passage up and down. We also had a
card that hung on a hook on the side of the ladder to tell her
whether I was up there when she came in. It was green on one
side and red on the other. Whenever I went up, I would flip the
card to red, and turn it back to green when I descended.

The ladder ran straight up the wall of the closet into the attic
through a three-foot-square opening. A wooden cover sealed the
hole and had to be pushed up and slid over to the side like a
manhole cover in the middle of a street. The opening was right
in the center of the floored area that became my layout, so when
you came up the ladder, your head popped up right in the midst
of another world.

It was a world that had become very important to me since
Ben's death—a place where I could be away and be alone and

use my constructive talents to build something that didn't remind me of him. Since Ben and I had been interested in cars and model houses, never trains, trains had suddenly become my new passion.

I had received the train set for Christmas when I was seven. It wasn't new—my parents could never have afforded such a gift—it came from my uncle who had accumulated a rather extensive American Flyer set over a number of years and then lost interest. It's the one Christmas gift from my childhood that I can still remember vividly. The train layout took up the whole living room with two switches, a huge steam engine that puffed smoke, and what seemed like a mile of freight cars trailing behind. And I can remember hearing strange noises in my sleep that Christmas Eve and wanting to believe that Santa was really out there bringing me something. It was my father, up the whole night setting it up.

It would be four more years, however, before I would put any real interest into the train. After the initial Christmas excitement, the set was boxed and put in the attic, where it remained until I discovered it again after Ben's death. It's not that I forgot about it entirely; it was just an inconvenience. My father and I tried setting it up a couple of times that first year, but it was too much trouble for the short time the family was able to tolerate having it up and running in and around the living room.

It was a large "S" gauge train, much larger than the standard "HO" trains whose sophisticated layouts can be accommodated on nothing larger than a Ping-Pong table. This train needed a whole room for even the simplest of runs, and after a few weeks everyone in the family, myself included, grew tired of stepping over it.

Then, last year, while I was rummaging through stuff in the attic where I found a box filled with memories of the hobby I had pursued with Ben—garage doors for our model houses; bundles of tiny shingles for the roof, tapered and stacked and tied together with string; scale model trees made of twigs dipped in shellac and then covered with bits of colored yarn for autumn leaves—leftovers from an imaginary world only Ben and I understood, I had also discovered the train box that sent the wheels of my rusty imagination rolling again. Sitting up there in the attic, holding the big eighteen-wheel locomotive in my lap, I suddenly saw the possibility of making a permanent layout right there under the rafters. There was enough room, where the roof peaked, to floor a fifteen-by-fifteen-foot area with at least four feet of sitting space.

My parents had jumped at the idea. They were probably happy to see me interested in a hobby again. The only opposition came, of course, from my sister, whose arguments were quickly overcome by my parents' enjoyment of the happy proposition that the train set could be up and used without being a permanent disruption in the house.

My dad had put the flooring down, and I started designing the layout from ideas I got from a model train magazine. I found out how to build a mountain range out of plywood supports, chicken wire, and paper-mache. I made two tracks go on a grade up the side of the mountain and one go right through it, in and out of a long tunnel.

What I loved best was the prospect of nailing down the track. No more uneven lumps over carpet; no more having to check for open track that had been kicked by careless feet. Now there was actually a place in my house where I could make my own world come true, free from the encroachment of the real one. I could leave it and come back to it whenever I wished and know it would never be in anyone else's way.

This was the way I wanted it. This was the way I had always wanted it with Ben, too, but he never let me get away with it. I wanted an imaginary world out of everyone's way, but Ben wanted a world that clashed with everyone else's. He wasn't satisfied with just his imagination; he had to play it out all the way. To him, it was *all* real. There was no imagining; there was only living out your ideas. He thrived on the confrontation. He would have gotten bored with my train set because it made no impact on the world outside my attic.

Ben was the one who had been unwilling to keep his jokes to himself. He had to share them with the whole congregation. And Ben's obsession with the Edsel car couldn't rest as his own personal hobby. It had to take us all the way to the mayor's office of the city of Pasadena and the front page of the local paper.

Small waves were even felt as far away as the Ford Motor Company in Detroit.

Life without Ben was much safer than it had been with him, and I tried to tell myself it was better, though something inside me told me it was not.

"Hi, Sis!" I said after sneaking down the ladder and jumping out of her closet. I had just finished spray-painting the mountains and sprinkling the wet paint with spongy imitation grass when I heard the car pull in the driveway. "How'd it go?"

"Jonathan! You scared me again. You've got to stop doing that!"

"I had the card turned to red. You just didn't look."

"Oh, so I'm supposed to stop and check the ladder in my closet every time I come into *my* room so I'll know if *you* might be *dropping in* on me? I'm sure I'm going to do that!"

"Touchy, aren't we? What happened? Did you run into someone at the racetrack?"

"Of course not. I drove the car perfectly. Ask your father."

"Wait a minute. Just because you can drive doesn't mean you can start talking like Mom."

"You'll have to come next time."

"Well, okay," I said. "I guess it's safe."

"Of course it's safe. Safer than I am in my own room, with you barging in on me at any time!"

We always went to church twice on Sundays. Sunday morning, of course, was more formal. I had to wear a suit, which I didn't like doing, but I had to admit I was starting to look good in one. Sunday night, though, I usually wore a sport shirt and corduroy pants. My favorite shirt for Sunday nights was a green checkered short-sleeved one that had a flap in front that folded under the collar and buttoned down the side instead of the middle. I liked the way I looked and felt in it.

How I looked had only started to be important to me in the last couple of months, and it had nothing to do with Margaret. Margaret was never someone I thought of as a potential girlfriend. She was only associated with Huntington Beach, one week out of the year. She may have been my first kiss, but it was a distant kiss, made even more distant now by the news I'd gotten from the sermon and from Matt that morning.

On the other hand, there was the daughter of the assistant pastor—I could see her almost every time I went to church, which was at least four or five times a week. She was the one I had skated with during every Couples Skate at the last all-church roller-skating party in June—every one except one. My mother had insisted I skate once with my sister.

Couples skating was the only time you could hold someone's hand without it becoming a big deal. Well, it was a big deal, but it would be even bigger if you were just holding someone's hand for no other reason than you liked them.

I knew she liked me, because after the first skate she waited for me in the same place every time they announced "couples only," and she would smile and blush when she saw me skating toward her. I also noticed her hands were always cold and sweaty when we skated together, but then again, so were mine.

It was hard not to be nervous during a Couples Skate. The lights would dim and turn soft colors, the mirrored ball in the center of the ceiling would send stars of light whirling everywhere, and the music would be something romantic like "Theme from a Summer Place." It was the closest I ever got to dancing at that age—the closest the church and my parents would let me get all the way through high school, in fact.

"I had a girl, Donna was her name. . . ." It was no coincidence that this song by Richie Valens was my favorite at the time, because Donna *was* her name, and she was the best-looking girl in the eighth grade.

I wasn't supposed to be listening to pop music, of course. It was forbidden in our house, but not necessarily outside our house—a strange rule, but for some reason Becky and I never questioned it. So my diet of rock 'n' roll came from the hour or so it took me to deliver the papers on my newspaper route. I had inherited my sister's big red transistor radio when she got a new, smaller turquoise one for Christmas, small enough to fit in her purse. I strapped the big red thing on the handlebars of my bike and cruised my route, music blaring. I thought I was pretty cool with V-necked handlebars almost as high as my head, print-stained newspaper bags hanging down from the rubber handlebar

grips like saddlebags, and the radio nestled in the bottom of the
V just like a radio in a car.

"I had a girl, Donna was her name. . . ." Ben wouldn't have
liked the fact that I skated every couples skate with Donna Ivory.
He wouldn't have liked it a bit. Not that he would have had
anything against Donna. It was her father. I didn't like her father
either, but time has a way of making you forget.

Three years ago, Ben and I had revealed to the whole church
that Pastor Ivory had secrets with junior high girls. In our spying
around the church, we had both seen and heard evidence to that
effect. Ben had insisted we do something about it, since we were
convinced that my sister was next on his list, so we used our
Scripture-illustrating platform for this arresting piece of information. Needless to say, that little message had put an end to our
activities altogether. The ensuing investigation turned up nothing. The pastor was exonerated, and we were banished from behind the organ pipes for good.

But Ben never forgot. He never trusted Virgil Ivory, so I
knew he would not be happy with my interest in his daughter. I
would even carry on imaginary conversations with Ben over this
issue. In many ways, the Ben I had known at ten became my
conscience at thirteen.

"Come on, Ben, give her a chance," I would say, even out
loud, as I was pulling papers out of my saddlebags and skimming
them down driveways. "She's not Virgil, you know; she's his
daughter. Besides, she's the cutest girl in the eighth grade. You
even used to think she was cute three years ago."

The problem with these one-way conversations in my head,
however, was that they did not always stay one-way. I had come
to know Ben so well that my knowledge of him sometimes came
back by way of a response. It was almost like I had a double
conscience: my own, and what I knew Ben's would be. For instance, to the little piece of rationale about Donna Ivory, I could
almost hear Ben say, *She may be cute, but she's dangerous. She's Virgil's daughter for heaven's sake. There's no way you can get around that!*

I was thinking about Virgil's daughter as I applied the butch
wax to my short hair and tried to comb it into a flattop, but with
a cowlick on each temple, it ended up looking more like the
picture of Stonehenge in my Western Civ book with its pillars

leaning up against each other. The green shirt was ironed and ready, and all I could think about was seeing Donna and when the next all-church roller-skating night was going to be.

At church that night they announced it. There was going to be a Back-to-School skate the first week of September. They'd had such a good turnout for the last skate that tickets would be going fast. "Better get yours soon," Pastor Ivory said.

Donna was sitting two rows in front of me, and when her father announced the skate, she glanced back at me and turned red. Her friend, Marcie Baker, elbowed her and they both giggled. I felt a rush of importance. I knew they were talking about me.

"Hi," I said when I found her afterward in the narthex.

"Hi." She smiled as the two girls who were with her vanished on cue.

I stood there for a moment feeling awkward.

"Going to the skate?" I said. *Oh great! Be obvious, Liebermann.*

"Sure. How about you?"

"Yeah. I'll be there."

There was another awkward moment, and then I said, "Well, better be going. See you later."

"Bye," she said.

I walked away feeling stupid. Actually, though, most of our conversations were about like this. I liked thinking about Donna while I got ready for church. I liked skating with her on Couples Skate when the rink wasn't so crowded and I could look at her smiling next to me as the wind created by our rolling wheels pulled the hair back from her pretty face and showed her glowing temples. I fell in love every time I heard "Oh, Donna" on my red transistor radio. But I could never talk to the real Donna very well.

That's because there's nothing going on in her head worth talking about.

Shut up, Ben, I can handle this.

There was still time to spare before my parents were ready to go—they were always among the last to leave church—so I went searching through the lower level of the sanctuary and the Christian Education building until I found the janitor, Harvey Griswold.

"Grizzly," as we called him, was a deaf mute who had Ben and me to thank for his job. We were the ones who had discovered that he could read and write and was much smarter than anyone around the church imagined. When the deacons found out he could read and respond to memos, they decided to cancel their plans for replacing him.

Grizzly was smartest of all about things that had to do with God, so I had a pretty good idea he might have something to say about angels.

I found him in the junior high room setting up chairs. I always scared him when I came upon him working late in his silent world. That was a real turnabout because he used to be the one who scared us all the time with his odd mannerisms, his wiry hair, and the grotesque, monotone sound that came out of his mouth when he got excited and forgot he couldn't talk.

I tapped him on the shoulder and he jumped back, letting go of a stack of folding chairs that fell like dominos with a crash. I started picking them up as he scolded me with his finger.

"Can you roller-skate?" I asked as I moved along with him while he pulled up one chair at a time and set it neatly in place. I suddenly realized that I had never seen him at the roller rink on skating night.

You had to remember to have Grizzly's attention when you talked to him so he could read your lips. Now he looked at me more closely and made me repeat my question. Then he shook his head "No."

"Have you ever tried?" I said as he reached for another chair.

He shook his head again.

"Why don't you come to the next church skate?" I said. I was pretty sure that all he needed was an invitation. Most people thought Grizzly was a miserly soul who preferred to keep to himself. That was only because most people left him to himself; he had no choice. Ben and I had found out that Grizzly was actually quite a sociable character hungering for new adventures.

He only shook his head again.

"Why not?" I said, forming the words carefully.

He balanced a folded chair against his leg and took out his writing pad.

"NO WAY TO GET THERE," he wrote and held it up for me.

"My parents can pick you up," I said, and he frowned.

"TOO MUCH TROUBLE."

"No," I said. "No trouble at all. Why don't you come with us? I'll talk to my parents."

He shrugged and acted disinterested, but I imagined he was overjoyed inside. Then I remembered what I really wanted to ask him—why I had gone looking for him in the first place.

"Do you believe in angels?"

He smiled broadly and wrote, "I HAVE ONE BEHOLD-ING THE FACE OF GOD RIGHT NOW."

"Have you ever seen an angel?"

"PROBABLY BUT DIDN'T KNOW IT."

"I know what you mean. I'm not sure, but I think I might have been kissed by an angel and didn't know it until now."

Grizzly got a wistful look and stared off for a moment before he wrote again.

"YOU ALWAYS KISS AN ANGEL WHEN YOU FALL IN LOVE."

Something clicked when I read that statement—like it did so often when Grizzly explained things. Suddenly I realized I wasn't in love with Margaret. I had been in love, for a while, with the idea of being kissed in the bunker, but now I knew the truth. I was in love, all right. I was in love with an angel.

"Do you think that if we have our own angels in heaven who are always looking at God, that when we go to heaven, we could send one down here to check out the friends we left behind?"

It was too much for Grizzly to get all in one sentence. He motioned with his hand for me to try again.

"You have your own angels in heaven, right?"

He nodded.

"If you died and went to heaven, could you send an angel down here to—?"

Now, the second time around, he grasped my concept before I had fully stated it. His mouth went into the shape of an "Ahhh" sound and an ugly groan came out of it that completely contradicted the delight on his face.

He unfolded the chair that was leaning against his hip and sat down to think. I did the same.

"BEN," he finally wrote and held up to me. I looked at him quizzically.

"BEN'S ANGEL," he added. I smiled. He was following my thoughts. Then he finished it: "KISSED YOU?"

"Yes!"

"WHERE?"

I pointed to a place on the edge of my right lip. Then he lifted his hand slowly and, with a look of great wonder, touched the spot.

I found myself wanting to pour my heart out to him right there. Throw him all the questions . . . all the details. Try and figure out all the ramifications. But I was obstructed by the communication barrier between us. At the same time, there was such a sense of wordless communication between us that talk seemed hardly necessary. At least it was comforting to know that in the matter of angels, I had someone who could understand.

After a moment he wrote, "NOT SURE I SEE ANGELS BUT HEAR THEM ALL THE TIME."

How could a deaf person hear angels?

"What do you hear?" I formed the words with my mouth without making a sound. It was a way that Ben and I had discovered we could talk in secret to Grizzly without anyone hearing. Often I talked to him this way even when no one was around, like right then.

"SINGING ANGELS," was what he wrote, and I remembered old rumors about unexplainable singing in the church. Maybe that was the one thing Grizzly could hear. It would make sense—that he should hear something we could not, if he could hear anything at all.

Then he wrote one more thing, going back to our original conversation.

"CAN'T SKATE."

"Sure you can," I said. "You can learn. It's easy."

Grizzly only shook his head and again held up this last written message to emphasize the fact that he would not be talked into roller skating. I had to laugh, though, because the last two entries looked like one sentence on Grizzly's pad: "SINGING ANGELS CAN'T SKATE."

He had a good laugh when I pointed it out to him and wrote: "BUT NO PROBLEM FLYING!"

5

Devil or Angel

The Back-to-School All-Church Skate Night was held where it always was held, at the Ramblin' Rose Roller Rink on the Arroyo Seca, a euphemism for a dry riverbed that ran into Los Angeles from the backside of Pasadena. At the north end of this riverbed you could see the picturesque Rose Bowl nestled in front of the San Gabriel Mountains (at least on a clear day); at the south end, just before the riverbed narrowed into a concrete wash, was the Ramblin' Rose.

The roller rink was only a block away from where the Pasadena Freeway began. In 1961, freeways were rapidly becoming the main arteries of southern California. Their subsequent hardening would necessitate numerous bypass operations, but at that time hardly any of the negative associations with these clogged thoroughfares had surfaced.

Freeways were looked upon as just one more bright hope for a more convenient future that already included automatic dryers, dishwashers, air conditioners, electric blenders, and push-button just about anything—advancements that would completely change the look and lifestyle of the modern family. Alan Shepard had made the first U.S. space flight; now Zenith brought the Space Age into the living room with Space Command TV, featuring a remote control "Space Commander 400"—"NOTHING BETWEEN YOU AND THE SET BUT SPACE!"

This was a time of great national optimism. America had its youngest elected President and a glamorous First Lady in the

White House. The era that would become known as Camelot captured the hopes of the best and the brightest and swelled our dreams for the future. The sores of civil unrest in the South had not yet festered to the national breaking point, President Kennedy had not yet been cut down on a humid Dallas afternoon, and most Americans paid no attention to the military advisors being sent to aid the tiny Far Eastern country of South Vietnam in its battle against Communist aggression from the north. At his inaugural in January of that year, John F. Kennedy had announced, "Let the word go forth from this time and place, to friend and foe alike, that the torch has been passed to a new generation of Americans." A new generation was reaching out its hand to a future full of hope and promise.

But the only thing important to me right then was that Donna Ivory was holding out her hand for me as I skated toward her during the first Couples Only skate of the night. My heart skipped when I saw her. The cutest girl in the eighth grade was waiting for me! I took her hand and we skated out onto an almost empty rink spotlighted with twirling stars.

Only a fraction of the number of people on skates actually made it out on the rink as couples, and most of these drifted in later—mostly high school and college age kids, and they always took a while to pair up. In 1961, this was as close as evangelical Christians ever got to dancing, which heightened the pressure on these pairings. Many a hope was dashed and many a dream came true during Couples Skate. The boys had to build up enough courage to ask, and, sometimes, the girls had to think about it for a while. Couples like Donna and me, who already had each other reserved, got the jump on an almost empty floor.

I liked that part about Couples Skate as much as I liked holding Donna's hand—the fact that for the first few minutes it felt as if we had the whole floor to ourselves. Even with the rolling wheels and the wind rushing past your ears and the soft music, it was almost quiet compared to the noise and congestion of All Skate with kids darting here and there and beginners trying to balance themselves like sailors on a slippery deck in a stormy sea.

But on the second Couples Skate that night I started to notice a heavy feeling, and it surprised me when I realized it was associated with Donna. I was actually getting bored skating with her. Things that had never bothered me before began to annoy me. For instance, whenever I wanted to skate faster, Donna, who was a poorer skater than I, would always pull back. Also, she never wanted to try anything different, like switching sides or locking arms or skating under another couple making a bridge. She just wanted to hold on tight and skate around and around. She never even talked much; she just smiled this pretty smile whenever I looked over at her.

I liked it when we did talk because then I would have to put my ear right up to her lips in order to hear her over the rolling wheels—so close that her delicate voice and breath buzzed and tickled my ear. Or, in order to hear me, she would have to lean in so close that I could smell the fragrance of her hair. But mostly she would just smile, shake her pretty brown hair, and say in a voice I could never hear, "I can't hear you! Tell me later." I wasn't even Grizzly, and I could read those lips.

I guess also I was beginning to realize that I had almost no contact with Donna apart from the Couples Skate. In fact, that particular night I was rather lonely because none of my usual friends were there. Not even Matt.

By the third Couples Skate, I almost didn't want to take Donna's outstretched hand. I felt like she was grabbing me and holding me back. Maybe that's why the devilish impulse to play rough came over me, just to create some excitement. So without slowing down, I skated up to her, grabbed her hand, and jerked her up from the bench. Her body lurched forward and her feet drummed on the rubber flooring mat to try and get her balance as I pulled her toward the skating floor. She still had not righted herself as we entered the rink, so I pulled her up with a jerk, and in the process she cracked like a whip, broke away from my hand, and went flying across the floor, unable to stop until she crashed into the wall on the other side.

"Gosh, I'm sorry," I said, rushing over to her, trying to hide my amusement. "I didn't mean to let go—"

"Why did you do that?" Her face was livid with anger and embarrassment.

"I'm sorry. I just wanted to have a little fun."

"If that's your idea of fun. . . !" Just as she turned to skate away from me, I heard the familiar introduction of one of my favorite songs by Richie Valens.

"Listen," I said, skating up behind her, "it's our song."

And just in time, I began singing, "I had a girl/Donna was her name." Of course, since this was church night, there were no popular records played, but whoever played the organ kept doing versions of all the latest hits. We always thought it was a great joke on our parents that we could hear these songs we weren't supposed to know, and we would often slip notes of requests to the guy at the organ. Matt usually kept him busy with requests most of the night.

For one lap, Donna and I skated like this—with me trailing behind her and singing. I thought she might go for an exit, but she didn't. Finally she turned around and looked at me, and the smile had returned to her face. I skated up to her and saw that she was blushing. I assumed her shyness was from hearing her name and realizing that I was making a deal out of it. Like magic, the song saved me. Taking my arm, she slipped her hand into mine as if nothing had happened and we skated off dodging stars.

As we skated, I started listening to the words of the song in my head. It's funny how you can know words to a pop song before you have even thought about them, and it wasn't until that skate that I realized this song was about a breakup. I'd always been so into the mood of the song—the music, the pathos, the name, and the fantasies of Donna in my mind—that I never paid any real attention to the lyrics. The chorus was all I really knew, and the chorus was only "Oh, Donna" a hundred times, it seemed, until it faded away.

But now I heard, "I had a girl/Donna was her name/Since she left me/I've never been the same./'Cause I love my girl/Don-na-a-a where . . . can ya be?"

I had *a girl*, I thought. Past tense. And even as we skated together, her hand felt cold in mine. Was it over? Had it ever started? I didn't even know what it was supposed to feel like to have a girl, but if this was it, I was pretty sure I didn't want it. All we ever did was skate together, and that was starting to make me feel trapped.

I looked over at her, and she had this exceptionally soft and gooey look on her face. It made me almost want to throw her into the wall again.

Couples Skates always ended with the lights going up and the familiar "ALL SKATE SLOWLY AND CAREFULLY" announcement coming over the speakers, followed by a deluge of little skaters and growing congestion. Donna and I usually split up at that point, with a final squeeze of clammy hands, and went back to our friends. This time was no exception, and I was happy to be free of her and skating on my own. I wiped my sweaty palms on my jeans and lost myself in the crowd.

Matt must have come in late, because I had spotted him standing beside the rail during that last skate. I started scanning the blurry faces looking for him as I coasted along. Suddenly Donna came up beside me and gave me a little shove. She was with her friend Marcie Baker and a relatively new girl to our group named Donna Callaway. I'd thought the new girl was kind of homely, but on skates there was a different quality about her. She obviously knew what she was doing with eight wheels on her feet.

"Donna wants to skate with you on the next Couples Skate," said Donna Ivory. "Why don't you?"

It seemed kind of odd, but they were all smiling at me, so I went along with it.

"Okay," I said. Just as they were skating away, Matt rolled up behind me.

"What was that all about?" he asked.

"Donna wants me to skate with that new girl, Donna Callaway. Isn't that a little weird?"

"Well, at least you'll get the name right."

"You should skate with Donna Ivory," I said, knowing that he probably wouldn't. I had never seen Matt on a Couples Skate.

To my surprise, he responded, "Maybe I will." *That does it*, I thought. Margaret *was* an angel. Only an angel would be able to make Matt actually want to be with a real girl instead of just talk about them.

"What do you suppose those girls are up to?" I said, wondering why Donna would set me up with someone else.

"Leonard says you should never try and understand women. I suppose it's the same with girls. Maybe they're just practicing."

Suddenly Marcie and the two Donnas passed us at a high rate of speed. Donna Callaway went right in between Matt and me, almost throwing us both off balance. I had fallen only once in the last three skate nights, and I wasn't about to let a girl spoil my record. We were just starting to chase after them when the buzzer sounded and the announcer came on the microphone.

"CLEAR THE FLOOR PLEASE. ALL CLEAR."

"All clear" always meant they were setting up for the Speed Skate—the only time all night you actually got to skate as fast as you wanted. It was my favorite skate. You got to lean over into the wind and feel yourself fly. It was always scary on the corners because I was never sure how to turn at high speed, so I just locked my legs and leaned and hoped my skates wouldn't slip out from under me.

I also liked this skate because it was always men and boys. It wasn't a "Men Only" skate, but it turned out that way. I guess the girls didn't like going fast. And after my last boring Couples Skate with Donna, I was ready to be rid of women in general and get out there with the guys.

The three rink attendants placed yellow cones down the center of the floor to keep people from cutting across and the buzzer sounded. Then the organist started playing "The Flight of the Bumblebee" and a number of guys streaked onto the rink. Some of the little boys were the fastest. They had such a low center of gravity that balance was no problem for them. It was just full speed ahead!

Just as we were starting to jump into the action, Matt grabbed my arm. "Look! Who's that?" he said, pointing to a blond-haired figure speeding faster than anyone.

"Holy Toledo, it's Donna Callaway!" I said.

She was incredible—fast but fluid, moving with ease and grace. She even kept her feet going on the curves, one inside the other. I'd tried that a little bit on All Skate, but never while going that fast. Flying past all those men and boys with their rigid and jerky movements, she looked like a swan among ducklings.

"Wow!" said Matt. "Look at her go! Come on, let's get out there."

"Wait a minute," I said, watching my future couples partner fly by.

"What? This is the only skate of the night worth coming for. Come on. We're wasting time!"

"No, you go ahead," I said. "I gotta go pee."

"Pee later," he said a little too loudly. "Come on! What's wrong with you?"

"Go on. I'm going to sit this one out."

"Wait a minute," said Matt, dragging out the words for emphasis. "You're not going out there because of Donna, aren't you? Too chicken to be beat by a girl?"

"I just need a rest before the next Couples Skate."

"I'll say, if you're skating with *her*," Matt said and swung himself around the railing and out onto the floor.

I couldn't take my eyes off Donna Callaway. Her curly blond ponytail flew behind her like it was holding on for dear life. She dodged in and out of the skaters around her, her legs moving in a constant pumping rhythm that seemed to keep time with the music. She was flying like a bumblebee, I thought, and if I went out there, I'd get stung.

Suddenly my legs felt like they weighed a thousand pounds, and I decided I'd take that pee I was lying to Matt about. Sitting in the stall would use up more time, so even though I didn't have to go, I took up residence on the toilet in the last stall.

What was I going to do now? The next Couples Skate would be coming up soon. How could I putter along next to that speed demon without looking like a fool? What if she wanted to go fast and ended up pulling me along like I pulled Donna? Suddenly the thought crossed my mind that Donna Ivory might have set this whole thing up on purpose, just to humiliate me for throwing her up against the rail. I should have been suspicious about her getting over her anger so quickly.

As I mulled these thoughts over in my mind with "The Flight of the Bumblebee" still reverberating through the walls, my eyes slowly focused on something on the inside of the stall door. I was glad my pants were down because I almost went to the bathroom anyway. There, scratched into the flesh-colored paint of the aluminum door, were the words "Ben B. was here."

It wasn't anything like the writing in the bunker. It was in lowercase letters except for the *B*'s, so I couldn't tell anything from the *n*. It was relatively new, however, because the door had received a fresh coat of paint since our last skate in June. These doors were always covered with writing, and I could still see the indentations of former marks that had been painted over. Now this one had only this message and someone's phone number who wanted a good time. It was hard to pass this off as a coincidence, not when it said "Ben *B*. was here."

Now I knew there were plenty of Bens in the world, but how many Ben B's could there be—and in Pasadena, no less? I pulled my pants up and returned to the rink a bit shaken, my concern about skating with Donna Callaway now diminished by comparison.

Matt was just coming off the floor from the end of Speed Skate and greeted me with, "Don't look now, but your fly's open."

Sure enough. I guess I really was spooked.

"Matt," I said, looking both ways and zipping up, "have you been to the bathroom yet?"

"I go three times a day, whether I have to or not."

"Seriously. I mean *this* bathroom."

"No, I haven't."

"Well go check out the stall on the far left . . . the back of the door. I'm going skating."

It was All Skate time again and I welcomed a chance to lose my thoughts in the crowd. Halfway into thinking I was either imagining things or going crazy, I realized I wasn't skating alone.

"You all right?" It was Becky. "You look like you just saw a ghost or something."

"I'm okay." I almost started to tell her about the writing, but I didn't want to shout about angelic graffiti over the noise of All Skate. There was too much to explain. I still hadn't told her about what we'd found in the bunker—not because I didn't want to, but because I just hadn't figured out how to tell her yet. My sister and I teased each other a lot, but I knew if I got serious, she would listen. She was good about that, especially when it had anything to do with Ben.

"I'll tell you later," I said.

"Is it about Donna?"

She would have to remind me.

"Which one?" I said, perking up.

"Oh, there's more than one now? What other Donna is there?"

"Donna Callaway."

"Oh, you mean Roller Derby Queen?"

"Wait until the next Couples Skate," I said, hiding my trepidation behind a cocky smile.

"Gosh, Jonathan," she said just before she skated off, "for an eighth grader, you really know how to pick the babes."

Rolling, rolling, rolling. The constant turning of wheels on ball bearings. The low hum of rubber on hard wood. Rolling feet, stomping amateurs, gliding experts—among them, Donna Callaway, skating backwards on the other side of the rink. Yes, backwards. I found the nearest exit and swung myself clumsily off the floor just ahead of Matt, who had been trying to catch up with me from behind.

"Okay," he said, out of breath, "I got the phone number. Now who's going to call the guy for a good time?"

"Not that! Come on, Matt, you know what I mean. Didn't you see the writing about Ben?"

"Yes," he said, turning serious. "Are you surprised that it's somebody in our group?"

"How do you know that?"

"It doesn't take a genius to know that somebody had to do it today to put today's date on it."

"Today's date? I didn't see any date."

"You're kidding," he said, his eyes going wide on me again. We both turned at the same time and stomped toward the rest room. The rubber mats around the rink were made to keep people from rolling. You couldn't skate on them, you had to tromp.

Once inside the bathroom, we had to wait for someone to vacate the end stall. We washed our hands and combed our hair a number of times while some old guy in there kept clearing his throat and blowing his nose. You can always tell old people by the way they clear their throats. It's like removing gravel from the bottom of a dumpster with a big shovel. That wasn't all he was clearing. The smell made us almost leave.

Finally a white-haired, unshaven man in a red and black checkered lumberjack coat came out of the stall. He nodded at us, winked at me, and vanished out the door.

"Pee-yooo!" said Matt, holding his nose. "I'm not going in there, that's for sure!"

I swung the door open and found it just as Matt had said. Under "Ben B. was here" there was a newly scratched 9/13/61.

"You're right," I said, "today's date."

"And that wasn't there before?"

"Nope."

"I think we'd better keep an eye on this wall," said Matt, trying to talk while holding his breath. "Who knows what's gonna show up next."

"Matt, this is weird. I don't like it."

"Wait a minute," he said, breathing freely again, though still making a face. "Have you ever seen that man before—the one who was just in here?"

"No."

"Don't we have the whole place reserved just for our church?"

"Yeah, but I don't know everybody in the church . . . and he could be someone's guest . . . someone's grandfather or something."

"But, Jonathan, did you see that coat he was wearing? It's 80 degrees outside!"

We stared at each other for a couple of seconds until we recognized that the same thought had entered our minds at the same time and we bolted toward the door and stood for a moment outside, scanning the crowd.

"You go left," I said, "I'll go right. If you see him, stay with him until we meet up."

When we rejoined each other, almost directly opposite the rest rooms, Matt said, "See anything?"

"Nope. Nothing. I even asked at the desk if anyone works here who fits his description."

"Or his smell!" said Matt.

"You *are* thinking what I'm thinking, aren't you?"

"That he was an angel?"

"He has to be."

"But, Jonathan, how could someone from heaven make a BM that smells so bad?"

"Ben's angel would!" I said. "No doubt about it."

Suddenly we were interrupted by Donna Callaway.

"Jonathan! Where have you been? I've been looking all over for you. The Couples Skate is almost starting."

I hadn't even noticed the lights go down and the music soften, but I did notice Donna Callaway's rosy cheeks and dancing eyes.

"Come on," she grabbed my hand, "we'll be late!"

Matt shrugged his shoulders as Donna pulled me toward the nearest entrance to the rink. It was going to be this way the whole skate, I could tell—Donna pulling me, that is.

Actually, it wasn't so bad. Once we got out on the floor, she skated at an easy pace. The first thing I noticed was that her palms were dry. The second thing was how she glided along next to me. There was no pushing and pulling like there always was with Donna Ivory. And the third thing was that it was easy to talk to her.

"Where were you for so long?"

"Looking for someone."

"I thought you'd be looking for me," she said, her eyes bright.

"I was looking for a stranger. Someone we saw in the rest room."

"Did you find him?"

"No."

"Is he dangerous or something?"

"Probably not, but you never know."

"Sounds creepy to me."

"Don't worry. He's gone now."

Donna looked convinced that I had just saved her from some menace. "Good! Let's skate!" she said, casting doubt on what it was we had been doing up until then.

She charged ahead, pulling me into a faster clip. I was surprised at how easy it was to move along with her, except for the turns. On the corners she crossed her outside foot inside the other like I had seen her do earlier, and my stationary feet felt like they had lead poured in them.

"How do you do that?" I asked, coming out of the turn after holding on to my stiff legs for dear life.

"Easy. Try it with me."

"No!" I shook my head, terrified. As we approached the next turn, I froze my feet and nearly tripped her up.

"Slow down next time and I'll try," I said. She did, and to my surprise I crossed my feet over twice.

"Hey!" I shouted. "It works!"

"Of course. You're a good skater."

By the time we had taken three or four more laps, we were crossing our feet in unison on the turns as if we were partners in a skating exhibition. The organ was playing "Moon River," and for a minute it seemed like we were skating on it. Everything was spinning past Donna's face as she glided effortlessly along the floor, and somehow I was able to skate better than I ever had, just being with her.

"I love this song, don't you?" she said.

"Yes," I said. "Where'd you learn to skate so well?"

"Right here. I take lessons every week. That older guy over there—that's Lenny. He was a two-time national champion. He thinks I could take the state this year if I concentrate."

I didn't need to read lips in order to hear Donna Callaway talking on the skating floor.

"Take the state in what—roller derby?" That was the only official skating I knew about.

"Oh, I can do that too. Want me to show you?" And she crossed her arms as if to throw me a body block.

"No thanks!" I shouted, grabbing her hand back. "I believe you. Wow, state champion. That's boss!"

"Hey, look! There's Matt and Donna," she said. "Let's go skate under them."

I hardly believed it at first, but there they were—skating together. Jealousy welled up inside me, even though I was having such a good time with Donna Callaway and actually preferred skating with her. There was no rational reason for the feeling; it was just there. I also was surprised to see Matt and Donna Ivory talking so much—more than she had ever talked with me. So much so that they didn't notice us coming.

"Comin' through!" Donna Callaway shouted, and they had to lift their arms to let us under, or split apart. They chose the former. Looking back, we both motioned them under us. We did this back and forth a few times until Lenny came over and gently told Donna we probably shouldn't do that anymore.

"You're spoiling the romantic mood," he said with a smile. Seeing Donna talking with the head attendant made me remember the mysterious character in the rest room. Maybe she knew something about him.

"Since you spend a lot of time here," I said as we separated from Matt and Donna, "you wouldn't happen to have ever seen an older guy in a red and black checkered lumberjack coat around, would you?

"Is that the man you were talking about earlier?"

"Yeah."

"No, I don't remember ever seeing anyone like that."

Couples Skate was coming to a close. The music had stopped, some couples had already left the floor, and the entrances were jammed with little kids waiting for the All Skate announcement. Matt and Donna were already off, and I caught a glimpse of Donna and Marcie leaning over the rail watching us. Donna was glaring at Donna Callaway, but she didn't notice. We just kept skating and holding hands. It had seemed like the longest Couples Skate I had ever taken, and I was sad it was over.

"Thanks for skating with me," she said, squeezing my hand and not letting go. It felt nice to be thanked. Donna Ivory never thanked me; she just expected that we would skate together. Then I remembered that she had set this whole thing up. Why? And why, since she had suggested it, was she angry with Donna Callaway?

"Thanks for calling last night, too," she said as we slowed down and started coasting to an exit. "I don't understand, though, why you wanted to know if I was coming to the skate if you weren't planning on skating with me."

"I don't know what you mean," I said, puzzled.

"Last night, when you called. You know, that was the first time any boy ever called me just to talk."

I was speechless. What was she talking about? I hadn't called her. I was about to tell her that when "ALL SKATE SLOWLY AND CAREFULLY" came on the loudspeaker and kids started pouring in from the gaps in the railing.

"Hey, I have an idea," she said, leaning in and shouting over the noise, "you want to come get an ice cream bar with me? My grandparents gave me extra money. Come on; I'll buy. The machine's over here."

Too confused to raise any objection, I followed her over to the exit near where Donna and Marcie were standing. Just before we got there, she grabbed my right arm with both hands.

"I'm sorry I have to do this, but I promised." At which, to my total surprise, she swung me around once and sent me flying toward the crowded exit. I tried to grab the railing but there were people on either side blocking it. My skates stopped dead on the rubber matting, sending me sprawling on the ground headfirst. Two skaters had to jump out of the way to avoid hitting me.

"First time on skates?" said a smart-aleck high school kid, and I picked myself up as quickly as possible, trying to dust off the knees of my new blue jeans that would not totally yield the ground-in floor dust.

I couldn't believe Donna had done this to me after she had been so nice. I went to the rail to see if I could find her. Instead, I spotted Donna Ivory and Marcie rounding the far turn, pointing in my direction and laughing. So I was right! They all had this set up to begin with!

I jumped into the moving mass of skaters and headed for the far turn as fast as I could move. Donna and Marcie must have seen me coming, though, because they swung off at the nearest exit and headed straight for the women's lounge. *Dumb, dumb*, I thought. I should have waited until they caught up with me and then gone after them. I skated around a couple more times looking for Donna Callaway or Matt but found neither, so I decided to stop and watch for them in the moving crowd.

What on earth was going on? The writing on the bathroom door . . . the phone call I supposedly made to Donna . . . getting thrown by her . . . nothing was making sense.

Suddenly I heard a feminine voice singing behind me, "Don-na-a-a where can ya be?" I turned around to find Donna Callaway standing there grinning and holding two ice cream bars.

"No hard feelings?" she said. "Here." She held out an ice cream bar. "This is from me. The throw was from Donna Ivory, I swear."

"I figured," I said, thanking her for the ice cream. "But why didn't she do her own dirty work?"

"She didn't think she was a good enough skater. Besides, I figured it was my only chance of skating with you." She blushed as she said this, and the redness of her face made the freckles on her turned-up nose stand out. She wasn't pretty, like Donna Ivory, but I decided she was cute. Really cute, with a bit of a pixie smile.

"Where is Donna, anyway?" she said. "I thought she'd be around here enjoying her triumph."

"I think she's hiding in the girls' room."

"Are you mad at me?"

"No. You really creamed me, though. Do you really skate in roller derbies?"

"No, my coach just taught me a few moves for fun. You got my best one."

I liked talking to her. She was like a friend. Donna Ivory was almost too pretty to talk to; I could never think of anything to say.

"I suppose you'll be skating the last skate with Donna," she said.

"I don't know now. I didn't know she was so mad."

"She's not mad. She just wanted to get back at you as a joke."

And her joke had backfired when I met this other Donna, but I didn't say that. Instead I said, "What kind of skating do you do, if not the roller derby kind?"

"Freestyle skating. It's a lot like ice skating. We do routines to music. You should come to one of my practices sometime."

"I'd like that."

Suddenly I heard someone calling my name over the crowd noise. It was Matt.

"Jonathan," he said, coming up behind me, quite agitated, "you need to come with me right now."

"Why?" I said. I didn't want to leave Donna right then.

"I can't tell you now. Just come with me."

"Is it in the ba—" but Matt jerked me away so fast I didn't get to say "bathroom."

"I guess I'll see you later, Donna," I said as Matt kept pulling on me. "Thanks for the ice cream bar!"

"Thanks for the skate." She gave me a puzzled look and a wave.

"What's the deal, Matt?" I said as I lost sight of her in the crowd. "Why did you jerk me away like that?"

"Because you were starting to say something about the bathroom, and believe me, you don't want to be talking to anyone here about the men's bathroom."

"Why?"

"Because your initials are in it now."

"What? Are you kidding?"

"No. Yours and Donna's."

"Which Donna?" I said. We had started out on the opposite side of the rink from the men's room and it seemed to be taking forever for us to get there.

"That's what's *really* weird. At first it was Donna Ivory, but now it's Donna Callaway. Who knows who it will be by the time we get back there. Do you know any other Donnas?"

Now I was beginning to suspect something. Matt had come in late, and after that I'd discovered the "Ben B. was here." Then we'd gone back and found the date. Now this.

"Matt, are you doing this?"

He stopped dead in his tracks when I said this, and the fright on his face was enough to at least keep me from pressing him any further—that, along with a little anger at being mistrusted.

"Okay, okay . . . sorry."

"Look," he said, stopping near a bench around the corner from the bathroom door, "you go see for yourself. I probably shouldn't be hanging around there too much anymore."

"Sounds like you've had to go to the bathroom a lot tonight," I said, still not believing him completely.

When I got in the bathroom, someone was in the end stall, so I stood in front of the mirror messing with my hair. Suddenly I felt uneasy. What if the person in there, looking at my initials right that moment, was someone who knew me? So I slipped into the other stall. I tried to look under the wall, but all I could see was a pair of roller skates. Then I looked at my own feet and realized that if the guy next door was checking me out, he would notice my pants weren't down, so I dropped them and waited. (When you're thirteen, you expect everyone to be looking under the partition because that's exactly what you would do.)

A number of questions entered my head while I sat there. How many people in this church *didn't* know me? Hardly any. My father was the choir director, for heaven's sake. How many "J.L.'s" were there in the church? How many "D.C.'s?" I decided right then and there to dump my idea of skating with Donna Callaway on the last Couples Skate.

When the coast was clear, I went over to the other stall and studied the writing. It was just as Matt had said. "J.L. + D.C.," but it wasn't a curved *C*. It had a straight vertical back line, the top and bottom of which clearly bore evidence of once being an *I*.

I came back out and sat next to Matt.

"Fly's open," he said.

Not again, I thought as I went for my zipper, only to find it was up.

"Just kidding."

"Come on, Matt, this is no time for jokes!"

"So what do you make of it?"

"I don't know," I sighed. "One thing's for sure: we've got to stay away from that bathroom or I'm gonna get charged with this."

"But what if Ben's angel adds to the message again? Don't you want to know?"

"You can look if you want. I'm not going in there anymore."

"So you don't think it's an angel doing this?" said Matt.

"I said, I don't know what to think. It could be someone playing a joke on me or trying to get me in trouble."

"Well, one thing's for sure," said Matt, looking off to the side, "you're going to be in big trouble if you don't skate the last skate with Donna Ivory. She's expecting you to skate it with her."

"How do you know?" I looked in the direction he was looking and saw Donna sitting in the spot where she usually waited for me for Couples Skate.

"She told me."

"Well, what if I don't want to?"

"You can probably kiss your girlfriend good-bye."

"That would be almost worth it, seeing as I haven't kissed her yet."

"She watched you talking to Donna Callaway and she didn't look very happy."

Donna Ivory looked over our way for an instant and then looked away when she saw we were watching her.

"I don't get it," I said. "She's the one who set me up with Donna in the first place."

"She probably didn't expect you to have such a good time."

"You weren't having such a bad time yourself. Why don't you skate the last skate with her? She talks to you more than she talks to me."

"So I guess this means you're skating with Donna Callaway," he said, changing the subject. "The writing's on the wall."

"That's the very reason why I'm *not* skating with her."

As it turned out, I didn't skate with either one of them. I had had it with Donnas for the night. Instead, I skated with my sister, who welcomed the idea because she had just been jilted by her present love interest on the last skate of the night. So Becky and I represented the lonely hearts club, and Matt ended up skating with a stone-faced Donna Ivory, whom I would not speak with again for a long time—something that would delight Ben, I thought. And as far as I could tell, Donna Callaway went home early.

The last song of the night was Bobby Vee's "Devil or Angel," which captured the evening perfectly. It would be a while before I would figure out who was what.

The one person who finished the night happily was my mother, who told me later that it made her proud to see Becky and me together on the last skate.

6

Pearly Gates

The Colorado Avenue Standard Christian Church was a typical middle- to upper-middle-class evangelical church. It was white on the outside and white on the inside, except for one family who always had a whole pew to themselves about three rows back on the left side—a row that could always be spotted by the bright colors the mother wore and the feathered hats, which always ensured a wide gap in the row behind her. That was the Pearl family, consisting of the mother, Netta, and her three children, Isabelle, Issac, and Isaiah, evenly spaced at nine, seven, and five years of age. The father had passed away before they started coming to our church. He had built a successful business before his heart attack, the sale of which had netted Netta a tidy sum that put her in a wider circle of opportunity than her more disadvantaged neighbors. She said that it was primarily because of our excellent Sunday school program for her children that she had left the First Apostolic Holy Ghost Church of God in Christ down on the Arroyo near the roller rink; but she had left her old neighborhood as well and moved into a predominantly white area of Pasadena.

In 1961, the Pearls were not called African-American or even "black." They were Negroes. And there were still vestiges of the derogatory term "nigger" hanging around then. My uncle, who grew up in the South, still called Brazil nuts "nigger toes," and little kids still used the popular coin-toss nursery rhyme, "eenie meenie minie mo, catch a nigger by the toe."

The Pearls had been coming to our church for almost a year, and Netta had made it clear she had every intention of making the Colorado Avenue Standard Christian Church her permanent church home. She had gone through the membership class and had even been baptized. Pastor Beamering had handled the whole affair splendidly and set a great example of acceptance and love, even when it meant losing two families and living with the ongoing ire of three more who decided to stay and make life miserable for him.

That wasn't all he lost. He also lost some water in the baptistery when he baptized Netta. It actually didn't happen when Netta went down; it happened when he tried to get her up.

Netta Pearl was big—250 pounds big. Yet she wasn't necessarily what you would call fat. A bit plump perhaps, but not fat. Fat is ugly and Netta was not ugly. She was big and wide and beautiful in the way that a mother's large lap is beautiful.

Pastor Beamering had anticipated some difficulty with the baptism, and I heard my father telling my mother that Jeffery T. had even considered using the help of Assistant Pastor Ivory, but then decided that this event already had enough attention drawn to it by virtue of Netta's color without adding insult by obviously adjusting tradition to cope with her size. That proved to be a fateful decision, since Pastor Beamering lost control of Netta going down. Had she been only fat, she might have been more buoyant; but Netta Pearl was just *big*, and she sank right out of Jeffery T.'s hands, causing the water level in the baptistery to rise considerably.

When he couldn't pick her up from his normal position, facing the congregation, Pastor Beamering quickly maneuvered himself around her, putting his back to us, so he could lift with his stronger right arm. His first attempt sent a wave of water over the front side of the baptistery as he slipped from her and fell back against the wall. The second, to the relief of everyone, finally brought Netta up out of the water. All of which only served to convince her that being rescued from her underwater tomb was all a part of her real salvation. She raised her hands, jumped and shouted "Glory to God!" and sloshed out more water over the edge of the baptistery until Pastor Beamering finally managed to calm her down with a prayer. This is why it would always be remembered at the Colorado Avenue Standard Christian Church that the last row of the choir were baptized simultaneously with Netta Pearl.

And now this intimate connection between Netta and the

choir was about to take on an even greater significance, for Netta Pearl's attempts to roost somewhere in our church had finally landed her smack-dab in the middle of the front row of my father's choir loft.

For almost a year, her efforts to enter some arena of the life of our church had been met with a good deal of resistance. Through all this disappointment, her countenance remained perpetually optimistic. Netta had a way of brushing off prejudice— taking it with a grain of salt and laughing back a comment that always diffused the anger. Her spirit, like her frame, was big enough to absorb anything, and now that patience was finally going to receive its reward.

My father was visibly nervous as we drove to church. Not only because it was Netta's first Sunday in the choir, but because she was starting off with the biggest bang possible—a solo.

"Don't be so concerned, dear," my mother said, "you know she has a remarkable voice."

"Oh, I know that, honey, it's just that you never quite know where she's going with it. I'm not sure Milton can follow her, and she's definitely not going to be following him."

Milton Owlsley was our church organist, and Netta Pearl was going to severely test his fastidious musical sensibilities.

"Milton is dreading this morning, and so am I. I wish Jeffery hadn't insisted she sing in the choir without at least talking to me first."

"And what would you have done?" asked my mother. "Turn her down, like the Ladies Aid Society and the Sunday school superintendent? I think that's just awful. She's got to know that the third and fourth grade classes are doubling up due to lack of teachers—one of her children is in the class!—and then they tell her they don't need any more teachers. To tell you the truth, I'm surprised she's still around here."

"Well, sometimes I wish she wasn't," said my father.

"Walter!"

"I'm sorry. . . . I didn't really mean that . . . and you're right, I wouldn't have turned her down. But I certainly wouldn't have started her off with a *solo*. I still can't believe Jeffery promised her a solo on her first Sunday!"

"He was probably trying to make up for her other disappointments, dear. What song did you decide on, by the way?"

" 'The Love of God.' "

"The one Stuart Hamlin sings?"

"Yes, and George Beverly Shea. It's the only one I could find that she knows. Ann, I told you, the woman can't read music! Jeffery gave me a 250-pound woman who takes up two chairs in choir practice and can't read music!"

"Yes, but she can sing," said my mother.

"Boy, can she ever," said Becky. "I sat in front of her once, and my ears were buzzing afterwards."

"Does she really take up two chairs?" I asked, and my father nodded his head.

"Now you two be careful," warned my mother. "Netta Pearl is simply a large woman, and a very fine person, I think."

"Mom, 'large' isn't the word," said Becky. "She's colossal!"

"She's a house," I said.

"All right, that will be enough. I think we are all in for a real treat this morning."

"I wish I could feel that way," said my father, taking a turn we didn't usually take. "I hope you're right."

"Dear," said my mother, looking suspiciously at the houses and streets we were passing, "where are you going?"

"To church, of course."

"You haven't taken this way in years."

"Haven't I?"

"My goodness, you *are* nervous."

"I'm just fine," my father said, squaring his jaw.

Despite the slight detour, we got to church when we normally did, around 9:15. Sunday school was at 9:30 and church was at 11:00. I went to the choir room first with my father. I didn't want to get to Sunday school early. It wasn't cool to be early. Besides, I didn't want to risk the fact that Donna Ivory might be there early too.

When we walked into the choir room, Netta was already there with one of the other choir members.

"Hi, Mildred . . . and, Netta, don't you look nice this morning," said my father, half swallowing his words. She had on the loudest clash of bright color I had ever seen. Netta smiled and nodded proudly.

"Walter," said Mildred, a regular in the choir, standing next to a pile of choir robes slung over a few folding chairs. "We don't have a proper size robe for Netta."

"That's all right," said my father, getting out the music folders and giving them to me so I could start passing them out on the chairs. "It doesn't have to be a perfect fit this morning. Anything close will do. We'll have Claudia take care of fitting her after the service."

Mildred gave my father a look that clearly said he had not grasped the gravity of the situation. This didn't register with him, however, because he was buried in a hymnal at the time.

"Excuse me," I heard Mildred say to Netta under her breath, and then she went over and whispered to my father, "She can't fit into any robe we have."

"Oh," he said, following Mildred's eyes over to where Netta was sitting. "Oh," he said again when he saw with new understanding what she was wearing. "Are you sure you can't find anything?"

Mildred nodded her head slowly. "Claudia will have to make up something this week from two of the other robes or we'll have to order from the factory, if they even have such a size."

"Well, she'll have to wear . . . what she has on," said my father with a certain pain in his voice. "Can you do something about the hat, though?"

Mildred went over and broke the news to Netta, who seemed quite relieved. But my poor father was going to be in for it this morning.

Sunday school had already started when I got there. All morning long, Donna Ivory gave me what I was expecting to get, the cold shoulder. She was like a porcupine with imaginary needles that stuck me if I got within three feet of her. I hardly ever looked at her, yet I always seemed to know right where she was all the time. I could feel her icy stare on the back of my head.

The more I thought about it, though, the less concerned I became. *There's got to be more to having a girlfriend than waiting for the next church skating night*, I thought.

I also found myself looking over at Donna Callaway a lot that morning, but she wasn't terribly friendly either. It made me wonder if they were in this together, the same way they'd plotted to knock me off my skates. I decided, as I listened to the Sunday school lesson, which was about some woman in the Old Testament who drove a tent peg through a guy's head while he slept, that I didn't want to have anything to do with girls anymore. I would play with my trains and maybe invite Matt over after church.

"Matt, do you want to come over to my house this after-noon—that is, if it's all right with my parents? I don't think it will be any problem."

"I'll have to check with Leonard and Bernice," he said. "I'll let you know after church."

Although I'd been wanting to show Matt my train layout, it was a pretty big step for me to invite him over, whether he could come or not. It was the first time since Ben's death that I had asked anyone over.

———————

My father's worst fears came true that Sunday in church. The choir was the green-robed backdrop for the colorful floral display that was Netta Pearl. It was not Netta *in* the choir; it was Netta *and* the choir.

On the choral numbers, like the Call to Worship and the Prayer Response and the Doxology, she made up her own part. Though she got all the words right, the notes were her own. In spite of this, however, she never sang a wrong note—that is, a note that didn't fit. It was simply not a note that was in the music. It was a note no one else was singing—a note, indeed, that no one in the Colorado Avenue Standard Christian Church ever knew existed before Netta Pearl.

Netta had been listening to these same choral responses for almost a year, and she'd been holding all those beautiful notes inside, waiting for this moment. No, she didn't need music, she didn't need directing; she needed to be cut loose. And once freed, it was Netta's voice filling every corner where sound could go in that church.

You could look at it from another perspective, of course. My father's worry over Netta having a solo on her first Sunday was unfounded. In truth, it was irrelevant, because every piece of music the choir sang was Netta's solo anyway. And by the time she got going, her outlandish dress actually seemed appropriate.

Though it turned out to be just one more solo for her, still, when Netta Pearl sang the anthem, "The Love of God," something happened—something that took everyone beyond the walls of the church to a place outside of time and space, a place they'd never been before. Someone said it was "the Throne of God." Pastor Beamering, never one to miss the opportunity for a pun, said it was the "Pearl-y Gates" Netta took us to.

The song was not new to most of us, but the way Netta sang it made it seem like we had never heard it before. She sang every word like it was a place to park. Her wide mouth brought forth rich vowel sounds that seemed to belong to another language. Her voice was not high and angelic, like the sopranos we were used to; it was low and deep and rich, rolling over you like a vast ocean.

I noticed the words of the song for the first time that day:

The love of God is greater far
Than tongue or pen can ever tell;
It goes beyond the highest star,
And reaches to the lowest hell

Every word erupted into a picture. Tongues wagged, pens went off pages, stars shot by at warp speed, and hell burned.

In the beginning, Milton Owlsley fought with the time Netta was taking over these words. He would play a musical pattern and then have to wait for her to catch up with him. This was the type of song that needed to be stretched out, and Netta was taking it as far as it would go. It seemed like words were blooming as she sang them, with blossoms as big and bursting as the ones on the floral print of her dress.

The guilty pair, bowed down with care,
God gave His Son to win;
His erring child, He reconciled,
And pardoned from his sin

For some reason, when Netta sang these words, I understood them. Maybe she sang it slow enough so I could really think about the words, or maybe she had some spiritual gift of interpretation. The guilty pair was Adam and Eve. She didn't say that; Adam and Eve just popped into my head. Of course . . . that made sense.

Most of the congregation was transfixed—even the people who had been giving Pastor Beamering a bad time about accepting the Pearl family. Our church had never heard anything come from the depths of the soul the way "The Love of God" came from this woman.

The only people who weren't getting it were my father and Milton. My father was waving his arms, trying to direct Milton. He was not directing Netta—he was smarter than that—but he was trying to interpret Netta to Milton. It wasn't working. My father's arm-waving would have been a distraction were it not for the hold Netta had on the congregation. And it certainly wasn't helping Milton, who kept running ahead of each phrase and waiting for her to catch up.

By the third verse my father realized his directing was of no consequence and stopped. Milton realized something too, for he stopped keeping time altogether and just played the chords behind Netta's notes, moving them around her voice when she moved. That's when it all came together. That's when everyone stopped fighting and allowed Netta to paint the most beautiful picture of all.

Everyone was with her now, and Netta knew it. She approached this last verse rocking on each foot and closing her eyes to balance her giant frame so her soul could reach down to the bottom of that deep well from which she drew the bittersweet waters of generations of suffering, hope, and grace—of rejection by men and acceptance by God in a place where there was no earthly home but a heavenly mansion.

> Could we with ink the oceans fill,
> And were the skies of parchment made;
> Were every stalk on earth a quill,
> And every man a scribe by trade;
> To write the love of God above
> Would drain the ocean dry,
> Nor could the scroll contain the whole,
> Though stretched from sky to sky.

Milton had it now. Milton was off the page, and they were in sync. He opened up the organ and Netta opened her big wide arms and the choir actually swayed to the time that was outside of time as they sang behind her.

> O love of God, how rich and pure!
> How measureless and strong!
> It shall forevermore endure—
> The saints' and angels' song.

Netta finished, Milton's hands came up off the organ keys, and though applause might have been called for, there was none. Not right away. Only a reverent hush. Pastor Beamering, a veteran of the unexpected in church, though it had been a while since he'd had to consider it, slowly mounted the pulpit and stood there motionless.

It was a strange silence. Not uncomfortable, but a silence that rendered speech inoperative. There was nothing to say—nothing that could be said. It was appropriate silence. Silence with a finish. Finally, slowly and methodically, way after the natural time for applause had passed, Pastor Beamering began to clap. All alone at first, then joined by a random few, then gaining force, then thunderous and seemingly unending.

Netta Pearl found the nearest chair, which happened to be one of the oversized platform chairs, and sat down, wiping her perspiring face with a hanky as the genuine appreciation continued unabated. Then, from sheer exhaustion, it stopped and the normal sounds of humanity returned to the sanctuary. Throats cleared, noses blew, coughs were expelled, seats were retaken, bodies rearranged themselves, Bibles and hymnals were moved about, and children were whispered to or shaken by the arm.

"Open your Bibles, please, to the eighth chapter of Romans, verses 38 and 39." Pastor Beamering paused for the zip of Bibles being pulled out of the backs of pews and the feathering of a thousand pages to rise and fall. "We will continue our study on angels next week, but today, inspired by this exceptional reminder of the love of God, I want us to focus on that on which even angels long to look."

What could that be? I wondered. *What do we know that angels don't? How can we be smarter than angels?*

" 'For I am persuaded, that neither death, nor life, nor angels, nor principalities, nor powers, nor things present, nor things to come, nor height, nor depth, nor any other creature, shall be able to separate us from the love of God, which is in Christ Jesus our Lord.' May the Lord add His blessing to the reading of His holy word."

Then, without dropping his eyes to read them, he began quoting the song Netta had just finished singing.

" 'The love of God is greater far than tongue or pen can ever tell; it goes beyond the highest star, and reaches to the lowest hell.' The man who wrote these words, and the man who wrote the Scripture we just read, both knew the same thing. They knew that the greatest, the single most powerful, most sure thing in all the world is the love of God. Regardless of what happens to any of us, it is and will be our most valuable possession." He paused. "Just how high is the highest star?"

"High," came a deep voice from somewhere. Pastor Beamering halted a second, then went on.

"And how low is the lowest hell?"

"Low." The voice came again from somewhere near the pastor.

"Does any one of us know?" And this time, Jeffery T. waited for the response.

"No!" came the voice, growing in strength.

People strained to see where the odd echo to Pastor Beamering's dramatic words was coming from. It didn't take long to realize it was coming from the platform—more specifically, from Netta Pearl, who was so caught up in the extraordinary events of the morning that she forgot she was not in the First Apostolic Holy Ghost Church of God in Christ.

"I'll tell you who knows," said Pastor Beamering, spurred on by the fact that his once-dead congregation was suddenly giving him what every pastor craves: instant feedback.

"God knows!"

"Glo-ry!" went the echo.

"No matter where you go—high or low—God has been there first."

"Yes He has!"

"He came from heaven . . ."

"Uh-huh . . ."

"And descended into the depths of hell itself . . ."

"Mercy!" The echo was coming short and quick now.

"For you and me."

"Amen!"

Netta had started answering Jeffery T.'s appeals almost in a whisper, but each successive burst grew louder until it was a verbal duet. By now, though, the poor congregation was a mixture of amusement and horror.

Pastor Beamering, knowing he had to do something, turned to his new cohort on the platform and said in a kind voice, "Netta, honey, if you keep this up, I'm never going to get my sermon in edgewise."

That broke the tension in the room with laughter and woke Netta up to the fact that she was in a Standard Christian church full of white faces. She laughed harder than anyone and quieted down after that, leaving Pastor Beamering to develop his extemporaneous sermon on the love of God. It was one of his best, recalling the days when the unexpected from Ben and me threw him into depending on something other than his notes and pre-thought words and messages.

The part of that sermon I remember the most was when he talked about the "saints' and angels' song." He said that the love of God was a song that saints could actually sing better than angels, because angels had never been sinners. Only saints knew what it meant to be a sinner saved by grace, he said, and that statement had gotten one last "Amen" from Netta—one that everyone felt, but she expressed for us. Standard Christians were not accustomed to seeing themselves as sinners.

After the service I looked for Matt and ran into Grizzly instead. Actually, he was looking for me, since I was his primary source of interpretation. As it turned out, there had been some plumbing emergencies in the rest room of the old educational wing, which kept him out of the service. His keen visual perception of people, however, told him something was up.

"WHAT HAPPENED IN THERE TODAY?" He already had it written on his pad in anticipation of finding me.

"Netta Pearl is what happened," I said by only moving my

lips. He stared at me, unable to make the read.

"Netta Pearl," I repeated.

"WHO ATE A PEARL?" he wrote down, and then I remembered he couldn't read proper names unless he already knew who you were talking about.

Taking his pad in my hand I wrote, "NETTA PEARL." He brightened and nodded his head, stretching out his arms real wide with a question mark on his face.

"Yes, the big Negro woman," I said, again by only moving my lips. "She sang with the choir. It stopped the show."

"LIKE BEN!"

Well . . . yes, just like Ben, though I hadn't thought of it until he wrote it down.

"HAVEN'T SEEN PEOPLE LEAVE CHURCH THIS HAPPY SINCE BEN."

Grizzly was always one to keep the memory of Ben alive. Most everyone else was afraid to bring it up. I never understood that. I loved talking about Ben, though sometimes I resisted. He would always be in my life through my memories of him, and now maybe even through his angels.

"WHAT DID SHE SING ABOUT?"

"She sang about the angels' song," I mouthed. I knew he would like that, and he smiled when I said it.

"It's in the song," I said, and I got out the bulletin where the words were written down and showed him the last line of the chorus: "The saints' and angels' song."

"BEN'S SONG TOO," he wrote, "BEN'S A SAINT NOW—BEN AND THE ANGELS SING."

"When do you hear angels sing?" I asked. "Is it a certain time?"

"ONLY WHEN ALONE."

"When *you're* alone?"

He nodded.

"During the day? Night?"

He thought for a minute and then wrote, "COULD HAPPEN ANYTIME NO ONE HERE."

"May I listen with you sometime?"

He welcomed the idea with joy, nodding vigorously.

Just then we were interrupted by one of the deacons who

informed Grizzly that another toilet in the education building was backing up and they needed him right away. So with a wave of his pad, he was gone.

I went back to looking for Matt but never found him. Instead I found Donna Callaway sitting on a bench in the narthex, waiting for her grandparents who were in line to see Pastor Beamering. It was a longer line than usual because Netta Pearl was greeting people along with the pastor.

This had come about more through the natural course of events than by any pastoral design. I knew how these things worked from observing Pastor Beamering deftly turn potential disruptions by Ben and me into events that flowed into the course of the service as if they had been planned.

Netta Pearl was still on the platform when Jeffery T. finished his sermon, since the choir had exited after her solo while she was caught up in the applause of the congregation, leaving her alone there. Pastor Beamering's usual close to a service was to start the congregation on the final hymn and then walk down the center aisle during the second or third verse so that he could give his benediction from the back of the church. This left him in the advantageous position to greet the first worshipers who wanted to speak to him or shake his hand on their way out.

So rather than leave Netta sitting alone on the platform, Pastor Beamering had taken her arm and escorted her down the aisle with him during the hymn. (Of course Netta kept singing all the way down, bringing her big voice into close proximity to those on the inside aisle and even closer to the beaming face of Pastor Beamering.) Thus, the first greeters to get to the pastor after the benediction found that Netta Pearl was there to greet them too, with a wide grin, big arms, and an even bigger heart.

"Hi," I said to Donna, sitting down next to her on the cold wooden bench.

"Oh, hi, Jonathan," she said with a little flat spot in the middle of her voice.

"Why didn't you stay for the last skate?" I asked.

"My grandparents were with me, and they were getting tired," she said, looking down. "Besides, I didn't want to watch you skate with Donna."

Her bluntness took me a little by surprise.

"I didn't skate with Donna."

"You didn't?" she said, brightening.

"No, I skated with Becky."

"Who's Becky?"

"My sister."

"Oh," she said, trying to hide her pleasure. "Donna's so pretty."

"I think you're pretty."

She bit her lip and looked over at her grandparents who had finally made it to Jeffery T. and Netta.

"Why don't you come to my practice this week?" she said, suddenly turning her whole body in my direction and looking straight at me, her ponytail bouncing behind her head.

"When do you practice?"

"Every day after school."

"Every day?"

"And two hours on Saturday."

"I have to deliver papers after school, but I might be able to come on Saturday. I'll have to talk to my parents."

"Saturday would be great! I practice in the morning at ten o'clock. Why don't you call me again this week and let me know if you can come."

Again? There was that mysterious phone call stuff again. It made me wonder, if I didn't call her, would she hear from me anyway? I thought about trying to get to the bottom of it right then and letting her know it wasn't me who called, but she was so happy and I liked where this whole thing was going, so I didn't say anything.

Just then Donna's grandparents started in our direction, and she quickly excused herself and joined them before they ever came close to the bench where we sat. She seemed embarrassed, and I wondered if it was because her grandmother was in a wheelchair. I wondered also where her parents were. Maybe they didn't go to church.

The last few people were waiting to speak with Pastor Beamering, and Matt was still nowhere in sight. I was about to go look for him when my mother came and put her arm around me and headed me toward the pastor and Netta Pearl.

"Come on, Jonathan. Let's let this woman know what a fine job she did this morning."

I started to wrestle away from her, but Jeffery T. had already spotted us.

"Jonathan!" he said, clasping his hands together and washing me all over with his pastorly glow. "I heard you came by the house this week. We've wondered where you've been. Let's not become strangers now." He thrust out his hand and flashed me his big shiny grin.

"Hi," I said while he shook my arm vigorously up and down.

"Netta," my mother said, "that was the most glorious thing I have ever heard. I'm so happy you had a chance to share your wonderful talents with us, and I certainly hope there will be more of this." She winked at Pastor Beamering when she said this.

"Why, thank you, Mrs. Liebermann . . . and this is your boy, here? You know, we nevuh met."

"You haven't? Well, this is Jonathan."

"Hullo, Jonathan," and something in the way she said it made me swell up inside. The tone of her voice made it sound as if I were someone very important she had been waiting to meet. When I put out my hand, she totally enclosed it with both of hers. I had never touched a Negro before. I don't know what I was expecting, but I found nothing unusual about her hands except that they were big and warm and kind.

"How old are you, Jonathan?"

"Thirteen."

"Thirteen," she mused. "A year of comin' out. A year of discoverin'. What have you discovered since you been thirteen, child?"

I didn't know what to say. No one had ever demanded creative thinking from me on such short notice. She gave me no mercy. She just stood there smiling and waiting, her eyebrows perched expectantly atop the big bony ledges over her broad nose.

"I . . . uh . . . I found out angels are real."

"Splendid!" she said, and Pastor Beamering smiled an especially big smile. Of course, not knowing I had been kissed on the lips by an angel, he was probably thinking my revelation had come through his sermons. "And just how did you find this out?"

I looked up at Jeffery T.'s hovering smile.

"Through Pastor Beamering's sermons," I said, hoping not to be questioned further.

"Have you evuh met an angel, Jonathan?" she said, dashing my hopes. I did not want to explain any further. Fortunately Netta saved me by answering her own question.

"I have," she said.

"Really?" said Pastor Beamering.

"Yes suh. The night my husband died. I awoke and saw two tall men a-talkin' softly at the end of my bed. It was the very moment George died, and though his body lie next to me, when the angels left, they was three of them. It made it so much easiuh to take. It was the most peaceful feelin' I've evuh known."

"Well—" said Pastor Beamering, breaking the mood of the moment and clasping his hands as though preparing to speak.

"What a beautiful story," my mother said slowly, interrupting his attempted closure.

"Yes," said Jeffery T. "A beautiful story, indeed. Well . . . I'm ready to wrap this morning up and go get some dinner. Netta, would you care to join us? We're just going down the street to the cafeteria."

"Oh, no thank you, pastor. I have a roast waitin' in the oven."

"Thank you again for your important part in this morning's service, said Mrs. Beamering."

"Oh, mercy me, it's Him you should be thankin'. He's the one done give me this voice."

7

Up the Tower

"Now what am I going to do?" said my father as we pulled out of the church parking lot and headed down Colorado Avenue toward Beedle's Cafeteria.

"About what, dear?"

"About Netta Pearl, of course. Thanks to Jeffery, I now have one very large Negro woman who has turned my choir into nothing more than a gospel backup group. I have an organist who suddenly wants to learn to play like Booker somebody and the sports cars—"

"Booker T. and the M.G.'s, Daddy," said Becky.

"—whatever they are. Where am I going to get music for this? If Netta Pearl is going to be in my choir, everything will have to be changed to accommodate her, for heaven's sake. Everything!"

We sat at a signal light in silence. We could feel the tension coming from the front seat, and Becky and I kept looking at each other, trying hard not to laugh.

"To tell you the truth, sometimes I wonder what I'm going to do with Jeffery," my father finally blurted out. "He's the one who always seems to set up these situations and then expects me to solve them. Sometimes I wish I could just wipe that silly little grin right off his face!"

"Walter! I can't believe you're talking like this."

Becky and I grinned fake smiles at each other, both of us silently wagging our bottom lips like a ventriloquist's dummy. The two of us had a running joke about Pastor Beamering that likened him to Edgar Bergen's Charlie McCarthy—the shiny face, the plastered-down hair, the hard head, and the smile that never changed.

"Well, it's true, Ann. I asked him that very thing . . . 'What are we going to do now?' . . . and he just smiled at me and said nothing. Nothing! All he did was smile at me. Honestly, I hate that . . . that—"

"Honey, cool down. We're almost to the restaurant."

Hearing my father talk about his frustration with Pastor Beamering reminded me of playing games with Matt. He would always beat me. Not only at gin, but any other games we played at the beach, for that matter, like chess or Chinese checkers—or even Ping-Pong in the youth room at church. Somehow he always managed to win. The worst was Ping-Pong. He never hit the ball hard; he'd just keep lobbing it back to me—regardless of where or how hard I hit it to him—until I finally got frustrated and smashed it off the table or into the net. I *hated* it when he did that. In the Bible that I got for graduating from the sixth grade into the junior high department, Matt actually had the nerve to write, "Since you'll never beat me at anything, vaporize!" Jeffery T.'s silent smile, like a dummy without a hand inside it, was just like Matt's lob return, and I imagined my father wanting to smash the pastor's smile down his throat right about then.

"I'm taking her out of the choir, Ann," he said as we pulled into Beedle's parking lot.

"Oh, honey, you can't do that after one week."

"Actually, it's not like that. Technically, she's never been *in* the choir. I honestly don't think she ever could sing just one part along with the other women. I *am* seriously thinking about having her only sing once a month. What do you think about that? Once a month could be Netta Pearl Sunday."

"I think we'd better go have dinner with the Beamerings and talk about this later."

My father rarely took us out to eat, but when he did, it was most likely to Beedle's Cafeteria. Beedle's was only a few blocks from the church and served an inexpensive buffet dinner that was popular with the Sunday church crowd. Once every couple months we would have Sunday dinner there, usually with the Beamerings.

I hated Beedle's. You had to wait in line for half an hour in a long, empty hallway. The food wasn't too bad once you got it, but nothing like my mother's Sunday dinner. I always thought that if you were going to go out to eat, it should be better than what you could get at home, and you shouldn't have to stand in line for it. Not so at Beedle's. Becky and I always changed the *d* to a *t* on our place mats and pretended we were hunting for beetles in the food. Once my father found a gnat in his salad. We told him it was a beetle without its shell, which we were sure he had already eaten.

"That was the crunchy part, Daddy," said Becky.

I always got halibut, not because I particularly liked fish, but because it was the best thing there. It was lightly battered and baked and looked like a giant, overweight cornflake. The best part about it was the tartar sauce Becky and I would squeeze out of little thimble-sized paper cups.

It was just as well that I hadn't found Matt after church, because I wouldn't have been able to have him over anyway. I had forgotten that we were going to Beedle's. Every time Becky or I tried to have a guest come along when we were going out, my father would get this pained look on his face, and my mother would say that it probably wouldn't be a good idea this time. If Matt had found me after church, I would have had to go through the embarrassment of un-inviting him on account of my father's face.

To add to my dismay, the Ivorys were also there that day, and Pastor Beamering was trying to get enough tables together to accommodate all three families. I breathed a sigh of relief when his attempts failed. Besides, they were too far ahead of us and were well into their meal by the time we got through the line.

The worst part about being at Beedle's Cafeteria, however, was not the food or the line; it was Pastor Beamering. His voice was as loud as it was from the pulpit. That afternoon, for instance, the entire restaurant knew all the details of his attempts to get our three families together at one seating. For a moment it seemed like one older couple sitting at a table next to the Ivorys might get up and move, but the man was hard of hearing and never got the message from his wife that the pastor of the Colorado Avenue Standard Christian Church was bearing down on them. I was rooting for the old guy all the way and was happy to see him stay put. I wanted to be as far away from Donna Ivory as possible. As it was, she kept her eyes away from me at all times.

Then there was Pastor Beamering's prayer over the meal. Believe it or not, he would actually stand up, stretch his long arms out over the three tables it took to seat our families, and bless the food *out loud!* That's when I would drop my napkin and go under the table for it.

Once through the line, you could cut back into it for seconds. After the pastoral buffet prayer, which usually had the Gospel story somewhere in it for anyone who might be listening, I surfaced with my napkin and immediately went back for my favorite part of the meal that I had forgotten to get the first time: the corn muffins. They were real tasty with lots of butter melted into them. I put two muffins on my plate and returned to my seat, only to have Peter and Joshua reach over and snatch them away. That was the other thing I didn't like about eating out with the Beamerings. The Beamering boys would always tease me. Part of this was probably because I was the youngest and they didn't have Ben to pick on anymore, but part of it was to show off for my sister's benefit.

There was a time when they used to tease her along with me. No more. My sister's sudden blooming had changed all that. Almost overnight, she went from being someone Peter and Joshua wanted to tease to someone they wanted to impress. Now they just teased me.

When I came back from my second muffin trip, Pastor Beamering was waxing on about Netta Pearl.

"Did you see the look on Mable Buecher's face when Netta started rockin' and rollin' on the second chorus? I thought she was going to roll over and die right there on the spot."

I caught Becky's eye and knew we were both thinking the same thing. If he thought "The Love of God" was rock 'n' roll, he had some big surprises coming.

"And Milton! Did you get a load of Milton? She actually had him going there. Do you know what he told me?"

"No," my father said, and I wondered if there was another version of Booker T. and the M.G.'s coming up. Sure enough. . . .

"He said he was going to start listening to Booker T. and the Emcee's—some rock group he knows about with a lot of organ in it. Can you believe that? Milton Owlsley, of all people!"

I looked around the table and it was obvious that everyone, including my parents, after being corrected by my sister, knew the pastor hadn't gotten the name of the Booker T. group quite right, but no one dared say anything to him. At moments like these I felt Ben's absence sharply. Ben would have said something. He was the only one who could. Without Ben around, Pastor Beamering got away with too much.

"You know, Walter, people weren't sure at first, but by the time she was done, they loved her. They want to hear more, Walter. They are going to hear more, aren't they?"

"Well . . . uh . . . sure. You can't have talent like that around and not use it. It's just that—"

"Good! I have a feeling this is stirring something among us. I haven't heard the church buzzing like this since Ben and Jonathan had them going. Right, Jonathan?"

"Yes, sir. By the way—"

"Well, Walter, what can you say about this morning?"

I surprised myself by trying to get a word in about the rock group, but what could anyone say after Jeffery T. had said it all?

"I'd say she had them eating out of her hands, Jeff."

"Boy, you can say that again."

Because I felt it had to be done, I wrote "IT'S BOOKER T. AND THE M.G.'S on a napkin and slipped it to Mrs. Beamering on the way out. She was the only one who could correct the pastor, but never in public. It was suddenly important to me to make sure Pastor Beamering got the name right. Maybe it was because I knew it would have been important to Ben.

"Well, that helped a lot," my father said sarcastically when we were back in the car driving home.

I noticed that I now had a nice big tartar sauce grease spot on the front of my pants, proof we'd been to Beedle's.

"You can talk to him alone tomorrow," said my mother. "He's much more cooperative when he doesn't have an audience."

"The whole restaurant is his audience," said Becky.

"Yes, Becky," said my mother. "That's all part of being a pastor."

"What, being obnoxious?"

"No, being firm and outspoken. If you can't say something

nice, young lady, then don't say anything at all."

"Daddy, can I drive again today?"

"Not today, sweetheart. I have work to do for tonight's service."

"Darn."

"I wanted to have Matt over today," I said, "but we went out."

"I'd be happy to have Matt over anytime. Why not next Sunday?" said my mother.

"Okay, I'll ask him. And do you think someone could take me to the roller rink next Saturday morning?"

"The roller rink? What for?"

"Donna Callaway has invited me to come watch her practice."

"So the Roller Derby Queen won the contest of Donnas," said my sister.

"Cut it out," I said to her. "She's not a roller derby skater."

"She practices roller skating?" said my mother. "Why?"

"She's entering competitions and stuff."

"I've never heard of such a thing, have you, dear?"

"What?" said my father, obviously somewhere else in his thoughts.

"What happened to Donna Ivory?" asked my mother.

"Nothing. I'd just like to see Donna Callaway skate, that's all. And she invited me."

"Well, I don't know about this," my mother said. "Someone would have to be with you at the roller rink. How long does she practice?"

"Two hours. You could just drop me off and come back later."

"I don't know. That sounds like a date to me, and you're not old enough to date yet. And besides, I'm not sure who this Donna Callaway is. Are they new in the church?"

"I wouldn't even be with her, Mother, I'd just be *watching* her."

"I think your father and I need to discuss this. Donna Callaway . . . do you know her parents, Walter?"

My father made no reply. His mind was still on something else—Netta Pearl, most likely.

"She always comes to everything with her grandparents," said Becky. "Her grandmother's in a wheelchair."

"Oh, so *that's* Donna Callaway. Your father and I definitely need to discuss this at another time."

"Why? What's wrong?"

"Never mind. We'll discuss it later."

I flashed my sister a gee-thanks-a-lot look, which she returned with a how-was-I-to-know? shrug.

I spent most of the afternoon up with my train set laying track in and around the completed mountains. I had already put a switch inside the mountain so that one track went in one side and two came out the other. I also had built up one of those tracks inside the mountain so it came out on top of the other. It was the high road and the low road railroad. While I worked, I thought about taking the low road and getting to Donna's practice regardless of what my parents decided.

My train layout was more exciting to work on now that I was within sight of getting all the track up and actually running the trains. It had taken almost a year to get to this point because I never had any concentrated time to work on it. I figured one good vacation period should do it—maybe Thanksgiving, or for sure by Christmas.

Often I was distracted along the way by ideas that had nothing to do with setting up the trains. My little model town had sidetracked me for months. Once I saw some ¼-inch plywood that my father was about to throw away and got the idea for raised city blocks. By cutting the plywood into rectangles with rounded corners, I was able to define the streets of my town with real curbs. I even cut notches in the plywood where I wanted driveways to be and formed ramps down from the curb level out of plaster of Paris. Then I painted the streets black and the curbs and sidewalks gray, making lines for cracks in the sidewalk. Ben would have been proud. Sometimes I imagined he was watching me from heaven. I didn't know whether people in heaven could do that or not, but it seemed like anything should be possible from up there. Sometimes I thought I heard him say, "No, Jonathan, that's a dumb idea . . ." and things like that.

In some ways I think I looked for excuses to slow down this project because I felt that completing it would be boring. There would be nothing to do but run the trains. It was much more fun to imagine and create than to actually play with the trains. None of the people who had seen my layout understood this. They couldn't understand why it was taking me so long to get my trains running. But I loved thinking about my layout, dreaming up creative ideas for it or talking to Ben about it. I loved finding odd things that would take on new significance when placed in the scale of my layout, like barrel candy that turned into real barrels when painted and stacked against the walls of a warehouse. It had been the same with the houses Ben and I worked on. The point was not to complete them but to enjoy the process.

That night church went by slowly. I had big plans for me and Donna Callaway after church. Whatever it was about her that concerned my mother had only made me more determined to see her skate and, if need be, find out about her parents myself. From my mother's tone, that seemed to be the big problem—her parents. Her parents, and now mine. We needed a place to talk away from all eyes, and I knew exactly where that would be.

All during church I fingered the little penlight flashlight that I had tucked away in my pocket. She might be frightened at first, I thought, but when she discovered how special a place it was, she would be impressed. The only problem was going to be slipping in the door without being seen. In my favor was the fact that the turnout at church was light that night, especially among our junior high group. Fewer friends to have to shake off.

Donna was sitting a few rows behind me, and at the conclusion of the service I caught her eye and pointed to the back of the church. When I got to the narthex, she was already there.

"Hi, Jonathan," she said, and her voice sounded like water dancing over smooth rocks.

"Can you come with me? I want to show you something."

"Sure . . . but . . . where are we going? My grandparents don't like to stay long on Sunday nights."

"This will only take about five minutes."

"Okay, just a minute." And she worked her way back through the exiting flow of churchgoers to find her grandparents.

"No problem," she said when she returned. "They're talking

with some friends anyway. I have to be at the car in ten minutes, though."

"Good. This way," I said, and led her to an unmarked door along the back wall of the church. Glancing around to make sure there were no spying eyes, I unlocked it—thanks to Grizzly—opened the door, and pulled her into the darkness.

"Jonathan, what are we doing in here?"

I quickly got out my flashlight and lit up her startled face.

"Up there," I said, pointing the little beam at a vertical ladder that went up the back wall of a tiny room no bigger than a closet. "Can you climb that?"

"Yes. What's up there?"

"Follow me and I'll show you."

I handed her the light and started up the ladder. I didn't need to see; I knew every board in this place by heart. I sat on the landing and waited for her.

"Oh, wow, this is boss up here. How did you ever find this?"

"Exploring," I said. "Look over here," and I pointed out the little window that looked out over the church from high up on the back wall of the balcony.

"This is really swell. I can see my grandparents down there. What's with this place?"

"It used to be a bell tower, and the bell ringer would stand here and watch through the window for the service to be over so he could ring the bells right after the benediction."

" 'Every time a bell rings, an angel gets its wings,' " she said.

"What's that?"

"Oh, just a saying I know. So no one uses this place anymore?"

"No. Ben and I used to be up here a lot. It was our hideout. We used to play tricks on the church from up here, too."

"Who's Ben?"

"He was Pastor Beamering's son and my best friend. He died a couple years ago. Look over here. You can see outside."

I showed her the vent where you could look through the slats and see the front steps of the church and the sidewalk below. A quiet mist must have been falling during the service because the street and the sidewalk were wet and people were moving quickly to their cars. The faint swish of tires on Colorado Avenue attested to the gentle precipitation.

"Wow, you can see everything from up here," she said. "I can see why this would be a perfect hideout."

Then she started shining the penlight around the inner walls of the little room.

"Careful," I said, "that will show up in the window."

"What's that?" she said, stopping the light at a crumpled piece of paper tacked to the wall. She looked closer and read out loud, " 'Saturday, January 17, 1959. There is a God-shaped vacuum in the heart of Ben. There is a Ben-shaped vacuum in the heart of God.' That's beautiful. Did you write that?"

"No. Ben did. He slipped that into my hand just before he died."

"How did he die, anyway?"

"Heart failure."

"I'm so sorry. I can tell he meant a lot to you."

I was glad she wasn't shining the light in my eyes right then.

"How come you're always with your grandparents?" I risked, knowing we didn't have much time.

"I live with my grandparents."

"What happened to your parents?"

"I don't know."

"Have you always lived with your grandparents?"

"As long as I can remember."

"I can't imagine what that would be like."

"My grandparents are okay."

"No, I mean not knowing where your parents are."

"I manage."

"Don't you have any idea?" I hoped I wasn't pressing too hard.

"No," she answered in a voice I didn't quite trust.

I decided I'd gone far enough with my questioning. "I'm going to come see you skate on Saturday."

"You are?"

The change in her voice made the moment. I knew right then that nothing would keep me away from that rink, even if I had to do something bad to get there.

"Better check on your grandparents," I said, not knowing what to do with my emotions at that moment. For a second the flashlight caught her face, and her eyes seemed to reflect more light than they were given.

"Oh dear," she said, looking out the little window, "they're not there anymore. I better go."

"Here. I'll hold the light for you down the ladder. You go out first. I'll wait a while up here."

"Jonathan, why is everything so secret?"

"This is a secret place, and—" I caught myself.

"And what? It's my parents, isn't it?"

"It's my parents finding out about your parents, I guess. I'm sorry I even brought it up."

"That's okay. It used to bother me, but I'm used to it now. Anyway, I'm so excited about Saturday. No one's come just to see me before except my grandparents. My routine is getting ready for competition, too. You have no idea how happy this makes me." She threw her arms around me and gave me a big hug.

"Please don't tell anybody about this tower," I said.

"If anyone can keep a secret," she said, sounding slightly offended, "it's me."

When she reached the bottom of the ladder, she looked up at me, her face radiant in the small beam of my penlight. "Thank you, Jonathan," she said. "I love your tower! See you Saturday!" And a shaft of light lit up her bouncing ponytail as she slipped out the door.

8

Practice

"Matt," I said over the phone, "you've got to help me."

It was Monday afternoon, I had just finished delivering my papers, and I was calling him from a pay phone next to the corner market because I couldn't risk being overheard at home.

"What's the problem, Casanova?"

That comment came from the night before. Matt had been at church, but I hadn't seen him until I came down from the tower. I stayed up there as long as I could without raising suspicions. It was so wonderful to feel that secret place warmed by smiles and voices again. It had become so lonely there that I wouldn't go up, even though it was such a special place to me. Without Ben, it had become an aching place. But Donna's smile had changed all that, and I imagined Ben was smiling, too.

Without even knowing it, Donna had opened up a way for me to meet my memories again. Her face lit up that dark place in the tower much like the face of Margaret, the angel, lit up the bunker. Donna's was a younger face, with freckles and a turned-up nose, and though she was not an angel, she did have fine, curly blond angel hair.

Matt had figured something was up by the time he ran into me in the parking lot.

"Hey, where have you been?" he had said. "I've been looking all over for you."

"Oh . . . nowhere in particular. Just . . . wandering around."

"You wouldn't have wandered into a dark closet somewhere, would you? The same one I saw Donna Callaway coming out of with a big smile on her face? Was there perhaps a little kissy-face going on in there? Huh? Huh?"

In the excitement of showing Donna the tower, I had forgotten to relock the door once we were in. I remembered noticing the door open and close once while I was still up in the tower, shortly after Donna left. It must have been Matt, looking for me and finding what he thought was an empty janitorial closet. That was what most people in the church thought that door went to. So he had put two and two together and come up with Donna and me smooching in the closet. The sacrifice I had to pay to keep Matt from knowing about my secret tower was to leave his "kissy-face" allegations unchallenged. *Not that costly a sacrifice*, I thought. Not really. Thus my new moniker: Casanova.

"You've got to invite me over to your house on Saturday morning," I said over the phone, ignoring his comments.

"Okay, you're invited. What's up?"

"I've got to figure a way out of the house for a few hours. Donna Callaway has—"

"Aha!" Matt interrupted. "Why did I know this had something to do with Donna Callaway? Didn't you get enough in the closet?"

"Shut up and let me finish," I said. "Donna has invited me to watch her roller-skating practice Saturday, but my parents aren't going to let me go."

"How come?"

"I'm not sure. I think it has something to do with her living with her grandparents and not knowing where her real parents are."

"So? What else is new?"

Suddenly I realized I had come very close to describing Matt's circumstances as well. The phone felt dead and heavy in my hand for a few seconds.

"So—" he said, "go ahead. What's your plan?"

"Well, I thought maybe you could invite me over and I could pretend I was riding my bike to your house but go to the roller rink instead."

"Why do all that?"

"You have a better idea?"

"Sure. Why don't you have your parents bring you over to my house, and I'll get Bernice to take us both to the roller rink and pick us up later. We're not far from there."

"I know. That's why I was going to ride my bike and maybe go to your place later and have my mom pick me up."

"Yeah, but it's a long way over here from your place. I can't believe your parents would let you ride a bike five miles in traffic but they won't let you see a girl who doesn't have any parents. It's not her fault. Don't they know that?"

This kind of injustice was probably familiar territory for Matt.

"Well, anyway," he went on, "you don't need to do all that. This way, you don't need to lie either. You really are coming to my place. Have someone drop you off here in time for Bernice to get us to the rink."

"Wow, Matt, that's a swell idea."

"What time does she practice?"

"From ten until noon."

"So I'll invite you to come around nine. And why don't you stay for the whole day."

"Really?"

"Sure. We got to make this look normal. I wouldn't invite you over for only a couple hours. I'll talk to Bernice and call you right back."

"Give me enough time to get home."

"You're not at home?"

"No. I'm at a pay phone."

"Slick, Jonathan. Real slick."

"Hey, Matt . . . thanks. Thanks a whole lot."

"I'll call you in a few minutes," Matt said. "Bye."

I thought I got home awfully fast, but Matt hadn't waited.

"Hi, Jonathan," my mother called to me as I came in the back door and started washing the newsprint off my hands in the laundry basin next to the kitchen.

"Matt called," she went on from where she was standing skinning carrots at the kitchen sink. "He wants you to call him, and his mother got on the phone and invited you over for the day on Saturday. I figured you'd want to go, so I told her you'd love to come."

"Okay, I guess." I tried not to sound too excited, and then I got a daring idea. "I was hoping to go to the roller rink, though."

"I think it would be best for you to go to Matt's house," she said in her serious adult voice that she was silly enough to think still worked on me. I could even predict what was coming . . . *Your father and I* . . . and sure enough: "Your father and I haven't had a chance to discuss this Callaway girl anyway—"

"Mother, she's not the 'Callaway girl.' That sounds like someone in a soap commercial. Her name is Donna, and it's not her fault that she doesn't have any parents around."

The sudden silence felt like a brick wall between us. I had never spoken to my mother quite so directly before, and I was surprised at how easily it came out. I thought of trying to soften what I had said, for the sake of peace, but I was enjoying the impact too much.

My mother stood there rigidly, braced against the sink and staring out the kitchen window with a totally blank expression.

"Jonathan," she said finally in a soft, more natural voice, and then she turned to me, "you're right. We are not being fair to her. Your father and I have nothing against Donna. We don't even know her. There *are* things about someone's background, however, that are important to find out about because a family shapes a person and their beliefs. We are just not comfortable with you spending time with her until we know a little more about the situation."

"You know, Matt doesn't know who his parents are either," I said.

"Matthew is adopted," she said.

"Yeah, by two people who are as old as Donna's grandparents. They're probably in the same Sunday school class. Do you know what Matt calls his parents when he's away from them?"

"No, what?"

Suddenly I realized I might be carrying my argument a little too far. Pretty soon she wasn't going to want me to be with Matt either. I had to go ahead with this one, though, since I'd set myself up.

"Leonard and Bernice."

That actually made my mother laugh and released a little tension.

"Does he really call them 'Leonard and Bernice'?"

"Yes, but not when they're around."

We both shared a laugh and then she said, "I still think it's good that you spend Saturday with Matthew. We can see about Donna later. Okay?"

"Okay, Mom."

"See . . . if you just leave things to the Lord, they have a way of working themselves out, don't they?"

"Yes. They sure do," I said, and this couldn't be working out any better for me, I thought, but I wasn't sure what the Lord had to do with it. I was doing a pretty good job by myself. I did know that the Lord didn't care about Donna's background, though; He cared about Donna, and that's just how I felt, too.

My mother put her arm around me and pulled me to her. "You're still my little baby, and I'm not ready to let go of you just yet."

Saturday morning would not come soon enough. I tried to keep my mind on schoolwork and off Donna and the roller rink caper, but it was hard not to relish not only the thought of seeing her skate, but the overall success of my plan to get there. The only slipup that could possibly happen would be for Matt's mom to mention something to my mother about the skating rink, but Matt had such control over his mother that he probably had her properly counseled on this matter. When it came to scheming, Matt seemed to cover all the bases.

One of the things that made the week go a little faster was the fact that it was collection week for my newspaper customers, so I had that to do on top of my schoolwork and my paper route.

Dingdong! "Collecting for the *Star-News!*" I felt like a dingdong myself doing this. I hated collecting money. I didn't like interrupting people, and I didn't like the trouble some of them gave me over the $1.50 monthly charge.

Then there was the fact that half of them weren't home when I first came by, and I had to keep track of that and go back the next day, and sometimes the next day after that. If I was unable to catch them at home, they would then owe me for two months the next billing week. That was the worst, because when somebody owed for two months they almost always disputed the fact.

"Didn't I just pay you?" they would always say.

With the exception of a couple old ladies who had them but could never find them, most people never kept the receipts I gave them, so it was usually my word against theirs. I would show them in my book how I still had last month's tab, but they would say that I must have forgotten to give it to them. I would eventually get my money, but not without going through all this hassle.

Most of my customers were nice to me, though. A few even gave me a quarter tip each month, and the Watermans always gave me two dollars and told me to keep the change.

My favorite customer by far was at 332 Live Oak Street, the home of Molly Fitzpatrick. 332 Live Oak Street was where Ben Beamering's face met the back end of a Pontiac station wagon before dawn one Sunday morning when the front wheel of his bike jammed while he was helping me with my Sunday paper delivery. That accident was the beginning of the end for Ben and the beginning of my friendship with Molly.

Molly Fitzpatrick, a retired nurse, had been instrumental in helping get Ben to the hospital and, later, in properly diagnosing his ensuing problems as a heart infection. Molly had also helped me face his death, and she constantly maintained the reality of his current place with the saints and angels in heaven.

Though Molly was a Roman Catholic, we shared a strange spiritual connection. In some ways, I saw Molly's faith as being stronger and more real than a lot of folks I knew at the Colorado Avenue Standard Christian Church. There was not a trace of pretense in her. Saints, angels, miracles, blessings, curses, prayers—it was all real to her. It wasn't a question of whether you believed it or not; it was the way it was.

She was particularly fond of the saints, and her favorite book was one on the lives of the patron saints, many of whom were first-century martyrs for the cause of Christ. That same book had been on Ben's bedside table the last week of his life. He especially loved the stories of the martyrs, and when questioned about the Roman Catholic origin of these stories, he had been quick to point out that in 100 A.D. there were no Catholics or Protestants, only people who believed. That's the way I always thought about Molly. She and I were believers just like the early Christians.

Unfortunately my parents didn't see it this way and didn't like me spending much time with her, so my times with Molly were pretty much limited to collection week. I would tell my parents I was going out to collect, but one of those nights I would only collect from Molly. And I would always collect much more than $1.50. I would collect a piece of cake and a cup of her hot Irish tea and some new slant on life from Molly's book of experiences.

I knew Molly would be in her element on the topic of angels, but first I decided to find out what she thought about Donna. The tea was ready, like it always was, when I got there at about five o'clock on Friday afternoon. The late afternoon sun made the yellow walls in her kitchen look buttery.

"So what ya been doin' these days, Johnny?" she said, pouring two cups. She was the only person I liked calling me Johnny. Her accent made it roll off her tongue naturally.

"I'm going to the roller rink Saturday to watch a friend skate.

I've seen her at the church skates and she's really good, but this will be different. She has a routine and everything, and she's trying to make it into competition."

"Really. I didn't know they had such a thing. What do you suppose they do?"

"I don't know. That's what I can't wait to find out. My parents don't know I'm going, though. They'd be real mad if they found out."

"There ya go again, a-flirtin' with disaster," she said with a wink of her red eyelashes. "Now what is it this time?"

"They don't want me to be around Donna because she doesn't have any parents."

"Now wait a minute here, everyone's got a mum and a dad. She's just not growin' up with 'em, eh?"

"Yeah, that's about it. She lives with her grandparents."

"Here, here, to the older generation! More power to 'em. What's she like, laddie?"

"She's okay . . . and boy can she skate!"

"Sounds like she's learned to believe she's important without the help of the two people in the world who have that as their job. That takes a lot of courage. Must be one strong little girl."

"Why can't my parents see that?"

"They will, Johnny, they will. Give them some time. Sure you want to give them somethin' more ta be upset over by doin' this?"

"I promised Donna. You should have seen the look on her face when I told her I was coming."

"Aye. So you've made up yer mind."

"Yep."

"Well, you'll be lettin' me know how it turns out, I'm sure."

"Guess what, Molly? I've been kissed by an angel," I said, eager to move on to the next subject I wanted her opinion on.

"Her name wouldn't be Donna would it?"

"No, it was Margaret." I went on to tell her about the writing in the bunker and the bathroom of the skating rink and about my theory of Ben commissioning angels from heaven. I told her, as well, about saving Matt's life and the voice in the water.

"That was most definitely the work of an angel. I've heard many similar stories."

"But you're not sure about Margaret and the writing?"

She smiled. "It does sound like our Benjamin, but savin' lives is a little more in the line of angelic duty. Angels are very busy, you know, with very important things. The archangel Michael once took two weeks to answer the prayer of Daniel because he was busy fighting off demons in Persia. I'm not sure too many angels have time for writin' on bathroom walls, if you know what I mean. If little Benjamin did get one to do this for him, I'd be thinkin' the case was under serious review up there."

I left Molly's more sure about what I was going to do on Saturday, but also more aware of the cost should my parents find out somehow. If the plan exploded in my face, I would simply have to take the consequences.

I left, that is, and got about as far as my bike, when I turned around and went back to the front door.

Molly was expecting me. She opened the door before I had a chance to knock and said it for me. "Collecting for the *Star-News*, right?"

I always had too much on my mind when I left Molly's to be thinking about newspaper bills.

Saturday went off with only one hitch. My dad got me to Matt's house by 9:30, but when I walked in the door, Matt informed me that Bernice had an early morning hair appointment and had already left with the car.

"Why didn't you call me?" I said.

"I didn't need to," said Matt. "We'll walk. It won't take us longer than twenty minutes to get there."

It took over thirty minutes, and we got there about a quarter past the hour.

"Oh no, it's locked," I said when we tried the front doors to the rink.

"Maybe there's a back door," said Matt.

We ended up circling the whole building, which wasn't an easy thing to do. There was a five-foot wall we had to climb and junk in the alley of a warehouse next door to work our way through. And when we finally got to the back, we found nothing but a long, unbroken wall.

"Gotta go back to the front," Matt said. "We'll just have to pound on the door."

So we went back through the junk and over the wall, and I was just about to knock when Matt said, "Wait a minute. Look at this. It looks like a doorbell." He pushed the button and we could hear a buzzer go off inside the door. We looked at each other sheepishly.

Before long a heavily tanned lady with dyed red hair slid open a window next to the door.

"Sorry, we're closed to the public," she said in a husky voice.

"We're friends of Donna Callaway," I said.

"Oh. Just a minute, then."

The smell of varnish was the first impression I had walking in; I didn't remember noticing that at the church skates. *It must make a difference when the rink is empty*, I thought. There was, in fact, much that was different about the skating rink that morning. No music, no crowd, only the voices of Donna and her coach echoing off the floor, the lonely clap and roll of one pair of skates, and the constant hum of the soda fountain machines.

When I first looked out at Donna that day, I saw not a girl but a whirling dervish. She was spinning like a top, her arms and legs a blur of movement and her ponytail horizontal.

"Matt, look! Can you believe that?"

"I'm looking, I'm looking! No, I can't believe it. I didn't know you could do that on roller skates."

The coach, a short, muscular man in tight black pants and a black T-shirt, was holding a stopwatch and calling out to her as she spun: "Nice camel . . . now sit . . . good . . . change . . . and sit again . . . good! That's your second spin. Now skate and get set for a double salchow."

"A double what?" said Matt.

"Got me," I said.

Donna hadn't seen us come in, or if she had, she didn't pay us any mind. She was giving her coach and her work total concentration.

"Okay," said the coach as he glued his eyes on her from the center of the rink. "Now I want you to set up for a double toe walley, keeping in mind you're going to come out of it into your final spin in the center of the rink, so you should start the toe walley about—" and he skated over to the spot, "here."

"Okay. Ready?" He looked at his stopwatch. "You can do it now. We're coming up on three minutes so far. Perfect. Start your double right . . . now! Beautiful! Now spin . . . camel . . . jump . . . back into a camel . . . and out! There it is. You did it! That's a typical program. Lots of work yet on the individual parts, but that gives you the whole picture."

Weak applause came from the other end of the rink, and Matt and I looked over to see Donna's grandparents proudly lending their encouragement. Matt and I joined them enthusiastically, and for the first time Donna looked our way.

"Okay, break time. We'll start working on the jumps next."

Matt and I were both speechless. We had just seen Donna Callaway spin, jump, twirl in midair, and somehow land without falling, then fly across the floor with her arms out as if they were lifting her beyond the realm of gravity that confined the rest of us mortals to walking on the ground.

As soon as her coach announced the break, she skated directly over to us, the wind of her movement laying the short little skirt of her one-piece outfit softly around the tops of her legs. Her face was red and radiant with a smile.

"Hi!" she said as she glided into a stop at the railing, her chest heaving rapidly. "I didn't expect you to be here. What a surprise!"

"I said I'd come."

"But my grandparents said you weren't coming. You were going over to a friend's house instead."

"How did your grandparents know that?"

"They called your house last night to see if you needed a ride. Didn't you know that?"

Must have been while I was at Molly's, I thought. *And my parents didn't even tell me.*

"Well, we're here, and I never was *not* going to be here. I wouldn't miss this for anything. That was boss! I didn't know you could do stuff like that on roller skates."

"I know. Most people don't know that. You can do everything that can be done on ice skates—some things, even better. They've had regional championships now for five years. That's what I'm practicing for. Lenny's getting me ready for the Southwest Pacific Regional Championships next June in Bakersfield. I'm so excited."

"Wow . . . June, and you're already starting?"

"Well, we've got all the jumps and spins decided. I haven't picked my songs yet, but I have until the first of the year for that."

She broke into an even bigger smile as we stood there smiling back at her in amazement. She let out a little nervous laugh, looked down, and then looked over and waved at her grandparents. When they waved back, she pointed at Matt and me, and they smiled back and nodded.

"Well! I have to get going!" and she skated off, bouncing and dipping her shoulders as she worked up speed, and then she leaned back and glided into a turn with her arms trailing casually behind her. I had never seen anything so beautiful in my life.

"What was that white stuff all over her?" said Matt.

"I don't know, but it makes her look like an angel," I said.

"Yeah . . . move over, Margaret," he said. "Did you really kiss her in the closet?"

I looked at him and a line from somewhere popped into my head. "That's for me to know and you to find out."

"You turkey."

"Hey, I just discovered what the white stuff is," I said. "At least where it's coming from," and I went over to a break in the railing and wiped a finger across the floor. "Look." A fine white powder had built up in a line on my finger.

"What is it, do you think?" he said.

"Beats me, but look, it's all over the floor. We'll have to ask Donna."

She was at it again out on the rink, and this time her coach was working her harder. He didn't seem nice at all. Sometimes he spoke harshly to her, and I didn't understand that.

"Concentrate, Donna," I heard him say. "Dominic is going to be here soon, and I want you to be able to put this jump into a sequence. Now I know you can do this. Get your mind on it or I will have to ask your friends to leave."

"Uh-oh," I said to Matt. "Maybe we'd better back off a little."

We moved away from the rail and started walking toward the

fountain area near where Donna's grandparents were sitting. The tanned lady who had let us in the door was working in an office area behind the skate rental desk, and Matt went over and got her attention.

"You boys want something from the fountain, I reckon."

"Sure . . . what you got?"

"All I can give you right now is a soda. Everything else is shut down."

"Could we get a cherry Coke?" asked Matt, reaching into his pocket for money. "Good, we'd like two, please." I faked like I was going for my pockets, and Matt said with a grin, "It's okay. It's on Bernice."

As she started to pour the Cokes, the door buzzer went off and she left the glasses and went to the front window. She let in a slight, salt-and-pepper-haired man carrying several books. He followed her back to where we were waiting at the counter and laid his books down. I glanced at them and saw they were music books. *101 Pop Favorites* was one. *Popular Broadway Show Tunes* was another.

"I'm pourin' these here boys some Cokes. You want something?"

"Actually, do you have any coffee made?"

"Sure do. Just a second," she said. She pumped cherry syrup into our Cokes, gave them a stir with a long spoon, and then slid the glasses in front of us.

"Hi, I'm Dominic," said the man, who looked vaguely familiar to me. "And who are you?"

"I'm Jonathan, and this is my friend Matt."

"Hi, Jonathan . . . Matt. You friends of Donna's?"

We both nodded.

"She's something, isn't she?" he said, turning on his stool to where he could see her fly by.

"Yeah," I said. "We had no idea."

"Really? This is the first time you've seen her skate?"

"Yes. Except for the all-church skates."

"We didn't even know you could do this stuff on roller skates," said Matt.

"Oh yes. You can do just about anything you want to if you set your mind to it."

The lady was back with a pot of coffee.

"Thanks, Peg," the man said as she poured him a cup. "So you boys are probably from the Standard Christian Church on Colorado, right?"

"Yeah, how'd you know?"

"I know that's where Donna goes. I play the organ for all their skates."

"Of course," said Matt. "I knew I'd seen you before. Do more Top Ten songs!"

"You like that, huh?"

"Yeah. I loved it when you did 'Teenie Weenie Yellow Polka Dot Bikini' last time. That was boss."

"Well, I figured since you kids can't hear the records, I can at least give you the songs."

"Why have records anyway, when you're sittin' in the only skating rink in all of southern California with a live organ," said Peg, "next to the most popular player around?"

"Flattery will get you everywhere," Dominic said to her. "Who's the organist over there at your church now? Is it still Milton Owlsley?"

"Yes, it is," I said.

"I went to school with Milton. Funny guy. As persnickety as they come. Good church organist, though."

I thought of Booker T. "He's loosening up some," I said.

"Milton? Loosening up?"

"Well, we have a new Negro singer in our choir, actually a soloist, and she and Milton got going last Sunday. Now he wants to learn to play like Booker T. and the M.G.'s."

That made Dominic almost fall off his stool with laughter.

"Hey, Dominic!" shouted the coach from the center of the rink. "Get over here!"

"Uh-oh, duty calls," said Dominic as he got up, still laughing. "Tell you what. If Milton wants some help with his Booker T., you have him give me a call," and he handed me a card: *Dominic Dimucci—Organist, Entertainer Extraordinaire*. He walked off laughing. "Milton Owlsley playing Booker T. Jones. This I gotta see!"

As Dominic made his way to the organ, Matt and I twisted

on our stools so we could watch Donna jumping and twisting in the air.

"Wow," I said to Matt. "They bring the organist in just for Donna."

"No, not 'just for Donna,' " said Peg from behind us. "She's our best. Gonna go a long way, that girl."

We watched for a few minutes as Donna started to move with the music, and I saw right away how important the music was to the whole thing. It was the glue that held it together and gave life to each movement. There was something different about the way Donna moved her body when she skated to the music. Her moves took on a flow and became less mechanical. She seemed to be working especially hard on a particular jump that I would later learn was called an axel. It was to be the opening jump of her routine.

Time and time again she fell—more times than she made it. Her coach kept repeating, "The better you get, the more you fall. The more difficult the jump, the smaller the margin of error. To do the great jumps, you have to do everything perfectly."

I marveled at her stamina. No matter how many times she fell, she kept getting up. I imagined her body as being nothing but black and blue.

"She's very brave," I said.

"Or crazy," said Matt.

"You think this is all crazy?"

"I didn't say that."

"You suggested it, though."

"Well, she sure is punishing herself," he said. "I don't think I would do it."

"I'm not sure I would either. I wonder what makes her go?"

I looked over at her grandparents and wondered if it was them. Her grandmother was pretty feisty for an elderly woman confined to a wheelchair. I had seen her on the move in the parking lot a few times and noticed how well she could get around.

"Hey, Matt, what do you say we go meet her grandparents."

"Sure."

We started over to where they were sitting, and her grandfather got up and pushed his wife over to meet us.

"Hi! I'm Jonathan, and this is my friend Matt."

"Yes, we've seen both of you boys at church," said Donna's grandfather, reaching out his hand. "I'm Harold Finley and this is my wife, Murietta."

"Most people just call me Granny Finley," she said, reaching out her hand to me. But I hesitated taking it. I had never met anyone in a wheelchair before, and I wasn't sure I wanted to touch her.

"It's okay," she said, still holding out her hand. "I'm like anyone else from the waist up."

I shook her hand and so did Matt, and I felt bad about hesitating.

There's certainly nothing wrong with her grip, I thought, as I checked to see that my fingers were all there. Matt, too. In fact, being Matt, he had to say something.

"Wow, you're pretty strong for—"

"For an old lady?" she finished. "You're darn tootin' I am. Have to be to operate this contraption. It's awful nice of you boys to come out here and encourage Donna. She's been talking a lot about you, Jonathan. You're Walter Liebermann's son, aren't you?"

"Yes."

"Well, what do you think of our little girl?" asked Mr. Finley.

"I think she's very talented—and brave, too," I said.

"That she is," he said.

"Brave and foolish," chimed Mrs. Finley. "It runs in the family."

Just then a faint cry shot across the hard maple floor and Mrs. Finley grabbed her husband's arm. "What was that?"

I turned to see Donna crumpled on the floor. It was not an unfamiliar position for her, but something was different this time. She wasn't getting up, and when she tried, she fell back to the floor with another soft cry.

"Harold, she's hurt," said Mrs. Finley, and off she went, rolling herself over to a gap in the railing. We all followed, and instinctively I started running out on the floor toward Donna.

"Stay out of here!" yelled the coach, waving me off sharply. "You've already caused enough trouble!"

I backed up, bewildered.

"Donna, Donna!" he said, slamming a fist into his hand. "You don't try a double when you haven't got the single down yet!"

"Peggy!" he shouted. Peg was already on her way out to them. Together they knelt at Donna's feet and started removing her skates. She winced and bit her lip when they worked on the left one. Tears glistened on her cheeks in the overhead light, and she looked over at us and shook her head and tried to smile.

The coach removed the sock from her left foot and held her ankle in his hands.

"Does this hurt?"

"No."

"Does that?"

"A little."

"Does that?"

"Ow! Yes!" and her body jerked back in pain. I looked over at Mr. and Mrs. Finley frozen at the rail.

"Now you've done it!" said the coach, and he stood up and turned his back to her, then spun back around. "I've seen this before. This will take, at best, three months off your schedule—at worst, four or five—which would put you out of the running."

"It's okay," Donna said through her tears, with gritty determination. "I can do it."

"Honey, Lenny's a little upset," Peg said to Donna. "Don't pay him any mind right now. He don't know what he's sayin'."

"I tell you, Peg, I've seen this kind of break before. I know exactly what I'm talking about."

"Lenny," she turned to him and spoke sharply, "will you leave the diagnosin' to the doctor and help me get her up!"

The two of them lifted Donna, and she braced herself on their shoulders, walking on her good foot. Our little group had huddled at the nearest exit from the rink, so we all backed away to let them through.

Donna smiled at me and said, "Well, you got to see part of a practice at least."

"Want my chair?" said Mrs. Finley.

"I'm all right, Granny," said Donna. "Don't worry."

"Where will you take her?" asked Mr. Finley.

"St. Mary's," said the coach, and a choking blackness came over me at the sound of those words.

9

St. Mary's

"Molly?" I said on the phone from the kitchen of Matt's house as he stood there listening in on my side of the conversation. "This is Jonathan. I need your help. Remember Donna Callaway, the girl I talked to you about yesterday? Well, she broke her ankle in practice today—at least that's what her coach thinks happened."

"I know, can you believe it?"

"Well, that's why I'm calling you. They took her to St. Mary's, and I knew you would know who's the best doctor over there for this kind of thing."

"Dr. Sanderson? Orthopedics?"

"Sanderson," I said to Matt, covering the phone. "Can you help me remember that?" He got a piece of paper and wrote it down.

"No kidding. The Dodgers? Really?" I covered the phone again. "This guy is the doctor who handles all the injuries for the Dodgers."

"I was hoping you'd do that. Gee, thanks, Molly."

"No, I'm at a friend's house."

"Well, I don't have a ride right now, but my friend's mother is due home any minute." Matt shook his head in disagreement.

"No, that's okay, you leave the Lincoln in the garage. If you can call over there, I'm sure that will be enough."

"Oh yeah, it's Callaway. C-A-L-L-A-W-A-Y. Donna Callaway."

"Oh, they left the rink about a half hour ago."

"She seemed to be in pretty good spirits, but her coach isn't doing very well, though."

"Yes. Competition is in June."

"I hope so too."

"Thank you, Molly. You're the greatest!"

"Oh yeah." I looked down at the round black and white telephone dial. "It's Sycamore 7–9729."

"Okay, bye." I hung up the phone and let out a big sigh.

"The Dodgers, huh?" said Matt. "He must be pretty good."

"Yeah, well Molly Fitzpatrick knows the best."

"How do you know her again?"

"She's a retired nurse who knows everybody over at St. Mary's. She's the one who helped out a lot with Ben. That's how we met her. He ran into the back of a Pontiac right in front of her house."

"I guess if you're gonna crash, that's a good place to do it. What was that about the Lincoln in her garage?"

"Oh, she's got a mint condition 1939 Lincoln Zephyr that never goes out on the road except for emergencies. You should have seen the ride she gave me once to see Ben in the hospital. She doesn't even have a license. When do you think your mother's going to get home?"

"If she's shopping, you can wait till the cows come home," came Leonard's voice bellowing from the next room. Matt confirmed his words with a knowing look.

"How far is it to St. Mary's from here?" I said.

Matt's dad was now in the kitchen with us. "It's about three miles," he said. "Too far to walk." He started rummaging through some papers next to the phone. "Now where does she keep that number for the taxi?"

A taxi? I had never ridden in a taxi in my life. I would never have even thought of it. Southern California was not known for its taxis. Probably because it was so spread out that it got too expensive. But Mr. Wendorf was calling one.

The taxi was there in ten minutes, and Matt's dad gave us money for a round-trip fare, plus tip, plus enough to buy lunch. "That's just in case you end up staying there for a while, which you probably will," he said. "Call when you're ready to come back, in case Bernice is home."

"That's as nice as I've ever seen your dad," I said as we pulled away from Matt's house.

"Yeah," said Matt. "He has streaks like that. You never can tell with him."

"I've never been in a taxi before."

"You haven't? Leonard puts me in taxis a lot when Bernice is gone."

We drove rapidly through light traffic, and it seemed like I was living out a scene on "77 Sunset Strip."

"The Dodgers!" I said. "Do you know what that means?"

"It means he's good."

"It also means he's the best at getting people over their injuries the fastest. They gotta have players back in action as soon as possible. This couldn't be better for Donna, and Molly's probably calling him right now."

As we pulled up to the emergency entrance, the choking feeling returned, but I pushed it back with a new sense of duty. I had a feeling I was going to be able to help Donna. This new challenge overcame even the awful memories of Ben dying in this very same hospital.

Because of all the time I'd spent at St. Mary's, I knew just what to do. Ben and his mom had taught me all about hospitals. They made this place hop, and I was ready to do the same.

In the emergency room we immediately ran into Lenny, Peg, and Mr. and Mrs. Finley.

"Oh, it's you again," said the coach. "Haven't you caused enough trouble today?"

"Lenny, stop it," said Peg.

"Don't pay him any mind," she said to me, "he's just upset."

"Where's Donna?" I asked.

"They took her inside."

"Has she seen a doctor yet?"

"We don't know anything."

I headed right for the emergency door and barely heard, "Wait a minute, you can't do that," as the door closed behind me. There were three empty beds and one with curtains pulled around three sides of it. I walked around the curtain and found Donna sitting there with her leg up on the table.

"Jonathan!" she said. "How did you get in here?"

"I walked in. How are you doing?"

"It hurts. But I'm okay."

"Has anyone seen you yet?"

"Just a nurse."

"Good. I'll be right back."

"Don't leave. I don't like it here by myself."

"Don't worry, I'll be right back."

I walked back out into the waiting area, and Lenny and Peg rushed me as if I were the doctor.

"How is she?" Lenny said.

"She's fine. No one's seen her yet. Matt, why don't you go keep her company."

I went to the window and asked the emergency receptionist, "Is Doctor Sanderson in the hospital today?"

"Just a moment I'll check." She looked up and down a couple pages and stopped halfway down the second one. "Yes, he is on duty, but he wouldn't be down here. He's not on call for emergency today. Doctor Howard is."

"Could you tell me how I could get in touch with Doctor Sanderson?"

"Well, that would be difficult. He's most likely doing his rounds about now. He could be anywhere in the hospital."

"Would you page him for me, please?"

"I don't know . . . I have to have a reason. Who are you, and why do you want Dr. Sanderson?"

"I'm Jonathan Liebermann, and I would like Dr. Sanderson to take care of Donna Callaway, the girl in emergency right now."

"I'm sorry, that won't be possible. Only Dr. Howard will see patients in emergency today, and he's on his way over here right now."

Suddenly I heard the deep drawl of a southern accent behind me. "Jeanne, you're looking mighty pretty today." I turned around to see a tall, handsome man in a physician's coat smiling behind me. He had dark hair with touches of gray, and he winked at me through a winsome smile.

"Oh—" the receptionist lost her breath for a minute. "Doctor Sanderson! Why, thank you."

"Jeanne, have you got a Donna Callaway here?"

"Why, yes, doctor, she's . . . right inside."

"Thank you. You know, if you were any prettier, nothing would get done around here. We'd all have to just stop and look."

Dr. Sanderson turned and went through the door, and I relished my vindication long enough to smile smugly at the bewildered, blushing receptionist. *Molly Fitzpatrick strikes again!*

The little group huddled in the waiting area was very impressed with Dr. Sanderson, and even more so when he predicted a speedy recovery.

"I've treated lots of these types of injuries," he told us about an hour and a half later, after he'd set Donna's ankle. "Fortunately, it's not a complex fracture. This is the same break you get sliding into second and catching your cleats on the bag. We can probably have her back in skates in less than two months. That is, if she cooperates with our therapy program. Otherwise it will take longer."

"She'll cooperate," said Lenny.

"I'll cooperate," said Donna cheerfully as a nurse wheeled her out of emergency in a cast up to her knee and ready to go home.

Mr. and Mrs. Finley smiled broadly, happy that Donna had been cared for so well.

"Thank you, doctor. We're so grateful to you for taking such good care of her," said Mrs. Finley.

"Thank this young man here," he said, putting a big hand on my shoulder. "He's the one responsible for getting me down here."

"We are thankful to you, Jonathan," said Mr. Finley, "mighty thankful."

I felt hot and embarrassed and couldn't think of anything to say that didn't sound stupid.

"You certainly seem to know your way around this place," said Peg. Lenny was standing around outside the conversation, a little less agitated than before, but not willing to take part in the award ceremony that was going on.

"My best friend was in here for a while," I said.

"Hey, Granny," said Donna, suddenly grabbing the wheels on her wheelchair and rocking back and forth, "I'll race you to the car!"

"You haven't got a chance!" said Mrs. Finley, whirling

around and gliding toward the door. Donna tried to follow, but was prevented from doing so by the nurse.

"No you don't," she said, "not as long as I'm in charge of you. Besides, you don't have a license to operate this vehicle."

"But I ride in Granny's all the time," Donna protested, and with a quick jerk she pulled away from the nurse and followed Mrs. Finley out the door.

"Wait a minute!" yelled the nurse, running after her. "You come back here!"

Everyone laughed, even Lenny, and we all rushed outside to watch Donna rolling after her grandmother and the nurse running after Donna. Finally the nurse caught up with Donna's wheelchair and barely dragged her to a stop, like a dog owner trying to get control of a St. Bernard that had just spotted a fleeing feline. Mrs. Finley lifted her hands in victory as she crossed an imaginary finish line.

"And some folks still wonder where Donna gets it," said Mr. Finley, shaking his head.

A big surprise was waiting for me when we got back to Matt's house later that afternoon. We had used the money Mr. Wendorf gave us to get lunch at the hospital and still had enough left for another taxi ride home, even though we figured Matt's mother was probably home by then. I wanted to enjoy being in charge a little longer.

I had walked into a situation that froze everyone around me and I had been the one to act. I had been able to accomplish something positive out of all the pain I had experienced losing Ben, using knowledge and the resources I wouldn't have had otherwise. Minor consolation, maybe, but consolation nonetheless.

Such feelings were short-lived, however, because waiting for me at Matt's house was the one thing that could sap all my confidence right then. It was my parents' blue and white Ford Fairlane parked out in front of Matt's house.

"Oh no!" I said as soon as I saw it.

"What's the matter?" said Matt.

"My parents are here!"

"So?"

"Then they know. They know I went to the roller rink!"

"But you're a hero now. You saved the day for Donna."

"They don't know that!"

"Relax, Jonathan. They'll come around."

"You don't know my parents."

I sat glued to the backseat of the taxi while Matt paid the driver. "Do you have any money left over?" I said. "Can't we have him drive us somewhere else?"

"Jonathan, come on! Stop making such a big deal out of this."

"You don't understand, Matt. I once got the belt just for talking in class. This is my first real lie."

"It's not a lie. You never said you weren't going . . . Jonathan! Would you get out of the car? We already paid this guy!"

"Okay, okay, I'm coming."

Matt's parents and my parents didn't know each other very well. Mostly because of the age difference, I think. That, coupled with the reason my parents had come—their anger over my disobedience—made for a room full of superficial smiles.

It had all been precipitated by an innocent phone call to Matt's house that afternoon to find out when they should come get me. I could just imagine Leonard's response: "Well, that depends on how long they plan on staying at the hospital."

"The *what?*" That alone would have been enough to get my folks in their car and over to the Wendorfs'. I had no idea how long they had been there, but it was clear, as soon as they saw me, that they were ready to go. There was a brief conversation, most of which had to do with how Donna was doing, as my parents feigned concern. Matt made a feeble attempt to share my hospital heroics with everyone, but no one seemed interested. The whole atmosphere was very uncomfortable, and in minutes we were out the door.

I took my last look at Matt before entering what felt like my transport vehicle to a penitentiary. It was my final look at freedom, and it angered me to see Matt standing there so casually. *How does he get away with treating his parents the way he does?* I wondered. *Hasn't he ever been in this situation before with them?* He was almost laughing at me, and I hated him right then.

The ride to our house took ten minutes. For the first five there was nothing but silence in the car. Painful silence. Then, as if on cue, we all tried to speak at exactly the same time and no one heard or understood anyone else until we all stopped and waited again through another, shorter silence.

"Dear," said my mother to my father, finally, "you said you would do this."

My father got that look he gets when he has to do something he doesn't want to do.

"Jonathan," he said in a nervous high voice, "your mother and I are very disappointed with your behavior today."

"Disappointed?" said my mother. His token sentence was the gate that opened the floodwaters of her frustration. "We are speechless. This is so unlike you, Jonathan. I never would have believed in a thousand years that our darling little boy would ever mislead us like you have done. You knew how we felt about you seeing Donna Callaway and yet you purposefully, *deliberately* disobeyed us. We are shocked, Jonathan. So much so that we haven't even been able to determine the appropriate punishment yet."

I tried to speak. I wanted to explain why I liked Donna and how important it turned out for me to be there, but there was this huge obstruction in my throat and tears in my eyes and I was sure my voice could not get around all that.

"Do you have anything to say for yourself?" said my mother.

I opened my mouth and out came a weak and cracking, "No."

"I'm just so *disappointed* in you," repeated my mother.

As we drove in the driveway, I noticed my father eyeing the rearview mirror.

"There's someone driving in our driveway behind us," he said. "Now who could that be?"

I turned around and recognized the car immediately. I had helped Donna get into that car earlier that afternoon. It was her grandparents. I didn't look very long behind me, but I thought I only saw two people in the car.

"Oh no, isn't that Donna Callaway's grandparents?" said my mother.

"I'm afraid so," said my father. "He's getting Mrs. Finley's wheelchair out right now."

"What on earth would they be coming over here for? Jonathan, do you know anything about this?"

I didn't answer. I was already out the door and headed toward the front yard to greet the Finleys.

"Jonathan!" shouted my mother, though controlled enough to keep her voice from carrying to the front yard. "You come back here this instant!"

I stopped as my mother got out of the car and came up behind me. "We are not through with our discussion, young man. I want you to march inside to your sister's room. We will finish this later."

Most kids were sent to their room. I was sent to my sister's room. My room was open to the dining room and within earshot of conversations in the living room—something my mother obviously wanted me removed from, given the nature of the impending guests.

My sister's room was separated by a hallway and two doors, both of which were shut soundly behind my mother as she left me there. But I had a plan. I immediately climbed the ladder to the attic and crawled past the boards of my train layout to a place I surmised was over the living room. I had never tried it before, but I was hoping to pick up something of the conversation below. I did even better. I found that the ceiling light in the living room cut an opening through the insulation, so by lying down across the rafters and placing my ear right near the electrical box, I could hear every word.

I heard my father say he didn't want to see these people right now. And I heard my mother say she didn't either, but they were here and they should make the best of it, and maybe this was a chance to find out about Donna's parents. That was the part I wanted to hear more than anything.

"Do we have anything we can serve them?" my father asked.

"Put some water on for tea. I think there's some Cheese Whiz and Ritz crackers we can put out. We were going to go shopping this afternoon, remember?"

"Yes, and I was going to do the yard when we got back."

"There they are," said my father when the doorbell went off.

I heard a rushing of footsteps and a chorus of cheery greetings at the door. My mother excused herself immediately to the kitchen amidst the vehement protests of Mr. and Mrs. Finley to not bother with anything. They were very apologetic about their unannounced mission. Nonetheless, my mother insisted on making tea.

I knew exactly what nervousness my father was going through right then. He hated being left to entertain people he did not know or like. Small talk filled the time until I heard a tray of tinkling china being carried out with the teapot and matching teacups, eliciting the usual comments.

"Yes, this whole set belonged to my great-grandmother in England."

"Your *great*-grandmother! Well I'll be."

"What a pleasant surprise to have you drop by," said my mother as everything seemed settled in the living room. "We just heard about Donna. I'm so sorry for her. How is she?"

"Oh, she's doing quite well," said Mrs. Finley, "thanks mostly to your son, Mrs. Liebermann."

"Oh, please call me Ann."

"We'll only be a minute," reiterated Mr. Finley in a kind and sincere voice, "but we had to stop by and congratulate you on raising such a fine boy. I've never seen anyone take charge like that in a hospital before, have you, Murietta?"

"No," said Mrs. Finley, and I heard the clink of a cup meeting its saucer. "What he did was remarkable for a boy his age. I've spent a lot of time in hospitals, and believe me, I know the power of the white coat and the clipboard. Your son was not intimidated in the least."

"And the doctor he was able to call in for Donna—" Mr. Finley interjected, "he's the best in southern California. Injury specialist for the Los Angeles Dodgers? My stars—"

"I kept saying to myself," said Mrs. Finley, " 'Who is this boy? Where did he come from?' "

At this point, there was a pause.

"You have heard what happened in the hospital?" said Mr. Finley. Then, "Murietta, I don't think they know."

Following was an embellished account of the proceedings of the afternoon—how I had marched right into the emergency

room and found Donna alone and assigned Matt to stay with her
while I attempted to get the receptionist to find Dr. Sanderson,
and how he had shown up at the most opportune time, taking
over the situation with his expertise. How the coach who was
blaming me in the beginning ended up thanking me in the end.
(That part was a little exaggerated, I thought. I didn't remember
him showing me any thanks.)

I listened to all this with pleasure, except for the pain of my
awkward positioning in the rafters. At least I was pleased right
up until they mentioned the "retired nurse" who was my inside
track on the best doctors in the hospital. I didn't need Molly's
name coming up right then. I rested my head against a beam in
the attic, keeping score: two strikes *for* me . . . one strike
against. . . .

During this recounting of the hospital scene, my parents remained deathly quiet. I imagined their faces with blank smiles
on them—masks for the confusing mixture of pride and anger
that must have been going on inside. Then something strange
happened. As I listened, for an instant I thought they were talking not about me, but about someone else. Something about the
words they used and the way they said them made me think
about Ben. It was the same way I used to hear people talk about
him, and us, when we were together—when I had been his accomplice in crime. That's when I realized for the first time that
in some ways I was becoming like Ben. It made me smile inside
to think that something about Ben was continuing on in me.

What I couldn't figure out was why Donna's grandparents
were at my house. What made them come over and deliver this
news personally? I began to surmise that Donna might have had
a hand in it. While waiting for Dr. Sanderson to look at the X-
rays and prescribe the proper treatment, I had told her that my
parents didn't know I was at the roller rink and that they
wouldn't be happy about it if they found out.

"It's because I don't have any parents, isn't it? Isn't that why
you asked me about my parents up in your tower?" she had said,
and I had said it probably was, though that made no difference
to me.

Donna's part in this unlikely visit seemed confirmed by the
fact that, at the end of it, Mr. and Mrs. Finley themselves vol-

unteered the topic of Donna's parents. My parents never would have brought it up. In fact, in Mrs. Finley's words, "Everyone talks to everyone else about these things except the people who are directly involved, so if your son and Donna are going to be friends, we want you to know straight from the horse's mouth, and we will be happy to answer any questions that we—"

Right then I would have heard the truth about Donna if it weren't for the Green Leaf Tree Service Company that trimmed trees for the city of Eagle Rock. Though the trees on our block were new and small, they kept them cut back severely to encourage thickness. I had seen the trucks out front when we drove up, and when the tree-eater started up, I knew that finding out about Donna was going to have to wait.

The tree-eater—that's what Ben and I called it—was shaped like a funnel. The tree trimmers fed branches in the wide end, and the churning blades inside chomped them up and spit little pieces of tree out the small end into the bed of a waiting truck. The thing made a high whining sound that dropped down to a low grind when it was fed, then slowly returned to its satisfied scream. Unfortunately, when the tree-eater was running, especially right in front of your house, it was so loud you could hardly hear yourself think. And through the attic vents it was even louder.

I descended the ladder, put my ear to the bedroom door, but still heard only the whining tree-eater. I cracked the door and could see the edge of Mrs. Finley's wheelchair backed up near the hallway. Someone must have used the bathroom and left the hall door open. I might be able to sneak down the hall and get another listen.

Whether my mother was reading my mind or trying to shut out some of the deafening noise, I don't know, but just as I got to the door a familiar arm reached out and closed it, shutting me out for the last time. Just before the door closed, however, I was able to pick up something about a place called Camarillo. That was as much as I got.

Frustrated, I lay back on my sister's bed and listened to the rise and fall of the moaning tree-eater devouring the forbidden history of Donna Callaway.

10

Go, Granny, Go

Donna's ankle healed quickly. The two months Dr. Sanderson had predicted turned out to be more than enough time, and in six weeks she was practicing again, much to her coach's delight. Part of that was because of the doctor's expertise, but most of it was because of Donna's desire. No one was more driven than Donna, unless it was her coach, Lenny LaRue.

Lenny was a fanatic about roller skating, and in 1961, if roller skating was anything more than a form of light recreation to you, you would have to have had a large measure of fanatical blood skating in your veins, because 1961 was a down time in the history of roller skating in America.

In 1900, Levan M. Richardson of Milwaukee, founder of the Richardson Skate Company, developed the modern roller skate, and by 1910 there were over thirty-five hundred roller rinks in the United States and eight million people flying around them on skates. A large percentage of those eight million were women. In fact, roller skating was the first organized recreation in which great numbers of ordinary American women and girls participated. I know all this because, inspired by Ben's files, I started one of my own that year on roller skating.

This skating boom rolled to a crawl around 1918, however, overcome by other, more lively, suddenly affordable attractions such as radio, picture shows, automobiles, high fashion, live entertainment, and dancing—a time better known as the "Roaring Twenties." But the stock market crash of 1929 and the Great Depression that led into the 1930s gave skating another chance as it became one of the few affordable diversions most Americans could enjoy. Then, an international event altered the course of skating forever when the 1932 Winter Olympic Games in Lake

Placid, New York, gained national attention for ice skating and brought a new star into the hearts of a nation—a glamorous and athletic acrobat of freestyle and grace, Sonja Henie.

Suddenly everyone wanted to skate like Sonja. But ice skating was seasonal, and there were only a few very expensive indoor rinks. So those dreaming about doing spins and jumps went to their closets, pulled out their neglected roller skates, and took to the dusty neighborhood roller rink to discover, lo and behold, it was all possible on wheels.

Thus, a new sport emerged. Roller skating for recreation suddenly became roller skating for dance, freestyle, and show. Even Fred Astaire and Ginger Rogers took to roller skates in the film "Shall We Dance?" National skating associations were formed to organize the many figure and freestyle competitions springing up in cities and towns across America, giving promising skaters a national championship to work toward. And in 1942, ten years after the Lake Placid Olympics, roller skating finally claimed its own answer to Sonja Henie in the form of a traveling review known as the Skating Vanities, featuring the exquisite skating talents of a nineteen-year-old sensation named Gloria Nord.

The Skating Vanities took their spectacular show on the road for twelve years while roller skating basked in its glory days. It was a dazzling spectacle on wheels, including musical comedy, acrobatics, speed skating, clowns on skates, and even the Rollerettes, a precision skating chorus of twenty-four women—a rolling version of New York's famous Radio City Music Hall Rockettes.

But the undisputed star of it all was the petite, blond, Hollywood-bred, dancer-turned-skater, Gloria Nord. In the words of one of her admirers, "You knew she was the star because she made her first entrance of the evening from atop a seventeen-foot ramp. As she glided down to the stage, a full complement of strings swelled to a crescendo. At the bottom, she melted into a full split and rose to find herself wrapped in the arms of her handsome skating partner. The audience was enraptured. Then the couple sped around the stage in a flashing, twirling display of lifts, turns, and dips. The audience was thrilled."

But as the 1950s came to a close, roller skating vanished

almost overnight, replaced by rock 'n' roll, sock hops, and cruising the boulevard in scooped-out Chevys and Fords. Gloria Nord made her last appearance on skates in 1960, and it was as if she twirled one last time and was gone without a trace. The only thing left behind was the bump and grind of roller derby "this Saturday night at the Olympic Auditorium," or the "All Skate" and "Couples Only" down at the Ramblin' Rose. Though national and world figure and freestyle competitions continued, the popularity roller skating once held, and the fact that it had been carried to the theatrical, heart-stopping level of the Skating Vanities and Gloria Nord, was remembered by only a few, among them Lenny LaRue and Donna Callaway.

Lenny remembered because he was a three-time national champion who'd once skated with the Skating Vanities. Donna remembered because Lenny made sure someone never forgot. Lenny could not bring back his glorious past, but he could instill his hope for the future in the youthfulness and natural talent of Donna Callaway. Thus, Donna was living in the middle of an anachronism—a leftover world struggling to survive in the minds of a few who remembered its glory.

In spite of Donna's grandparents and their glowing report of my gallantry at the hospital, my punishment for going to the roller rink against my parents' wishes turned out to be bad enough. Whatever happened in our living room that day seemed to make my parents even more set on thwarting any opportunity for my budding friendship with Donna to grow. I had hoped that the Finleys' visit would soften their anger somewhat, and maybe it did. Maybe what they really had in mind for me was far worse than this, but this was bad enough. For they told me that I was absolutely forbidden to ever enter the Ramblin' Rose again.

"Not even for an all-church skate?" I protested.

"No. You may go to the church skates," said my mother. "That's a different story entirely. Your father and I don't like the bad crowd this other kind of skating draws."

"What do you mean?" I said. "What other kind of skating?"

"The kind Donna is learning," said my mother. "It's no different than dancing. It's worse, in fact—the way they throw their legs around in those little skirts . . . well, it leaves little to the imagination."

"Mother, it's incredible. It's not bad. You should see what she can do!"

"No. I don't need to see anything of the kind, and I don't want you anywhere near the kind of crowd that hangs out at that roller rink when the church isn't there. The only time you may go is when godly people take over that place. Apart from that, it is no less a den of iniquity than a dance hall."

That had pretty much been the end of it, except that she warned me that any more visits to Matt's house would have the full cooperation of Mr. and Mrs. Wendorf to enforce this new policy on behalf of "your father and I."

"No problem," Matt said when I delivered the verdict to him the next day in church. "We can still go. Bernice will keep it quiet."

"You've got to be kidding," I said. "Your mom would lie for you?"

"She'll do anything I want her to."

"No, I couldn't do it anyway. It's too risky. My parents would find out one way or another. There must be a way to get them to change their minds. If they could just see Donna skate, they'd know it's not what they think."

"Why not have them take you to one of Donna's practices so they can see for themselves?" said Matt.

"Are you kidding? My mother entering that 'den of iniquity'?"

But impossible as it seemed, that was just what came to pass. And as had happened so many times before, Mrs. Beamering ended up playing an important role in bringing it about.

The six weeks of Donna's recuperation wedged a slight opening in my parents' attitude. It was a leverage brought about by the continued kindness and appreciation Mr. and Mrs. Finley lavished on me and on them. But it was Mrs. Beamering who cracked it wide open one Sunday at Beedle's Cafeteria. In a conversation about some of the debilitated members of the congregation, the subject of Mr. and Mrs. Finley came up, which then spilled over into Donna and, finally, skating. My mother was speaking in a judgmental tone about a style of dance skating that she knew next to nothing about, and Mrs. Beamering twisted her words right out from under her.

"The way they move their bodies—" said my mother.

"I know," said Mrs. Beamering, "isn't it amazing? You know, we saw the Skating Vanities in Houston the year before we came out to California, and it was one of the most spectacular things I have ever seen. Don't you think so, Jeffery?"

"Splendid!" said Pastor Beamering. "Absolutely splendid! Twirls . . . flips . . . I still can't figure out how they landed on those wheels all the time, and so smoothly!"

"Donna can skate like that," I chanced, ducking the icy stare of my mother.

"Can she?" said Mrs. Beamering. "I'd love to see that sometime. I thought that kind of skating went out with Gloria Nord. Is that how she broke her ankle?"

I dared not open my mouth again.

"Yes," said my mother, reluctantly.

"Poor child," Mrs. Beamering went on. "How serious is her injury, Ann? She'll be able to skate again, won't she?"

My mother knew the answer to that question. She was an unwitting expert on Donna's progress. The Finleys had been showering her with reports about Donna, which she received politely and never spoke of again.

I continued to keep my mouth shut during this conversation, however. Mrs. Beamering knew exactly what she was doing. She had a way of turning things around on my mother without embarrassing her. I knew Mrs. Beamering was up to something because she was questioning my mother for answers she'd already had from me. I'd had more than one conversation with Mrs. Beamering about my forbidden relationship with Donna, which she had obviously been pondering, waiting for the moment that came that afternoon at Beedle's.

"She's recovering quite well I hear," said my mother. "I'm sure she'll be skating again in no time."

"You know what, Ann? Why don't you and Becky and I go watch her practice sometime. I'd love an excuse to get away from all these men knocking around my house."

"That would be . . . lovely," said my mother as I almost choked on a dry corn muffin.

"I think it's wonderful what that little girl is accomplishing," said Mrs. Beamering, "after all she's been through."

What has she been through? I wanted desperately to ask, but dared not. This was far enough for one conversation—farther than I thought anyone would ever get with my mother on this subject.

"Do you think Martha's serious about this 'girls only' outing to the roller rink?" my father said in the car on the way home from Beedle's.

"Of course she's serious. Martha always means what she says. You should know that by now."

"I don't want to go to the roller rink with you and Mrs. Beamering," said Becky.

"Ouch!" That was Becky responding to my jabs in the back-seat. I didn't want her setting back this new development.

"Do I have to go along with this 'girls' thing, Mother? . . . Ouch! Stop that, Jonathan!"

"I'll go," I volunteered.

"I'm sure you would, Jonathan," said my mother.

We rode in silence for a few blocks as we all thought about the conflict from our own perspective.

"I think it sounds like a good idea," said my father, most likely thinking about his professional relationship with Pastor Beamering.

"And why do you say that?" said my mother.

"Well . . . it would give you a chance to see firsthand what this . . . this skating business is all about."

"I know what it's all about, Walter. It's about dancing and secular music and risque costumes and the appearance of evil."

"Well then, why do you suppose the pastor's wife wants to go?"

"Walter, you know they're more liberal than we are. They come from a different part of the country."

"They come from the Bible Belt, Ann. The south is much more conservative than California. Maybe things have changed, honey. They saw the show. What was it, the Skating—?"

"Vanities, Walter. The Skating *Vanities*. And that's just what I mean. What kind of clean, wholesome group would call itself the *Vanities*? It's vain, I tell you, just like its name, and how can anything 'vain' be honoring to the Lord?"

"Good, then we're not going," said my sister. "Ouch! Will you *stop it!*"

"I didn't say that," said my mother. "I have a commitment now. I didn't say no to Martha, and once she gets going on an idea, there's no stopping her."

"Why do I have to go? Why not just you and Mrs. Beamering?" said Becky, holding me back at arm's length this time.

"Because she wants you to come, and I do too. We've been talking about the three of us doing something together for some time now. That part of it would be very nice. She thinks of you as her own daughter, you know, being that she wishes sometimes she had one of her own." My mother paused for a moment or two, then turned to my father again. "I don't know, Walter. Sometimes I think my constitution is lacking. Why can't I stand up to her? Martha has a way of twisting things around and suddenly I'm supporting what I am against."

"I know," said my father as we turned into our driveway. "Jeffery does the same thing to me all the time. I wouldn't have Netta Pearl in the choir if it weren't for Jeffery putting words in my mouth. I guess that's why he's a pastor."

If ever I wanted to be invisible, it was the following Saturday when Becky and my mother left to go see Donna practice at the Ramblin' Rose. They were meeting Mrs. Beamering there and then going out for lunch afterward. The closest I got was Matt's house, since my mother agreed to drop me off there while they were at the rink. Matt wanted to sneak over and watch, but I didn't want to risk messing up the possibility of something good happening, which was exactly what came about—something beyond my wildest imagination.

My mother and Becky were in pretty good spirits when they left me at Matt's, but nothing could have prepared me for the complete reversal of my mother's position when they returned. First of all, they were later than expected by about two hours. Then they returned in such a giddy mood that I could have easily mistaken my mother for one of Becky's dingbatty friends. But most of all, my mother, in the period of a few hours, had gone through a metamorphosis that defied reason. The same mother who'd left in utter condemnation of the sport of skating returned such an avid supporter of it that it made me instinctively jealous of her sudden inside track on Donna's life and career.

Apparently Mrs. Finley had turned out to be the life of the party. Even my sister had had a good time. "Funny as a hoot," my mother kept saying all the way home, and she and Becky would look at each other and start laughing for no apparent reason.

"Well, this is certainly a surprise," said my father at the dinner table that night. "What on earth went on out there at the rink today?"

"Girls' day out," said my mother, sounding a little like Bernice. "And Mrs. Finley turned out to be one of the funniest people I've ever met. Martha just kept her going, too. The two of them must have gone on for at least two hours at that restaurant. I can't remember when I've laughed more in my life."

"What was so funny?" asked my father.

"Everything," said Becky. "She's got this mousey little voice and yet she's so tough. Could you pass me the string beans, Jonathan?"

"She's as tough as nails," said my mother. "What makes it so funny is that she laughs about being in a wheelchair. It makes you feel uncomfortable at first. Didn't you feel that way, Becky?"

"Yeah," said my sister. "She says all the things you're thinking and it makes you feel awful at first, and then you realize she's joking."

"That's exactly right," said my mother, sliding a piece of fried Spam onto her plate and passing the platter to me. "She tells all these jokes on herself until suddenly you find you are joining in with her. I've never felt so free around a person in a wheelchair before. Usually I'm much more nervous. And then you find out all the things she's done in that wheelchair!" she said, looking over at Becky.

"Oh yeah," said Becky, "it's incredible. She's traveled all over the country. Gone on hikes. She rolled herself on trails up and down the Grand Canyon."

"She still swims regularly at the YWCA—at her age! Honestly, Walter, it makes you not want to complain about anything ever again. Heavens to Betsy, we've got two legs and a future, and we haven't done half the things she's done without them. And then, as old as she is, she tells you what she's not done yet. You know what she wants to do next?"

"What?"

"Jump out of an airplane!" said Becky.

"That's right," said my mother. "She wants to go parachute jumping. Can you believe that?"

"And she will, too," said my sister.

"Yes," said my mother, "she's dead serious."

"Or seriously dead, if it doesn't open," laughed my father, but no one thought it was funny.

"Becky, tell them what she said that time she cut her leg."

"Oh yeah. That was hilarious. Once she was working outside in her garden and she cut her leg pretty bad—"

"She's paralyzed from the waist down, you know," my mother inserted. "Can't feel a thing."

"Yeah, so she doesn't even know about this cut, and she doesn't discover it until she's been outside for a while, dragging herself around, and suddenly she gets to feeling kind of dizzy, and she looks down at her leg and sees this awful cut caked with blood and dirt—"

"Yuk!" I said.

"And guess what she says?"

"What?" I asked.

" 'Well would you look at that,' she says. 'That must really *hurt!*' "

We all laughed.

"You know, she and Donna had a wheelchair race at the hospital," I recalled, suddenly feeling free to mention the unmentionable, "and Donna never caught up with her."

"Speaking of Donna, Jonathan, I owe you an apology," said my mother.

This was monumental. Never before had my mother apologized to me. Once when I found a way to see Ben in the hospital against her wishes, she later admitted she was wrong to forbid me, but that wasn't exactly an apology.

"I judged this skating business before I really knew what I was talking about. You are right about Donna. She's terrific, and I hope she wins the competition. She's a lot like her grandmother—overcoming a lot of difficulties with a real flair, and my hat is off to both of them."

"What difficulties is Donna overcoming? What did happen to her parents?" I asked, and the old concerned look reappeared for a minute on my parents' faces.

"Jonathan, it's really not necessary for you to know that," said my mother. "What's important is that Donna is a wonderful girl and she needs support, and your father and I are sorry we stood in the way of what has been a very genuine caring on your part."

"I never stood in the way of anything," said my father.

"You could have stopped me," said my mother with a firm look.

"Does this mean I can go see Donna practice this week?" I asked.

"Well, not with your paper route, but certainly next Saturday. I may even go with you."

"Me too," said Becky.

Great! I thought. *How about the whole family?*

11

Under the Desk

For the next few weeks my attention was almost completely taken up with the skating aspirations of Donna Callaway. Part of that time included the Christmas holidays, meaning Donna went into extended practices every day, and almost every day I (and sometimes Matt with me) was there at the Ramblin' Rose cheering her on. I can't say I understood her aspirations, but I admired them. I admired Donna's endurance and her hard work, and I was fascinated by a world totally unlike the one I'd known up until then.

Gradually, Peg started asking me to do a few odd jobs around the place. I moved boxes, carted deliveries around, and wiped down tables in the fountain. Oh yes, and she had me touch up the inside of one of the stalls in the men's room "where some jerk named Ben had to leave his mark for posterity on our freshly painted stall." Luckily she hadn't noticed that the accompanying initials were the same as Donna's and mine. I liked doing this kind of stuff. It made me feel like I belonged there.

I think Peg gave me the jobs so I wouldn't get bored, but it was never boring being with Donna. Most of the time at the rink, of course, she couldn't be with me. So I had taken to putting on skates and joining her on the floor while she warmed up and when she took breaks from her arduous routines. Lenny had softened his tight hold on Donna's practices once he saw the value of someone giving her attention other than himself. Being able to have company on her breaks was helping her relax more, which meant she was more able to concentrate when she went back to work. Though Lenny still made me feel like an intrusion, he allowed my presence as part of his "work hard, play hard" ethic.

Donna was even trying to teach me a few simple tricks, providing herself with a little comic interlude at my expense. I could now do fairly well with the backward scissor steps and was just learning my first simple jump: taking a half turn in the air and landing backward while immediately going into the scissors— though I hadn't experienced the scissors part at the end of this jump, since so far I had landed on everything but my wheels.

"And I was hoping we could skate in the pairs competition this year," she kept teasing as she would give me a hand up.

Sometimes, while Donna skated, I explored around the rink, though there was not much room for exploring. Lenny kept as tight a control on his private affairs as he did on his skaters. His office was declared "off limits," and its location made that easy to enforce. It was like an inner sanctum—two closed doors away from the public part of the rink.

First there was the front counter from which the general public rented skates and skate time. Directly behind that were four long rows of skates racked like books in bookshelves and marked by size. Hidden behind the last row was the first door that opened into Peg's office. Peggy Lane, her name to those who knew her when she was a competition skater, was the general manager of the rink. She booked all the lessons; she handled the public; and as far as I could tell, she ran the business.

Her relationship with Lenny was an odd one that I never could quite figure out. They were best of friends, partners in business, and constant companions, but they were not married, nor did there ever appear to be any romantic involvement between them. Often Lenny would talk about having a date, and Peg didn't seem concerned at all. Whatever their relationship was, they were the kind of people who were suspect in my world, so I steered pretty clear of both of them. That seemed to be the way Lenny wanted it anyway, although Peg could be friendly in her own rough sort of way.

Lenny's office was through another door behind Peg's office, and I had never been that far in until Lenny himself, to my surprise, sent me there. Maybe I was making a nuisance of myself wandering around aimlessly, or maybe it was because Lenny was getting used to having me available, but that day he sent me into his office to get a bag of plaster of Paris for the floor. Though some of the newer rinks had plastic-coated urethane finishes on their floors, the Ramblin' Rose still had its original varnish coating that was too slick for the more involved tricks of freestyle skating. A light dusting of plaster of Paris was necessary to cut the slipperiness of the varnish enough to give the wheels the grip they needed. This was the strange white powder Matt and I had discovered the first time we came to watch Donna skate—the fine angelic dust that mysteriously settled on everyone and everything inside the rink.

Being on special assignment to Lenny's office didn't give me much time there, but it was enough to set me wondering. As soon as I entered the room, I could see why Lenny needed someone like Peg running his affairs. There were skates and parts of skates on shelves on one wall and along the floor below. Trophies were scattered in and around skate wheels, wheel trucks, and toe stoppers. The plaster of Paris in a sack in the corner had dusted the skate bags near it. A full set of barbells occupied the opposite side of the room. But it was the wall behind his desk, visible over the piles of papers on it, that drew me like a magnet.

There was a sort of wall of fame there, with pictures and memorabilia of Lenny's grand and glorious skating past haphazardly arranged. Many of the pictures were framed and signed. Some were action shots; others were posed; all of them seemed to jump off the wall at me as if these people were living again in their glory. There were large companies of people, all in elaborate costumes and all on skates, that I took to be the Skating Vanities I had heard so much about. Other shots were more candid, taken on buses or in dressing rooms with the half-dressed scurrying from the eye of the camera. In all of them, though, their young and vibrant faces exuded confidence and joy. The camera had caught them in the middle of a dream come true.

One photograph especially caught my eye. It was the most prominent picture on the wall—an exciting action shot of a youthful Lenny with a skating partner that took my breath away. Lenny was skating with his legs spread slightly, toes out, and one arm outstretched in front of him towards the audience. His other arm was straight up, balancing the horizontal body of a beautiful woman on the palm of his hand. They couldn't have held this pose for very long, but the camera had it captured forever.

I was mesmerized by this picture, so much so that I almost forgot my assignment in Lenny's office. Lenny's face had no wrinkles, and his hair had no gray. And the woman . . . what was it about her? Even the way she held her arms and her body while hovering in such a precarious place defied gravity and awarded grace. Something about her seemed vaguely familiar. I could not turn my eye away. . . .

"Jonathan, you in there?" Peg called from the door of her office. "What's taking you so long with that plaster?"

"Coming," I sang out, grabbing the heavy sack of plaster of Paris and thinking fast. "I was looking for something I could roll this out with. It's very heavy."

"I know, but you're a growing boy," she said, crossing through her office and finding me struggling with the sack. "Come on, you can do it."

It *was* heavy—much heavier than I anticipated. Inspired by the picture I had been looking at, and somewhat curious as to just how hard it would be to do what Lenny did, I lifted the heavy sack up on my shoulder and got the palm of my hand under the bag to see if I could push it straight up from my shoulder.

"What if this were Donna?" I said, getting the sack only half-way up before it teetered and almost fell, but for my catching it with the other hand.

"We'd be going back to the hospital, kid," said Peg.

"Where have you been?" said Donna as I skated out to join her on a break. "You've got plaster in your hair."

"Really?" I said, shaking my head and watching a fine white mist float down. "I was trying to be like Lenny."

"What do you mean?"

"The picture in Lenny's office. Haven't you seen it?"

Donna looked like she'd just had white plaster thrown in her face. She twirled to a sudden stop in the middle of the rink and glared at me as I tried to stop gracefully but ended up crashing into the rail ten yards away.

"What were you doing in Lenny's office?" she said, skating over to me. "Don't you know that's off limits?"

"Well, yes," I said, shocked and surprised by the sharpness of her voice, "but he sent me there . . . to get the plaster of Paris."

"What did you see in there?" she said sternly.

"I—I saw lots of pictures."

"What kind of pictures? Who was in them?"

"Well . . . well," I stammered, totally confused by this line of questioning, "one was of Lenny holding his partner up with one hand. I tried to do it with a sack of plaster and—"

Suddenly she turned on her wheels and skated off, looking like she was going to cry. Lenny was just coming back into the rink, and Donna went into a jump followed by a camel spin in the middle of the floor and then skated over to him and barked in a curt, military manner, "Let's get to work."

Lenny looked over at me like he was wondering what I had said to put her in such a testy mood, but he didn't pursue it. He went right ahead with practice, probably happy for the opportunity to focus all this energy into her performance. As it turned out, she successfully, and quite beautifully, completed that morning, for the first time, the axel loop/double mapes combination she had been working on since coming back from her broken ankle.

At the noon break she was more like her usual self.

"You were great this morning," I said, happy to see her smile return, but still nervous about saying the wrong thing.

"Thanks," she said with a blush.

The Finleys smothered Donna with congratulations and then sent us off to the fountain area, where Peg had a couple hamburgers and two cherry Cokes waiting for us at a table. The rink was quiet except for the whirring of the refrigerators behind the empty counter. I watched as Donna sucked up her entire Coke, right down to the slurp at the bottom, without stopping.

"Thirsty, huh?"

She leaned back and let out a big sigh.

"I'm sorry, Jonathan," she smiled.

What a relief! I thought.

"Gosh, I—I'm sorry, too . . . I didn't mean to—"

"It's not your fault. It's not you, Jonathan, it's really Lenny I'm mad at for letting you into his office. I don't get him sometimes. He's up to something."

"What's the big deal with being in his office?"

Donna stared coldly at the uneaten hamburger in front of her.

"It's okay," I said hurriedly. "If you don't want to tell me—"

"No, you might as well know . . . my mother is probably in those pictures, Jonathan." She said it so matter-of-factly. "She and Lenny used to be skating partners."

I felt like I had been hit in the stomach. That was it! The woman Lenny was holding up had to be Donna's mother. As soon as she said it, I knew. That was why she looked so familiar. Donna would hold herself just like that if she were flying in the air.

"You want to see the pictures?" I said. "It's not hard to slip in there, you know."

"No!" she said quickly and emphatically.

"Why? If she's your mother. . . ?"

"She left me when I was four."

The words hung there like they had been torn out of a book and thrown on the table.

"You haven't seen her since?"

"No."

"Doesn't she ever write you?"

"No. Nothing. Can't we talk about something else?"

Donna reached down into her glass and fished out a Maraschino cherry, bit off and ate the little red fruit, and then put the stem in her mouth and started moving her tongue around just behind her lips.

"What are you doing?" I asked, welcoming the distraction.

"Tying the stem in a knot with my tongue."

"You can do that?"

Her face went into all kinds of silly contortions that made me laugh until she finally produced the stem between her teeth, tied in the middle in a tight little knot.

"Yes," she said through her teeth.

"How did you do that?" I asked, staring at the stem but noticing more the pretty mouth around it.

"Practice," she beamed, using her favorite word and handing me the knotted stem.

"I'll cherish it forever," I said, examining it and then putting it in my pocket.

The smiles slowly fell off our faces and a heaviness returned.

"She fell," Donna said, deciding for some reason to give me one more piece of information. I didn't get the significance at first. Who fell? Her mother? So? Everybody fell. Even the best, Lenny always said. The harder the thing attempted, the greater the chance of falling. But Donna wasn't finished yet.

"My mother fell in the World Competitions in 1952," she said, watching the ice melt in her empty Coca-Cola glass, "and she hasn't gotten up since."

She set her straw aside and drank the little bit of water that had melted in that short time, then set her glass back down in front of her, still focused on the ice as if she were melting it with her eyes.

I looked at her flat expression, and then I stared into my glass for a while. I didn't know what to say. I felt a deep pain inside me and another pain near it that I didn't understand. One was an actual physical pain, the other was deep in my heart. Finally I reached into my own glass and pulled my cherry out from under the ice.

"Here," I said, dangling the fruit by its stem over the middle of the table. "You can have mine. I don't like these."

Donna leaned in and snapped the cherry off with her teeth,

leaving the stem in my hand. I looked at it curiously and then popped it in my mouth.

"You'll never get it," she said, eyes suddenly gleaming. Then she started laughing at how funny I looked trying to tie a knot in a cherry stem with my tongue for the first time. I started making all kinds of funny faces that made her laugh some more. Finally, I overdid it completely—falling back in my chair and putting my whole body into the act, which sent her tumbling uncontrollably into roaring fits.

"I give up," I said, spitting the stem across the table, where it bounced once and landed in her lap. She picked it up, put it in her mouth, and started in with that talented tongue again.

"Ta da!" she sang, pulling it out of her mouth in seconds and holding it up for me. "You want to cherish this one too?"

"All right, what's so funny over here?" said Lenny, bringing up a chair and squinting through the smoke of his cigarette. Unlike Peg, who was a chain smoker, Lenny liked to have just one smoke during his break.

"It's Jonathan," Donna said, stiffening a little at his presence. "He always makes me laugh."

"So how's your little jump coming along, Johnny?"

"Great," I said. "I've got everything down but the landing."

"Do you think he'll ever make it as a skating partner?" Donna's coach said to my coach.

"I have my doubts," she said.

I did try, but never wholeheartedly and always more to amuse Donna than to satisfy any ambitions of my own. I felt strange enough in this skating world Donna was involved in; the people I met were nothing like the people in church or my middle-class suburban neighborhood. When it came to skating, I was definitely an "all skate" person. Lenny and Peg and Donna were part of a harder, darker world.

Lenny even dressed the part; he always wore black. He must have had a closetful of black T-shirts and stretch pants because that was his uniform, whether he was skating or not. The T-shirts showed off a muscular, though not bulky, chest. Lenny was small and compact, about 5'6"; at thirteen, I was almost as tall as he was. He was built a little like a fireplug—as if God had taken a taller man and squished him down a foot. The features on his face seemed large for the rest of his body, especially his eyes; they were always red and wet and protruding slightly, making them appear ominous and buglike. His hair was his most attractive asset—thick and black with handsome streaks of grey. He always wore a gold chain around his neck, and when it popped out of his T-shirt, you could see the St. Christopher medal that dangled from it. He claimed he had worn it since the days of his own competitions.

Skaters, I learned, were often superstitious, since so much was riding on one performance. When you thought about it, it was hardly fair. Donna, for instance, was well into her third month of practice specifically for the state competitions in Bakersfield in June, and she had six more months to go. Four days a week for nine months that would all boil down to one 3½-minute performance—a performance that could be adversely affected by nothing more than a faulty ball bearing or a bad night's sleep. Compare that to a baseball player who gets 160 games over the course of a season to prove the same thing. A ballplayer can have off days and make quite a few errors (they even keep track of them) and still end up with a good year. A skater got 3½ minutes, and one little mistake could ruin the whole thing.

Sometimes I wondered what made Donna skate, but finding out about her mother explained a lot. Even though she was angry at her mother for leaving her, she still must have admired what her mother had accomplished or she wouldn't be pursuing it herself. Perhaps she was hoping to find something of her mother in the steps and routines of her skating.

Meanwhile, Lenny was hoping to shine again through her youth. I looked at him as I thought about this and his wall of memories. Just then he exhaled, sending a plume of smoke across the table so that it stung my eyes.

"We're right on schedule," he said to Donna. "Time to start thinking about your music."

"Let's go sneak into Lenny's office," I said as soon as he left. It was a perfect opportunity. Donna's grandparents hadn't returned from lunch, Lenny and Dominic were going to work on some music at the organ, and Peg wasn't anywhere around. Probably out running an errand.

"Jonathan. . . ." She bit her lower lip and looked off at the rink, sighed, then looked back at me. "I'm not allowed to go in there; don't you understand that?"

"No. Not when there are pictures of your mother on the wall. Donna, she's so pretty," I said in my sweetest voice possible. It was suddenly the most important thing in the world to me— to get her in that room. "Come on, we could slip in there right now and no one will know. They'll think we went over to the Rocket Cafe or the market."

"I don't want to see the pictures," she said, but she was less convincing than before. We both stared off at nothing for a moment until she spoke again.

"Is she really pretty?"

"Yes! You'll go then?"

"I have to go to the rest room first. Wait for me at the front counter."

When she returned she announced that Peg was cleaning the bathrooms.

"Great. That's even better. Come on!"

"I don't like this," she said as we passed through Peg's office. Then, "What a mess!" as we entered Lenny's office.

But when she saw the wall of fame she said nothing. Having already studied it, I now studied Donna instead. She stopped and stood perfectly still, staring at the collage of memories on the other side of the messy desk where she steadied herself. She looked at me with wonder, as if to get her bearings in the present, and then back at the wall. She moved in slow motion around the desk and right up to the pictures, reaching out and touching them gently, one by one, as if a quick movement might disturb the people in them.

"Look, she's over here," Donna said softly, "and over here."

"And isn't this her?" I said, pointing to a group shot.

"Yes," she said, now smiling.

"I told you she was pretty," I said.

"She was," Donna said. "Like Lenny. Look how handsome he was."

We both ended up staring at the prominent picture in the middle, the one with Lenny lifting Donna's mother.

"How did they do that?" I asked.

"They were the best," said Donna.

"Look what I found," I said, picking up a program from a shelf under the pictures on the wall.

"Oh! It's the first program of the Vanities. I've never seen this one!"

I held it up for her. "Skating Vanities of 1942" it said on the front over a picture of a petite blonde sitting on a white table lifting up her short chiffon skirt to show off her pretty legs.

"That's Gloria Nord," said Donna.

Suddenly we heard someone entering Peg's office next door.

"Quick! Under the desk!" I whispered.

We tucked ourselves under, and I prayed whoever it was didn't need to come behind it. It was Lenny, and fortunately, whatever he was looking for was in the pile somewhere on top of his desk. When he left, we let out deep breaths and then started giggling. Even though it was safe to come out from under the desk, we stayed huddled there together and looked at the Skating Vanities program I still had in my hand.

"Look! There's her name. Esther Callaway," Donna said, her voice so close to my ear that I could feel her breath. She was pointing to a list of the Gae Foster Rollerettes: "The twenty-four pulchritudinous girls that share thirty-nine local, city, state, and national crowns."

" 'Pul-chri-tu-di-nous' " I read. "That's a mouthful!"

"Do you know what it means?" she said.

"No, but I can find out."

"Look, there she is again," said Donna, quietly worshiping her mother's glory.

It was easy to spot her mother, even in the group pictures. She had wide-set eyes, a high forehead, and a turned-up nose just like Donna's. In fact, she was young enough in these pictures that the resemblance was striking.

We found her in four pictures in the program, and we also found Lenny listed among the Roller Boys, though it was hard to tell which one he was in the only picture that included them, since they were dressed like wooden soldiers with plumed hats that made them all look exactly alike. The Roller Boys were in the back line of a formation that had the Rollerettes formed in a V in front of them. And closest to the camera, at the point of the

V, was a beaming Esther Callaway.

It was right then and there, with our knees to our chins and our noses in the program of the 1942 Skating Vanities, under the messy desk of Lenny LaRue, in the inner sanctum of the Ramblin' Rose Roller Rink in Pasadena, that I fell in love for the first time in my life. And under that desk I kissed Donna Callaway's cheek, which seemed to make one hurt lessen and another one worse.

12

The Dark Talks Back

"Come on, Matt, tell me the truth," I said when I had him cornered in the lower level of the church the following Sunday. "Tell me the truth or Grizzly here is going to turn you into hamburger!"

None of the other kids in the church, Matt included, shared my friendship with Grizzly. To them, he was still the retarded janitor—the scary deaf-mute making guttural, half-human, half-animal sounds from the dark, unlit catacombs of the church. They continued to see him the way Ben and I used to see him, before we found out he was intelligent, and kind, and probably the most loyal friend anyone could ever have. Sometimes, that misconception was something I could use to my advantage. This time, it proved to be very effective in helping me extract some important information out of Matt.

I had done a lot of thinking since Donna and I snuck into Lenny's office and found her mother on the wall. Suddenly everything had gotten very complicated. No sooner did I leave the rink that afternoon than I felt confused. While I was with Donna, I had been brave and gallant. I had handled the news about her mother, reunited her with a memory, and even kissed her under the desk. But afterward, all I could think was: "Oh no . . . what have I done?"

For so long it seemed like I didn't know enough about Donna Callaway; now it seemed like I knew too much. I started feeling that a certain degree of her happiness—perhaps even her success in skating—was going to be connected to me somehow. As exciting as it had been to be close to her, there was a whole lot inside of me that wanted to turn around and run. Caring for Donna was now going to cost me something, and I wasn't sure I wanted to pay it.

I had come to this same point with Ben. I could play around with ideas forever, but acting on them was another thing entirely. I always wanted to pull back, while Ben wanted to make something big out of his actions. I believe now that part of that was because he knew intuitively that he did not have long to live. Strange thoughts for a ten-year-old, to be sure, but not necessarily a ten-year-old who knew he had a hole in his heart. And now I had a kind of hole in my heart—an emotional hole—an aching for Donna that only being with her and doing something about it would solve, and yet being with her *meant something* now. I was no longer only a cheerleader or a spectator. I was a player who wasn't sure he wanted to be put in the game. And there was no Ben around to push me through the barriers.

So as soon as I had gotten home from the rink that afternoon, I had gone up the ladder in my sister's closet and played with my trains until my father pulled the fuse on me. My parents and even my sister had tried to get me to come down, but I was blissfully entangled in switches and engines and imaginary towns and freight delivery runs that desperately needed me to run them. It wasn't until my father literally cut off the electricity to the attic that I finally came down. Still, my mother had a warm plate of food waiting for me in the oven.

That had all happened on the Thursday after Christmas. For the next two days I stayed as far away from everyone as possible, especially Donna and anything to do with skating. With the exception of my paper route, I spent most of the time in the attic with my trains. Once in a while I would think about Donna and then push the thought away. Thinking of Ben didn't help either, because I knew Ben would have had me down from the attic *doing* something, and right then I didn't want to do anything but be alone.

Saturday night my mother had tried to get through my wall of silence.

"What's wrong, Jonathan?" she said while she tucked me into bed. "Do you want to talk about it?"

"No."

"Is it Ben, honey?"

Of course it was Ben. It was always Ben in some way. It was his raw faith and what it made me do, and how it changed my life whether he was there or not—whether he was alive or dead didn't matter. Yeah, it was Ben all right.

"Do you miss him?"

Did I miss him? Actually, right then, and for the last couple days, I had wished with everything I had that he would go away. But it's kind of hard to send someone away who is already gone.

"Remember, you've got him right here," she said, laying her hand on my heart, and that was the worst thing she could have said. It was the worst because I loved him and hated him. I wished he would go away and I hated him for leaving, all at the same time.

"Good-night," she said, kissing me on the forehead.

I always had my hardest times over Ben at night. That was when the two of us used to have our best talks—lying in bed on sleepovers staring out at the dark. Some nights I didn't even want to go to bed because I knew as soon as my head hit the pillow I would be wide awake with memories.

That night, however, for some strange reason, Ben didn't seem so far away. The one time I wanted him out of my life, he seemed closer than ever. In fact, it seemed like he was right there. And then I had gotten this crazy thought that if he was right there, it would be just like it always had been. I wouldn't see him or touch him. I would just talk to the dark, and the dark would talk back.

And so I did.

"Ben?" I said out loud.

Speak, Lord, for thy servant heareth.

What? What was that? My mind must have been playing tricks on me.

"Ben!" I said it again and lifted my head off the pillow, only to see the familiar dog patterns on the curtains silhouetted by the moonlight. I rested my head back on the pillow and there it was again—that voice!

Scale the highest mountain.

I can't even be sure anymore if I actually heard this voice. I've tried to both explain and explain away that night so many times since then that what actually happened escapes me. However it happened, whether I heard the voice, whether someone else would have heard it had they been there, or whether I only heard it in my brain, doesn't really matter—didn't matter then—because the important thing was the words. They were specific words. Definite messages. And I remembered every one.

"Ben?" I said his name again, only because that was all I could think to say. The voice, or whatever it was, didn't sound like Ben's—more like a deep whisper. Ben's whisper was weak and thin, or at least that's the way I remembered his voice last, from a hospital bed.

Sing our song.

That was it. That was the end of the messages. What kind of strange thing was this? Two or three more entreaties to Ben went unanswered, and then my mother had come out to comfort me, concerned over my attempt to awaken the dead.

"Did you hear anything, Mother?"

"Only you calling."

"No other voices?"

"No, Jonathan. You were just calling for Ben in your sleep."

After she kissed me good-night for a second time, I had gotten up and written down the messages. It wasn't really necessary. There was no way I would ever forget them. But I did it anyway.

Speak, Lord, for thy servant heareth.

Scale the highest mountain.

Sing our song.

I awakened the next morning thinking back on all the encounters Matt and I had had with the supposed supernatural. Suspicious that he might have had more to do with this angelic stuff than any real angels, I had found it most convenient to dismiss these occurrences as coming from the Matt Wendorf school of practical jokes—until the events of the night before made me go back through everything in my mind one more time: the writing in the bunker, the meeting with "Margaret," the writing in the bathroom stall, the strange man in the checkered coat, and the unexplained phone call to Donna Callaway. Was any part of it real? I knew from the look on Matt's face in the rest room of the roller rink that he had been up to something. But how much?

So that Sunday morning I was determined to find Matt at church and get to the bottom of this. I ran into Grizzly first, outside the educational building.

"I have to talk to you," I told him, "in private."

He led me into the old building, down the stairs, and through the gym into a back kitchen that was only used for banquets. Matt and I knew that kitchen well. A window there looked out into a loading area below ground level, and from it you could look up a wall and see people walking along a railing that bordered a path at the edge of the parking lot. Leave it to Matt to find the one place in church where, if the wind was right, you could peek under a skirt blowing in the updraft.

I took the piece of paper with the messages out of my pocket and smoothed it out for Grizzly on the counter.

"I heard these voices last night in the dark. Three very clear messages. What do you think?"

Grizzly studied the paper for a few minutes looking puzzled. Then he underlined the first message with his finger, *Speak, Lord, for thy servant heareth*, and looked at me questioningly.

"That's the first thing I heard."

Grizzly rubbed his chin and then got out his pad and wrote: "WHO SPOKE FIRST?"

I had to think a moment.

"I did. I called out Ben's name."

That made Grizzly's face light up.

"What? What is it?" I hated waiting for Grizzly to write. He was so slow at it.

"YOU . . . CALLED . . . ANGEL . . . ANSWER."

"Wait a minute. That's not right. That would make me the Lord and the angel would be my servant."

At that, Grizzly nodded his whole torso up and down to say that I had it precisely. Then he wrote: "MINISTERING SPIR-ITS."

He was right, but I had never thought about it quite that way before. Angels were actually our servants. Grizzly started writing "PASTOR BEAM—" but I impatiently grabbed the pencil from him and said, "I know what Pastor Beamering said. I was there too. What about the rest of this?"

Grizzly stared at the messages for a while and the wrinkles of puzzlement came back to his face. Then he took the pencil back.

"RIDDLES," he wrote finally. "SOMETHING YOU MUST DO."

That was when I had glimpsed through the window, out of the corner of my eye, the unmistakably white legs of Bernice Wendorf, with Matt following right behind. They were on their way from the parking lot to church, and a brilliant idea hit me. I knew a way to coerce Matt into telling me the truth, once and for all, about our experiences with angels.

"Wait here," I said with a hand on Grizzly's arm, "and scare Matt to death when I bring him back. He knows something about this."

So when I brought Matt down to the kitchen, Grizzly not only looked scary, he had found a huge meat cleaver and was waving it madly in the air. That's when I had pushed Matt up against the wall and demanded the truth.

"I'll talk! I'll talk!" he screamed, his eyes saucer-wide. "What do you want to know?"

Grizzly was playing it to the hilt. He had roughed up his hair, and he was emitting the most horrible sound out of his twisted mouth, which was drooling and foaming to such an extent that he even had me a little scared.

"I want to know if you were behind any of these so-called angelic visits we've had in the last few months." I had him pinned to the kitchen wall by both shoulders while Grizzly moved around behind me grunting and groaning. Though my face was right in front of his, Matt's eyes were not on me at all; they darted from side to side, waiting to see where the awful face behind me was going to pop up next. "I want to know the truth, starting with the writing in the bunker."

"Okay! Okay! I'll tell you everything! Just tell him to put down that . . . that meat-cutting thing!"

I waved Grizzly off and loosened my grip on Matt's shoulders. Grizzly stopped waving the cleaver and settled down, but kept on breathing like he was gargling.

"The only thing I faked was the stuff in the bathroom at the roller rink," he said, straightening his clothes and never taking his eyes off Grizzly, who had gone to rocking in a slow swoon.

"What about the bunker?"

"I don't know nothin' about the bunker. I didn't do a thing there."

"And Margaret? Did you really see Margaret the next day after I left?"

"It's just like I told you," said Matt. "Honest."

"Did you ever call Donna Callaway and pretend to be me?"

"No! I don't know anything about that. The only thing . . . in the bathroom at the roller rink—"

"Yeah?" I said, with Grizzly gurgling down my neck.

"I did everything but change the *I* to a *C*. I swear, I didn't do *that*. I wouldn't lie about that because it freaked me out. There was nobody in there but that old guy."

I stepped back and relished his misery for a while before I let him go.

"And by the way," I said, smiling, "Mr. Griswold's only faking it. He's really a nice fellow."

Matt looked at Grizzly, who broke into a smile, and back at me and never changed his expression. "I think you're both crazy!" he said and bolted out the door.

I looked at Grizzly and we both laughed. Then he found a napkin and wiped the drool off his face.

"Boy, did we have him on the ropes! What was that stuff coming out of your mouth? How did you do that?"

He opened one of the cupboards and held up a package of baking soda with a sly smile.

"Wow, that's boss! We'll have to remember that."

I jumped up and sat on one of the counters and tried to think about what all this meant. Some of the stuff had been a hoax, but not all of it. Now I knew the voices in the night were real. Matt hadn't been up to as much as I'd thought, which didn't make me very happy. I was hoping it had all been him, because then I could have dismissed the former encounters and figured out some way to explain the voices. Now there was too much to explain away, and I was being pushed again outside of my comfortable places.

While I was thinking, Grizzly had been writing, so I looked over his shoulder.

"BEN'S ANGEL IS AT IT AGAIN!"

Yes, Ben was still messing with my life, and now I had to find out why.

13

Mr. Whitney

By the time church was over that morning, it was obvious that Donna was now avoiding *me*. It came as no surprise. I hadn't been at her last two practices, including the one on Saturday, and I hadn't missed a Saturday practice since I first started going to them. On top of that, I hadn't even called her, and by the looks she gave me in church, it didn't appear that any angels had done any calling on my behalf lately, either. The nearest I got to her Sunday morning was five feet behind her in the parking lot as she walked rapidly to her car.

"Donna, stop, please! Let me talk to you."

No acknowledgment whatsoever.

"I found out what pulchritudinous means!"

For that, I at least got her to turn around and glare at me.

"It means 'endowed with physical beauty'!" I said loud enough to be heard by more than a few.

Donna just turned and walked the rest of the way to her grandparents' car without looking back.

The real blow, however, came the next day when I showed up at the rink only to have Peg announce to me through the window that Donna didn't want any guests that day. I wasn't even allowed to have a name. "Donna is not entertaining any *guests* today."

All this only made me more determined to find out what the angelic messages meant. I knew if I was really supposed to help her, and if God and His angels and even Ben were in on this, sooner or later she would have to come around. This thing was obviously bigger than just the two of us.

There were still a couple days of Christmas vacation left, so with the rink closed to me, I knew exactly where to go next. I told my mother I was going for a bike ride and then I headed for 332 Live Oak Street.

"Johnny, come on in! It must still be your vacation," said Molly. "I know it's not collection time, so what brings you by?"

"I've been hearing from angels, Molly," I said, happy to have someone I could talk to directly about this without having to wait for them to write down their responses.

"You have, have you? And what have they been sayin' to ya?"

Once again I pulled out the piece of paper with the messages on it. Molly had to go to the next room and get her glasses.

"Mother Mary," she said as she studied the paper, "I've never heard of anything like this."

"Do you think I'm crazy?"

"No, Johnny, of course not."

"Grizzly and I figured out the first one was the angel responding to me calling for Ben."

"Who's Grizzly?"

"Oh, that's Harvey Griswold, the janitor at our church. He can't hear or talk, but he knows a lot about angels. Says he hears them sometimes in the church."

"People with problems like that know a lot about things the rest of us miss," said Molly. "I've seen it time and time again in my years at St. Mary's."

She kept studying the phrases and lifting up her glasses as if the words might change on her somehow, depending on which way she looked at them. "Well now, that last one has to be a song that angels sing, right? . . . since it says, 'Sing *our* song'?"

Of course. I hadn't even thought of that, probably because it was so obvious.

"But this other one about scaling the highest mountain . . . I wouldn't know how to take that. It could be a vague idea about doing something difficult, or it could be a particular mountain you're supposed to climb, takin' it lit'rally, I suppose. You have any difficult things waitin' to be done, Johnny?"

"Well, yes, but Ben was never vague about anything," I said. "If he's behind this, there's a trick somewhere—something you have to find out in a book, I bet."

"*Scale the highest mountain,*" Molly repeated, and shook her head.

"What's the highest mountain around here?" I asked.

"There's Mt. Wilson and Mt. Baldy. Do those mean anything to you?" said Molly.

"No, nothing. We sometimes go on family picnics to Mt. Wilson."

"Well anyway," said Molly, waving her glasses, "neither one is even close to bein' the 'highest' mountain. Do you know what the highest mountain in the world is?"

"Mt. Everest maybe? I'm not sure. I *do* know what the highest mountain in California is."

"And what would that be?"

"Mt. Whitney," I said. "I just learned that in geography the week before vacation. It's 14,494 feet high. It *was* the highest mountain in the United States until a couple years ago when Alaska became a state."

"There you go," said Molly. "If you just learned it, it would be fresh on your mind. Angels know about things like that. And it does qualify for the highest mountain—in California, did you say?"

"But what does that mean, then? Am I supposed to climb Mt. Whitney?"

"It may."

"Holy cow! How am I going to do that?"

"Either that, or as you say, laddie, there might be a bit of a trick to it."

I went home and read up on all I could find about Mt. Whitney in the *Encyclopedia Britannica*. Nothing rang a bell. Then I remembered a classmate at school who'd recently done an oral report about mountain climbing, so I called him up and found out that you could *hike* Mt. Whitney and it wasn't even that hard. There was an easy trail up the back side all the way to the top. *Hardly scaling it*, I thought. When I asked him if there was a hard way, he said, "Yes, and a number of experienced climbers have died trying."

What could scaling Mt. Whitney possibly have to do with anything anyway? I thought. Was I going to risk my life on a possible interpretation of a riddle from a voice in the dark?

I decided to call Matt and found him still mad about the day before.

"That man's a nut case. They should have put him in Camarillo years ago. You know you didn't have to do that; I would have told you the truth."

"Matt, it was just a joke, and Grizzly's not a nut case. He's very smart. You know that foam in his mouth?"

"Yeah?"

"That was baking soda. He came up with that on his own. He's not dumb."

"Just keep him away from me, all the same. He's creepy."

"What was that you just said about Camarillo? What's that?"

"It's some place where they send all the crazy people. It's a hospital, I think, for the retards. Why?"

"Oh, I just heard someone mention it the other day and wondered what it was. Hey, Matt, do you know anything about Mt. Whitney?"

"It's the tallest mountain in California, I think."

"Anything else? Anything unusual?"

"Isn't there something about it being right up next to Death Valley, the lowest spot in the country?"

"Oh yeah, I remember that. I wonder if that means anything."

"What're you talking about?"

"Never mind. It's nothing important. I'll tell you later. What are you doing tomorrow?"

"Nothing much. You want to come over and go to the rink?"

"Yeah. Only Donna might not let me in."

"Uh-oh. 'I'm Mr. Blue, wa-o-wa-ooo . . .' What happened, lover boy?"

"Donna thinks I don't like her anymore."

"Do you?"

"Oh yeah. In fact, I'm trying to help her out, but she doesn't know it yet. I'll tell you about it tomorrow. It's all about angels and stuff."

"Hey, I'm sorry about messing around with that writing in the bathroom. I only meant it for fun. I really didn't think real angels would be interested in your love life."

"Let's just call it even, okay?"

"Okay. It's a deal. See you tomorrow."

"Hey, Matt, wait a minute. You still there?"

"Yeah, I'm here."

"You *do* know it was an angel that helped me save your life last summer, don't you?"

There was a long pause on the other end of the phone. I really didn't know why I was bringing this up now, but it had been bugging me for months.

"Matt?"

"What are you talking about?" he said.

"When you almost drowned last summer . . . at Huntington Beach."

"I didn't almost drown."

Now it was my turn to pause.

"I just bumped my head, that's all."

"Matt! I pulled you out of the water! You weren't breathing! And if a voice hadn't told me right where you were, it would have been all over for you! I'm sure now it was a real angel. You didn't know that?"

"Gosh . . . no . . . I honestly thought I only bumped my head . . . Oh no! Does that mean you did *mouth to mouth*?"

"No. I didn't need to. I kicked you by accident and you spouted like a whale."

"Oh good, because I'd hate to think of you kissing me. Yuck! Gee, I guess I should say 'thanks.' "

"I think you should thank your angel. I wouldn't have had a chance of finding you if it weren't for him."

"Or *her* . . . hey, maybe it was Margaret."

"Yeah," I laughed. "Maybe it was."

It might have just been my imagination, but it seemed Matt was different after that. More friendly and interested in what I was doing. At least he didn't balk at my reporting the next day of angels in the night. In fact, after that phone conversation, Matt never joked about angels again.

That night I looked up Death Valley and nothing clicked. I didn't really think the message meant to actually scale the mountain, but I had nothing more to go on. Maybe Molly was right. Maybe it meant to do something difficult. Maybe I was already doing it. Maybe the point of the riddle was to get me out of the attic.

I also looked up Camarillo in a book on California that we had on our coffee table and found out it was just as Matt had said. There was a mental institution there, the largest one in the state. The picture was getting clearer. When Donna said her mother hadn't gotten up since she fell in 1952, maybe that was exactly what she meant. I wondered how much Donna knew. Sometimes she talked like she didn't even know if her mother was alive.

The next day Matt and I rang the buzzer at the door of the Ramblin' Rose at 11:30 A.M. and Peg came to the ticket window again with the same announcement. "Sorry, no guests."

"Would you tell Donna that I hope she has a great practice," I said, "and if she wants to see me, I'll be over at the Rocket Cafe?"

"Sure will, but don't get your hopes up."

"So how long are we gonna hang around here?" said Matt as we walked over to the cafe.

"I don't know. I haven't thought that far."

The Rocket Cafe was directly across the street from the Ramblin' Rose and was the closest thing to a diner you could find in California. It was a bit out of place next to the desert-like Arroyo Seca and owed most of its business to the roller rink. Since that business had been faltering, so was the cafe. There were rips on some of the swiveling bar stools at the counter, and the jukebox didn't work, much to Matt's disappointment. Everyone from the rink was on a first-name basis over there, including Matt and me.

"Hey, look who's here," I said as we stood just inside the door. It was Dominic Demucci sitting alone in a booth, and when he saw us, he motioned us over.

"You boys want to join me?"

"Sure," I said, and we both slid into the ribbed burgundy seat across from him.

"Want a donut or something?" he asked as the waitress came over and brought us water and silverware.

"Maybe just some hot chocolate," said Matt.

"I'd like that too," I said. "What are you reading?" It didn't look like a normal newspaper—more like a magazine on newsprint paper.

"Oh, it's all about the local music scene—clubs and gigs and studios—things like that. Where's Donna? You two are usually inseparable."

" 'I had a girl,' " Matt sang, " 'Don-na was her name.' "

" '*Had*' is right," I said.

"Lovers' quarrel?" Dominic asked, raising his eyebrows.

" 'Wo, wo, wo, tra-ge-dy,' " Matt kept up his musical commentary.

"What is this?" said Dominic. "A walking Hit Parade?"

"I'm making up for the jukebox," said Matt. "I know all the Top Ten. Ask me anything."

"So what's the problem with you and Donna?" said Dominic, ignoring Matt's challenge.

"I missed her practice a couple times and now she thinks I don't like her anymore, I guess." Of course I didn't tell him that the last time we were together was the closest we'd ever been and that I'd gotten scared and stayed away.

"So she's giving you the cold shoulder."

"Yeah. She won't even let me in the door."

"I wouldn't worry. She'll get over it. These skaters are a stubborn lot. They have to be to keep getting up off the floor over and over again."

The waitress brought our hot chocolates, and my eye caught a book on the table next to Dominic, probably because several words on the cover jumped out at me: "crossword puzzles, riddles, word games."

"Are you good at riddles?" I asked.

"It's my business. I'm a songwriter too, you know."

"Maybe you can help us," I said. "Someone gave me a message in the form of a riddle. It's something I have to do, and I think it may have something to do with Donna's competition."

"What's the deal? Have you guys been seeing Madame Zar lately?"

"No, nothing like that," I said, and Matt started in on the chorus of "Gypsy Woman."

"Cool it, Matt," I said.

"So where did you get the riddle?" Dominic persisted.

I looked at Matt and decided I had nothing to lose.

"From an angel," Matt said, beating me to it.

"No kidding? An angel talked to you?" Dominic said to Matt.

"No. To me," I corrected.

"I've heard about this kind of thing," he said, not at all put-off like I thought he'd be. "So what's the riddle?"

" 'Scale the highest mountain,' and I'm already pretty sure the mountain is Mt. Whitney."

"Hmm," said Dominic, taking a sip of his coffee and staring out the window. It was overcast and drizzly outside. "Climbing a high mountain would be the obvious—"

"I know," I said. "I'm hoping it's not that."

"Completing some difficult task would be the less obvious."

"Yeah, that's part of it. But I think there might be a trick to it."

"Well, let's see. It *is* interesting that it uses the word 'scale.' Why not just 'climb'?"

"Maybe 'scale' is angel talk," said Matt.

"Maybe," said Dominic, "but it might mean something else. It's also a musical term, you know—like in a musical scale. Hey . . . what did you say that mountain was again?"

"Mt. Whitney," I said as Dominic started sifting through the pages of the paper he was reading.

"There it is," he said. "Just as I thought."

"What?" I said, getting excited. "What did you find?"

He folded the paper back, put it on the table, and pointed to a section called "Recording Studios."

"Whitney Sound Studios," he said. "I thought I remembered that name. I did a gig there a couple years ago. Mostly religious music. It's the only studio in L.A. with a real pipe organ in it."

"Holy cow! Matt, I bet that's it! Where is it?"

"Address and phone are right there. It's on Lankersheim in Burbank."

"Matt, do you think Bernice could take us there?"

"No, but we could take a taxi."

"I'd help you guys out, but I gotta meet Lenny in a couple minutes," said Dominic.

"That's okay. We'll get there," I said. "Thanks for helping with the riddle!"

"No problem. Good luck. Hey, don't forget this address."

He wrote it down on a napkin and gave it to me. I put it in my pocket while Matt tried to wrestle some money out of the watch pocket of his blue jeans.

"Save your money for the taxi," Dominic said with a wink. "The hot chocolate's on me. Just put in a good word for me next time you hear from that angel."

"You bet!" I said, sliding out of the booth. "And thanks!"

14

Once More With Feeling

"I hope this is okay," I said, having second thoughts about flagging taxis near the Arroyo Seca.

"You got any better ideas?" said Matt.

I really didn't. Bernice was shopping and my father was at the church, and anyway, how could we possibly explain to anybody what we were doing?

Well, you see this angel gave me a clue about scaling the highest mountain, which we think might have something to do with Whitney Sound Studios in Burbank, so we want to go over there and see if we're on the right track, but we don't really know what to look for once we get there, or what might turn up next. We're just trying to figure out the next piece of the puzzle and go from there.

"You sure you have enough money?"

"Plenty," Matt said. "I do this all the time, remember?"

"Whitney Sound Studios," Matt said to the driver as we hopped in the backseat of a taxi that pulled up right then. I handed him the napkin with the address.

"You sure you want to go to Burbank?" said the driver, looking us over closely.

"Why?" I said.

"That's going to be eight or nine bucks," he said. "You boys got that kind of money?"

"No problem," said Matt as the driver took off down the Arroyo Parkway. Neither one of us noticed anything familiar about the red and black lumberjack coat he was wearing.

" 'Scale the highest mountain,' " I quoted the angel as we got on the Pasadena Freeway, "could turn out to be Whitney Studios. It's just like something Ben would do."

"You still think he has something to do with these angels?"

"Positive."

"So what are we going to do once we get there?" asked Matt.

"I don't know. I've been thinking about that. I doubt we can sneak in without knowing our way around."

"So why don't we just go in the front door with a reason?"

"What reason?"

"What do you do with studios?" Matt said. "You rent them, right? We're just checking it out for a recording project."

"You think they'll believe two kids are going to rent a studio?"

"Act like you know what you're doing and you can get away with almost anything."

"You're right about that," I said. "I did that in the hospital and it worked. Of course I had a little help from Molly."

"Well, if all this angel stuff you're talking about is really true, we've got some friends in higher places than Molly."

"Look, there's City Hall," I said.

"Dum, de dum dum." We both did the "Dragnet" theme at the same time.

Though it was less than half an hour away, the Los Angeles skyline might as well have been Baltimore to me. It seemed that far away from home, and my apprehension grew as the buildings grew closer together and the familiar friendly sights of residential suburbia gave way to rows of duplexes, apartments, and industry. I had never been this far away from home without my parents knowing it. We had to get back without them finding out or my name was mud.

I watched the meter click to six dollars when we turned onto the Hollywood Freeway, and I thought I caught a worried look on Matt's face. I was ready to say something to him about it when the driver spoke up.

"What are you boys doing in Burbank?" He was an older Negro man who looked like he hadn't shaved in a few days. Stubby gray whiskers salted his black skin and a missing front tooth made a hole in his smile.

"We're going to check out a recording studio," I said.

"Did I hear you boys say something about angels?"

"Uh . . . yeah," I said.

"The Los Angeles Angels," Matt inserted, thinking fast.

"I always liked them Angels," said the driver. "Even if they was in the minors. I'd rather see Steve Bilko at the plate than any of them players the Dodgers are sending up there right now."

"Yeah," said Matt. "I saw the Angels and the Bakersfield Saints once. Bilko hit three home runs in one game."

"Ah yes," said the driver. "The Saints and the Angels. Those were great games. Never knew who to root for, though. So what kind of music you boys play?"

"Uh . . . we don't play. We're just checking the studio out for some friends of ours," I tried out our new line on him.

"Oh, I get it. You're producers."

"Yeah," said Matt, smiling at me. "That's it. We're producers."

"I like gospel music," the driver said. "Aretha Franklin and Ethel Waters are my favorites. They're gonna be singin' gospel music in heaven and the singers ain't gonna be white," and he turned around and winked at us while the taxi drifted over one lane. Matt looked over his shoulder nervously. "Unless, of course, you think we'll all be white when we get to heaven."

I'd never thought about it, but I had to admit, in my pictures of heaven there were no colored folks. That is, not until Netta Pearl. She was one colored person I knew would be in heaven for sure.

"Maybe when you die and go to heaven you'll be black like me," said the driver, and he turned back around and laughed loudly.

A few minutes later he pulled up to the curb. "Well, here you are, boys," he said. "Whitney Sound Studios, at your service."

The meter read $8.70, and Matt pulled a ten dollar bill out of his pocket.

"No, you keep it," said the man, pushing the money away. "You'll need it to get home. Record me some heavenly gospel music instead."

We stood on the sidewalk with our mouths open as the taxi drove away.

"Guess what?" Matt said. "This is all the money I have. How did he know that?"

We both looked up from the ten-dollar bill at the same time and saw only an empty street.

"No . . . you don't suppose—" said Matt.

"Did you notice his jacket?"

"Yeah," he said. "It was just like the coat that guy had on in the rest room at the roller rink."

"But the guy in the rest room wasn't a Negro," I said. "I'm sure of that."

"Maybe they just use the same coat," said Matt.

"Maybe . . . but a Negro angel?"

"Why not?" said Matt. "I just hope he wasn't right about us changing color in heaven."

"I'm just glad you still have your ten bucks. How were we supposed to get home?"

"Your parents would come get us," said Matt.

"*My* parents?" I said. "My parents would kill me if they knew I was out here without permission."

"I know. You've got to get your parents to relax a little bit."

"That's easy for you to say," I said, frustrated with his casualness.

The studio didn't look like anything from the outside. There was only a glass door with WHITNEY SOUND printed on it in small letters.

"If a Negro angel with a missing tooth brought us here," said Matt, "no telling what we're going to find inside."

What we found inside was a small waiting room with a desk that appeared to have someone temporarily away from it. There were notes and papers on it and a calendar book open to May, 1962. The phone was off the hook.

Two hallways opened off the room, one on either side of the desk, and when we heard the clicking of high heels echoing down one, we quickly ducked into the other. It led down blank walls to a thick open door where we could hear the muffled sound of music coming from inside. It was almost dark in the room except for the light spilling into it through a window in the door to another room—a sort of room within a room. The door to that room was closed, and there appeared to be two men in there listening intently to what we could only hear faintly.

"It's okay," whispered Matt. "I doubt they can see us. It's too dark in here."

As our eyes slowly adjusted to the dark, we inched our way along the wall inside the big room until it turned back out of view of the window. There we slid down to a sitting position and studied our situation.

The room we were in was large with a high ceiling. The walls were mostly covered with wood, except for large rectangular panels of cushiony type material every few feet. There was a piano in one corner and an organ console next to it. I pointed to the stacks of organ pipes behind and above it. It was the pipe organ Dominic had mentioned.

Microphones and music stands were scattered around the room. Black wires stretched to each of the mike stands, coiling next to them like snakes. Everything was quiet, except for the muffled music coming from the room behind the window.

"I bet this is where people sing and in there is where they record it," I said.

"Brilliant," said Matt. "As a producer, you probably should know that."

Suddenly we heard high heels coming down the hall and stiffened. Then the music got loud for a moment as the door to the inner room was opened. That brief opening was enough to hear a few lines of a familiar song.

"Did you hear that?" I whispered. "It's Netta's song—the first one she sang in church about the love of God."

I had only heard "how rich, how pure," but that was enough to recognize it.

"And I know that voice too," I said, but I couldn't place it. When I heard the door open again to "the saints' and angels' song" I knew where I'd heard that voice before.

That voice made me think of lying in bed with a fever, listening to the radio. It was definitely a radio voice. Then I remembered that my mother would always find "The Hour of Decision" and play it for me when I was sick in bed. "The Hour of Decision" was a daily broadcast from wherever Billy Graham was doing his latest crusade, and the voice I heard spilling out through the briefly opened door was the same unmistakable, rich velvety voice I had heard at my bedside.

"Matt, that's got to be George Beverly Shea."

"Do you suppose he's in there?" said Matt.

"Let's see if we can get a better look."

The high-heeled shoes had disappeared back down the hall, so we snuck out into the room, more daring this time.

"This way," I whispered, and we followed the back wall over behind the organ console where we could get adequate cover for our spying. From there we could see three men in the room, and the one standing farthest back looked awfully familiar.

"Is it George?" said Matt.

"I think so."

"Which one is he?"

"He's the one standing up in the back, I think."

The other two men were sitting down at a big control board, facing the window. Seeing them there, facing out at us with light pouring out of the window, made it seem like they were commanding a spaceship and we were some alien enemy being hunted in the darkness. I shuddered when I thought of how vulnerable we were out there and wondered what on earth we were doing.

The music had stopped and all three were talking together when suddenly the two men at the controls stood up and headed for the door that opened into the room where we were hiding. One of them reached toward the wall and suddenly the lights went on above us. Matt and I ducked down behind the organ console and looked at each other in horror.

"You sure we can do this over?" said a voice as steps approached. *He was heading straight for the organ!*

"Yes," said the other one. "That's the beauty of three tracks."

Matt managed to crawl out under the bench before the man got there and escape behind a baffle that stood a couple feet from the wall where the organ pipes were housed. But I was caught under the bench of the organ, trying to make myself as small as I possibly could as the man sat down right above me.

"Okay. Let's fire this baby up."

I knew I had to get out of there before he turned on the organ, because I was sitting right on the pedals that played the big bass notes. Just as I heard a click on the console, I rolled out the back side of the bench and around behind the baffle. A whirring sound and a sudden rush of air filled the pipes, disguising my exit, as the wall behind me seemed to breathe in a huge gulp of air.

I was surprised not to find Matt behind the baffle, but there was a door there, slightly ajar, opening into where the organ pipes were housed. I slipped inside just as the organist hit the first note. He must have been playing a joke on the other guys because he had all the stops open and played a chord that sounded like the opening of a tragic melodrama. I must have jumped three feet when he did it.

Matt jumped too, which was unfortunate, because at the moment he jumped, he was exploring on top of a ladder that went up into the smaller pipes, and the blast of that opening chord threw him off the ladder and down fifteen feet into the big pipes below.

I knew nothing of this because the music drowned out the thud and his cry when he landed. All I could do was search for him amidst the darkness throughout the thunderous playing of

"The Love of God." The pipes bellowed and shrilled. The low ones seemed to reach in and tickle my heart; I could feel them before I heard them. And more than once I jumped when a pipe went off right next to my ear.

I went up and down the ladder two or three times, completely miffed. Where could Matt have gone back there? The only light was higher up where the smaller pipes were open to the room. I couldn't see anything down below.

It wasn't until the organist released the final chord of the song that I heard a faint whimpering coming from down in the pipes, and I barely made out Matt's voice, still trying to conceal himself.

"I can't move!" he cried in a kind of shrieking whisper.

"Once more with feeling," came a voice through the loud-speaker in the room.

"No, wait!" I shouted from up in the pipes. It was their turn to be surprised.

15

A Record for Donna

My father got a big surprise, too—several, in fact. Not only because he got the call from the studio and because he had no idea that his son was in Burbank, but also because my mother and Becky were out with the car, leaving him home alone to deal with the awkward and totally unexpected visit of Lenny LaRue.

Apparently Donna's performance had fallen off so dramatically in the last few days that Lenny had stopped by on a personal mission to try to patch things up between me and his skater. It made me chuckle when I heard it—to think Lenny would be that desperate for Donna's performance. But that's why Lenny was at my house when the call came in from me; and that's why he was the only available transportation to get my father to the studio.

Now Lenny may have kept a messy office, but he somehow managed to keep the cleanest black and white '55 Corvette in southern California. And to this day, whenever I need a little imaginary entertainment, I merely picture that thirty-minute ride to Whitney Sound Studios, and the unlikely pairing of Lenny and my father, top down on a misty January day, in Lenny's '55 Corvette.

The serious questioning process didn't begin until Matt was on his way to the hospital and my father and Lenny got there. All the immediate attention was directed toward getting Matt free from the organ pipes and making him as comfortable as possible until his parents arrived.

With Matt gone, however, everyone was demanding some sort of explanation from me. It was during that explanation that the whole thing came to me—the purpose of our trip to the studio and the solution to the mystery behind the angelic messages. I hadn't realized until I started answering questions that all the information was in; it only needed to be sorted out properly. And somehow, as the questions were thrown at me, one by one, that's exactly what happened.

What were you doing here in the first place?

"We were checking out the studio."

Why on earth would you do that? Are you planning on recording something?

"Actually, yes." I was thinking right then of the taxi driver who'd told us to record some heavenly gospel music and keep our taxi fare. And I was thinking of "The Saints' and Angels' Song," which was what I was already calling "The Love of God" in my mind, once I had connected it to the third message whispered to me by an angel in the night. And I was thinking, most importantly, of Donna skating to that song—skating effortlessly and gracefully, twirling and jumping and making long sweeping turns with her arms and hands, writing the love of God with the graceful twist of a wrist on the imaginary parchment of the sky.

Strangely enough, I had seen these images in my mind while the organ blasted away next to my ears and I searched for Matt. I had wanted to stop and dwell on what I was imagining with such clarity, while at the same time feeling anxious about not finding Matt. Now I knew why I had seen those things. It was all finally making sense.

And just what are you planning to record?

Probably they were thinking they were humoring me with this question, not expecting me to have an answer ready for them—but I did.

"Netta Pearl and the choir singing 'The Saints' and Angels' Song,' " I said, convinced now that it had to be Netta. George Beverly Shea had probably recorded the song already—not to mention the one they were working on that day—but no one could sing it like Netta. Only Netta Pearl had the emotion to compete with the excitement of Donna's skating. Together, they would make heavenly gospel music dance.

What? You want to record Netta Pearl and the choir? Why on earth would you want to do that?

"So Donna can have something to hand the judges—a recording to skate to, made just for her."

I couldn't believe how I was thinking on my feet. I couldn't believe what was coming out of my mouth. I remembered Ben talking like this, but it was not like me to be so quick and so confident.

Little did I know when I revealed all this that there was something in this idea for everybody. The momentary silence that greeted me was indicative of the wheels that were turning. I only thought they were trying to figure out what to do with me.

Instead, as it turned out, Lenny was thinking about how this would get Donna and me back together and Donna back to work. And even though it certainly wouldn't be a song he would choose, the idea of making a custom recording especially for a 3½-minute routine was something that hadn't been done yet at Donna's level of competition. It would give her a definite advantage.

Then there was my father, who was upset with me, on the one hand, for sneaking away to the studio without asking; but on the other hand, here he was in the same room with two of the most revered names in Christian music, Loren Whitney and George Beverly Shea. The thought of experiencing a recording studio and having his choir recorded by the likes of the present company was a tantalizing proposition, aside from the preposterous nature of the events that had brought this odd group of individuals together.

And then there was Loren Whitney, with at least a three-hour session and a master record to cut. He had something in this, though perhaps the least at stake. That was probably why he was the one who responded first.

"Well, it looks like we've got ourselves a pretty ambitious producer here," he said. That made everyone laugh and loosened some of the tension. It also made everyone wonder if there was, in fact, something to this crazy notion I had. That's when my mother and Becky showed up, announced at the door of the control room by the high-heeled lady, who by then I had learned was named Grace.

"Walter . . . I got your note," said my mother. "Jonathan, are you all right?"

"Yes, but Matt's not. Can I go see him now?"

"Where is he?" my mother said, looking at my father, worriedly.

"Mr. and Mrs. Wendorf took him to St. Mary's. It looks like a broken leg."

"Oh dear," said my mother.

My father turned to Mr. Whitney and said, "Was there any damage to the organ?"

"None whatsoever. It's the boy we're concerned about."

"Was it a bad break?" asked my mother.

"It didn't break the skin, if that's what you mean," said Mr. Whitney.

"By the way," said my father, "this is my wife, Ann. Ann . . . Loren Whitney."

"How do you do."

"And, Ann," he could not conceal the admiration in his voice, "this is George Beverly Shea."

"Oh—" she said, taken by surprise, "Mr. Shea—what a privilege to meet you."

"Hello, Ann," said Mr. Shea in a deep voice that rendered my mother speechless for a few seconds.

"Well," said my father, clasping his hands together, "I suppose we should let you gentlemen get back to work. This whole thing has been such an intrusion upon your time and I apologize."

"Nonsense," said Mr. Whitney. "In fact, you're welcome to stay and sit in on the rest of the session. We're just doing some taping for a radio show."

My father looked interested, but my mother spoke. "We need to go see how Matt is, dear."

"Of course," said my father.

"You're welcome any time," said Mr. Whitney, shaking my father's hand. "And, Jonathan, no need to sneak in anymore." And then he handed me his business card and said with a wink, "Call me later about that recording idea. I'm sure we can work out something."

I looked at my father, who turned and shook George Beverly Shea's hand. Then Lenny shook hands all around and filed out with us.

"I'll meet you over at the hospital," he said, and I thought it was a bit odd for Lenny to be that interested in seeing Matt.

Most of the drive to the hospital was taken up with my father trying to spell out to my mother what had happened. He told the story while Becky and I sat quietly in the back. I was only brought in to complete parts he didn't know yet. When he told the part about recording Donna's song, however, I noticed that he didn't present it as an entirely ridiculous idea—indeed, he made it sound almost as if it were a logical reason for us to be there, though certainly not an excuse for not letting them know where I was.

As we pulled into the hospital parking lot, an all-too-familiar heaviness pressed in on my chest. I had Donna's brief hospital visit to combat memories of Ben, but I still could not make this feeling go away. Besides, I knew Matt's injury was worse than Donna's because my parents had called the hospital before leaving the studios to find out that he was being admitted and would be there at least overnight. He had a multiple fracture; he had broken his leg in three places.

"I don't want to go in," I said at the last minute as everyone started getting out of the car. My mother looked at my father with an aren't-you-glad-you-weren't-hard-on-him look and turned around and patted my hand.

"It's okay, honey. This is nothing like Ben. Ben had problems long before his accident. You know that now. It's just a break; and breaks heal."

"It's a bad break."

"It will heal just the same."

As obnoxious as Matt could be sometimes, I was starting to like him, and liking someone who was about to spend the night in the hospital was just a little too familiar.

"No. I'll wait here. You guys go ahead."

My mother flashed my father a worried look and said, "Why don't you and Becky go see how Matt is. I'll stay here with him."

My father looked like he wanted to protest, but my mother had a look of resolve on her face that kept him from saying anything.

"Tell me about this recording idea," she said as soon as they were out of sight, surprising me with her interest. At first I thought she was only doing this because she was trying to get my mind off my fear of St. Mary's Hospital, but the more we talked, the more she convinced me she was genuinely interested.

I told her all about recording Netta Pearl—everything except the angels, that is—and as I talked, she grew more excited.

"I think it could be a wonderful idea, Jonathan," she said, "something the whole church could get behind."

"You really think so?"

"Yes I do. It's a great opportunity for the Gospel, too. Pastor Beamering would like that. Donna would be skating as a testimony to the love of God."

It was almost as if she was convincing herself, too. Maybe she was seeing this as a way all her objections to skating could be overcome—as if Donna's skating could be sanctified through this song and the purpose behind it.

I hadn't even thought of the effect Donna's performance might have on an audience. Up to that point I had been too busy solving angelic riddles to see any broader ramifications. Now my mother was opening the door to a bigger purpose.

I liked being with my mother right then. She had turned sideways in the seat to talk to me, leaning her head back against the window with one arm resting on the top of the seat, and I thought she looked very pretty. I wanted to ask her why she couldn't be like this more often, but I didn't.

"Does Donna know about this idea?" she asked.

"No. Do you think she'll like it?"

"I think she'll like the fact that you came up with it and that you've risked life and limb to pursue it."

"I risked Matt's limb," I corrected her, and we both smiled.

"I don't know," I said, "she doesn't want to see me right now. The last two times I showed up at the rink, Peg told me she was not 'entertaining any guests today.' "

"That won't last long," she said. "In fact—"

"What?" I said, following her moving gaze to the lane leading to the hospital and whatever it was that caught her eye right then. What it was made me excited, scared, and embarrassed all at the same time. It was an immaculate black and white '55 Corvette with Lenny's silver-streaked hair waving in the wind from the driver's seat, and a familiar blond ponytail bobbing around next to him.

"Why are they here?" I said.

"To see Matt and probably to see you."

"Not me."

"And why not?"

Now I was really confused. I was enjoying being with my mother right then, but not sure what to do about running into Donna with her around. That's when my mother surprised me the most.

"I'll go on in," she said. "You come with them." And she left me.

I wanted to run after her and give her a big hug, but I didn't want to lose track of the Corvette. Lenny was heading for the other side of the hospital, and I had to run as fast as I could without slipping on the wet pavement. I rounded the far side of emergency just in time to see them already walking toward the back entrance.

"Donna!" I called out.

They both stopped and turned around, and when they saw it was me, Lenny said something to Donna and went on through the door, leaving her standing there waiting for me. I tried to slow down and look cool, but it was no use; I was entirely out of breath.

"What . . . are you . . . doing here?" I said, grabbing for air.

"Lenny told me what happened."

"Oh."

"I hope Matt's okay," she said.

"Me too."

"Lenny also told me about the song. I actually think he likes the idea."

"Really?"

She was looking all over except when she spoke; then she looked right at me.

"Do you like it?" I said.

"Oh yes! I like it a lot. I've always liked that song, and with Netta Pearl singing it—I know I could skate to that. But you don't think it's really possible, do you? I mean . . . the choir and everything?"

"It's starting to look that way. Even my mother seems to be excited about it. I bet the whole church would get behind it. You'd be skating for everybody."

"Wow, I never thought about it like that, but I guess you're right."

There was an awkward silence when I wanted to apologize but I didn't know how to say it, or I was too proud, so I didn't say anything. Neither did she. All I was hoping for was some kind of sign that everything was okay, and her excitement seemed to telegraph that.

"Let's go find Matt," she said, but I hesitated, immobilized by the old fear again.

"Come on!" She smiled and grabbed my hand, pulling me into the hospital in much the same way that Margaret had pulled Matt and me into the dark of the Bolsa Chica bunker.

16

Milton Play Motown; Netta Goes Downtown

"No! Never!" said Matt when I started telling him how things were shaping up for the recording of Donna's song. It was three days after the accident and he was home and uncomfortable in a cast all the way up to his hip. "I never want to hear that song again!"

"But, Matt, you and I have to be the producers. Mr. Whitney said so."

And he had, too. My father was the one who made the initial call to inquire about the estimated costs of such a project and to pursue the idea further. He and Jeffery T. had decided to go at least that far with it. When my dad found out that it wasn't nearly as expensive as they had feared, the level of talk and anticipation had jumped considerably, and word was already spreading around the church that Netta Pearl and the choir were going to become recording artists.

"Well, you'll have to just produce it without me!" Matt insisted.

"Matt, it wasn't the song that broke your leg."

"I don't care," he said. "Haven't you ever barfed up vegetable soup because it was the last thing you had to eat before you got sick and you know you'll never be able to eat vegetable soup again? It's kind of like that."

"I know what you mean," I said. "That happened to me once with macaroni and cheese, but I got over it. You'll get over it. The session won't be for a couple of weeks yet."

"A couple weeks won't be enough. I'll never get over 'The Love of God,' " he said. "So it's really going to happen, huh?"

"It sure looks like it," I said. "And that part about us being producers is for real, Matt. Mr. Whitney made a big deal about it when my father talked to him. It was his only condition for giving us a good price. You and I had to be the producers. So you see, you have to do it."

"So what are producers supposed to do anyway?" he asked.

"Tell him what we like and what we don't like about what's happening."

"That doesn't sound tough. I do that all the time. How do you know so much about this?"

"I've already talked to Mr. Whitney a couple of times and that's what he told me. He said not to worry about it; we'd know just what to do."

"Sounds like you and this Whitney guy are real tight."

"I'm taking the deposit over right after this and picking a date for the studio."

"Well pick one far enough away so I can forget that song for a while."

"It has to be as soon as possible. Donna needs the recording to build her routine around."

Things were moving fast. The day before had been Netta Pearl Sunday, and though my father had tried to keep the news quiet until plans were a little more finalized, it was impossible.

"You wouldn't believe the things people were asking me yesterday after church," I said as Matt tried to get in a more comfortable position on his bed.

"Like what?"

" 'Does Netta Pearl really have a recording contract with Motown Records? Is she singing a duet with George Beverly Shea or Aretha Franklin? Is Billy Graham really going to be there for the recording? Who's directing, your father or Cliff Barrows?' Honestly—the things people come up with."

"What does Milton think about it?" Matt asked.

"Milton is in seventh heaven. He's sure the single is going to go gold. Pastor Beamering is wondering if he'll get to preach at the competitions, and Netta is already planning what she's going to wear to the studio."

"It's only a recording," said Matt. "No one's going to *see* her sing!"

"Yeah, but try telling her that. Besides, it's 'Hollywood,' or at least the next town over. That's close enough for Netta."

"I thought it was expensive to record. Who's going to pay for all this? Donna's grandparents don't seem the type to have a lot of money."

"The choir has already taken up a collection that will cover most of the recording session. It's seventy-five dollars an hour for a choir, and Mr. Whitney thinks it will take about three hours, including setup and takedown."

"Now you're starting to sound like a producer."

"Oh yeah, there's also this businessman in the church who's going to pay for the pressing of five hundred singles because he knows he can sell at least that many in the church alone."

"Wow!" said Matt. "A lot has happened in a few days."

"So you're in on it—even if you do hate the song?"

"Yeah, I'm in. Here," he said, handing me a pen, "sign my cast."

So I signed it "Get well fast. Jonathan. P.S. There are easier ways to play an organ!"

It didn't take long for the whole church to get caught up in the recording idea and even the skating competitions. There was already talk about taking a busload of choir members to Bakersfield to see Donna perform, and once the recording was out, they had to make that two buses because of all the families and friends. By the time we did the recording, the businessman who was financing the pressing had to increase his order to take into account relatives and friends of church members who'd already signed up for copies of the single.

Donna was a little taken aback by all the attention, but Lenny knew how to handle that. He had been through stardom before. He knew how fickle an audience could be and how foolish a fad could become if you didn't keep focused on your original intent. He'd watched roller skating go from the Skating Vanities to Roller Derby, so he knew you didn't get too excited about anything other than your performance and your own personal goals.

"To compete well in the competitions," I heard him say over and over to Donna during those final months of practice, "to know you went up there and skated your best, to walk away with your head up, that's what you're looking for. Nothing more, but nothing less than your best. *Your* best. No one else's. Regardless of what the judges say, you want to know in your heart you skated the best you possibly could."

We set the recording date for the last Saturday in January. That gave Matt some time to get to where he could at least move around on crutches. It also gave Lenny, my father, and Milton Owlsley time to reconstruct the arrangement of the song to fit the 3½-minute requirement. That meant a Saturday session with Donna and Netta Pearl at the Ramblin' Rose to try and work it all out. It took some doing, in that the song, the way they sang it in church, was over five minutes long.

"We'll have to cut it down," Lenny said, and everyone agreed except Netta.

"Couldn't I just sing it faster?"

"You'd have to sing it like Alvin and the Chipmunks," said Dominic, who was sitting in on this session more because of his curiosity over watching Milton play Motown than anything.

"You know, Milt, I gotta hand it to you," he said afterward, "you make a pretty good Booker T." That made Milton's buttons almost pop off his shirt.

We ended up cutting out the second verse. Two verses and two choruses took exactly three minutes to sing, which left half a minute for the introduction and a key change transition between the second verse and the last chorus. That was the climax of the song and everyone's favorite part. Netta would repeat the last line, "Though stretched from sky to sky" (except when she sang it, it was more like "sta-retched"), while Milton transposed it up one key, and for a split second there was a gaping hole that Netta's big voice would rush in and fill with, "The love of God, how rich and pure. . . ." That was right when Donna planned on landing with her arms outstretched from the biggest jump of her routine, and the music would catch her.

As the day of the recording session finally approached, it seemed half the congregation wanted to come, but the number of people had to be limited to what we could fit into the small control room. That turned out to be Donna, Donna's grandparents, my mother and father, Lenny, Pastor and Mrs. Beamering, Mr. and Mrs. Wendorf, and Matt and I.

"What about the sister of the producer?" argued Becky, and I had relished the rare power to refuse my sister.

"Well, after all the nasty things you've done to me," I strung her out . . . "you can come."

Loren Whitney had an engineer to help him, and though he had co-workers who were perfectly capable of running this session without him, he took this project personally. He was a very kind and accommodating man who seemed to have taken a special liking to Matt and me and treated us like adults. More than that, he treated us, just as he had promised, like producers. I had been thinking that his insistence on our being the producers was just a way of being nice to us, but that was clearly not the case. Even though he ran the session, he consulted with us often, and he never made a decision without our okay. A number of times during the session he said to Lenny or my father or Milton or Netta Pearl, "Well, what do Matt and Jonathan think?" This was nothing short of an irritation to all of them.

Donna also was brought into the actual recording, since having a general idea of certain moves she wanted to perform at particular junctures in the song allowed us to embellish portions of it appropriately. This usually amounted to Netta stretching out a note, or coming in late on another one to allow for a twirl or a jump to be completed.

What should have taken an hour, however, ended up taking two, and most of that was due to having too many people voicing their opinions. My father had an awful time of it out in the studio, having to deal with forty-five opinions from the choir and occasional outbursts from Pastor Beamering or Lenny actually running out into the studio to try and influence the recording.

"No one will go into the studio unless I say so," said Mr. Whitney after the second infraction. "Is that clear?"

But the worst place of all was the control room itself. It was too crowded to begin with, and then people kept offering their unsolicited remarks and observations. Jeffery T. wanted to make sure certain words came across with sufficient clarity to convey the message of the song. Bernice and my mother took exception to some of Netta's more breathy sections which they thought were too "jazzy." Lenny kept trying to make the music more uptown, Milton Owlsley wanted it more Motown, and Netta Pearl simply wanted to go all the way downtown with it.

I watched Mr. Whitney grow more and more exasperated, until at exactly the hour mark, he announced that everyone must clear the control room except for the producers and the skater. Matt and Donna and I sat quietly while the adults filed out red-faced. There was some laughter when the door closed behind them, but mostly we got down to work.

The real turning point came when Netta got so nervous after a couple more attempts at the song and the interruptions of varying opinions that she broke out in heavy perspiration and almost fainted.

"She's just too uptight," I said in the now-quiet control room as forty-eight people stood with taut nerves on the other side of the glass. "They need a break."

"Good idea," said Mr. Whitney. "Come back to it fresh. Matthew, you tell them. Here, just press this button and talk into the microphone."

"All right, you guys," Matt's voice made its effect on the other side of the glass, "we're going to take a fifteen-minute break. There's stuff to drink out in the waiting room. Everybody relax. You're doing great. Donna can't wait to skate to this!"

"Matthew, where did you learn to be so natural at the microphone?" asked Mr. Whitney.

"We have a special radio elective at our school. One of the shop teachers used to be a DJ. We have our own broadcast booth and our own station that covers three blocks."

"I didn't know that," I said.

"Yep," he said. "I'm going to be a DJ someday."

"Well, Matthew, you have the talk-back microphone from here on out," said Mr. Whitney. "Look at them out there. They're loosening up already."

"And I have an idea how we can loosen up Netta Pearl even more," said Donna. "There's nothing wrong with Netta that a few minutes with Granny Finley wouldn't cure."

"Perfect!" I said.

So Donna went and got her grandmother while we rolled back the tape and got the machines ready for another try. Then we watched Granny Finley roll right up to where Netta had nearly collapsed in a chair. She patted Netta's face with tissue and started talking to her, and in seconds Netta Pearl was laughing so hard she was bouncing up and down and crying all at the same time. And the effect of this lightheartedness passed on to the rest of the choir. You could see the heightened animation through the window, as if Granny Finley somehow pumped everyone full of happy juice. Suddenly, everyone remembered this singing along with Netta was once fun to do.

That gave me the next idea.

"I think the problem with everyone out there is they don't have an audience. Netta needs an audience to perform to. She's lost without it. Why don't we leave Granny Finley out there?"

"Better than that," said Donna. "What about everyone else waiting in the reception room? Would there be room in the studio for them? They could be the audience."

"If they'll behave themselves," said Mr. Whitney.

"I think they will now," I said.

"Great, then," Mr. Whitney said. "Donna, why don't you go invite them back in; and, Jonathan, you come help me set up some chairs. Matthew, the controls are all yours. Just don't press that red button over there. That will start the tape rolling."

Matt sat proudly at the console with his leg up on a chair while Mr. Whitney and I started setting up chairs in the studio.

Suddenly Matt's voice came over the microphone: " 'I'm just a lonely boy/Lonely and blue/I'm all alone/With nothin' to do.' "

Mr. Whitney smiled and waved him off.

Matt came right back with, "That's number seven this week, kids, 'Lonely Boy' by Paul Anka. And number six and holding for yet another week in our Top Ten countdown is 'Rama Lama Ding Dong' by The Edsels, followed by our leading gainer, from out of nowhere, 'The Love of God' by Netta Pearl and the Colorado Avenue Standard Christian Church Sanctuary Choir from Pasadena!"

That made everybody laugh even more, and cheer too.

"You're good, kid," said Mr. Whitney as he and Donna and I came back into the control room. "You've got a future in this.

"Okay," he went on, "let's run this down one more time. I have a good feeling about this one."

Happy to be back in on the action, Pastor Beamering waved his arms at us through the window.

"Oh no, what is it now?" said Mr. Whitney.

Matt punched the talk-back button. "Yes?"

"I'd like to lead us all in prayer," Pastor said in a faint voice that was faint only to us because he was not near a microphone. Jeffery T. Beamering never had a faint voice in his life.

"Why didn't he think of that sooner?" Mr. Whitney said on our side of the glass.

Matt clicked on the button and looked at Mr. Whitney for the answer.

"Go right ahead," said Mr. Whitney, pushing the volume up on the microphone nearest Pastor Beamering, which unfortunately happened to be right in front of Netta Pearl.

"Dear heavenly Father," he began, his voice stronger now in the control room, "we thank Thee for this opportunity to use these voices and this studio to glorify thy name—"

"YES, LORD!" boomed Netta Pearl, nearly sending us through the roof.

Mr. Whitney quickly fumbled for the volume control on Netta's microphone while Donna and I fell on the floor with laughter, followed by Matt's scream because I knocked against his leg when I landed.

"Sshhhh!" Mr. Whitney said over everyone's giggling. "They might hear us out there. Wow. Do you think the Lord heard that one?"

"I'm wondering if I will ever hear anything else again," I said.

" . . . and lead us not into temptation . . ." Pastor Beamering had them into the Lord's Prayer now. Then he finished up by praying for Donna, that she would skate her best to the glory of God, and for the proclamation through everyone of God's great and glorious love.

"In Jesus' name, Amen."

"Amen!" said Netta Pearl, her voice back down to a low roar.

"Play ball!" said Mr. Whitney, and he started the tape.

The presence of an audience to sing to changed everything. Netta glowed. The choir sang out at twice the volume (we knew that because Mr. Whitney had to pull their recording volume down to keep the dial from going into the red). Even Milton stretched out and found that magical spot with Netta that they had discovered that first Sunday.

Somehow, everyone stopped trying to make it happen and let it happen instead, and the result pleased everyone. They got it the first time; everyone knew it; and there was great joy and celebration.

"Mercy, is that me?" said Netta Pearl as we played back the recording through the studio monitors.

"Glo-ry!" she said in a hushed whisper, and people listened humbly, overtaken by the quality and the depth of their own voices.

They all said it was Pastor Beamering's prayer that did it.

17

Route 99

North of Los Angeles 109 miles sits the rural community of Bakersfield. It is situated in the southernmost part of the Central Valley, which stretches five hundred miles to the north and lies between the golden hills of the Coast Range to the west and the purple Sierra Nevadas to the east. This fertile valley forms the largest and most important farming area west of the Rocky Mountains and produces almost every kind of crop imaginable. The upper portion of the valley, north of San Francisco Bay, is known as the Sacramento Valley. The larger, southern part is called the San Joaquin Valley. Each is named for the river that cuts through its valley floor and flows to the Sacramento Delta.

This is the heartland of California, and it resembles the Midwest in both lifestyle and terrain more than it does the mountains and the beaches, those things people normally associate with California. This is John Steinbeck country, dotted with small towns, dusty roads, shanty homes of migrant workers, and row upon row of orchards, vineyards, and farmland flourishing in the fertile soil.

Bakersfield is the gateway to the San Joaquin Valley from the south. To get there from Pasadena you must travel the "Grapevine," the popular name for that portion of California Route 99 that crosses the San Gabriel Mountains north of the Los Angeles basin—the route we traveled that June day in 1962 to attend the roller-skating competitions in Bakersfield.

Air conditioning was not standard in cars then, and once we hit the valley, which opened before us like a broad plain, my father regretted not attaching the water cooler. We always took the water cooler on our annual trip to visit relatives in Texas, but that was through the desert in August. My father didn't think it was going to be that hot in the Central Valley in June, but it was. Like a furnace.

"The temperature must have gone up twenty degrees over the Grapevine," he said as we came down off the mountain and hit the first long stretch of road in the valley. Our windows went down immediately, and Becky and I stuck our faces into the hot, dry wind.

"No, no," said my father. "Hands and arms inside the car. That goes for heads too."

"What's that smell?" Becky said.

"Fruit trees," said my mother. "There are miles and miles of orchards here, and all kinds of crops."

The San Joaquin Valley was known for its almonds, apricots, cherries, figs, grapes, nectarines, olives, oranges, peaches, plums, and walnuts, and the hot sun beating down on all those fruits and nuts created a rich aroma that rushed to meet you.

"That's not only crops I'm smelling," said Becky.

"And a few stockyards too," said my father.

"How much longer to Bakersfield?" I said just as we came up on a sign that read Bakersfield 30, Fresno 138, San Francisco 323.

"Looks like about half an hour," said my father.

"We're way ahead of the buses," I said, studying the straight, steamy road that wiggled in the heat behind us before it started winding back up into the mountains from which we had just come. "They're nowhere in sight."

"Donna's still back there, isn't she?"

"Yep," I said. "Comin' right along."

I had been keeping an eye on the Finleys' '39 Plymouth. Sometimes older cars overheated in the mountain passes, but they didn't seem to be having any trouble. Mr. Finley did drive quite a bit slower than my father, however, which meant we were traveling slower than we would have if we weren't traveling in a caravan.

"Do you see Lenny up ahead?" I asked.

"I haven't seen him since the other side of the mountain," said my father.

"With that car, he's probably already been there for half an hour," I said. "Do you have the directions to the Civic Auditorium, Mother?"

"Yes, Jonathan. I've told you three times now, I have them right here."

"Relax, little brother," said Becky. "Everything's going to be all right."

"I'm not worried," I said, "just excited."

"Well you've been keeping your eyes glued to Donna's car since we left Pasadena," she said. "It's a wonder you're not carsick from looking backwards all the time."

The last four and a half months had been relatively uneventful. Once Donna had a song, her practicing took on a much more focused direction. She spent the first month after the recording session deciding exactly what she was going to attempt to do and the next three learning how to do it, piece by piece. It wasn't until the last four weeks, however, that she actually started putting the whole thing together.

A good program consisted of elements you did well, along with elements you stretched to perform. A skater might perform flawlessly, said Lenny, but if the skater's program was below his or her perceived abilities, it would not be judged as highly as a routine that included more difficult elements, even though they might not be perfectly executed. In other words, the judges wanted to see you reach. The best scores came when skaters attempted something slightly beyond their grasp and seized it.

So Donna's program was constantly in a state of flux right up to the day of her performance. That also meant she never skated her routine twice in exactly the same manner. What she attempted on a particular day—in a particular second, even—depended on her mental confidence and her physical strength at the time. The slightest thing could alter it.

Donna's physical strength and stamina continually amazed me. Watching someone skate freestyle in a performance or competition is deceptive. The audience sees only the finished product, and the practiced style and grace make it look easy. But I'd had the privilege of watching Donna learn, of knowing what went into creating that style and grace, seeing the bruises come and go on her legs, and hearing her grunt and groan in practice as she put her body through incredible paces. I saw the gritty face before the smile went on.

There had been no more angelic visitations since I'd received the messages that landed us at Whitney Sound, proving what I now believe to be the case: that their purpose was to get me over the barriers that had kept me from being involved with people I cared about. The angels were like Ben, poking and prodding me until I found myself doing Ben-type things, saying Ben-type things. And I still hold that they performed these functions in my life because, in fact, they were sent by Ben.

I did try and hear angels with Grizzly once. We even stayed overnight in the church one Friday night, and though no voices awakened us, I felt like I'd had a kind of angelic visit in just being alone in the sanctuary with the moon shining through the stained-glass window overhead and Grizzly moaning hymns out of the hymnbook as I sang along. Many people would have thought the sound of his voice grotesque, and I would have been one of them if I didn't know him. But that night there was truly something beautiful and clear and honest about his sounds. They expressed a love for God more beautifully than words could.

I also believe, to this day, that Ben had a hand in getting Donna and me together; that he had picked out my next friend—someone to replace him. Someone with his tenacity, his frankness, his faith, and his obtuse relationship to society and what most people regarded as being cool. What a surprise to discover his choice was a girl!

And now we were finally on the long-awaited trip to Bakersfield to see her skate. Even Matt, who had gotten bored with Donna's practices and hardly come to the rink at all during the past couple months, was coming too. I told him the producers had to be there, so Leonard and Bernice were bringing him, somewhere in the caravan behind us.

Everything had been leading up to this, and I had a feeling that something more than just the competition was going to take place.

This was the first year the Southwest Pacific Regional Championship was being held in Bakersfield rather than Los Angeles. Roller skating had atrophied to where it was too small for L.A. The Pan Pacific Auditorium had swallowed it up the last few years, and the city never even stopped to notice. Not to mention the expense. The entire event lasted for a whole week, and, depending on your classification, there could be a few days between qualifying and the finals, if, in fact, you were fortunate enough to get that far. That meant a few nights' lodging and meals for out-of-town contestants, and in L.A. that was pretty steep for the budgets of most skaters and their families.

By contrast, in Bakersfield the regional championship was a big deal. And this being the first year there made it even bigger. The city was rolling out the red carpet. Bands were going to play, the mayor and a number of councilmen were going to attend; there was going to be more press coverage over this than the championship had had in years.

It was definitely a big event for the Colorado Avenue Standard Christian Church. Rolling behind us were two buses full of choir members and their families, along with a number of people, like us, who were driving their own cars so they could have the freedom of staying or returning, depending on the outcome. The buses were only coming for the day, for Donna's qualifying skate. If she went on to the finals, she would skate again sometime during the next two or three days. Most people, of course, didn't have the time or money to put into that kind of commitment. My father, for instance, was not real happy about not knowing exactly how long we were going to be staying. He liked to plan his trips months in advance and keep to a certain predictable schedule. He was prepared to stay for one night if necessary, but no longer than that. Becky and I were hoping for at least one night in a motel.

"This trip was not in my budget for this year," he had said. "If the finals are later than that, we'll have to go home and come back up for it."

There had been some consideration as to when to bring the buses. Everyone would prefer to see the finals, but then again, if Donna didn't make it that far, they would miss her entirely.

"Of course she'll make it to the finals. Our Donna? She's the best!" That was pretty much the sentiment around the church, but Lenny made it clear to my father that even the best can have their bad days. If they wanted to be sure their trip up to Bakersfield would be rewarded by seeing Donna skate to their recording of "The Love of God," they had better plan on coming to the qualifications. Let people decide individually what they wanted to do after that.

"Besides," Lenny said, "Donna needs the support to qualify. It's much harder to qualify than to win. If you make it to the finals, you have already won in a way. The pressure to qualify is much greater."

And so it was decided—which meant that Donna's qualifying skate would undoubtedly be accompanied by the biggest entourage in the history of the regional championships. And if the mayor of Bakersfield wasn't impressive enough, we had the mayor of Pasadena himself, Mayor Seth Wilson, in our caravan, still driving the 1958 Edsel convertible that had made him Ben's lasting friend and, as a result, a member of our church. He and his wife passed us twice on Route 99, once on the uphill grade and once on the straightaway into Bakersfield on the other side of the mountains—the reason for these two passes being a stop to put their top down once they hit the heat of the valley floor.

"Dad, you're going too fast again," I said. "I can hardly see them."

"Well, Mayor Wilson just passed us and waved us on," he answered. "Now he'll think I'm some kind of old fogy."

"Let him think what he thinks, dear," said my mother. "We can't lose the skater."

As I looked back at the wavy impression the front of the Finleys' Plymouth made through a mirage, I thought of the cherished box I had seen on Donna's lap as I closed her in the backseat of their car before we left the parking lot of the church. It was a package she had received in the mail—a total surprise—only three days earlier. She'd probably held it on her lap all the way up Route 99.

Frustrated over not being able to get anything more out of anyone about Donna's mother, I had finally asked Donna herself if she knew anything about Camarillo.

"Who told you about that?" she had snapped.

"No one. I figured it out."

"Jonathan, I'll tell you everything I know. My mother's alive, I think, but what state she is in, I do not know. I have not heard from her in nine years. I don't even know if she knows I exist. Granny says that when I'm old enough she will tell me the whole story. Apparently I'm not old enough yet, because I haven't been told. In the meantime, anything that would remind me of her has been removed or forbidden, like the pictures in Lenny's office."

That's why the box sat in Donna's lap right now, and the note was probably still inside, right where it was when she first opened the box three days ago.

Once the recording was completed and the routine worked out, the only other item to be decided was what outfit Donna would wear for the competitions. For a while, when she was going to skate to "La Paloma" by Billy Vaughn and His Orchestra—the song Lenny wanted her to skate to until Netta Pearl and the Colorado Avenue Standard Christian Church Sanctuary Choir came on the scene—she was going to wear a Spanish-style costume with a matador's cape. "The Love of God" called for a more traditional approach, however, and when Donna would start to question what she should wear, Lenny would say he had it all taken care of, not to worry. Well, that speech had gone on right up until a week ago, and Donna, in a panic, had tried to get her grandmother to help her make an outfit.

"I have to know I have something," she told me. "If whatever Lenny has in mind doesn't pan out, I won't have anything."

It was unlike Lenny to push things that late, and also unlike him not to have an alternative plan. That's why Donna was so confused.

"He must be absolutely sure or he wouldn't do this. It's just not like him," she kept repeating.

"But what if I don't like it or it doesn't fit?" I heard her say to him. "What will I do then?"

"You'll like it," he kept saying. "Trust me."

Well, she didn't really trust him. She couldn't with something this important. And she didn't get any help from Granny Finley either. Oh, Granny hemmed and hawed about doing this or that, but there was always something in the way—some excuse that kept her from getting to it.

"I honestly think they're in cahoots," Donna told me.

Out of frustration, she had finally designed her own outfit and was halfway through making it when the package arrived. She was so excited she couldn't tell me about it over the phone. Since it was summertime now and I was out of school, I rode my bike to her house. It took me over an hour to get there, and she was waiting for me on the front porch with the box on her lap.

"Open it," she said.

I looked at my hands all wet with dirty perspiration from the handlebar grips on my bike that were covered with three years of newsprint. I showed them to her and she ran inside and got me a towel, which I used to wipe everything I could find on my body to wipe. It was almost 80 degrees and I had just ridden over five miles uphill.

"Open it!" She had no patience.

I removed the top of the box and there was a note lying on tissue paper.

"Read it," she said, eyes sparkling. "Read it to me. I want to hear what it sounds like out loud." So I read.

Dear Baby,

Here's the outfit I wore in my first performance. I would have been about your age then. It is still my favorite. I made it as simple and comfortable as possible. I sure hope it fits. The fur collar comes up the back and wraps around your throat, but unfortunately I have lost some of the snaps. The collar is kind of special to me. It can be snipped off and worn without it, but maybe you can fix it. If you don't like the suit, just give it to the Goodwill, but please keep the collar and save it for me.

Good luck. I'm real proud of you.

Love, Mama

Donna could only look at me with eyes shining and her legs pulled up under her chin.

"Read that last part again," she said. "That part about keeping the collar."

" 'Please keep the collar and save it for me,' " I read.

"You know what that means? That means I'm going to see her again sometime . . . sometime soon, maybe!"

It was the greatest gift she could have received. And Lenny was right. It fit. It fit like it was made for her. Granny helped her fix the snaps, and she had done a dress rehearsal in it the day before.

It took your breath away just to watch her glide through the air in this outfit. It was white with sequins and rhinestones in front and a short satin skirt gathered slightly. In the back there was a deep plunge lined with white feathery fur that came up to the tops of her shoulders and then wrapped around her throat like a furry ribbon. It was that final touch that set it off. The furry band seemed to make her eyes sparkle and her hair dance.

This had, of course, raised a whole set of new questions. Lenny obviously had some kind of contact with Donna's mother, enough to be confident that the outfit would arrive by the time she needed it. How much did he know, and what was his relationship with Donna's mother anyway? Was he, in fact, Donna's father? That question crossed my mind, though I never told Donna. If he wasn't her father, he certainly fulfilled that role for her in many ways.

It would also help to explain the attention he gave her—attention that was out of proportion to the significance of the event. The competitions were important within the circle of amateur skating, but not as important as Lenny made them. Anyone could go to Bakersfield as long as they were associated with a club. There was no prize money except at the world level. It was simply a passion for some people and an enjoyment for others. But to Lenny it seemed to be much more than that.

" 'Welcome to Bakersfield'!" my father read triumphantly as we passed the sign, " 'Gateway to the San Joaquin Valley.' Get out the directions, dear. Tell me what to do."

"Well, nothing until we get into the center of town."

I had an important box with me, too—a surprise for Donna that she didn't know about yet. My mother had helped me with it. It was a small delicate wrist corsage made of tiny fragrant orchids.

My mother and I had gone to the florist the day before to get flowers to give to Donna after she finished skating, and I had spotted the corsage in a refrigerated display case. It was in a box with a cellophane window just like the box the model Edsel came in that I had gotten Ben for his birthday right after I first met him. Knowing what I knew about Donna's outfit, I could imagine how terrific this would look on her wrist. We wondered about it getting in the way of her skating, but the saleslady assured us she could tie the flowers down well and make the elastic especially tight.

"She could direct a Beethoven symphony with this on when I'm done with it," the lady said, and so we took it.

I reached down under the seat where the box was riding and looked at it again.

"Better keep it out of the sun," my mother said, noticing it in my lap. "Why don't I keep it with me and you can get it from me when you're ready?"

I handed it to her and imagined Donna's excitement. Maybe this would be her second best gift.

The Civic Auditorium was in an older part of town that didn't look anything like southern California. Nothing in Bakersfield did, as a matter of fact. Everything was flat, and there were few trees or tall buildings. The older part seemed a little like the Old West with buildings that had facades for faces. The auditorium itself was nondescript. Back in Pasadena it would have been a supermarket.

We pulled into a gravel and dirt parking lot that was already filling up with cars. I spotted Lenny's Corvette well up the line, but he was nowhere in sight.

We waited for Donna, and a small crowd of our caravan

started to form, then Donna and the Finleys, and finally the buses about ten minutes after that. Just before the buses arrived, Lenny showed up with Donna's official packet.

"We don't have as much time as I thought," he said. "They've moved you up two hours, Donna. You're skating at one o'clock now. That's only two hours away. Jonathan, here are the tickets. You see that everyone gets one. I'm going to take Donna in and get her familiar with the floor."

It was eleven o'clock in the morning and we were already wiping the perspiration from our faces and foreheads.

"Don't worry, folks," Lenny said. "It's air conditioned inside." That was welcome news to everyone.

The buses pulled in on a cloud of dust I could taste.

"Mercy, where are we?" said Netta, first one through the door. "This sure ain't Hollywood, honey."

She was in a bright pink and green floral outfit with new white shoes that she looked down at disgustedly as she stepped off the bus into the dirt.

"Where's the red carpet? Who was it said Bakersfield was puttin' out the red carpet for us? I could use one of them right now."

Netta's bus emptied out in a very jovial mood. I could hear singing from the back, and I asked if that had been going on all the way up.

"No, just the last hour," someone said.

"If this place ain't air conditioned, I'm gettin' back on the bus," said Netta, fanning herself with the program I was handing out with the tickets.

"Don't worry," said Granny Finley. "They wouldn't be able to skate if it wasn't."

That made everyone want to go inside as soon as possible.

The inside of the Bakersfield Civic Auditorium looked pretty much like a school gymnasium to me. The large floor was marked for basketball, and the backstops were pulled up to the high ceiling. There were about fifteen rows of bleachers on either side and a grandstand of red theater seats at one end. The other end was the officials' platform, backed by a ceiling-to-floor curtain with the emblems and initials of the Roller Skating Rink Operators Association of America (R.S.R.O.A.) and the United

States Federation of Amateur Roller Skaters (U.S.F.A.R.), the two organizations that sponsored this competition.

The Southwest Pacific Regional Championship was attended by clubs from Arizona, Nevada, and California. Winners from here went on to the nationals and then the world competitions. Donna, entering as a freestyle skater, would be skating in the Freshman Girls Singles group at one o'clock. Since there was always the possibility that competition times might be changed, as they had already done with Donna, it was a little chancy coming up on the same day as the qualifications. Most coaches brought their teams up the night before and gave them time to get acclimated. Lenny had a different philosophy.

"Coming up early only makes you more nervous. All your patterns are altered. You stay awake half the night because nothing is familiar. Better to spend the night in your own bed, drive in, and skate. If you qualify, then you will probably have a couple of days to adjust, but by then you already have a successful skate under your belt to ward off the jitters."

So having Donna arrive only two hours before her qualifications was actually within the parameters of Lenny's overall plan. Lenny's other skaters, whose qualifications were the next day, were not coming up until then.

Our contingent equaled almost half the crowd that was already assembled inside, though more people were filing in all the time. Most of our group were already wandering around inside when the Wendorfs drove up.

"She's on in an hour and a half," I said as I met them getting out of their air-conditioned Thunderbird.

"Whew, it's a furnace out here," said Leonard. "I told you it would be like this."

"Don't worry, it's cool inside."

"Good thing," he said, "because we would have turned around right now."

"Oh, Leonard, come on now," said Bernice. "We're here for Donna and the choir. Speaking of Donna, there she is right now."

I turned around to see Donna heading toward the parking lot. She waved at us and smiled as she went to the Plymouth and unlocked the door.

"Well she certainly looks calm for a girl who's going to be on the ever-lovin' spot in a few minutes," said Mr. Wendorf.

No sooner had he said this than we were shaken by a blood-curdling shriek from Donna. By the time I got to her, she was slumped in the backseat of her grandparents' car with one hand over her face and the other holding a wavy piece of round plastic with a large hole in it. It was the recording of "The Love of God" by Netta Pearl and the Colorado Avenue Standard Christian Church Sanctuary Choir, all curled up and melted by the San Joaquin sun through the back window of a '39 Plymouth.

18

For the Love of God

"Surely someone here has another record with them," said Mrs. Wendorf.

"Doesn't Lenny have one?" I said.

Donna just kept shaking her head and crying. "He sent me out here to get mine because his was not in his briefcase."

"I'll go get him," I said.

"No, I'll go," said Matt, holding me back and moving out as fast as his healing leg would allow.

"I just knew something like this was going to happen," Donna said, staring hopelessly at the curled-up disk of vinyl in her lap. "Things were going too well."

"Now now, honey, don't give up," said Mrs. Wendorf. "There are a lot of folks here. Something will turn up."

And something about what she said started the wheels turning in my head. She was right. There *were* a lot of folks there—a lot of just the right folks, too.

Matt returned with Lenny who, when he saw the ruined record, threw his hands up in the air and began pacing back and forth in exasperation. Then he pointed to me.

"Go round everybody up. There's got to be another record in this group somewhere."

"Where shall I tell them to come?"

"We'll have to meet outside. There are no rooms available."

"Come on, Matt," I said, and we rushed off together.

There was one tree near the parking lot of the Bakersfield Civic Auditorium and everyone squeezed to get under its shade, wondering what this was all about. Some sat down on the sparse grass and the rest stood around the edges of the shade. Lenny got everyone's attention.

"Folks, we have some bad news. Unfortunately the only copy of the recording we have with us is now a melted piece of plastic. Does anyone here have a copy with them?"

There was a long silence. Then someone spoke.

"I'd be glad to go home and get mine."

"There's no time," said Lenny. "Donna skates in an hour."

"Couldn't they give her a new time, later in the afternoon?" asked Mrs. Beamering.

"I can make an appeal, but it's highly unlikely anything will happen. These judges have no reason to be flexible. Besides, in the time it would take someone to go back to Pasadena, they'll be into another event."

"What normally happens in a case like this?" asked my father.

"They have a backup recording that they play, and the contestant has to do their best to improvise, or perhaps borrow someone else's record."

There was another long, sad pause. Donna was sniffling while Granny Finley held her hand.

"Wait a minute—" I blurted out. Eyes turned to me, and I suddenly realized I had succeeded in something I had not intended: I had everyone's attention. My own private thoughts were about to intrude upon this meeting with what was becoming obvious to me, but not necessarily anyone else. Lenny was glaring at me, probably wishing, right then, that I had never come into his life. Probably thinking how much easier it would have been for him if I hadn't. He would be at these competitions right now with a predictable song and with a few skaters and their immediate families, not a caravan of buses and cars and these strange religious fanatics.

"Well?" he said. "We're waiting."

"We may not have the record," I said, "but we have everyone here . . . everyone who made that record . . . don't we? Why can't we just do the song?"

Murmurs welled up in the group as Lenny thought out loud, "A live performance . . . while Donna skates. . . ."

"I like this boy!" said Netta Pearl. "I'm game! Show me to the microphone!"

"They have an organ," chimed Milton. "I saw the console on the platform." And the murmurs rose higher in approval.

"Not so fast now," said Lenny. "You're right, Milton, they do have an organ. In fact, Dominic has been hired to play it for the dance competitions. But the problem is the judges. I can tell you right now, they'll never go for it."

"What if we just did it before they have a chance to decide whether they like the idea or not?" said Mrs. Beamering to a chorus of affirming comments.

"Donna would be disqualified," said Lenny. "No question."

"Sounds like it all rests with the judges," said another voice from the choir.

"Let's pray for the judges right now," said my father. "Pastor, would you lead us?" And all heads went down.

"Wait a minute," said Lenny and heads came back up. "You pray for them if you want; I'll go *talk* to them. In the meantime, you should be ready to sing, just in case. Sit together in the bleachers as close to the platform as you can. Milton, find Dominic and have him get the organ ready. I know he's here somewhere. The only way this *might* work is if we present the idea to the judges right before Donna skates."

He glanced at his watch. "It's twelve o'clock. I'm supposed to be turning in Donna's music right now. I'll alert them to the problem and try for a possible time slot tonight or tomorrow. If that fails, and I'm confident it will, Donna will present this 'live music' idea to the judges right before she skates. You'll have to be ready on the spot in case they go for it, but I'm pretty confident they won't." And he stepped over the legs of a few choir members sitting on the grass and headed back to the auditorium at a brisk walk. He appeared to be eager to get out of the way of our impending prayer.

"Ain't never seen a man so confident about all the wrong things," said Netta as we watched him go.

"I'm confident that the Lord has us here for a reason," said Pastor Beamering. "Let's pray." And then he led us all in a prayer, punctuated every few phrases by the "amens" of Netta Pearl—a prayer that pushed over, pulled down, and bound up judges, thrones, kingdoms, authorities, powers, dominions, rulers in heavenly places, and the devil's strongholds from here to eternity. I opened my eyes when he was done and checked to see if the Civic Auditorium was still standing.

Next, my father took over.

"All right, how many altos do we have? Altos? Line up, please. We don't have much time. Sopranos over here. Tenors? . . . Marv, thank goodness you're here. . . . Basses? . . . Come on, people," and he clapped his hands. "I know it's hot, but we need to go over this at least a couple times. The sooner we get it, the sooner we can get back inside where it's cool."

The print flowers on Netta's dress were already starting to wilt, Milton ran off to try and find Dominic, and Donna came over and grabbed my arm. Her face was bright again with hope and excitement.

"Jonathan, I can't believe this is happening! All these people! Jonathan, thank you. You are very brave." She kissed me on the cheek and turned and headed back to the auditorium.

The choir went through "The Love of God" a couple times with Netta until my father was satisfied that they remembered it. By the end of the second time through, a small audience had formed and applauded the parking lot performance. Then we all went inside.

At the opposite end from where the judges sat was an area, just outside the rink wall, which served as a sort of "on-deck circle" for the skaters. Only the next three skaters and their coaches were allowed in there, but Matt and I sat near it on the edge of the bleachers where we could see and hear what was going on. Seven girls were skating in the Freshman Girls Singles competition, and Donna was number three.

At a quarter to one she came out sparkling in her mother's

outfit. She had one new addition: a tiara in her hair made of silk flower petals that reminded me of the corsage. I looked down the bleachers to where my mother was sitting in what was now the sanctuary choir section, and she must have thought of it at the same time because she stood up and pointed at the box in her hand. I ran around behind the grandstand and brought it back to Donna.

She loved it so much she almost came apart. She put it on her wrist and twirled with it overhead and told me it was the most beautiful thing she had ever seen. Then Lenny saw it and he came apart too.

"No, absolutely not," and he glared at me and then back at Donna. "How could you possibly think of skating with something like that on your arm?"

Donna kept giving him the most pleading looks, but it was no use.

"Take it off!" he demanded in a voice so mean that she looked like she was going to cry.

I felt awful. I wished I had never given it to her. What a terrible time this was turning out to be for her. I began to wonder how she was going to be able to skate at all with her emotions as torn as they were right then.

A few minutes later they called for the warm-up, and all seven girls went out onto the floor to loosen up for four and a half minutes, during which time you could tell a lot about them. Donna and one other girl both had natural grace. The others appeared to be jerky in their movements. You could probably decide the finalists just by watching them warm up. This seemed to relax Donna a little and give her some confidence.

Finally, after they were all off the floor and the first three contestants were ready, a voice came over the loudspeaker: "And now for our first contestant in the Freshman Girls Singles competition, we have from Las Vegas, Nevada, Miss Percy Engleman!"

Percy came out to light applause and bowed in the center of the rink. She struck her opening pose as the first strains of "Moon River" came over the speakers. She skated well, but very mechanically, with little connection to the music. She could probably have skated just as well to any piece of music and done the three jumps and one twirl she attempted. She skated off to a polite round of applause.

Next was a girl from Sacramento. I didn't get her name, but the song was "Moon River" again. I was thinking only of Donna coming up next and wondering what she was thinking. At one point she bowed her head and prayed, and when she did, I prayed too. I opened my eyes a minute later to see her looking right at me.

"Thank you," she said.

"You'll do great!" I said.

She was taking deep breaths now and her chest would fill up and then collapse suddenly as she dropped her shoulders and let the air out with a sharp heave. The Sacramento girl finished and Lenny started giving Donna her last-minute instructions. He was speaking softly, up close to her, so I couldn't hear much. She listened with a stern face, unmoving.

"What's he saying?" said Matt.

"I think he's telling her what to tell the judges about the record and the choir and everything."

"Sure hope this works," said Matt.

"Me too."

"Contestant number three, from Pasadena, California, Miss Donna Callaway."

There was thunderous applause, relatively speaking, from Donna's supporters as she skated directly to the judges' table at the other end of the rink. They were on the ground floor with a red, white, and blue bunting covering the front of their table. Behind them on a riser was the announcer, the organ console, and the person playing the records.

"If I had his job, I'd do something about song selection," said Matt. "If I hear 'Moon River' one more time I'm gonna puke."

"Yeah, well in his job you gotta play what they give you. Lenny was right. Donna wanted to do 'Moon River' in the beginning, and he said everyone would be doing it."

"If I had that guy's job I'd pop something on like 'Duke of Earl' just to see what happens. That would mess them up, huh?"

It sure would, and from the looks of it, Donna was about to be messed up by that very thing—skating to a song she had not planned for. You could read the writing on the wall from the other side of the rink. Since she started talking to them, the judges' heads hadn't gone any direction but side to side. Side to side. Side to side. Donna turned around and skated back to Lenny, who met her at the rail right in front of us.

"I can't do it," she said, on the verge of tears again, but maintaining a regal posture.

"Yes you can, Donna. What's the song?"

"The theme from 'Exodus.' "

"That's fine. Now listen to me. Skate your routine from start to finish."

"But I can't," Donna protested. "I have to skate to the music. If I can't follow the music, I can't skate."

"Yes you can, Donna. Ignore the music. Just stick to your routine."

"Let me skate to the song with the choir and Netta like we talked about. I don't care about qualifying anymore. I just want to do my routine to this song—for the audience and for everyone who came up here."

"Donna," Lenny put his hands on her shoulders and addressed her nose to nose, "now listen to me. Pay no attention to the music. Remember what I told you: they're looking for content and performance. On any normal day you're better than any of these girls here. You watched them warm up. If you skate well, you'll qualify, and by the final we'll have five hundred records here, and the Mormon Tabernacle Choir if you want!"

"I don't want the Mormon Tabernacle Choir. I want Netta Pearl and the Colorado Avenue Stand—"

"I know, I know," interrupted Lenny. "I was just kidding. Donna, just skate. You'll do the song for the finals."

Donna managed a tough little smile and turned to skate toward the middle of the rink. She wiped under her eyes, heaved her shoulders one more time, and took up her sculptured opening position. When the theme from "Exodus" began, she went immediately into a dramatic twirl which went beautifully with the opening cymbal crescendo of the music, but that was not in her routine. Nor was anything else she did from that point on. I looked over at Lenny and he already had an angry look on his face, even though Donna had started out so well.

"No," I heard him say under his breath. "Stick to the routine." But Donna had other ideas, and for the opening minute they worked surprisingly well. She came out of her twirl with a smooth flourish at the cymbal crash that brought spontaneous applause from an audience eager to acknowledge any kind of success amidst an obvious challenge. They did not know what was wrong, but they knew Donna was fighting something—that she was good, but something was in her way.

Her first jump was right on target as well, and that too met with applause that seemed to give us hope. So far she was in another league from the first two skaters. But that euphoria was short-lived. Her second jump didn't connect at all with the music, and that seemed to visibly deflate her. Donna had practiced so long and hard with music that she was married to it. She could not separate a routine from the music that drove it. It was the only way she could skate. She had to express what she heard, and when she did not know what was coming, she fell apart. She did the best she could with what she remembered of the hit version of "Exodus," but the third jump was so far out of sync that it landed her in a heap on the floor.

For a while the music played on to a hushed crowd.

"Get up," I heard Lenny say, and I thought of Donna's mother—locked in some place for crazy people, still on the floor after all these years.

"Get up," I said under my breath. "Get up, Donna!"

But Donna didn't move.

"Is she hurt?" said Matt.

She wasn't crying or grabbing on to any part of her body like you would expect if she had injured herself. She was simply slumped over like a rag doll, like a puppet without strings, as if someone or something had sucked the life out of her and she had folded on the spot, all of her limbs going every which way.

I knew Donna was not hurt, at least not physically. Lenny knew too, and I'm sure that's why he did not run out immediately to try and help her. If she was not going to get up, nothing he could do or say would change that. She would have to decide this on her own. It was not a matter of broken bones. It was something more important than that. It was a broken spirit.

Suddenly I knew what I had to do. It was very simple really, though not that simple to do. It was deathly quiet now. The DJ had lifted the needle off of Ferrante & Teicher's version of "Exodus," and I realized that if Donna couldn't get up, I had to get up for her. Perhaps, in some small way, I could convey some courage by standing with her. When I did, the old grandstands squeaked and echoed through the silent hall and all eyes turned in my direction. I stood there for what seemed like a long time, but that was only because that simple act started a chain reaction of events that still move by the walls of my memory in slow motion as if time has stopped to savor each one of them.

The first thing was that my lonely squeak was joined by others in the hall—a few random creakings that gradually swelled into a huge chorus of rattling grandstands as the entire crowd got to its feet. I noticed that my mother, Mayor Wilson, and Mrs. Beamering were among the first to stand.

Then I heard the familiar booming voice of Pastor Beamering. He started quoting Scripture, of all things, and that voice, which at other times in public places had been such an embarrassment to me, seemed at this time the most appropriate thing that could happen.

" 'Wherefore seeing we also are compassed about with so great a cloud of witnesses,' " he began, " 'let us lay aside every weight, and the sin which doth so easily beset us, and let us run with patience the race that is set before us.' "

His voice boomed like it was amplified. It seemed to fall from the middle of the ceiling. It fell on Donna and awakened her spirit enough to get her sitting up.

" 'Looking unto Jesus,' " Pastor Beamering continued, quoting that familiar benediction, " 'the author and finisher of our faith; who for the joy that was set before him endured the cross, despising the shame, and is set down at the right hand of the throne of God.' "

That made me immediately think about angels. Whenever Pastor Beamering referred to the throne of God, I always imagined angels around that throne, and I wondered if angels were around Donna right then.

Another hush fell on the crowd when he finished. Everyone in the hall was standing except Donna, the three judges, and Granny Finley, or so I thought. I thought of Granny Finley right then because she was the next one to break the silence.

"Esther!" came that familiar voice barking out of the stillness. "Esther," she repeated, "get up!"

I strained, with the rest of the crowd, to try and see where the voice was coming from. I found an empty wheelchair before I found Granny, for she had gotten two strong men from the church to lift her up out of it and take her right up to the railing of the rink where her voice and her vision could address her granddaughter.

And yet it was not her granddaughter she was speaking to. Her gaze was not at Donna, but somewhere across to the opposite side of the rink.

"Esther?" I said under my breath.

"Who's Esther?" said Matt.

"Esther," I repeated. "Esther Callaway! Matt, it's Donna's mother! She must be here!"

Matt didn't know the story so he did not understand the significance; he just looked puzzled.

For the next few minutes everyone forgot about Donna and followed Granny Finley's gaze to the other side of the rink where a blond woman sat in a wheelchair, locked in the grip of Granny's stare. Suddenly it was not Donna we were pulling for, but Donna's mother, because she was trying, with every ounce of her strength, to get up out of her wheelchair. The crowd was focused on her as if they knew. Did they? Did they know it was this woman that Donna was skating for? Did they know she was the one who had not been able to get up for nine years?

Esther Callaway's arms shook as she pushed the dead weight of her body up out of the chair. Her jaw was set in determination, and the rest of her face distorted itself through the strain of her efforts. She got her arms straight, but her lower body flew out in front of her, uncontrolled. Her legs were not paralyzed like Granny Finley's; they had merely become useless through a mental paralysis—a way of thinking that had held her captive for so long.

Two spectators helped steady her, but she brushed them off, somehow managing to get her balance long enough to take two short, faltering steps to the railing, where she grabbed on and straightened herself with a great air of dignity and a determined grace. There she stood, at the rail, alone, shaking and looking straight at Donna.

"Glow-ry!" said Netta Pearl under her breath but loud enough to be heard in the hall. She didn't know the story either, but she knew a healing when she saw one.

Donna and her mother were now locked in each other's gaze, reunited after so many years in front of all these witnesses. Though in their eyes, the witnesses fell away right then. For an instant it seemed there was just the two of them in the whole world.

I saw Donna's lips move slowly, as if she were awaking from a trance. "Mama" was what I'm sure she said, though there was no sound. Esther Callaway held her own against the rail and finally spoke through the tears in her voice.

"Baby," she said, and immediately I thought of her note to Donna that began the same way. She must have called her this in her mind all along.

"Get up!"

Though the tears were welling up in Donna's eyes—tears of joy I was sure—at those words they went away, and a bright, confident smile swept across her face. Suddenly those magical words reminded her of where she was and what she was doing— indeed, of what she was yet to do.

Slowly, Donna stood up, and those who were there will confirm this: there was something odd about the way she did this. If you were to describe it as Donna getting up under her own power, you could not fully account for the strange way in which her body rose up off the floor. But if you explained it as Donna being lifted up by some invisible power, you would have it perfectly in your imagination—the way it looked to the undiscerning eye. Netta Pearl later said she saw them—two tall angels gently lifting Donna up by her arms—saw it as plainly as she saw the angels leave with her husband that night God took him home. And Donna herself will swear to it: that someone got a hold of her under her arms, lifted her up, and placed her on her wheels.

And as she rose, music started to fall from the rafters of the building, because that's where the organ speakers were housed.

"It's Milton!" said Matt. "He's at the organ."

"Way to go Milton!" I said.

The announcer ran over to the organ to try and do something about this unauthorized intrusion, but Dominic stopped him. The poor gentleman then turned around to get back to his beloved microphone, only to find a very large Negro woman in a flowery dress gripping it with both hands, leaving him no choice but to stand there helplessly.

The choir, of course, was already up with everyone else in the auditorium, but my father got a chair and stood up on it so he could get their attention. He had that look in his eye that he gets when he is about to lead a performance. It's a look that brings the best out of him and out of everyone else.

The whole building was suddenly caught up in excitement and anticipation. Donna was going to skate. The organ was playing. Netta Pearl was going to sing. The choir was going to back her up. Nothing was going to stop any of them now, and had the judges tried, they would have been overruled by the entire assembly still on their feet and waiting.

Milton hadn't started the official introduction to the song yet; he was ad-libbing something that sounded a little like "The Love of God" but wasn't quite it, like he always did in church when he was filling in between things.

Through all of this the announcer stood stone-faced, and the judges kept shaking their heads as if their necks were only jointed to move sideways. They pushed themselves away from the table and crossed their arms in front of their bodies as if to wash their hands of whatever was going to happen next, making it perfectly clear that nothing, after Donna's fall, would have any bearing on the official results of this competition.

Finally, Donna skated out toward the center of the rink, ready to take up her starting position once more. But suddenly she stopped short of it, as if she had forgotten something. Milton kept improvising and the audience dangled on a precipice of emotion. Then she turned and skated over to Lenny with her arm out in front of her, pointing to her wrist.

"My corsage, please," I heard her say proudly.

Lenny had no choice but to get it for her. And why not? The judges didn't matter anymore. Rules were out the window. Winning and losing were irrelevant. Donna was ready to skate, and she could skate it any way she wanted.

And did she skate! She skated up one side of the rink and down the other. She skated with a strength and a grace that exceeded anything I had ever seen her do. She skated into the darkest unknown of her abandoned childhood, throwing her body down, down, down, until she was a tiny ball spinning in a fetal position . . . and suddenly, when Netta sang the words, "The love of God . . . ," she spun out of that darkness as if she had a gleaming ball of light in her hands which she flung out against the wall of that homely auditorium where it cascaded down like glittering fireworks that became the sequins of her dress as she caught them and landed effortlessly from a double spin on those trained, muscular legs.

She skated into the deep psychological depression of a woman who for nine years had forgotten how to get up . . . at least until today. Yes, she skated for her mother, and her mother reveled in her every move—every nuance of perfection. And while strong arms held her grandmother up like Moses against the Amalekites, she skated for the lifeless legs of Murietta Finley, and the heart of Murietta Finley skated within her.

And as I watched her, she seemed to skate for me too—right into the Ben-shaped vacuum in my life, and with one wave of her outstretched hands she cleared it of the cobwebs of anger and bitterness that had built up there and replaced the emptiness with a sense of purpose and gratitude—with the knowledge that I had helped her come to this moment just as Ben had helped me, so many times, out of my comfortable loneliness. It was then that I realized I didn't need Ben anymore—didn't need to miss Ben anymore. I had Ben, in that all the things he had been for me, I was now learning to be for myself, and for someone else besides me. Ben was here. He would always be here—I knew that now—challenging me and testing me and making sure I did not hide.

And I suppose if anyone else there that day were telling this story, they would tell you where it was that Donna skated to in their own life, because that was the way it was. Every lonely, awful place in your life that day became a place that Donna found. She found it, skated into it without even asking, and came back out victorious. We all saw ourselves somewhere in what she accomplished, because her victory was our victory.

The irony of all this was that Donna was disqualified by the judges for falling on the prescribed number. It hardly mattered. Not to Donna, not to Esther Callaway, not to Granny Finley, not to Netta or Milton, not to Pastor Beamering or my father, not to the choir, not to me, and not to the crowd who stayed on their feet for minutes, cheering her performance. Bouquets of flowers rained down from the grandstands—flowers intended for the winners but they went to Donna instead.

Even Lenny was pleased, because Donna had accomplished what he always told her to strive for: to skate the best she knew how. And he knew, just like everyone knew, including the judges, that Donna could never skate any better than she skated that day. It was said that no one could.

And besides, Lenny had to like it. She kept to her routine. The only thing she changed was the very end. She was supposed to end kneeling. Instead, she ended with a spin that seemed to go on forever. And though her body was turning like an eggbeater, her arm, which she held straight up, seemed to move in slow motion, almost as if it were not attached. And on her wrist, turning softly as her head and shoulders fell back away from it, was the beautiful white orchid corsage I had given her, perfectly intact.

Acknowledgments

Three books on roller skating were valuable and fascinating resources to me for this story. *Winning Roller Skating*, by Randy Dayney (Chicago: Contemporary Books, Inc., 1976); *The Complete Book of Roller Skating*, by Ann-Victoria Phillips (New York: Workman Publishing, 1979); and most importantly, *The Wonderful World of Roller Skating*, by David Roggensack (New York: Everest House, 1980) from which I gleaned the quote in Chapter 10.

I am indebted to Bob LaBriola of the Fountain Valley Skating Center in Fountain Valley, California, for educating me on skating championships circa 1961, and for enduring the interruptions of a number of phone calls for follow-up details. I was also thrilled to find an actual program of the original 1942 Skating Vanities, starring Gloria Nord, at Sports Books in Los Angeles, and I have it now cherished perpetually in plastic wrap. Attempts to find the attractive Ms. Nord herself came up empty, even though she resided in nearby Newport Beach as recently as 1980. From the looks of her picture at 60, in David Roggensack's book, she would be a young 72 at this printing.

I would like to thank Clark Gassman and Bill Cole who served as resources for what the recording business was like in Los Angeles in 1961, and, yes, thanks to Loren Whitney himself, obviously an expert on the placement of the sixteen-foot organ pipes in his own studio—a studio which has since been sold. Thanks again to Dr. J. Jones Stewart for medical advice, and a special thanks to Gay Magistro for a letter to Anne, our daughter, which I borrowed almost word-for-word to create a very special note accompanying Donna's skating outfit.

Finally, thanks are in order to Kathy Cunningham for reading the manuscript, to Judith Markham for editing it, and to my children, Christopher and Anne, who were probably my most ruthless critics, being closest to the ages of the most important characters in this story. I am also indebted to Noel Stookey, whose exuberant support of *Saint Ben* has helped keep me fanning the fires of fiction. And most of all, to my wife, my deepest acknowledgments. Let the world know, all my best ideas are yours, Marti.

One final note to those who may be '60s music buffs. I must confess to stretching one piece of history for the purposes of my story. Booker T. and the M.G.'s were not famous until 1962 when their first hit, "Green Onions," went to number three on the charts. The Mar-Keys, who later became the M.G.'s when they hooked up with Booker T., would have probably been more familiar to Matthew and Jonathan when this story takes place in late 1961 when they had their own number three hit, "Last Night." It's conceivable that Booker T. and the Mar-Keys might have teamed up by late '61 and gotten some air-play and recognition as Booker T. and the M.G.'s, but not likely. That's something that probably only Booker T. Jones and Casey Kasem know for sure.